GORDON STEVENS

# *Kara's Game*

HarperCollins*Publishers*

HarperCollins*Publishers*
77–85 Fulham Palace Road,
Hammersmith, London W6 8JB

This paperback edition 1996

First published in Great Britain by
HarperCollins*Publishers* 1996



ISBN 978-0-00-734959-3

Set in Postscript Linotype Sabon by
Rowland Phototypesetting Ltd,
Bury St Edmunds, Suffolk

To the real Kara.

And to Mick, Steve, Ken and Jim,
on behalf of the people of Maglaj.

# PROLOGUE

The sun was orange and the sky was tinged with red. A shepherd's sky, they had called it in Maglaj in the old days. Blood sky, they had called it after the shelling and sniping had started and the graveyard was full and you were afraid to cross the bridge from the old town to the new. But that was at dusk, when the light was fading and the night was gathering. And now it was only two in the afternoon.

Amsterdam time; the same in Paris and Berlin. Four in the afternoon in Moscow, one in London, and eight in the morning in Washington. The shifts in time zone relevant because of what she had said four hours earlier and what would happen in eight hours' time.

The sky was deeper, redder. Perhaps those who clung to the old ways and the old traditions would have called it a sign, she thought; perhaps the women would have dipped their heads and hurried the children inside. Only now, because of the shelling and the sniping, they were inside anyway. Except when they went to the food kitchen, but that was a risk in itself.

'Tell them we're leaving,' she told Maeschler.

Somehow he had known, the captain thought. He pulled on the headset and pressed the transmit button on the left side of the control column.

Lufthansa 3216 taking off, the Strike committee in the Cobra room below Downing Street was informed.

Strike One, the political committee: the British Foreign Secretary and the ambassadors of the United States, France and the Federation of Russian States. Strike Two, the intelligence back-up: the Russian and American heads of station in London, the Frenchman from Paris, and Kilpatrick from Riverside. Knowledge of its existence and its machinations on a need-to-know basis, even within the governments represented.

'So what now?' Langdon asked. Langdon had been Foreign Secretary for three years.

'We wait,' Kilpatrick suggested. Because there's nothing else we can do, because we don't know what's going to happen or where Lufthansa 3216 will go after Amsterdam. Even though the SAS have been at Heathrow since ninety minutes after the hijack.

The images on the monitors at the end of the room changed: BBC first, ITV and CNN two seconds later, the picture on each the same. The Boeing 737 moving slowly, the words NEWS FLASH superimposed over the image, and the reporters describing the event and playing back the conversation which had preceded it.

Lufthansa 3216 moving, the women heard on the transistor radios most of them carried. Lufthansa 3216 leaving Amsterdam . . .

The demonstration outside the United Nations headquarters in New York had begun with one woman – seventy years old and a survivor of Auschwitz. In London it had been two women outside the St Stephen's entrance to the House of Commons. Now the area outside the UN building and Parliament Square itself were filled, with similar demonstrations in most European cities.

'Tower, this is Lufthansa 3216. Ready for takeoff.'

'3216, cleared for takeoff. Surface wind two two five degrees, eight knots.'

It was two days since Lufthansa 3216, with its hundred

and thirty passengers and crew, had been seized. Twenty-eight hours since the leader of the hijack team had issued her demand, and four since she had announced her deadline. Eight hours to that deadline now and four to the emergency session of the United Nations Security Council which would vote on the demand.

'Lufthansa 3216 . . .'

'Go ahead, Tower.' The words were picked up on VHF airband and transmitted live by the television and radio teams reporting from Schipol. 'Good luck.'

So what will the captain say, Kilpatrick wondered; how will the captain react? The captain was taking too long to answer, he realized; it wasn't going to be the captain who answered.

'Thank you, Amsterdam . . .' they all heard her voice.

'Lufthansa 3216 is airborne,' the operation commander informed Finn.

The holding room for the assault teams was in a building away from the main terminal complex at Heathrow, the Operations Room was on the floor above, and the hangar to the side was sealed and guarded, the 737 in it and the assault teams practising their approach and entry.

They had come in as soon as the hijack had been reported to Hereford – the advance team flying in in the Agusta 109, nothing about the helicopter to suggest its purpose and nothing about its markings to indicate the identities of the men in the back: the operations officer, the team commander, the assault group commander, the sniper group commander, a signaller, and the operations clerk. The rest of the teams screaming up the motorway in the unmarked Range Rovers and the plain white van with the back-up gear close behind. Nobody seeing them, of course; nobody, except those with a need to know, aware they were here.

'Which way are they heading?'

'Nobody's sure yet.'

Finn stood the teams down, left the hangar, and went to the Operations Room.

Lufthansa 3216 flying north, Strike was informed. Lufthansa 3216 still in Dutch air space.

For one moment she was no longer on the flight deck. For one moment she was back in Bosnia, the snow was on the ground and the cold of winter was tight around her. Flour was fifteen deutschmarks a kilo, the black marketeer next to her was saying. I only have ten – the other man was even more desperate than those around him – my wife and my children are starving, they haven't eaten for days. Take it or leave it, the black marketeer was telling him. The man was reaching into his coat, pulling out a gun and shooting the black marketeer. What good is fifteen d'marks to you now, he was saying. Was turning away and disappearing into the crowd. One day this would be *her*, she had thought; one day it would be *her* lying on the ground or in the snow. A bullet in *her* head and *her* blood running down *her* face.

'Ask Control for a routeing for London Heathrow,' she told Maeschler.

She's asked directions for Heathrow – the whisper spread round the women on The Green, in the middle of Parliament Square. She's bringing Lufthansa 3216 into London.

Bastard – Langdon turned to the other members of Strike.

You were right – the operation commander nodded as Finn came into the Ops Room. She's requested a routeing for Heathrow.

She was always going to – Finn helped himself to a coffee and settled at one of the desks.

Because at ten o'clock this morning she actually told us what she was going to do. Not directly, but in the way she specified the deadline in a number of hours – twelve to be precise – rather than as a time. Which means that where she'll be when the deadline expires, it might not actually be ten o'clock this evening. Therefore she was going to change time zones. Therefore she was coming to Heathrow.

Because Lufthansa 3216 had taken off from Berlin with thirteen metric tonnes of fuel – nine tonnes for the flight plus four reserve. And a Boeing 737 burned fuel at a rate of two and a half tonnes an hour. Which gave a flying time of just over five hours.

The hijack had taken place thirty minutes into the flight, plus the thirty minutes to return back over Berlin. So effectively you were down to four hours. Add Berlin–Paris, where the hijacker had first landed, then Paris–Amsterdam, where the hijacker had flown next, plus the usual in-flight delays and the fact that an aircraft burned more fuel when it was landing and taking off than it did when cruising, and you could knock another two and a half off. So when 3216 had taken off from Amsterdam it had less than ninety minutes' flying time.

Then run that against the first assumption that the hijacker was going to switch time zones. Throw in a second, that the Amsterdam stop-over was merely an interlude, and that the hijacker was targeting the Big Players – Paris, London, Moscow and Washington. And she was telling you where she was going next.

Paris was out because she'd already been there, and, in any case, it was in the same time zone as Amsterdam. And Moscow and Washington were out because of flight times. Which only left one.

*

'Lufthansa 3216. Route direct to Refso.' The Dutch controller's English was clipped and precise. 'Then Lambourne Three Alpha arrival.' Refso was the reporting point between Dutch and British air space; Lambourne, in Essex, was a navigation beacon on the route into London from Amsterdam, and Lambourne Three Alpha was the standard routeing from the Lambourne beacon into Heathrow. 'Contact London on one three six decimal five five.'

Maeschler leaned to his right and began to adjust the frequency.

'Check ATIS first,' she told him.

Because that will tell us the conditions at Heathrow, including which runway we're landing on. Which in turn will tell us our route in. And the authorities may not like the way we're coming in and might try to change it. And if they try, I want to know.

Maeschler glanced at the first officer and dialled up the frequency for Heathrow.

'This is Heathrow Information Charlie . . .' The details were updated every twenty minutes. 'Runway in use Two Seven Left. Surface wind two six zero, eighteen knots. Overcast at four thousand feet. QNH is one zero one eight.'

So now you know – Maeschler looked back at the woman in the jump seat. And everyone else will also know. Because anyone with the right set can pick up our messages on VHF, and those who can't can listen to them being played live on radio and television. Which you understood already, of course. Because you planned it as you planned everything.

Pity they didn't know much about the hijackers, Finn thought. Four of them, from the debriefs of the passengers she'd released. Two men and two women, all heavily armed, though there had been no indication how they had smuggled their weapons on board. But nothing apart from that, not even the names and aliases they were using. Because the hijacker had hacked a pirate programme into the computerized check-in system in Berlin, activated when the computer received confirmation that 3216 was airborne, and wiped all record of the passenger list. Therefore the security people hadn't been able to check which passengers were genuine, and which were the hijackers travelling under false passports or genuine passports assigned to someone sitting comfortably at home in Bremen or Copenhagen or Manchester.

He topped up the coffee, checked the television monitors against the right-hand wall of the room, and placed the two radios on the desk – one VHF tuned to the frequency 3216 was using, and the other a transistor so that he could listen to the press reports of the progress of 3216, and *ipso facto* the details the hijackers were receiving.

The Operations Room was silent, almost eerie. Just like one of the RSGs, Finn thought. He'd been down one once, part of an exercise. An attack on a Regional Seat of Government, one of the underground bunkers for use in the event of nuclear war: four levels in a hollowed-out hill in Essex. Everything ready for World War Three – desks and chairs and bunks, even the blankets folded on them and the notepads and pencils perfectly in position. Everything silent as everything was ready and silent in the Ops Room now. Everything waiting, except the Cold War had ended, the threat of the ultimate mushroom over the world had lifted, and the RSG had been decommissioned. Just like the Ops Room until twenty minutes ago. Then somebody had pressed the button: then the hijacker had requested a routeing for Heathrow.

It was one-thirty London time, Lufthansa 3216 over the North Sea. The nerves had gone from her stomach now, and her mind was calm.

. . . The next time the United Nations lets your people down . . . She remembered the moment he had told her. The corridor in the hospital, the night dark and freezing, the children crying and the Serb shells thundering outside. Adin somewhere on the front line and little Jovan in the makeshift ward two doors away.

Look down on me this day, she told them both. Pray for me, my husband. Smile at me, my son.

The next time the United Nations stands by and does nothing. She remembered why he had told her . . .

'Contact London,' she instructed Maeschler.

'London. This is Lufthansa 3216. Approaching Refso.'

Lufthansa 3216 approaching British air space, Strike was informed. About to leave Dutch air space. Now in British air space. Lufthansa 3216 now his problem, Finn thought.

'Lufthansa 3216.' They all heard the voice of the British controller. 'Standard Lambourne Three Alpha arrival for landing runway Two Seven Left.'

'What does that mean?' Langdon demanded.

Kilpatrick crossed to the telephones and asked the flight adviser to join them.

Lambourne Three Alpha was the standard arrival route for aircraft coming in from Amsterdam, the adviser informed them. He was settled uncomfortably at the end of the table facing Langdon. Runway Two Seven Left was the standard runway at that time of day for aircraft coming in from Lambourne.

'Which way do they come in from Lambourne?' Langdon leaned forward.

'You mean the route?'

'Yes.' Because Lambourne is to the east, Heathrow is to the west, and London is bang in the middle.

'Up the Thames and over central London.'

'Over the City? Directly over Westminster, Downing Street, and Parliament?'

'Yes.'

Lufthansa 3216 approaching the Essex coast, Strike was informed.

'Lufthansa 3216. Descend when ready to flight level one five zero.' Descend to fifteen thousand feet.

The air traffic control room was rectangular; low lighting and quiet atmosphere, no smoking and not even soft drinks allowed. The watch supervisor's desk was at the head of the room; along the left wall were four radar suites, each controlling a sector; another suite on the end wall farthest from the watch supervisor, and four more suites along the other long wall. At each suite were two radar controllers, headsets on and radar screens horizontal on the desk in front of them, the crew chief for the sector standing between them.

The watch supervisor checked the time, left his desk and walked the twenty metres to the third suite on the left. 'How's it going?' he asked the controller in the right-hand seat.

'Fine,' Simmons told him.

'How long can we leave it before we stop everything else?'

Because there are thirty-eight landings and thirty take-offs every hour at Heathrow at this time of day. Of course we'll clear a window for 3216, stop all landings and takeoffs. Do it too early, however, and we create chaos; too late and we risk adding to the problems.

'Twenty minutes window,' the crew chief told him. 'As soon as she leaves Lambourne.'

'Agreed.'

'3216 over Essex coast,' Simmons informed them. 'Two minutes to Lambourne.'

And at Lambourne he would direct 3216 left, so it would pick up the ILS, the Instrument Landing System, which would guide it on to runway Two Seven Left.

'Lufthansa 3216 approaching the point at which they turn for the run-in to Heathrow,' the intelligence major informed the Operations Room.

The room was beginning to fill.

So what are you thinking, Finn?

I'm hoping that my assumptions are correct, that's what I'm thinking. I'm hoping that the plans we laid this morning actually work. I'm hoping the preliminary diversion works, otherwise the press might see us approaching the aircraft and put it out on radio and television. And if they do, the hijackers will hear, and then they'll be waiting for us.

'3216 en route for Lambourne,' the intelligence major updated the Operations Room. 'Heathrow about to be closed down.'

A Boeing 737 has six doors – that's what I'm thinking, because that's what I have to think about. Two at the front, two at the rear, and two emergency doors over the wings. All doors can be opened by handles on the outside. Three toilets where the hijackers might hide: one at front on left, assuming entry is through the front port door, and two at rear. And I'm thinking this, and nothing else, because from now on I can only think of what is relevant for when I go on to Lufthansa 3216 tonight. And I must assume that I'm going on, because otherwise I won't be prepared. And if I'm not prepared, I'm dead.

'Hold,' the watch supervisor told the Clacton crew chief.

'Hold,' the crew chief told Simmons.

The supervisor put the phone down, left his desk and hurried to them. 'We need to re-route.'

Getting tight to do it, they knew. Plus 3216 was running out of fuel.

'3216 one minute from Lambourne.' Simmons's voice was almost mechanical.

'Why re-route?' the crew chief asked.

'Orders.' The reply was direct rather than blunt. '3216 can't go over central London.'

'Who says?'

'Downing Street.'

Oh shit, the crew chief thought. 'Which rules out a landing from the east. Which means a landing from the west.'

'That's what they've told us to do.'

'We can't.' Simmons's eyes were riveted to the solid line against the black of the radar screen, the last details of Lufthansa 3216's flight pattern trailing in a cone behind it.

'Why not?'

'Tail wind from the west is eighteen knots.' It was the crew chief. 'Maximum tail wind for a 737 is ten.'

'3216 thirty seconds from Lambourne.'

The supervisor turned, ran to his desk, and punched the number. 'This is the watch supervisor at West Drayton. We cannot divert 3216 from its planned course because that would involve a landing from the west, and the tail wind is too strong.'

'How much too strong?'

'The maximum permitted wind speed is ten knots and the actual wind speed at the moment is eighteen.'

'The west approach,' Langdon told him curtly. 'Do it.' Because there's no way I'll allow Lufthansa 3216 to fly over central London. No way I'll allow the bloody hijacker to fly over Westminster when I'm sitting in the Cobra rooms below Downing Street.

'3216 at Lambourne,' Simmons said calmly.

*

The layer of cloud was thin below them. It was time to turn left, she knew, time to angle towards London, pick up the ILS beam, then swing right and follow it up the Thames and into Heathrow. Because that was what Air Traffic Control had instructed the other flights from Amsterdam when she had sat listening to the airband at Heathrow four days before.

'Lufthansa 3216.' The voice of the controller sounded different. 'Turn right on to two eight five for landing on Zero Nine Left.'

Which is not what Control had told the other planes. Which was why she had made the Heathrow check. She sensed the way the first officer froze and Maeschler hesitated.

'They're re-routeing us.' She was still calm, still controlled. The Zastava sub-machine gun was across her lap, the M70 was in the shoulder holster and the grenades were in her pocket. 'We should be turning left, not right. Any course above two hundred and seventy means we're going north of the runway.'

'Correct,' Maeschler told her.

'Check ATIS again.'

'Runway in use is Two Seven Left.' The details on the automatic message were the same as earlier. 'Surface wind two six zero, eighteen knots.'

'Tell Control that,' she ordered Maeschler. 'Nothing else, just point out that they're telling us to land with an eighteen-knot tail wind and the maximum is ten.'

'Control, this is Lufthansa 3216. Repeat last directions.'

Something was wrong. Finn ignored the other men round him and listened to the exchange.

'Lufthansa 3216. Turn right on to two eight five for landing on Zero Nine Left.'

'Control, this is Lufthansa 3216. You originally told me to land from the east on runway Two Seven Left. Now you're telling me to land from the west on runway Zero Nine Left.'

'Affirmative, 3216.'

'But according to ATIS there's an eighteen-knot tail wind from the west, and the maximum tail wind for a 737 is ten knots.'

There was no reply.

Finn swung in his chair so that he could see the TV monitors. There had been no live pictures of Lufthansa 3216 since the Boeing had left Amsterdam, therefore ITV and CNN were replaying the takeoff from Amsterdam, and the BBC were running a studio discussion: a presenter and what Finn thought of as the inevitable panel of experts.

'What's ATIS?' the presenter asked.

'Airfield Terminal Information Service,' the flight consultant told him. 'It gives the latest airfield report to incoming pilots.'

'What's the difference between a tail wind of ten and eighteen knots?'

They stopped talking as Maeschler spoke again.

'Control, this is Lufthansa 3216. If I follow your instructions and land from the west, the tail wind will mean that I might run out of runway.'

For the second time there was no reply.

'Is that correct?' the presenter asked the panel.

'Yes.'

'So if they land from the west, they might not make it?'

'They should make it . . .'

'But?'

'There's a chance they won't.'

'And the authorities are aware of that but are still telling them to do it?'

Be careful, the expert warned himself. Wrong answer and he wouldn't be invited as an expert again; right answer and he might jeopardize his government contracts. 'So it would seem,' he agreed.

What's happening? one of the sergeants in the police unit supervising the demonstration in Parliament Square asked the woman next to him. Heathrow's changed the route in, she told him. Heathrow's told them to land from the west, but the tail wind from the west is above the permitted speed and it means they might run out of runway. Bloody politicians, the policeman said aloud.

'Control, this is Lufthansa 3216. Be aware we are fuel priority.' Lufthansa 3216 running out of fuel, they understood. 'I repeat. Be aware we are fuel priority.'

So what do I say, the radar controller stared at the crew chief, what do I do? 'She's turning.' He picked up the first movement. 'Repeat. She's turning.'

'3216 turning,' the crew chief told the shift supervisor.

'Lufthansa 3216 turning,' the supervisor informed Downing Street.

'3216 turning left,' Simmons told the crew chief. 'Confirm, she's turning left.'

'You mean right.' Because that's what we told her to do. That's what we were ordered to tell her.

'No, I mean left.'

There was nothing on VHF and there should be something. 'What's happening?' the BBC presenter asked the panel.

'One of two things.' It was the flight expert again. 'Either Lufthansa 3216 has turned north. Except that's what Air Traffic Control instructed, which seems unlikely.'

'Or?'

'She's disregarded Air Traffic Control and turned left, which would be the normal route in. Then she'd head south at an angle till she picks up the ILS beam, turn right, and follow the beam into Heathrow.'

'Over London?'

'Yes. Over London.'

'And as of this moment, all other air traffic into and out of Heathrow has been stopped.'

'Yes.'

'So the only plane which will fly over London in the next twenty minutes is Lufthansa 3216?'

'Yes.'

The cloud was around them. 'Locking on to ILS,' Maeschler told her. 'Beginning final approach.' The Boeing banked gently to the right, the cloud thinned and the ground was suddenly visible beneath them. The green of the fields below them, the silver of the Thames snaking away from them, and the grey of London in front of them.

. . . The next time the United Nations lets your people down you must have something the world wants, he had told her . . . The next time the UN fails you, you must have something which makes the world afraid of you . . .

CNN, BBC and ITV were all already transmitting pictures from Heathrow, BBC cutting with shots from Parliament Square, and ITV mixing with aerial shots of London from an Aero Spatiale Twin Squirrel jet helicopter.

So what are you thinking, Finn?

I'm thinking that I'm at the top of the ladder. The night's black as hell around me and the aircraft door is in front of me. Steve to my left, Jim and Ken tight behind; Janner and his team at the rear door, the helicopter hovering over the flight deck of Lufthansa 3216, the ops major counting down and the diversion about to go in. I'm in first, that's what I'm thinking. I go right, start looking for the hijackers. Steve goes left and checks the flight deck and toilet. Jim covers me and Ken covers Steve.

Although that's not all I'm thinking.

What do you mean, Finn? What are you *really* thinking?

'Lufthansa 3216 is approaching from the east.' The radio presenter tried to stifle the excitement in his voice. 'We are receiving reports that Lufthansa 3216 has passed over the Thames flood barrier and is about to fly over the City.'

'We have first pictures of Lufthansa 3216,' the voice of the ITV presenter was suddenly urgent, suddenly dramatic, the monitor showing the shot from the Twin Squirrel, the Boeing slightly below it.

Christ she's low, Finn thought. The television images were almost unreal – the empty runways at Heathrow, the people in Parliament Square, their faces turned up and their eyes searching the sky to the east. The aerial shot from the helicopter of Lufthansa 3216 tracking up the river.

Docklands was below her, Tower Bridge in front then suddenly below, and Westminster and Big Ben drawing her in as if she was on a piece of string.

Finn glanced at the BBC pictures from Westminster – the sky empty in the background and the Palace of Westminster in front, Big Ben to the right and the Churchill statue to the left.

'Lufthansa 3216, this is Heathrow Tower.'

'Heathrow Tower, this is Lufthansa 3216.' Maeschler, the captain, husband of a beautiful wife and father of two pretty children – the papers had found out and published a family photograph. Maeschler the hero who'd landed 3216 at Schipol even though the authorities had tried to stop him.

'3216, you are cleared to land.'

There was a slight delay.

'Thank you, Heathrow Tower.' Not the captain this time.

It's not the critic who counts ... she remembered the

words he had quoted at her, remembered again the corridor of the hospital. The doctors white with exhaustion, the nurses dropping with fatigue, and the United Nations still doing nothing to stop the shells falling on them. It's not the one who points out how the strong man stumbled or how the doer of deeds might have done them better . . .

'I can see Lufthansa 3216 . . .' The radio reporter had slipped through the police cordon and was standing on Westminster Bridge. 'Lufthansa 3216 is coming up the Thames towards me . . .' The Boeing was suddenly in shot on the pictures from Parliament Square, suddenly approaching Westminster. Passing over Parliament and framed for one incredible moment between Big Ben and the Churchill statue.

The credit belongs to the man who is actually in the arena, he had told her . . . Who strives valiantly and spends himself in a worthy cause . . . Who, if he wins, knows the triumph of high achievement and who, if he fails, at least fails while daring greatly . . .

What had he said the motto was?

Who Dares Wins.

Finn left the building and stood on the tarmac looking east. Heathrow was like a ghost around him, the skies and runways empty.

So what are you really thinking, Finn?

You know what I'm thinking.

Tell me anyway.

I'm thinking about a winter night behind the lines in Bosnia. I'm thinking about how the United Nations blew Kev and Geordie John to Kingdom Come that night. How Janner and Max only survived because someone who didn't know them risked everything to save them, even though she didn't have to. I'm thinking about how I told her that I owed, that the regiment owed, and that none of us would ever forget. Because if you can't help those who help you and yours, then who can you help? If you can't be loyal to those who are loyal to you and yours, then who or what the hell can you be loyal to?

In the sky to the east he saw the first flash from the wing lights of the Boeing.

But that's not all you're thinking, is it, Finn?

No, it's not all I'm thinking.

So what else, Finn?

I'm thinking about the other thing I said to her that night. About how I told her that the West would never help her people unless her people had something the West wanted. I'm thinking about what I said her people should do next time the United Nations let them down.

But there's something else, isn't there, Finn?

Okay, there's something else.

So what is it, Finn?

You want to know? You really want to know?

Yeah, Finn. I really want to know.

I'm thinking that it's her on Lufthansa 3216. Except it can't be her, because she's dead. But the hijacker on Lufthansa 3216 is doing exactly what I told her to do.

The Boeing was over the outer marker, over the approach lights. Next time the UN lets your people down, he'd told her . . .

The Boeing was over the lead-in lights, over the runway threshold. The credit belongs to the man who is actually in the arena, he'd said . . .

The tyres thumped on the tarmac. As long as the cause was a worthy cause, and the journey was just and right . . .

Hers was a worthy cause, which was why he'd told her. Hers was a just and righteous journey, otherwise he would not have set her upon it. Time to do it, she thought, time to take it to the last stage. Time to do what he'd told her, the way he'd told her. Change it all, he'd said; change the rules, the game, change everything.

Kara's Rules. Kara's Game.

Thanks, Finn.

# Kara's Game

# Book One

*Bosnia . . .*
*ten months earlier*
*January 1994*

# 1

The bridge was the problem. Because that was where the snipers were waiting for you. And you had to cross because you were on one side and the food was on the other.

Please God, may they not be waiting today. Please God, may they not get me. Because today my husband is on the front line, and because he's on the front line, probably only three hundred metres from the bridge, he cannot go for the food while I look after our son. Therefore I have to go, even though the food will only be a bowl of beans and a slice of dry bread. I cannot wait because my son has not eaten for two days and is crying with the pain. Because we have been under siege since August, and now it's January. And the nights are long and dark and the days are so cold I sometimes think I'm going to die, and the shells have been falling on my dear sweet pretty little town for as long as I can remember. Therefore I have to go for food. But because my husband is on the front line, waiting for the next attack, there is no one to look after my son. So I have to take my precious little Jovan with me. Because unless he eats soon he will die. But in trying to reach the food the two of us might die anyway.

Therefore, when I reach the bridge and begin to run across it, I will pray that the sniper who killed old man Samir yesterday and little Lejla the day before, is looking the other way, or moving position as the snipers do, or warming his fingers round a mug of hot coffee, or glancing up and downing a slivovic.

Therefore when I begin to run across the bridge I will hold my little Jovan in my left arm, so that my body will be between him and the sniper. And when I try to make it back across the bridge I will hold Jovan on my right, so that I am again between him and the sniper. Please God, protect me. Please God, may the shells not fall again until I and my little son are safely home.

Dear God, why did you decree that I should be born a Bosnian? Dear God, why have you allowed the war-mongers to tear my country and my people apart? Dear God, why have you decreed that the governments of the world do nothing; that the United Nations should stand back and allow this carnage?

She made sure the coat was wrapped tightly round the boy, that his gloves were on his hands and the scarf round his head, and pulled on her own coat and boots. Even though it was mid-morning the room was dark – just the glimmer from the makeshift candle on the table. They had lived in the semi-basement since the siege had started and the shells had begun falling. At first, and in the heat of summer, herself and Adin in the double bed and Jovan in his next to them. Now, in the cold, the three of them slept together. When Adin was not on the front line defending the town. Two days at the front and one off – that was the way the men fought now. Not just the soldiers but everyone. Sometimes she woke at night – when, that was, she was able to sleep – and imagined him staring into the black, the wire to the land mines clutched in his hand for the moment the enemy tried to storm the town.

She opened the door and checked outside. The snow was frozen hard, the sky was a deep grey, and the sound of small-arms fire rattled in the distance, at the head of the valley where the men were positioned. It was the usual pattern – shelling for an hour as the winter night broke into day, a handful of shells in the middle of the few hours of light, then a last barrage as the light left them. Always the snipers in the middle, though, like the tripwires in no man's land.

She lifted the boy in her arms, picked up the tin pan and lid, went outside, and closed the door. There was one other person in what had once been a street, scurrying as she herself was already scurrying, scarf wrapped round her head and tin container clutched in her hand. She nodded at the other woman and hurried after her, feet slipping on the ice and the air almost freezing her lungs.

The boy's face was already white with cold, and the houses around her were shell-damaged and wasted. Some families had moved, of course: across the bridge to the new town, but the new town was already packed with refugees.

Maglaj – pronounced Maglai – was nestled on either side of the river which had once flowed gently down the valley between the pine-covered hills rising to the west, north and east. Across the bridge, on the west side, was the new town with the shops and the school. On the east was the old quarter, its streets narrow and winding, the minaret of the mosque rising above the red-tiled roofs, and the cluster of more modern houses in the trees beyond.

She and Adin had come here eight years ago, after they both graduated from the University of Sarajevo, she in languages and he in chemistry. Until the conflict he had worked in the paper factory, just down the valley to the south of the new town, and she had taught in the school, on the northern edge. For three years they had dreamed of the day they would have a child, had almost despaired. Even now she remembered the morning the doctor had told her she was pregnant, even now she remembered how she had left school early and gone to the paper factory because she could not wait till evening for Adin to know.

The small-arms fire stopped, abruptly and without warning, and she froze, knew that the shelling was about to descend on them again, that she'd got it wrong. The rattle began again and she hurried on, her feet slipping on the ice which covered the bricks and the rubble, till she came to the last group of houses before the bridge.

The river was some seventy metres wide, and the bridge which spanned it rose slightly in the centre, so that from where she now stood she couldn't see the other end. The people were huddled in a line in the shelter of the wall, thin and tired and cold like herself. Only one other with a child, and all carrying shiny tin pots with the lids firmly on.

She held the boy against her and stood at the end.

'Sniper?' she asked.

'Sniper,' the man at the front nodded. He was rocking backwards and forwards, as if gathering momentum, as if winding up his courage. As if the fraction of a second he would save when he launched himself from the cover of the building would save his life.

Don't worry, she whispered to Jovan, soon we'll have food.

Going in ten, the man told them.

Go with him, go with a group, and she might have cover. But go in a group and the sniper might take more notice. Go and she and the boy might die, don't go and the boy would starve.

Going in five, the man in front muttered, perhaps to them all, perhaps just to himself.

Give the boy to someone else and offer to get their food for them, she thought. That way she might be killed but the boy would live. Except that if she made it across and couldn't get back, if the snipers pinned them down or the artillery destroyed the bridge, then she might never see him again. Then she couldn't protect him, feed him, make sure he at least survived.

Going in three, the man's lips moved, no sound coming out. The morning was suddenly colder. Going in two.

*

It was almost time to move, Valeschov thought; he'd been in this position too long, any longer and the other side might spot him and send their own sniper to target him. In five minutes he'd pull back, skirt behind the trees to the other position, grab something warm on the way. The metal was almost frozen to the skin of his cheek and his finger was stiff with cold. He checked that the settings on the telescopic sight were as he had set them when he had zeroed the rifle two hours earlier, and settled again. No movement on the bridge for the past fifteen minutes anyway, so perhaps they weren't crossing today. More likely they knew he was there, though, more likely they were gathered in a huddle in the shelter of the last building of the old town waiting for someone to be the first. He thought about pulling back his cuff and checking his watch, and decided it was too cold. Mid-morning, he knew anyway, feeding time at the refugee centre. Regular as clockwork. So someone would be breaking soon, because otherwise they wouldn't eat.

Going in one, the man at the front said. The stubble on his face was grey and his coat was torn.

Go with him, she decided, but make sure she was to his left, use him as protection. Except that was why he was counting, because he was hoping someone would go with him, and if they did he would run to the left so that whoever went with him had to go to the right, between him and the sniper.

'Now.' He launched himself forward.

She was moving, the boy clasped tight to her left side and the pan in her right hand. She was past the others and alongside the man, then suddenly clear of the protection of the building, suddenly on the bridge.

To her right the man froze in fear.

*

Time for it, MacFarlane thought.

MacFarlane didn't like it here. Okay, so the position gave them a good view across the bridge to Maglaj old town, and the building against which they'd parked was on the north side of the street and therefore protected them from incoming fire. But two, three times a day, sometimes more, it crucified MacFarlane to see the people crossing the bridge and being taken out by a sniper.

He pulled the parka tight against his light blue United Nations helmet, and checked the time. Eleven hundred hours, so everything should be quiet for the next four, except for the two or three shells they'd throw over round midday to keep everyone on their toes. The standard thirty artillery rounds this morning – he'd reported in as usual half an hour ago. Plus, he assumed, the usual thirty-five to forty this afternoon.

The jeep, parked in the lee of the houses, was white, with the letters UN distinctive on both sides as well as the bonnet, plus the words VOYNI PASMATRACI, Military Observer, on the front and back of the vehicle. There were four of them in the team: MacFarlane himself from Canada, Umbegi from Nigeria, Anderssen from Norway, and Belan from Belgium. They'd come in two days ago, when the various factions had agreed the ceasefire, been delayed slightly because the two sides had taken their time clearing the minefields from the road. Because Maglaj and Tesanj, fifteen kilometres away, were a so-called Muslim pocket isolated like an island in the Serb-held area to the north of the main front line. The sort of area the Serbs would seek to overrun prior to any final agreement.

And because there was a possibility of an agreement, there was another round of so-called peace negotiations under way in Vienna, and to give those negotiations a chance the two sides had declared a ceasefire. And as their contribution to the sham the United Nations was putting out its usual UN-speak. *The situation in Maglaj remains at levels consistent with previous days.* Except Maglaj was still under fire, but that was par for the course.

Perhaps the politicians were right, though. Perhaps another clutch of dead this morning didn't matter any more, perhaps another handful of women and kids in the makeshift morgue this afternoon really was insignificant in the greater order of things.

Goddamn Bosnia.

In front of him the bridge stretched in a curve to the shattered remains of the old town; above him the sky cleared slightly. Christ it was cold, fifteen under and every sign of falling.

'Cigarette?' The Nigerian offered him a Winston.

'Here goes.' It was Anderssen, the Norwegian.

MacFarlane saw the figure on the bridge, the head first as the figure came up the slight curve, then the shoulders, then the body.

The woman was tucked low and running hard, the scarf round her head was coming loose and the food can was flapping in her right hand. Her feet were sliding slightly on the ice, so that she was off balance, and her left arm was clutched round something. 'Christ.' It was meant to be a thought but came out as an exclamation. 'She's carrying a kid.' In her left arm, so that she was protecting it with her body. Sniper in position up to fifteen minutes ago, he remembered, please God may the bastard be taking a drink or moving position. Sometimes the men in the hills sprayed a machine gun arc across the bridge, sometimes a haphazard burst of rifle fire. Sometimes, if the man on duty was a pro, one single well-aimed shot. Then the figure would crumple and the bastard would wait to see if anyone came to help them, if anyone tried to pull them to safety. And then the bastards in the hills would play their little game, just as everyone played their games in the Balkans. Sometimes allow the body to be hauled away, sometimes use it as a bait to take out those brave or foolish enough to help.

Don't slip, he willed the woman, just don't slow down.

She was halfway across, her breath rasping and her legs beginning to slow. No sniper shot so far, thank God, no single sharp sound, no body stumbling and collapsing. She was three-quarters of the way over. He could see her face and make out her age. Late twenties, black hair and good-looking, the child a boy, probably four years old.

Thirty metres behind her another group appeared like puppets.

Time to get them later, Valeschov decided, time to wait for them to come back with their little saucepans of food. Because then they'd be moving slower, because then they'd be terrified of spilling anything.

The woman came off the bridge and slowed by the jeep.

Her lungs were screaming and her head was pounding. Thank God there'd been no sniper today, thank God she and Jovan had made it. She glanced at the soldiers by the UN vehicle and hurried up the street, keeping to the right for the protection the buildings offered. Before the war this had been the main area of Maglaj, now the shop fronts were boarded and the buildings around and behind them were pockmarked with holes.

The street was almost empty, only a few like herself scuttling for the food kitchen, and it was beginning to snow again, the first flakes settling like feathers. She glanced up at the sky, unsure whether she was looking at the snow or searching for incoming shells, then hurried across and disappeared into the side streets on the southern side.

The food itself – by which she meant the boiled beans and bread which was now their staple diet – was prepared in a kitchen beneath the radio station, and served in the school fifty metres away which the local Red Cross had taken over.

She turned the last corner, between the ruins of the houses. The line of people was five deep, the inside layer pressed against the wall and the outer layers packed against them, either for warmth or protection or both. She followed the queue round the corner, and round the next, then back along the third wall till she was almost at the front again. Today it would take hours, she understood, today she might not get the boy back across the bridge before the shells the Chetniks threw over at midday. She joined the end of the line, making sure she stood in the middle, and held the boy tight, smiling at him and whispering him a story. At least they were able to join the queue, at least she had a ration card which entitled her and Adin and Jovan to the food.

The queue shuffled slowly, someone occasionally pushing, but most of the men and women too exhausted to do anything other than wait. God it was cold – she shuffled forward another two paces and stamped her feet in a vain attempt to shake the numbness from her toes.

'You okay?' She tucked her head against the boy and smiled at him again.

'Okay.'

They reached the first corner, seemed to stand an eternity before they reached the next, even longer before they turned along the front wall and edged towards the steps and door into the school.

There had been no midday shells so far, so perhaps the Chetniks were letting them off today, perhaps there really was a ceasefire, perhaps the peace talks in Vienna really were achieving something.

They were inside at last, along the lime-green corridor and into the room at the other end. The wooden tables were on the left, the vats of soup on them and the helpers behind them, one woman checking the ration cards and stamping the backs with the date so no one would get double rations, and the others ladling the liquid and cutting the bread. The room seemed packed and cold, people milling with their soup cans, a few seeking a space to eat but most leaving. The floor was running wet and the smell of the beans hung in the air.

She felt in her coat pocket, pulled out the three ration cards, and showed them to the first woman.

Kadira Isak – the woman read her name. Adin and Jovan Isak. 'Where's your husband?' she asked.

'At the front,' Kara explained. 'He's due back this afternoon.'

'So you didn't get his food yesterday?' The woman checked the back of the card.

'No, because he was on the front line yesterday.' And therefore, although the boy and I could have done with his share, it would have deprived someone else.

The woman nodded, stamped the three cards to indicate they had received their food for that day, and nodded for them to move forward.

The beans were bubbling in the vat. Another woman ladled her two helpings, and the third passed her two slices of rough white bread.

'Three helpings,' she told them. 'My husband's back from the front today.'

The beans were white, without taste. She smiled her thanks, jammed the lid firmly on, put the bread in the plastic bag she'd carried in her pocket, and left. Outside it was snowing slightly more heavily. Thank God there was no sniper today, thank God she wouldn't have to run across the bridge.

MacFarlane saw her coming. It was funny how you remembered certain people, certain faces. Perhaps it was the child she was carrying or the way she was carrying him, perhaps the way she'd run across the bridge earlier. He smiled at her as she passed and watched as she approached the bridge.

Any more snow and he'd begin losing visibility, Valeschov thought. Christ it was cold. He held the Dragunov carefully, so it did not touch his face. A couple of hours to go, then he'd be off to the village two kilometres away for forty-eight hours' R and R. He peered down the sights and picked up the bridge. There were two places where the targets were soft and easy: the first was the bridge and the second was the street running from the school into the new town, parallel to the river and some hundred metres from it. Sniper Alley the locals would call it, and if they didn't they should.

No midday shelling today, so something was up. Not that they'd tell him, he'd be the last to know. Probably leave him up here to freeze his balls off unless he made sure they remembered him. The snow was heavier and the darkness was closing in, even though it was still early afternoon. He flicked the safety on and blew the snowflakes away from the sights. Christ it was even colder. He settled again and picked up the bridge. Someone was about to cross – it was strange how you could pick it up, almost smell the fear. Which direction, though, old town to new, or new town to old? Probably the latter.

New town to old – he saw the figure. Go for the first and not get lined up properly, or wait and hope there was a second? Perhaps just let off a few rounds and laugh at the way the bastards danced.

Thank God there was no sniper, Kara thought, thank God she didn't have to risk spilling the soup. She called it soup because it sounded better; when she and Jovan got home perhaps she'd add a few herbs she'd saved from the summer, make it taste better, at least make it taste of something. God she was cold, God how little Jovan's face was white and stiff. Please may Adin be okay, please may he make it home tonight.

Somebody didn't know he was there – Valeschov flicked off the safety. Somebody was walking rather than running across the bridge. Somebody liked playing Russian roulette. Perhaps he'd take them in one, perhaps he'd put a shot near them first, scare the shit out of them before he finished them off.

The river below her was grey and the sky above was lost in the snow. Why wasn't she running, she suddenly thought; why hadn't she waited to cross the bridge with a group? At least Jovan was on her right, away from where the snipers normally were. Run, she told herself. Don't run, because if you do you'll lose your nerve for ever. What the hell are you talking about – she came back at herself. You're on the bridge and even though there's no sniper you're in the open and exposed.

Take them now, Valeschov decided, it was too cold to be frigging about.

The swirl of snow closed round her, so she could no longer see even the end of the bridge. On the hillside above, Valeschov heard the crunch of footsteps behind him and turned.

'We're pulling out.' The sergeant was wrapped against the cold, his face barely visible. 'They're sending up the big stuff.'

'Thank Christ for that.' Valeschov flicked on the safety and eased himself up. 'Another hour and I'd have been a bloody snowman.'

Something was wrong. There had been no shells at midday, and no small-arms rounds that afternoon.

It was ten minutes to the time the Serbs on the hills above Maglaj began their late afternoon barrage – thirty rounds over a one-hour period, then more or less silence for the night.

MacFarlane swung the Nissan in a tight circle, drove to the dilapidated building next to the bank midway between the radio station and the school, and went to the ground floor of the block where the UNMO team had established its base.

The room was six metres by five, low ceiling and sparse furniture. The sleeping bags and American camp cots were against one wall, food and cooking items against a second, and a table and chairs in the centre. The windows were boarded against shrapnel, and the radio handset was on the table, coaxial wires running to the HF set mounted in the vehicle so they didn't have to go outside to speak to Vitez.

Umbegi brewed a tea and they waited.

Jovan's hands and face were cold. Kara closed the door, lit the candle, sat him by the stove and rubbed a semblance of warmth back into him. The semi-basement in which they now lived was crowded: the stove in the centre of the rear wall, the double bed to the right, which they also used as a sofa, and Jovan's smaller bed – which he no longer slept in – to the left, the table in the middle with the wooden chairs round it, and the dresser against the left wall, on it the family photographs and the radio (connected to the bike, which you had to pedal to get the power). The only other furniture was an armchair to the left of the door.

At the beginning of the siege they had boarded the windows with planks and moved the rest of the furniture to the floor above, leaving the top level empty . . . At the beginning the water and electricity had stopped almost immediately, so now they made their own candles and got their water from the well in the garden . . . At the beginning . . .

How long ago that was.

Jovan was playing on the double bed with the wooden toys Adin had made him. Kara knelt in front of the stove, opened the fire door, and added a little more wood. Not too much – even though every summer she and Adin made sure they had enough for the winter she was careful now, unsure how long winter would last. The boy's eyes stared at her through the halo of light round the wick of the candle. She poured his share of the beans into a saucepan, then half of her own. Perhaps it was caution, perhaps premonition, that she saved the rest. Then she cut half a potato and half a carrot into cubes and put them in. It was a luxury, but today they should celebrate; this afternoon Adin would be home from the front, even if only for a few hours, and today there had been no sniper waiting for her to cross the bridge.

Please God, may Adin be safe. Please may he really come home tonight. Please God, may this crazy war soon be over.

Outside it was dark.

At midday there had been no shells, and by now there should have been the late afternoon blitz, reminding them that the Serbs, the Chetniks as she called them, were on the hills above Maglaj and controlling everything that happened in it.

Perhaps that was it for today, Kara realized she was praying; perhaps the Chetniks had run out of shells, perhaps they were going away. Perhaps there really was a ceasefire.

Crazy war – the thought was more conscious this time.

First the Serbs had attacked the Croats and Muslims. Then, just under a year ago, the Croats had changed sides, and were now fighting with rather than against the Serbs. So villages and towns and areas were split. But even that was logical compared with what was really happening.

Take the small pocket containing Maglaj and, fifteen kilometres to the north, Tesanj. The pocket was an island, isolated in Serb-held territory, with the main front line with Muslim-held Bosnia to the south. On the west, north and east sides of the pocket the Serbs were attacking them; to the south the attack was coming from a combined Serb and Croat army. But in Tesanj the local Croats and Muslims were fighting side by side against the Serbs.

Even the term *Muslim* was misleading. At first the world called me a Yugoslav, she remembered telling an aid worker once; then it called me a Bosnian, and now it calls me a Muslim. But I've never been inside a mosque, don't even know how to pray. My mother's mother, my grandmother, who lives in Travnik, is a Croat. And my husband's grandfather, after whom we named our son, was a Serb.

She thought she heard the whine of the first shell or mortar, and froze. Braced herself for the impact then relaxed again. If there was such a word or notion as relaxing any more.

Don't look at the photograph, she told herself, because it will only make you cry. Because of all those in the photograph apart from her and Adin and Jovan, only her Croat grandmother in Travnik was definitely alive. The others – her parents, Adin's parents, their brothers and their sisters – had either been killed or had vanished in the ethnic cleansing by the Serbs or the bitter bloodletting between Croats and Muslims. Or perhaps they were alive, perhaps they had made it out and were in a refugee camp somewhere. Perhaps one day they would see each other again, take another photograph of the family happy and at peace with itself and the world.

Sometimes it was as if the West had abandoned her, had totally and cynically forgotten about her and the likes of her.

Forget it, she told herself; just concentrate on surviving

today, don't even think about tomorrow.

She made herself kneel again in front of the stove, made herself stir the beans. Made herself laugh at little Jovan as she poured his share into the small round plastic bowl, then poured the smaller portion she had allowed herself and broke a piece of bread for him.

Occasionally someone remembered, of course, occasionally a little aid got through.

The first time was before the siege proper had started. They had still been cut off and under fire, but some British soldiers had come. The Cheshires, she remembered the name of the regiment. Then there was the man with a beard from the UNHCR. And after that, when the days were short and dark and the cold and hunger were seeping into them all, the planes had come over and dropped food packages on to the town, but the wind had taken the food on to the hillsides. That night the people had gone out with torches, Adin among them, to search for the oh-so-precious packages. Even now she could remember standing in the doorway, little Jovan in her arms, pointing out the lights among the trees and laughing because it was like Christmas, seeing the lights moving in the dark as the people looked. Then the Chetniks had started to shell the wood, and the lights had scattered like fireflies on a summer night, and one by one had gone out as people ran or died.

There had been one more time the aid had come.

Adin was at home, so she had gone alone for the pan of beans. Had crossed the bridge and was scuttling towards the school when she had seen them. Four soldiers, but not as she had seen soldiers before. Not riding in tanks or jeeps like other soldiers, or like the UN monitors who'd come in to cover the so-called ceasefire. Combat clothes but no helmets or berets, big packs on their backs, radios on them, and all carrying guns. Always walking, always carrying everything they had with them. Always moving quickly.

The next day she had seen them again. Had heard them speak and spoken to them. And because she had spoken to them in English, because at university she had studied English, she always remembered them as English rather than British.

And because there was no one else, she had interpreted for them. Had picked up the word *laser*, and interpreted to the Red Cross about the planes and the food drops. That night, and for several nights after, the soldiers had disappeared into the woods; that night and for several nights after, the planes had come over and dropped the food exactly where the soldiers told them to. And the people had eaten. Then the soldiers had gone, and she had never known how they had come to Maglaj or how they had left or even who they were. Except that once she had asked them, and they had told her, but even then she had not understood.

'Eat up.' She wiped the bread round the bowl and made Jovan eat, spooned the beans into her own mouth and heard the swoosh.

Mortar, MacFarlane registered automatically. Incoming. An hour later than normal, but still more or less in line with the usual pattern.

Kara grabbed Jovan and pushed him under the bed, slid beside him.

Impact two hundred metres away, near the river bank of the old town – MacFarlane registered the fact automatically and entered it in his log.

Kara felt Jovan trembling and held him tight. Half an hour, perhaps an hour of hell, then it would be over till tomorrow.

Thirty seconds gone – MacFarlane didn't need to check his watch. Almost a minute, closing on two. Incoming –

he heard the whine, then the sound of impact. New town again, somewhere near the radio station. He waited another two minutes, perhaps slightly longer.

The incoming shell sounded like an express train. They're trying to make us afraid, Kara told herself; they've allowed us to settle into a routine, now they're changing it. The walls shook slightly as the round landed.

Old town, MacFarlane confirmed.

The half-hour stretched to forty-five minutes, then to an hour, an hour and a half, the shells and mortars still landing.

The Norwegian handed him a mug of tea, hot and sweet, and crouched beside him.

'What's up?'

'Not sure.'

The Chetniks were preparing for an attack, Kara suddenly thought. Please God, help Adin waiting among the mines and the snow and the ice of the front, please God save him.

It was six in the evening, three hours into the darkness of the winter night and the shells and mortars were falling now with a nightmarish regularity. Time to file his latest report. MacFarlane picked up the handset and squeezed the grip.

'Zero. This is Four One Delta. Over.'

Zero was the code for base, and base was in the radio room on the ground floor of the white-painted schoolhouse which now formed the Operations Centre in the BritBat – British Battalion – barracks just outside Vitez, fifty kilometres away. Vitez itself was one of the places the United Nations modestly called a *hot spot*: Croats laying siege to the Muslims in Old Vitez, and themselves surrounded by more Muslim forces in the hills outside.

'Four One Delta. This is Zero. Send. Over.'

'Four One Delta. As at eighteen hundred hours.' His

report going through Vitez to the monitoring centre in Sarajevo then to the politicians and the generals. 'Eighty ceasefire violations, all incoming.' He lumped the mortar and shells together. 'Forty small-arms violations.' Which was as accurate as he and his team could be. He split the message. 'Roger so far. Over.'

'Zero. Roger. Over.'

Message received so far.

'Four One Delta. Pattern of shelling appears to have changed. Maglaj old and new town under constant shelling for past two hours. Over.'

'Zero. Roger. Over.'

'Four One Delta. Roger. Out.'

Another shell landed fifty metres away. 'Bit close,' he suggested. The ceiling shook again, they ignored it and opened the ration packs.

Kara was still hungry and her nerves were beginning to fray. She held the boy tight and began to tell him his favourite story. Another round struck the old town, not that she could tell when the noise and vibration of one round ended and the next began. This can't go on all night, she tried to convince herself. The room was getting cold again, and the candle had died an hour ago. She crept out, flinching in anticipation of the next shell, felt in the black till she stumbled against the dresser, then found and lit another candle and placed it on the table. Then she pulled Jovan's mattress under the double bed, helped the boy wriggle on to it, and covered him with blankets. The shell landed a hundred metres away and she felt the shock, almost dived back under the bed and felt the plaster fall from the ceiling. Sometime this has to stop, she told herself, sometime the war has to end. Be all right, she prayed to her husband. Don't die. Don't let us die.

*

It was ten in the evening, six hours since the bombardment had begun.

'In Vienna negotiations are going well and the ceasefire is holding.' MacFarlane and the others huddled round the table and listened to the news on the BBC World Service. 'All sides have stated their positions, and the Bosnian Serb leader has emphasized once again that he believes peace is possible.'

'Zero. This is Four One Delta.' MacFarlane called Vitez on the net.

'Four One Delta. This is Zero.'

'Four One Delta. Update on Maglaj. The shelling is continuing. One hundred and twenty ceasefire violations in past four hours. Shelling has not stopped, repeat, has not stopped, since last report. Over.'

'Zero. Roger. Over.'

'Four One Delta. Roger. Out.'

They made themselves hot chocolate from the ration packs, and rolled out the sleeping bags on the camp cots.

'Two-hour shifts,' MacFarlane told them. 'Three men sleeping and one on duty for the shell count.' He laughed. 'Sorry, the ceasefire violation count.' Because we're UN, therefore we don't deal in anything as simple as shells and mortars.

Good man, MacFarlane, they understood, good leader. Kept you going when you might be inclined to wonder what the hell you were doing in a place like this.

'I'll do the first shift to midnight, Paul next, then Sven and Pierre.' Which meant that, theoretically at least, he would have to do another shift, beginning at six, but he was in charge and they would all be awake by then anyway. If they slept.

It was getting cold now, despite the Helly Hansen fleeces and Norgies – Norwegian semi-fleece army shirts – and thermals they were wearing. The Tilley lamp popped and died, and the black enveloped him. Another shell landed. Range a hundred and fifty metres, nothing to worry about. He switched on the mag light, refilled the lamp with kerosene, and lit it again. The night was quiet, only the sounds of breathing as the others slept or tried to sleep, only the constant crash of another round hitting another building. So the night's quiet, he thought. It was midnight. He updated the shell count, shook Umbegi's shoulder, took off his boots, and climbed into his sleeping bag.

At two in the morning he heard Anderssen replace Umbegi. In the past two hours there had been another sixty-two violations. He had lain awake and counted them, known the others were doing the same. At four Belan replaced Anderssen. Another fifty-eight rounds. There was no point sleeping any more, no point pretending to sleep, because no one was. He climbed out of the bag and put on his boots. Umbegi was making a brew. Umbegi was a good man. When the shit hit the fan, because the shit was going to hit the fan, Umbegi was the one he'd have at his shoulder. Christ, they were all good men.

Today he was going to die, he suddenly thought. Calmly and clearly and soberly. Today he and his men would meet their Maker.

'Zero. This is Four One Delta. Over.' He took the mug from Umbegi and called Vitez. Not that the peacemakers and the pen-pushers would know, because they would still be asleep.

'Four One Delta. This is Zero. Over.'

'Four One Delta. One hundred and twenty-seven ceasefire violations in the past four hours, all incoming. A total of three hundred and seventy-two in the past twelve hours, all incoming. Over.'

'Zero. Last report already sent to HQ.' Which was good, MacFarlane thought, because it meant the guys in Vitez were with him, supporting him, knew the trouble he was in and the bigger trouble which was about to engulf him. 'Will send latest immediately.' Even though the bureaucrats wouldn't read it for another four hours.

'Four One Delta. Roger. Out.'

The formal end of the message, no more communication.

'Cheers, mate,' the man in the room in the Ops Centre told him. 'Keep your head down. See you for breakfast.'

'Thanks, mate.'

It was six in the morning, the shells still falling like express trains. The room was cold and Jovan was shivering, crying slightly. Kara left whatever protection the bed gave them, lit a candle, placed it on the table, then relit the fire, watching the flames flicker then gather strength. I'm hungry: she saw it in her son's eyes. Tried to kindle the mental strength to reply.

It was seven o'clock, almost eight, the day outside getting light and the shells still raining down. Sometimes close, sometimes on to the new town on the other side of the river. Part of her mind telling her that soon the Chetniks on the hills would launch their morning burst of shellfire on the town, and that after that the shelling would stop, and then her only worry would be crossing the bridge to the food kitchens on the other side. Another part of her brain reminding her that the first thought was illogical, because the Chetniks had been shelling Maglaj all night and weren't going to stop now.

In Vienna the peace negotiators would be assembling; in Vienna the limos would be drawing up outside whatever hotel they were using and the politicians would be hurrying in, the newsmen clustered round them like bees round honey, anxious for every word they spoke. Most of the newsmen swallowing any line the politicians told them. MacFarlane logged the next round and waited for the next.

This is crazy – he glanced at the faces of the others. They

were soldiers, but here they were sitting in a house in a town being shelled and in which people were dying, yet they could do nothing about it. Partly because they were unarmed, in line with the agreement on the placement of UN military observers, but mainly because it was not their job. Not even the job of the United Nations, with its battalions of soldiers present in the country under the UNPROFOR plan, and with the naval power off the coast and the air strike capacity waiting on the runways in Italy. Because they were bound by their own rules of engagement. Or, and more accurately, their rules on non-engagement.

Except there was a way, of course.

Sure, it would mean bending the rules; sure it would assume that Thorne, the British general in charge of UNPROFOR, would understand not just what MacFarlane was asking but why he was asking it; that Thorne could get the necessary go-ahead from his political masters at the United Nations. But at least he could try. At least he could leave this place with a clean conscience.

He checked his watch and counted in the next rounds.

'Mummy,' Kara heard her son's voice. 'It's hurting.'

'What's hurting, my little one?' There were tears on his face. She took his head in her hands and held him against her.

'My tummy.'

'Let's see.' The boy was hungry, just as she was hungry. Which meant that she would have to risk the bridge again, except that today she couldn't because of the shelling. She opened his coat, pulled up the layers of sweater and shirt, and rubbed his stomach gently. 'Better now?' she asked.

The shell was close to the house. Please may Adin come home today, because if he doesn't we'll die. But please may Adin not try to come home today, because if he does the shells will kill him.

*

It was ten o'clock, the mortars and artillery shells still falling around them. 'Discussion time.' MacFarlane gathered his team round the table. 'It is my intention to inform General Thorne that at some time in the near future I may have to consider requesting him to call in an air strike.' The Tilley lamp was on the table, slightly off centre, the light illuminating their faces and the rest of the room in darkness. 'Comments on that line of action?'

'What reason will you give?' It was Anderssen, the Norwegian.

Because we all know that air strikes can only be called in under highly specific guidelines. And those guidelines exclude the protection of people like the poor sods dying outside.

The noise from the street was almost deafening, the walls reverberating and plaster falling from the ceiling.

'What I'll say is that we are confined to our operating base and therefore cannot properly fulfil our role as military monitors. That if we attempt to, one or all of us will certainly be killed. That if we try to withdraw we'll also probably be killed, and that if we stay inside we still run a major risk.'

'What about the people?' Because that's what we're really talking about here.

'The people are a moral issue. I'm dealing with a technical situation relating to UNPROFOR personnel.'

'Because that's the only way you stand a chance of calling in an air strike?' The Norwegian was looking straight at him.

Wonder what happened to the woman and kid on the bridge – MacFarlane sipped his coffee. Wonder if they're dead yet, and if not, how long it will be before they are. 'As I said at the beginning, it is my intention to inform General Thorne that at some time in the near future I may have to consider requesting him to call in an air strike.' He looked at them for confirmation.

'Air strike,' Umbegi said simply.

'Agreed,' said the Norwegian and the Belgian, almost together.

'Timetable?' Anderssen asked. Christ, it was daytime, but the temperature seems to be going down rather than up.

'We can't move, therefore Thorne will have to send in a couple of FACs.' Forward Air Controllers. 'Presumably they'd come in tonight.' Two teams, one each side of the valley because it was impossible from one side to get line of vision on all the positions which would be necessary to laser-guide the attack planes on to their targets. 'Which means that the earliest an air strike could be launched would be tomorrow.' Which was a long way off, but better than never. 'Agreed?' he asked them.

'Agreed.'

Two radio nets had been assigned them. The first, HF through Vitez, was so-called all-informed, in line with the standard system of communication where line of sight was a problem, and the second was direct to Thorne via a satellite.

MacFarlane ignored the first and chose the second.

'Zeus. This is Lear. Over.'

'Lear. This is Zeus.'

Thorne's signaller was never further than a room from the general; he travelled in the general's armoured Range Rover when Thorne went by road, and in the general's helicopter when Thorne went by air.

An UNMO team wouldn't be coming through on the direct net unless it was urgent, he understood. 'Better get The Boss,' he told the man apparently relaxed in the hard-backed chair next to him. The man left the office, nodded at the second man positioned in the corridor, knocked on the door of the conference room and went in without being told to enter.

The coffee cups were on the table; some of the men present wore combat uniform and the others civilian suits: Thorne in discussion with his military commanders and the representatives of his political masters.

'Lear on the secure net,' the minder whispered to Thorne.

In a way Thorne had expected it.

'Excuse me, gentlemen.'

The general was early fifties, tall and apparently slim build. He left the conference room, crossed to the office being used by his signaller, and waited till the man who was his constant shadow closed the door.

'Lear. This is Zeus. Send. Over.'

'Lear. Sitrep. The situation in Maglaj is becoming serious. I feel I should warn you that I may request an air strike. Over.'

'Zeus. I read your reports overnight. Justification? Over.'

Because we both know the UN prefers to sit on its butt rather than risk upsetting anyone's apple cart. And because we both understand the narrowness of the restrictions placed on such action.

'Lear. Shelling has been continuous for the past eighteen hours. We are confined to our base, but even if we do not leave it I am approaching the position where I can no longer guarantee the safety of my men. Over.'

'Zeus. How bad is it, Tom?' Thorne broke the formality. 'Over.'

'Lear. The worst I've seen, and about to go downhill fast. Over.'

'Zeus. The UN will request a stop to firing immediately. Decision on an FAC in two hours. Over.'

Which meant that Thorne would send his men in, MacFarlane understood. And once they were in position, and assuming the onslaught on Maglaj didn't abate, Thorne would request an air strike.

'Lear. Thank you. Over.'

'Zeus. Keep in touch. Out.'

He would brief the meeting on the development – already Thorne was working out how he would play it. But before that he would task Fielding. And while the politicians were busy pointing out the diplomatic implications and nuances and repercussions, Fielding would already be tasking Finn and Janner.

# 2

The room was on the first floor of the anonymous block on the left of the main gate of the British headquarters at Split. Half a kilometre away in one direction was the airport servicing this part of the Dalmatian coast, half a kilometre in another were the pebble beaches and what in summer were the clear blue waters of the Adriatic. Now the islands of Brac and Hvar hung like ghosts in the winter fog, and the damp mixed with the cold.

The eight bunks were along one wall, and the television set was in the corner. Finn slumped in an armchair and watched the news coverage of the peace talks in Vienna on the feed from the British Forces Television service, some of the other seven men with whom he shared the room also watching. Finn was early thirties, strong upper body and a little over six feet tall. Like the others he was dressed in camouflage fatigues, their packs and weapons by the bunks. Already that morning they had worked out in the makeshift gym on the ground floor.

According to a UN spokesperson, the ceasefire in Bosnia was holding, the report was saying. The images from the Vienna hotel where the latest talks were being held showed the politicians going in and coming out, and the international negotiators smiling and talking about the possibility of a breakthrough. The images from London were slightly different: the British Foreign Secretary commenting on the possibility of peace but being careful in the way he always was. The reporter was summing up the mood in

Vienna that morning, quoting direct from the Bosnian Serb delegates. Where the hell have you been for the past year and a half? Finn thought. The politicos have said the same thing a hundred times before and each time they were lying, so why the hell should we believe them this time?

Fielding came in. He was in his late thirties, with the air of physical fitness and strength which exuded from all of them.

'We're on standby.' The relaxation in the room snapped tight. 'Briefing in five minutes.'

Fielding's room was one along. The floor was wood, the walls a dull yellow, and the rumble of a UN transport taking off for Zagreb shook the ceiling slightly. There were two maps on the table: the HQ BritFor current situation map, and the Director General of Military Survey town map of Maglaj and the countryside immediately surrounding.

'Patrol Orders.'

Fielding followed the standard pattern:

Task, beginning with a summary of the operation.

'Maglaj. The UNMO team there reports that the town has been under continual bombardment since sixteen hundred yesterday. The UNMO team leader has spoken to The Boss, and warned that he may have to request an air strike in order to protect his people. The UNMO boys can't move from their shelter. The Boss wants an FAC in tonight to assess the situation in case he decides to go for an air strike.'

He ran through the other items under the task heading: country, politics, method of entry, role or target, approximate timings and durations.

He moved to the second heading.

Ground: description of area, enemy and own locations, boundaries, landmarks, minefields, entry RV and LZ – rendezvous and landing zones.

'You know the area,' he told the teams. Because they'd been in Bosnia two months and had familiarized themselves with the terrain. Even so he maintained the standard routine.

Met report: weather, moon phase, first and last light. Situation: the area of the operation, enemy forces and friendly forces. Civilians: restrictions, curfews, food situation.

They went through the details on the maps.

'The towns of Maglaj and Tesanj, fifteen kilometres to the north-west, are in a pocket surrounded by Serb forces to the west, north and east and by combined Serb and Croat forces to the south. Maglaj is in two halves, the old and new towns, divided by a river.'

They focused on the town map of Maglaj: the sweep of the river and the position of the Serb guns, then Fielding moved to the next heading of the briefing.

'Mission. To locate and identify any Serb artillery, tanks and armour, and to mark it for air strike.' He repeated the mission, then moved on to the next heading. Execution: general outline, entry and return; RV and LUP procedures – rendezvous point and lying up position. Exit phase, RVs and passwords.

Finn and Janner and their patrols would fly by helicopter to a forward position at the British Battalion base near Vitez. They would wait there for final briefings, plus the green light for insertion. At last light they would chopper the fifty kilometres to the Maglaj pocket. Both patrols would be dropped at the same time, Finn would then take his patrol to the hills on the west of the town, and Janner would take his to the east. The two groups would establish the positions of the guns or tanks shelling the town, and guide the attack planes in by laser if Thorne requested an air strike and the UN approved it.

'This is a hard routine patrol,' Fielding told them. Therefore there would be no cooking, because cooking might give their positions to the opposition. They would only take food which they could eat cold: tins of stew, beans, sausages, plus Mars bars.

They moved to the last heading.

Logistics and communications: arms and ammunition, dress and equipment, rations, special equipment including LTM – laser target markers – and medical packs.

'Any questions?'

'Why two patrols?' Finn asked.

'According to the UNMO team not all the firing positions can be observed from one side of the valley.'

'What are the chances of an air strike?' Janner this time. Which is to say, what are the odds we're going to freeze for nothing?

'Has to be a first sometime,' Fielding told him noncommittally.

They went into the details of the helicopter drop-offs and the OPs.

In an ideal world the drop would be at least five kilometres from where they would establish themselves, because helicopters could be seen and heard, therefore shouldn't land anywhere near where they were headed. Therefore the helicopter would drop them in the middle of the pocket, midway between Maglaj and Tesanj.

'What else do we know about Maglaj?'

'Ian Morris took a patrol in two months ago, organized some food drops. His sitrep's already on the way.' Sitrep – situation report. 'You'll have it before you leave Vitez tonight.'

They returned to their own room, the two teams splitting and Finn and Janner going through their own patrol orders, this time in more detail, each man in the patrol asking questions and throwing in ideas as he saw fit.

An hour later the two teams carried their bergens on to

the side of the helicopter landing site and crouched as the Sea King pilot ran through his pre-flight checks, then started the engines. The rotor blades were winding up and rain was falling. Each man was armed with his favourite weapons – Sig Sauers, Heckler and Kochs, Remington pump action shotguns, reduced and fitted with folding butts. In the bergens each carried spare ammunition, ration packs – non-essential items or those they didn't like discarded – and spare winter clothing. Satcom sets, for communication with Thorne and/or Split via Hereford; hand-held ground-to-air sets for communication with the pilots of the fighter team should an air strike be authorized; and mobiles in case the teams needed to talk to each other. Which was unusual, but which Finn and Janner had decided upon. Laser target markers and spares. Each man carrying his own medi-pack, plus two syrettes of morphine, name tag and wristwatch on parachute cord round the neck. Name tags because it wasn't a deniable operation.

'Okay,' the pilot told the load master. 'Bring them in.'

The load master jerked his thumbs up, and the two teams moved forward, ducking under what the pilot called the disc, the solid metal cutter of the rotor blades. The door was on the right-hand side, seats opposite it and the rest of the interior stripped bare. They climbed up and sat down, bergens in front of them and weapons on their laps. The loadie clanged the door shut, and the pilot lifted the Sea King off the tarmac, running forward to build air speed, then rising and banking slightly. Behind them the bleak grey of the Adriatic disappeared in the mist and the snow of Middle Bosnia beckoned from the hills in front.

It was eleven in the morning. Time to run the gauntlet of the bridge, time to try to reach the food kitchen. Except that today she wouldn't, because today the shells were still falling. On the hillside above Maglaj, Kara heard the soft *boom* of the gun and steeled herself in the silence as the shell rose on its trajectory, then she heard the sound of the express train as it descended, and the thump of the explosion somewhere in the new town.

'Mummy, my tummy's hurting again.' Jovan's eyes looked at her from beneath the bed.

She kissed him and told him that soon they would eat. She should go outside and get wood, she knew, should fetch more water from the well. At least she had the food she hadn't eaten yesterday, plus the portion she had brought home for her husband. She diced the two halves of the potato and carrot left from the day before, put them into the pan of beans, and put the pan on the stove.

They would eat first then she would go outside, because by then the shelling might have stopped.

The room was cold, despite the stove. She knelt by the boy and stroked his face. At least his cheeks and his forehead were warm – she would remember the moment later. At least he wasn't as cold as she feared he might be.

The ground below was cold and hard and bleak.

From Split the Sea King flew east then north-east over the coastal area of Croatia, more or less following the aid supply route codenamed Circle at an altitude of four thousand feet, then picking up Route Triangle, crossing the front line into the Muslim-held area of Bosnia, and skirting the Croat-held pocket defined by the three towns of Novi Travnik, Vitez and Busovaca.

Fifty minutes after leaving the coast, the Sea King dropped on to the LZ, the helicopter landing zone, on the edge of the British Battalion camp near Vitez, the roar of the rotors drowning the sniper fire from the Muslim forces in the ring of hills round the camp and the Croats in the village.

The camp was some two hundred metres square, circled

by a perimeter fence of razor wire and dissected by an internal road running north–south. To the south was the parking area for the white-painted APCs; to the north, protected by sangars and clustered tightly round the two-storey former school which now served as the Operations Centre, were the kitchens, dining block and sleeping units. The ground was a sea of mud, the ridges at the sides of the road and walkways frozen hard, and the camp seemed empty; the only movement was at the main gate as a pair of Warriors turned off the road.

Snow was falling and the temperature was below freezing. Welcome to Middle Bosnia, Finn thought. The loadie opened the door, the two patrols grabbed their weapons and bergens and followed the captain who had been waiting for them into the Operations Centre.

The building sounded hollow, footsteps in the gloom and voices echoing. The room they had been assigned was on the first floor. It was just after midday. They locked the equipment in the room then the others went to the cookhouse while Finn was taken to meet the base's commanding officer.

'Welcome to BritBat.' The Coldstream commander had done similar liaison jobs in Northern Ireland. 'Gather you're just using us for bed and breakfast. Anything you need . . .'

Finn thanked him and went to the cookhouse. The room was large, serving hatches on the right, and filled with tables, one area partitioned off for officers. Even here the men – and occasional woman – carried their personal weapons, mostly SA-80s, though some officers wore Brownings, either on their belts or in shoulder holsters. On the right of the door was a table, manned by a private, with a book for visitors and guests. Finn ignored it, picked up an aluminium food dish and plastic cutlery, joined the line at the hatches, and helped himself to a large portion of roast chicken and vegetables. It would be the last hot meal for some time; in the OPs they would eat cold, not even the smallest spark of a flame or heater to alert anyone to their presence. The hall was busy and the tables crowded. He joined the others, ate without speaking, then returned to the room in the Operations Centre.

For the next hour they pored over the map of Maglaj, confirming the drop points with the helicopter team, then working out the grid references of the locations where they would site their OPs. For the hour after that they checked and re-checked their equipment: radios and radio frequencies; spare batteries; laser equipment and PNGs – passive night goggles. Emergency plans in and out if either group ran into trouble.

Fielding flew in at three-thirty. The last briefing began in the room in the Operations Centre ten minutes later. Outside the light was fading fast and the snow was still falling.

'It's on,' he told them. 'You go at seventeen hundred hours.' They hunched round the table, coffee in plastic cups. 'The Boss will wait for your sitreps before he decides whether or not to request an air strike.'

'Latest UNMO report?' Janner asked.

'Maglaj is still under constant shelling. By constant they mean a shell every two to three minutes.'

'You said Ian Morris took a patrol in in November?'

'A ground team to laser in aid drops.' Fielding took the file from his day sack. 'Nothing much to help you.' He gave them the report anyway. Outside the snow had stopped and the sky had begun to clear.

Finn skimmed the report and handed it to Janner. 'The local interpreter, any way we can use her?'

'Probably not. With any luck you won't need to go anywhere near the town.'

It was four-thirty, the dark suddenly closing in outside.

They checked the equipment again, and confirmed again the radio frequencies on which they would be transmitting. It was fifteen minutes to five. On the LZ on the edge of the camp the Sea King pilot began his pre-flight checks. In low and fast tonight, himself and the other crew wearing night viewing gear, get the hell out as quickly as they could. The load master was outside, looking at him. He held up one finger – engine one starting. Two fingers – engine two. Both engines running. He ran through his cockpit checks then swivelled his fingers at the loadie, saw the thumbs up – all clear left and right. He released the rotor brake and the blades began to turn. In the shadows at the edge of the LZ the eight men appeared, bergens on their backs and weapons in their hands, thin white suits over their combat clothes – not pure white, because pure white stood out in the snow, but off-white and smudged with paint, tape round their weapons to break the shapes.

The load master jumped back in, waited for the pilot's order, then gave a thumbs up to the group to come forward. The sky above was clear, the first stars showing, though it was still too early for the quarter moon. The two patrols came forward, moving quickly, climbed in and sat on the seats opposite the door, bergens on their backs, weapons across their laps, and PNGs on their heads. The loadie gave Finn a helmet with built-in communications so he could hear the conversations between pilot and crew. Finn pulled off the PNG and put it on. The Sea King was in darkness, no interior or exterior lights. The loadie closed the door, and the Sea King rose from the ice and disappeared into the black. Flying south, away from the Maglaj–Tesanj pocket, then turning west then east on a deception course.

Land on or near the gravel road between Maglaj and Tesanj – Finn rehearsed the procedure again. Door already open. Land, then out fast, the cab hardly touching the ground, the pilot pulling away the second the last man was out. Maintain position, see what the opposition was up to, then separate, his patrol moving off first, then Janner's. Patrol order, guns carried in the ready position and with safeties off, and the countryside varying shades of green in the night viewing goggles.

They had been airborne thirty minutes, were flying low now, the sides of the valleys above them.

'Two minutes,' the pilot told the load master.

Two minutes – the loadie held two fingers up. Finn took off the helmet and put the PNG back on. In the cockpit the pilot and navigator were leaning forward, eyes straining for the changes in terrain. Behind them the loadie pulled open the door and leaned out, also checking.

'Radio mast one thousand metres at two o'clock.' The navigator to the pilot.

'Factory chimney two hundred metres at nine o'clock.' The loadie.

'Give them the one minute,' the pilot told the load master. The loadie swung back in and held up one finger.

'Confirm location,' the pilot asked the navigator.

'Location confirmed.' The navigator was still staring ahead.

'Thirty seconds,' the pilot told them. The rotors were thudding and the wind was gusting through the open door.

'Tail clear,' the loadie told the pilot.

The Sea King descended fast and hard.

Stand by – the loadie swung half in and mouthed the words at them.

The wheels hit the ground. 'Out,' the pilot told the load master. The loadie turned. Go – he mouthed at them. Go – his thumbs up told them. They were already moving past him, Finn's team first, then Janner's. Fanning to the sides of the Sea King in an all-round defence and looking for the enemy, looking for the trap. The blades were screaming above them and the snow was swirling round them. The Sea King lifted off into the blackness. Good cab, Finn thought, good driver. He rose, Ken and Steve and Jim rising with him, nodded to Janner, and began the walk in.

Two of his team were beginning to crack and MacFarlane's own nerves were stretched beyond what he had ever before experienced. If this is what the shelling was doing to them, then God only knew what it was doing to the civilians who weren't supposed to be used to this sort of thing.

The UNMO team were still in their base, crouched over coffee and cigarettes.

At around three in the morning there had been a slight lull in the express trains of the artillery shells and the spiralling screaming of the mortars. At six the intensity had picked up again, at seven he had filed his latest situation report via the HF channel through the radio net at Vitez. At eight, as the new day mixed from black to grey to the cold light of winter, he had spoken on the secure line to General Thorne, informing him of the situation, reporting that his team were under severe pressure, and asking whether there had been any Serbian response to the United Nations request of the previous day.

There had been no response, he was informed. FAC teams were in position, however. Thorne was waiting for their assessment, plus confirmation that the offending gun positions had been identified. Once this was received, and if the bombardment had not stopped or the Serbs had not responded, then an air strike request would be formally submitted.

Jovan was still asleep. Kara checked that he was as warm as he could be, and crawled from beneath the bed. Her head thumped with pain and she felt sick and exhausted.

In the sky over Maglaj she heard the sound of another express train. Please God, may it end today, please God, may Adin come home. Please may she and her son and her husband come through all this alive and together.

Yesterday she and Jovan had finished the beans, so today she would have to run the gauntlet of the bridge and the shells. Either that or she would have to dig into the supplies of potatoes and carrots she and Adin had grown last summer; but the sacks were already almost empty and the winter was not even half over. She pulled on an extra coat, laced up her boots, waited until another shell had fallen, and went outside. The cold took her breath away. She had two minutes before the next shell, she told herself, three if she was lucky. She grabbed a handful of wood from under the cover at the side of the garden, went back inside, and dumped it by the stove. Wait till after the next shell, she reminded herself. Get on with it, she thought; she had been cowering under the fear of the shells for too long. She went outside again. The bucket by the well was frozen to the ground; she kicked it loose, dropped it down the shaft, and heard the clank as it struck the ice. She pulled it up and dropped it again, heard the ice crack and felt the bucket fill. Heard the whine of the mortar in the sky and knew she should have waited. Froze like the water had frozen then heard the thump in the new town.

When she went back inside Jovan was looking at her. She kissed him and lit the stove. Tonight she shouldn't let the fire go out, she told herself; she had enough wood to keep it in. And if she ran out she could collect more from the woods on the hillsides above the house. Except that the woods might be mined – she wasn't sure, but Adin had told her to be careful, not to go anywhere near them. So she couldn't go to the woods, but she could salvage some scraps from the remnants of the houses down the road, as long as someone else hadn't beaten her to it.

'Mummy,' Jovan's eyes were large and staring. 'My tummy's hurting again.'

'Where?' She held him in her arms and felt his forehead. The skin was warm and slightly clammy, not cold as it should have been. She pressed his stomach carefully and gently, and felt the relief when he did not jerk in pain. Probably stomach cramp because he was hungry, she thought. She moved her hand slightly, to the right of his stomach and slightly down, and pressed again, felt him recoil in pain. 'Don't worry,' she told him, told herself. 'It'll be all right after I've made us something to eat.' In the sky above she heard the next shell.

'Location confirmed?' Finn asked Steve.

'Confirmed.'

Christ it was cold, but they wouldn't be here long. And they'd got themselves a good position. Hadn't been able to dig in, of course, but they hadn't expected to. Instead they'd found themselves an OP under the lower branches of some trees, which gave them at least some protection from the weather, plus having direct line of sight to the gun positions at the head of the valley and on the other side. Two of them up front and two at the rear covering them.

'Zero, this is Charlie Two One. Over.'

'Charlie Two One, this is Zero. Roger. Over.'

Finn spoke the details of his report and the grid references of the targets into the mike of the radio, then pressed the activate button. The computerized set scrambled the message and transmitted it on burst – fifteen seconds of report condensed into a micro-second, no possibility of it being intercepted, and no indication they were there.

'Zero. Roger. Out.'

His position could have been better, Janner was aware. They'd made it in easily enough, established the grid references of the gun emplacements and confirmed they were in direct line of vision for the lasers. But that was the problem: the ground on his side of the valley didn't allow for a base *and* a good OP. So the base was in a small indentation along a contour, from which he couldn't see the opposition but where the opposition couldn't see him, and the OP was fifty metres further forward on a slight lip, the two men in it lying motionless and the two behind covering them. The men in the forward position not able to move, but that was standard, except the ground behind the opposition emplacements was marginally higher than the OP, so the opposition was looking down on it and therefore able to see it. But only if they were looking, and they wouldn't be, because there was no reason to. The only time the opposition would know would be after the air strike, then the guns would be dealt with anyway. So there were no problems.

He contacted base, sent his report, then opened a can of cold beans and began to eat. Hard routine patrol, Fielding had said. Bloody right, Janner thought. Only six hours of light left, though, then he and Max could creep back and join Geordie John and Kev.

Poor bastards, he thought as another round struck the town in the valley below. The barrage was virtually non-stop now. Rather be here than there.

The call to MacFarlane was on the secure net.

'Update?' Thorne asked him.

'Ceasefire violations continuing at a rate of one round every two to three minutes, all incoming.' MacFarlane was also deliberately official.

'State of UNMO team?' Thorne asked.

'UNMO team in serious danger. Four shells have landed near UNMO position in past hour.' Four among the many that were still falling. 'There is a possibility that UNMO team is being targeted. If no response has been received from yesterday's approach to Bosnian Serbs, I formally request an air strike to protect lives of United Nations Military Observers.'

'Request being lodged immediately.'

So in two and a half hours, the time it took to process the request, the jets could be airborne from their bases in Italy. Thirty minutes' flying time, forty maximum; so by one-thirty, two at the latest, the jets could be over Maglaj and silencing the guns.

'Thank you.'

'Confirm you are visual with targets,' Thorne requested Finn and Janner via Hereford.

Confirmed, they both told him.

'Request for air strike being lodged now. Aircraft on RS 10' – a readiness state of ten minutes, which meant that the aircraft could be airborne within ten minutes of being scrambled. 'Aircraft call sign Thunder One.'

Assuming the UN sanction the action.

Jovan was slightly hotter. Kara wiped his forehead and talked to him about what they would do when the summer came and how he and she and his father would walk in the hills and pick the berries and the apples.

The shells and the mortars were still coming in. 'Roof of UNMO building has just received a direct hit,' MacFarlane reported on the secure net.

'Serbian authorities have been informed of request for air strike,' he was informed. 'UN procedures in operation. Thunder One on cockpit readiness.' The pilot in the cockpit and the engines running.

Perhaps he had become accustomed to the sound of the shelling, Janner thought, perhaps it was the temperature. The air cut through his lungs and the cold crept into his body. Two hours to go, he told himself, two hours before the Jaguar zipped over the valley and bombed the shit out of the bastards shelling the town. Two hours before he and Max could crawl out of the OP and join the others in the base position. Not that the base was any warmer than the OP, not that they would risk heating any food there.

It was all a game, of course. The Serbs were calling the UN bluff by not responding to the request to stop the shelling, and in just under two hours now the UN would call the Serbian bluff by taking out the guns in the hills.

The sky was a thin blue and the temperature was plummeting. God how he wanted something hot, Finn thought. Ninety minutes to go before the air strike. The Boss would have talked to both the UN and NATO by now, and the wheels would be rumbling, the pilots already briefed.

Jovan was going to vomit. Kara knew by the way he was holding his stomach and clenching his jaw. She held him in her lap, the bowl in her hand. Probably the food, she told herself, probably because she had put too much potato and carrot in, and he wasn't used to it. The jet of liquid shot from his mouth. 'It's all right, my little one.' She wiped the saliva from his lips. 'Now you'll feel better.'

The air strike was sixty minutes away, assuming the UN procedure took two and a half hours. 'Another round near UNMO HQ,' MacFarlane reported. 'Constant incoming, no cessation.'

'AWACS in position.' The Airborne Warning and Control System aircraft sitting high above them. 'Thunder One on sling shot.' The Jaguar waiting at the end of the runway.

The sky and the air had the awesome clarity of winter. 'Forty-five minutes,' Janner whispered, half to himself and half to Max. 'Wonder whether Belgrade's told the bastards on the guns.'

Jovan's temperature was rising, the sweat was breaking on his forehead and his breathing was slightly shallow.

'Where's it hurting?' Kara asked him. She undid his coat and gently felt his stomach, then his abdomen, to the right and lower. 'There, Mummy.' He jerked away in pain.

Thirty minutes to go – Janner counted down.

'Mission approved,' he and Finn were informed on the secure net. 'Confirm laser coding.' To ensure that the pilot received the correct target positioning.

'Charlie Two Two. Laser coding confirmed. Over.' Janner on burst, the transmission lasting a millisecond.

'Charlie Two One. Confirmed. Over.' Finn.

The guns pounded again

'Thunder One airborne,' the FAC and UNMO teams were informed.

'Confirm you are still in danger,' MacFarlane was requested.

'Confirmed.'

So what was she going to do? Kara held Jovan close and rocked him gently. Try to get him to the medical centre in Maglaj new town, which would mean running the risk of the snipers in the daylight and the guns even in the dark? Or stay here and pray the fever didn't develop and the pain went away?

The guns were still pounding.

'Thunder One over Adriatic,' the FAC and UNMO teams were informed. 'Thunder One crossing coast. Thunder One over Bosnian air space.'

'Magic Five Five.' The Jaguar pilot to the communications AWACS. 'This is Thunder One entering the area.'

'Roger, Thunder One. This is Magic Five Five. You are cleared to contact Charlie Two One and Charlie Two Two.'

'Charlie Two One. This is Thunder One. Radio check.'

Thank God, Finn and Janner thought.

'Roger, Thunder One. This is Charlie Two One. Loud and clear.'

'Charlie Two Two. This is Thunder One. Radio check.'

'Roger, Thunder One. This is Charlie Two Two. Loud and clear. Check position.'

'This is Thunder One. Now thirty miles south of Maglaj.' The Jaguar travelling at a mile every six seconds and losing altitude for the run-in.

'Roger, confirm target position,' Janner requested.

The first target – Janner's target – was camouflaged in a yard at the side of two houses, both empty except for the gun crews.

'Target as briefed.'

'Okay, Thunder One.' Janner switched on the laser marker. 'Lima on.'

The pilot saw the cross in the HUD, the head-up display, the L to the right indicating the laser was operating. He checked the code and selected the rocket on the weapons panel.

Four miles and twenty-four seconds out. Cross and L in HUD – he checked automatically. Everything okay.

Can't see target but I can see buildings, he thought.

The ground was a hundred feet below and he was following the course of the valley.

Three miles and eighteen seconds out.

I can see two buildings where the target should be, he thought.

Two miles and twelve seconds.

I can't see any guns. I can only see two houses.

One mile and six seconds.

Kara heard the thunder. What is it, Jovan asked. I don't know, she told him.

'Aborting run. No target in sight. I can only see two houses.' He was already a mile past the target.

'Yeah,' he heard the man on the ground. 'The guns are camouflaged in a yard to your left of the houses.' And you should have known that, because it was on my report.

Except somewhere along the line somebody forgot to tell you.

'Okay, Charlie Two Two. Coming round again. With you in forty seconds.'

'Okay, Thunder One. Lima on.'

In the winter light, the sun glinted on the laser sight.

'Thunder One. This is Magic Five Five.' The command and control AWACS. 'Are you task complete?'

The Jaguar was five miles and thirty seconds from the target.

'Negative, Magic Five Five. This is Thunder One. Will be in thirty seconds.'

'Thunder. This is Magic. Abort. Abort.'

The Jaguar was four miles and twenty-four seconds out.

Christ, the pilot thought. 'Magic, confirm mission abort and reason.' Because someone – somehow – might be playing silly buggers.

Three miles and eighteen seconds.

At the head of the valley the sun glinted again on the laser sights.

'Thunder One. This is Magic Five Five. You are to abort. I time authenticate Whisky Juliet.'

Each operation was coded for such a situation, the code changed every two minutes. The pilot checked the authentication code. 'Confirm reason for abort,' he asked.

Two miles and twelve seconds out.

'Thunder One. This is Magic Controller. Just fucking abort.' Meaning how the hell do I know?

One mile and six seconds.

In the house Kara heard the thunder again. Listen, she told Jovan. The planes are coming to stop the guns. The planes are coming to save us.

'Charlie Two One and Two. This is Thunder One.' The Jaguar was past the target and climbing hard above the hills to the north.

What the hell is this? Janner wondered.

What the hell's going on? Finn almost swore.

'Bad news. Just been told to abort the mission.'

'Why?'

'Sorry. Have to exit area. Good luck.'

Because the negotiators in Vienna have said they were on the verge of a breakthrough, so do nothing to rock the boat, Janner thought. He waited for the next salvo from the hills. One minute, two, three.

The guns have stopped, Kara thought. We're going to live, going to survive. Adin's coming home and little Jovan will be okay. Nine minutes since the last rounds, ten. Suddenly fifteen, twenty. The planes have done it, Kara whispered to Jovan: the United Nations have saved us. The blue of the sky had turned to purple and the purple was deepening into black, the first stars above them. Told you we could handle it, Janner knew the negotiators in Vienna would be telling each other, told you we could call their bluff. Kara held Jovan in her arms. Almost laughing, almost crying, not sure which but not caring.

The twilight was gone and the night was cold and hard, the silence hanging over the valley and the stars in the sky above it. They had already eaten today, Kara told her son, but tonight they would eat again, tonight they would celebrate. Then the fire in his forehead would cool and the pain in his stomach would go away.

The moon was coming up, pale and ghostly.

'In light of Serbian ceasefire at Maglaj, UN has ordered no further air action, therefore withdraw immediately,' Finn and Janner were told. 'UN have also decreed chopper pick-ups in Maglaj–Tesanj pocket might be deemed provocative, therefore patrol back through lines.'

'Get something inside us before we go,' Finn told his team. They took out the ration packs and opened the tins. Shone the torches on the map and plotted the route out.

'Time to go.' Janner's team confirmed the exfiltration and began to leave, Janner leading and the team strung at five-yard intervals behind him.

Jovan's temperature was suddenly soaring. The sweat was running from him and she could barely hear his breathing. 'Is it hurting again?' Kara asked him. 'Where's it hurting?' She undid his coat and felt his stomach, then his abdomen, to the right and lower. 'There, Mummy.' He was crying now, clinging to her, the fever burning. At least the shelling was over, at least she could get him to the doctor in Maglaj new town. At least at night the sniper wouldn't be waiting for her to cross the bridge. 'It'll be all right,' she told him. Please come home soon, she prayed to her husband, please be all right. She lifted the boy carefully and dressed him in his warmest clothes and coat. The night was dark now, but there was no time to wait till morning. She pulled on her own coat and scarf. What about Adin, what about if her husband came home that night? She hugged the boy again then sat at the table and began to write a note.

The thunder came from nowhere, the whine of the mortar and the express train of the shell. Oh no, she almost screamed. Not the shelling again. Not on the town. Not when she had to get Jovan to hospital.

Mortar, incoming – Janner heard the whine. 'Down,' he was shouting, already hitting the ground himself.

The mortar landed fifty metres away. Another shell was coming in, striking the ground a hundred metres down the slope. The bastards weren't going for the town, they were going for him. He and the others were up and moving, fast but orderly, running for the slight dip where they had established the base, the dip that might give them some protection. More crumps, suddenly more whines. The dip was fifty metres away, they were slipping on the ice, crashing into the branches of the trees. The mortars were landing again, closer this time. He heard the whine then saw the flash in front.

Oh Christ, he was aware he was thinking coldly and calmly, oh no. Not Kev, not Geordie John. The bodies were catapulting in the air, the earth and ice showering over him and the shrapnel hitting him. Oh Christ not me. The pain was somewhere on his face, somewhere in his chest, somewhere round his legs. Another mortar round was coming in. Head down and pray, he told himself, then check the others and get to the bunker. If he could find the others, if he could move.

The round hit the ground twenty metres from him and he felt the shock, waited two seconds then looked up. Max was on the ground five metres in front of him, moving slightly and moaning. At least he assumed it was Max, because Kev and Geordie John had been in front when the first round took them out. He half stood, made sure his legs weren't giving way, and shuffled forward. 'Legs have gone,' Max told him. 'Bit fucked up. Can't move.' Another round was coming in. Janner ignored it, unstrapped Max's bergen and grabbed his shoulder, tried to lift him, pull him. Tried to move him whichever way he could. It'll hurt like hell, old friend, he didn't need to say, but no option. Move if you can, he didn't need to tell Max, give me all the help you can.

The pain in his chest was gone, his body was suddenly numb, but his legs were holding. He was pulling, hauling. The dip in the ground ten metres from him, five metres, another round coming in and Max trying to walk, trying to get to his own shattered knees and help them both. Janner passed something, cold and bloody, realized it was Kev. Another round was coming in. This is the one, this time they've got us. He jerked Max forward and they slid into the dip.

'Maglaj ceasefire broken,' MacFarlane reported on both nets.

'Friendly forces under enemy fire,' Finn informed Hereford. 'Repeat. Friendly forces under enemy fire.' The other men in the patrol were checking the locations of the offending mortar and artillery piece. 'Serbs deliberately targeting Charlie Two Two.'

It was too late to call an air strike, the bloody decision-makers at the UN would be too busy wining and dining to make any decisions. Only one thing to do and one way to do it. Only one way of stopping the guns shelling the men on the other side of the valley.

'You have the positions?' he asked the others.

'Not moved since we targeted them earlier.'

'Charlie One to Charlie Two.' He used the motorola. 'Charlie One to Charlie Two. Over.'

'Charlie Two receiving.' Janner was on the floor of the dip, Max half across him and blood everywhere.

'Charlie One. What are you like?'

'Two missing, presumed dead. Rest of patrol in minimal cover. One injured, I'm also wounded.'

'You can walk?'

'I can try.'

'Give me twenty minutes.' Which was a bloody eternity. 'When they stop shelling, get as far out as you can. Romeo Victor is a group of houses over the ridge.' He gave Janner the co-ordinates.

Romeo Victor – RV – rendezvous point.

'Got that,' Janner told him.

'Oboe Oboe,' Finn told Hereford. 'Bringing out own wounded.' No code ranked above OO. When an SAS patrol signalled Oboe Oboe everything but everything stopped. 'Repeat. Oboe Oboe. Bringing out own wounded. Hot extraction. Landing site not secure.' He gave them the details. 'Will confirm co-ordinates. Radio silence from this point. Repeat. Radio silence.' Because where we're going and what we're going to do, we don't want anyone knowing. Because if they do then we're dead as well.

Time to forget the UN. Time to ignore the rules. Time to cut throats.

'Okay, let's do it.'

The shells and mortars were falling on the town again. Falling on somewhere else as well, somewhere in the hills, which she couldn't understand. But falling on the town again. Kara heard the thuds and felt the vibrations. Please God no, she prayed. Please God tell me what to do. Unless I get Jovan to the doctor's he's going to die, but if I try he'll be killed anyway.

'Finn and the boys are on the way,' Janner told Max. 'Be out of here soon.' He waited till the next round exploded then looked out of the hollow, shouted for Kev and Geordie John. Kept shouting for thirty seconds then ducked inside again as another round exploded.

Kev's body – assuming it was Kev – was ten metres away. It would be dangerous, but Kev would have done the same for him. Just enough time to get out and check if Kev had a pulse, if Kev was alive. So what would he do if he was? One he might be able to get to the RV, two no. And what about Geordie John? 'Be back,' he told Max. He waited till the next round exploded, slid out of the hollow and pulled himself along the ground. Pull Kev back in, which might be difficult, or waste time finding the pulse? Half Kev's head was missing, Kev hadn't even known what hit him. Geordie John presumably the same. Janner rolled back and tumbled into the hollow as the next round landed.

The bridge across the river, a kilometre and a half from the town, was thin and rickety, and swinging slightly in the night, the snow ghostly in the PNGs. The river beneath was cold and grey and running fast, but the bridge itself might be wired. Finn knelt and felt carefully around and under the first sections, the others covering him from the shadows. There were no wires. He nodded and ran across, allowing for the swing of the bridge, then slipped into the dark and covered the next man. There was no cold now, just the adrenalin. The last man came over and they turned up the slope.

The sites were a hundred metres apart, the support huts fifty metres back from them. Himself and Steve to take the first, Finn indicated, Ken and Jim to deal with the second. Knife job, no noise. Because if the guns simply stopped firing the soldiers in the back-up hut might think the gunners on duty had received a change of order, whereas if there was small-arms fire they might investigate. The guns were still pounding. One minute – they set their watches on count down.

Twenty minutes, Finn had said, therefore five minutes to go. The bastards had his range now and were pounding the shells in. 'You ready?' Janner asked Max. He'd discarded almost everything, destroyed the radios. Four minutes to go. 'It's going to hurt like buggery,' he told Max, 'but it's the only way.' It's going to hurt me as well, because I don't know where my head is going and the pain is in my legs again and my chest feels like it doesn't exist.

He ducked as the next round came in.

'Ready, Max?'

Christ, Max was a mess, his legs hanging disjointed and his face and body mangled as hell.

'Ready, Janner.'

He half-lifted Max so that his body was across his shoulders and Max could still carry his Heckler, still use it if he needed, and began counting since the last round. A minute between rounds now, never more than a minute and twenty seconds. In the distance the other guns and mortars pounded the town. Thirty seconds since the last round. Forty-five. Minute gone. He waited for the next incoming round. Finn would have done it. Finn and the boys wouldn't let him down. One minute twenty, one thirty.

Go – he heard himself shout, heard himself scream.

He was out of the bunker and trying to run. Max bouncing on his shoulders and telling him he was okay. Up the slope of the hill fifty metres, then turn along the contour line – he had worked it out on the map, knew exactly what he had to do, drummed it into his head so he would do it automatically. Christ, Max was heavy. Christ, his legs and his chest and his head were suddenly hurting. He was running slower now, little more than a stagger. Control it, he told himself, keep it calm and measured, just get up the first fifty metres and you're okay. Still no incoming rounds, still the wonderful blissful silence. Except for the pounding in his head and the heavy metallic rasping in his lungs. Thanks, Finn, thanks, lads. He turned right, along the hillside, the woods green in the night sights and his feet slipping on the ice.

'You okay?' he asked the man on his back. 'Okay,' Max told him. The rounds going into the town were like echoes in his head, the trees around him and the slope of the hillside making it difficult to move. He was walking now, holding on to the instructions Finn had given him and the directions he had instilled into his brain. Can't be far now, halfway there already, probably more. He was no longer walking, was on his knees, forcing himself forward. Bit like selection: when you think you've had it, that's the point you start really going. Bit like counter-interrogation: get your story fixed in your head and stick to it. So he was going well, going great guns, was getting there.

He was bent forward now, was on his hands and knees, the pain tearing at his chest and the ice and trees cutting into him. Don't think about it, don't think about anything. Just keep going. Finn and the lads will be waiting at the RV, and the chopper will already be airborne. Nice pint of beer at the end, nice fag to go with it. He was crying now, on his face and his front, reaching forward with one hand and grabbing anything, pulling himself and Max on, Heckler still in the other hand. Doing well, doing great, you old bugger. Christ he must have passed the RV point a hundred years ago. He reached forward again and grabbed the tree stump, pulled himself and Max up to it, lifted his face from the ice and reached forward again, felt for the next thing he could, pulled himself forward again. Tell Max to mind his legs on the stump, part of his mind warned him, tell Max to keep his legs clear.

The shelling on the town was continuing but the shelling on the hillside had stopped. Jovan's fever was burning now, his breathing shallow and his lips moving, as if he was praying. Kara knelt by him and wiped his face and hands. Don't worry, she told him, everything will be all right soon; you'll be okay soon. She wet the flannel and held it against his lips. Heard the scream.

Like an animal caught in a trap. Like a fox when its leg is torn off. Except that it wasn't an animal. It was a man.

Someone's hurt – her mind was numb with the cold and the shelling and the shock. Someone's been hit by a shell. Except there hadn't been a shell before the scream. Her mind was still numb. It's all right, she told Jovan, everything is fine. She dipped the flannel into the water again and cooled his face again.

Adin – it came out of the darkness, out of the black. Adin was outside. Adin had left the front line and was coming home. Adin was hurt, was trying to reach her and Jovan even though he was wounded.

Not Adin, it couldn't be Adin, because Adin wouldn't come that way. But could she take the risk . . .

She smiled at the boy and kissed him. 'I'm going to get

something.' She wiped his forehead again. 'I'll be back in two minutes to tell you a story.'

She pulled on her coat and laced her boots. Made sure Jovan was comfortable and opened the door, slipped through it and closed it quickly so as not to let the cold in. Crouched in the dark and listened for the sound, listened for her husband.

'Sorry, Janner.' Max's voice shuddered as his body was shuddering.

'All right, Max. No probs. Almost there.' The shells were coming in again, falling on the old town, falling near them. He was hardly moving now. One hand, the hand with the gun, trying to reach out and the other holding Max's wrist and trying to pull him. The night sights were getting in the way, but he and Max needed them to see where they were going. Fuck me, part of his mind was saying, the places you take me. Ten green bottles, part of his brain was singing as he had sung with his wife during the last stages of labour when their first child had been born. Ten green bottles hanging on the wall, and if one green bottle should accidentally fall. You're losing it, Janner; stop thinking about Jude, stop thinking about the kids. Because if you do you're finished, you're on the way out. The shrapnel was cutting through his chest now and the shells were bursting round him, his head was down and his face was scraping on the ice. You're making it, he told himself. Just keep it up, just keep going.

The shell was coming in. He heard it explode. Heard the other explosion which it detonated. Oh Christ, he thought. Oh Jesus bloody Christ. I'm in a minefield.

Kara heard Adin, saw Adin. Dark and black against the snow and the ice. The shells and the noise and the hell pounding down on him, pounding down on them both. She was lying on the ground, wriggling forward trying to protect herself from the bombs and the guns. Adin, she whispered, no noise coming out. It's me, Adin; please move, Adin. Don't be dead, Adin. The shell was coming in, close to them. She ignored it, ignored everything.

Saw him.

Christ the pain in his head and his legs and his chest. Forget the pain, pain only exists when you acknowledge it. Got to get to the lads, can't let the lads down after all they did so you could get this far, can't let Max down. Christ the bloody awful fucking pain. Don't give up, don't give up now, don't ever give up. Because you're regiment, because you're a Cornishman. Almost there now, Max. Almost made it.

He saw her.

Oh God – she felt the fresh fear. Not Adin, not anyone she knew. Not even a man. The shape in front of her was black and red, no face, especially no eyes. Just the face of something from another world staring at her.

Christ – he was reacting automatically, instinctively. Heckler coming up and finger on trigger.

The fear still froze her. Froze her body and her mind. Why no face, the panic screamed at her; why no eyes?

Janner's finger was easing on the trigger, mind and body functioning instinctively.

She understood why she couldn't see a face, why she couldn't see the eyes. She had seen someone like this before, seen four men like this before. Except then they had been helping her, then they had been disappearing into the woods at night, then the planes had flown over and the food had parachuted down.

'Ian . . .' she remembered the leader's name. 'English?' she asked. 'Aid,' she said. 'Food drops?'

Except that it wasn't Ian. Except that the man two metres from her was wounded and in pain. And the man behind him, the man he was carrying, was even more badly injured.

'English?' she asked again, her voice almost lost in the fear.

The eyes looking at him were wide with fright and the face framed green in the PNG was a woman's.

'English?' Janner heard the words again. 'Food drop?'

Ian Morris took a patrol in to organize a food drop – part of his brain pulled out of the numbness. Ian Morris had an interpreter – he remembered the briefing. A woman, not sure where she lived because she met them at their operating base.

'English,' he said. 'Friend of Ian's. Help me.' The voice seemed distant, as if it was no longer his. 'Two of us. Can't move any more.' It was as if the night was still and silent, as if the rounds were not falling round and on them. Got to trust her, got to trust someone. He took the pressure off the trigger and stretched out his hand towards her.

Their fingers touched, palms sliding across each other. Hers cold with ice and fear, his red and slimed in blood. She held his wrist, he hers, grip clamped like a vice. He tried to help, tried to pull himself and Max forward.

'Minefield,' he told her.

Oh God – she remembered what Adin had said, remembered the different explosions as she had left the house, as if the shells had detonated something else in the woods.

She let go his hand and he knew she was going to leave him. Can't blame her, a distant part of his brain told him. On her own and she might make it back; her and one of them and the chances were falling; her and two and they were all dead.

Another shell landed thirty metres away.

'You have a knife?' she asked. What am I doing, she thought. Why am I doing it?

What the hell did she want a knife for? Janner let go Max's arm, felt in his belt, and gave her the knife. 'Don't move,' she told him. Christ – he understood why she wanted the knife and what she was going to do.

Slowly, carefully, she eased the tip of the knife into the ground, pressed it through the ice. Repeated the procedure. Made sure the area between her and Janner was clear. Then she turned and edged up the track made by her knees and hands.

There were no mines, she began to think; perhaps Adin was wrong; perhaps they hadn't been laid. There were no mines, part of Janner's brain told him; he'd been wrong about the different explosion. He saw the moment she froze. Sensed – split second before – the metallic contact as the tip of the knife struck something. Leave us, part of him wanted to tell her, save yourself. Except save herself and he was finished. Why was she doing this, she wondered; why was she risking her life when Jovan was sick less than a hundred metres away? She marked the location of the contact with her scarf and moved past it, suddenly rigid with fear and almost unable to move. Came to the place where the animal tracks were all along the route, and therefore where she was safe. Except that animals were lighter than men. She turned and crept back to the two men.

'Can't move both of you.' She ducked as another round came in. 'I'll take you, come back for the other.'

Can't abandon Max, Janner thought. And if she takes one, no way she's coming back for a second. 'Can't leave Max,' he told her.

'I'll take Max and come back for you.'

No way she would come back, he understood, but no way he could get Max out by himself. No way he and Max would get out without her. And if she got Max out then he might just make it by himself.

'Okay.'

She crawled round him, half-dragged half-carried Max

along the track to the point marked by the handkerchief. Don't touch it, she told herself, make sure he doesn't. Another shell came in. She eased him round the scarf, made sure his trailing leg didn't touch it, hauled him clear of the woods and across the neck of open ground to the house. God he was heavy, God she could barely pull him. She opened the door, lifted him inside, and laid him on the floor.

Okay, Janner, he told himself. Nice and steady and you'll make it. His chest and legs and head were hurting again, and he could barely move. Christ, he couldn't move. Remember the scarf she put down, remember to be careful when you get there. Except he wasn't going to get there, wasn't going to get anywhere. In the sky above he heard another mortar, ducked and flinched as it landed and exploded, felt the tremor as it exploded. Close, he thought; too bloody close. Don't give up, a voice was telling him, never give up. His legs were trying to stand, his fingers were gripping the ice and his arms were trying to pull him. His body was shuddering and he knew he wasn't moving. The rounds were coming in again. Fuck, he thought, he was finished, and they hadn't even launched an air strike against the fucking guns that were trying to kill him. Fuck – the strength was almost gone now. Fuck – he was going to die. One more effort, he told himself, one more try. He stretched out his hand and felt the trembling, felt the shaking. Felt the woman's hand grab his.

'Help me,' she told him.

Didn't think you were coming back, he almost told her. If a squaddie was doing what she was doing he'd get a DSO, he thought, perhaps an MC. And if it had been in war and witnessed by a superior officer, possibly even the big one, possibly the Victoria Cross. 'Okay,' he said.

Even though he was now barely conscious, she noticed, he did not let go of his weapon.

The shells were still falling. They were almost at the scarf, were round it, the trees like ghosts above them and the rounds falling round. This isn't Bosnia, Janner thought, this isn't 1994; this is 1914, this is bloody World War One. They were past the scarf and almost at the edge of the woods, were through the garden and stumbling into the house, Jovan's eyes staring frightened at her. 'It's all right,' Kara told him, told the two men. She moved the table back to allow them more room, knelt by them and tried to help them. Both were badly injured, bones broken and bodies ripped by shrapnel. Oh God how can I help them? Oh God what can I do for them? What about my poor Jovan? Where is my husband?

It's all right, Janner tried to tell her, someone's coming for us. The blood frothed at his mouth and he made himself stop crying with the pain. It's okay, he tried to turn, tried to tell Max. Finn and the lads will be here soon.

She knelt by them and wet their lips, knelt by Jovan and wiped the sweat from his forehead.

The door opened and the two men came in. Guns in their hands, packs on their backs and goggles over their eyes. Moving quickly, closing the door and checking the room.

'Picked up your trail,' Finn took off his bergen and knelt by Janner. 'It's okay, Ken and Jim are wiping it, chopper's due in soon.' He pulled open Janner's jacket, took the syrettes from the parachute cord round Janner's neck, and gave him the morphine. First rule, even if the injured man was your best friend. Always use his morphine on him, never your own, because you didn't know when you yourself might need yours. To his left Steve did the same for Max, then marked the M on his forehead so the medics would know what he'd been given.

'Minefield,' Janner struggled to tell Finn.

'It's okay,' Finn calmed him. 'They know.'

'The woman saved us,' Janner tried to tell him. 'The woman brought us in.' His voice and breath were slipping. 'Interpreter for the food drops.' The morphine was relaxing him. 'Carried us out through the minefield. Max first. Then came back for me.'

Two more men came. 'Clean,' they told Finn. They slipped off their packs and pulled the makeshift stretchers together.

'Oboe Oboe,' Finn called Hereford again. 'Bringing out own casualties.' He gave Hereford Janner's and Max's NAAFI numbers, the codes agreed before, so that Hereford would already be checking blood groups, already getting things rolling. 'Cas-evac and hot extraction.' He confirmed the six-figure grid reference. Over the hill and into the valley on the other side. 'Confirm landing site not, repeat not, secured.' So the crew would know what they were flying into.

'Romeo Victor two three four five hours,' he was told. 'Cab already airborne. Medics on board.'

'Moving now.'

Kara held Jovan close against her and watched, body numb and mind bemused, Jovan pouring sweat and jerking in pain, and Kara trying to comfort him. Finn emptied his bergen and gave her the remaining ration packs, the other men doing the same.

'What's your name?' he asked.

She was still confused, still frightened. Still numb. 'Kara,' she told him.

'You were Ian's interpreter for the food drops?'

'Yes.' The response was a long time coming.

The others laid Janner and Max on the stretchers.

'We owe you, Kara. Janner and Max and I. And we'll never forget. Anything you want you have. Anything you need you get.'

'Take my son with you,' she asked him. 'He's ill,

he needs help. He's dying, and there's nothing I can do.'

Time to move it, one of the men was telling Finn, time to get going.

'I'm sorry,' Finn told her. 'I can't.'

Because it's going to be rough anyway getting to the RV. Because there may not be enough space in the chopper. Because we'd have to take you with us. Because the shit's going to hit the fan anyway after what we did on the hill to stop the bastards shelling Janner and Max. Because we don't know what the hell is waiting for us between here and the RV or at the RV itself.

'You said if there was anything I wanted, anything I needed.' Her voice was suddenly firmer, suddenly like ice.

He was picking up his end of the makeshift stretcher. 'Yes.'

'I asked you for something and you said no.' The voice colder, stronger.

Oh Christ, Finn thought.

'I saved yours,' Kara stood in front of him and stopped him leaving. 'Now you won't save mine.'

Because I can't. Because my sole function at the moment is to save Janner and Max. Because my sole responsibility and my sole allegiance is to them. But you said you owed, he knew the woman would say. Anything I want I can have. Anything I need I get. And all I've asked is one small thing, but you've refused me.

'I'll be back,' he told her.

Why commit yourself, Finn? Why say that? Why say anything?

'When?' She refused to move, refused to let him go. 'My son is dying, like your people are dying.' Therefore tomorrow, next week, next month, will be too late.

'Tonight.'

'What's your name?' she asked.
'Finn.'
'Don't let me down, Finn.'
She stood aside and opened the door for him.

# 3

The room was dark and getting colder. Kara sat at the table and watched the candle flame flicker, knelt by the stove and fed the remaining wood into it. The shells were still falling – somewhere, everywhere – but at least Jovan was sleeping.

It was midnight, closing on one.

The man called Finn would be back soon, because he'd said he would be.

Finn wouldn't be back, because he didn't exist and what she thought had happened that night had not happened at all. Except there was blood on the floor where she had laid the two men. So the man called Finn did exist, so he would be back.

Except he had his own to look after. But Finn had promised, and she had believed him.

It was one in the morning, going on two.

She was hungry now, crying now. She knelt by Jovan and felt the fever on his forehead – red hot and burning now. Knelt on the floor and began to wash the blood from it.

It was two in the morning, almost three.

The door opened and the men came in. The ice was frozen in their eyebrows and their faces were grey with cold.

Finn was taking off the strange thing he wore on his head, taking off the pack on his back, putting the gun he carried by the table, then kneeling by the bed and pulling little Jovan out, feeling his brow then his pulse.

Steve was helping her up, telling her she was cold and hungry and asking her why she hadn't eaten the food they'd left her.

'What food?' she asked.

He opened one of the packs, poured the contents into a saucepan, and put the pan on the stove.

Ken was tending Jovan, Finn spreading a map of Maglaj on the table and asking her where the hospital was. Steve took the pan off the stove, poured the stew into a bowl, and gave it to her. 'Easy, it'll be hot.' She took it and smelt the stew, was shaking, crying again.

'It's not a hospital, it's a medical centre.' She held the bowl of stew tight and showed Finn on the map.

The shells were still falling, the mortars still coming in.

Why did you come back? she asked at last.

Because I said I would, he told her. Any way to the new town other than over the bridge, he asked.

'No.' She was numb, confused.

Finn was emptying his bergen, cutting two holes in the bottom. 'We'll take three food packs with us, leave the rest for when you get back. You know how to use them now?'

Yes – she was nodding. But we can't go now, even though little Jovan needs to go. Because the shells and the rockets are falling and we'll be killed.

'Warm coat and boots?' Finn asked her.

'Yes.' She began to put them on.

'Where's your husband?'

'At the front.' She was still numb, still confused. 'Two days on and one off.'

'When's he due back?'

'He's already overdue.'

The others were standing, pulling on their bergens.

'What's his name?'

'Adin.'

'Leave him a note in case you and Jovan are still at the medical centre when he gets here.'

She did as he told her. Tightened the coat round her and laced the boots.

Finn lifted the boy from the floor, wrapped the coat and blankets round him, and slid him into the bergen so that his legs were hanging out of the holes in the bottom. Then he pulled the top over him and strapped the bergen on to his back.

'Steve in front, Ken looks after Kara. Jim behind. Put this on.' He gave her Janner's PNG.

'Why?'

'So you can see.'

She put it on and allowed Steve to tighten the straps, looked round and saw the world in shades of green, everything in tunnel vision. What's going on, part of her mind asked. This is not real, this is not happening.

They were out of the house – suddenly and quickly, no orders. The candle blown out and the door shut. Were going down the hill into the ghost of the old town. A shell was coming in and exploding somewhere to their right. The street and houses and figures of the others were a ghostly green through the ovals of the eyepieces. I don't believe this, she thought again, I can't believe this. The moon was up and the houses were like skeletons around them. They were moving in stages, she realized, sheltering in the lee of a building when a shell came in, then running in the lull after it had exploded, Steve in front as Finn had said, Ken grabbing her as she stumbled, Jim just behind them. Soon be there, my son. Soon be safe and well with the doctor looking after you.

They were crouching in the shelter of the last building of the old town, the bridge in front of them and the shells still coming in. Ken had pushed her forward so that she was beside Finn and to his left, Steve and Jim to his right, protecting her and the boy on Finn's back.

'Go.'

They ran on to the bridge. She no longer felt the cold. Her heart was pounding and her legs were moving automatically, Ken lifting her slightly so she seemed to be running on air. They were halfway across, almost three-quarters, almost there. In the still of the night she heard the sound of the express train. 'Down.' Ken pushed her, the others lying on the ground round her, Finn facing away from her, so that the boy on his back was protected, Steve facing Finn, his back upstream. The shell struck the building forty metres from them, then they were up and running again, suddenly across the bridge and into the comparative safety of the new town. They turned left, exposed now; turned right again. Came to the medical centre, opened the door, and tumbled down to the basement.

The steps were lined with people, mostly refugees but some locals afraid to move, more in the basement room. Staring at them, bewildered and frightened. The doctor recognizing her as she pulled the strange apparatus from her head. Finn knelt and Jim lifted Jovan from the bergen and laid him on the table in the middle of the room. The only light came from two Tilley lamps hanging from the ceiling, the shadows flickering across the walls.

I helped deliver this boy, the woman thought. 'What's wrong?' she asked Kara.

Jovan was crying with pain now, almost screaming. 'Here?' the doctor asked. She lifted his clothes and placed her hand carefully against his right lower abdomen.

'Yes.'

Kara felt the relief. 'Soon be okay.' She held Jovan's hand and comforted him, tried to reassure herself.

The doctor looked up. Her face was ashen, partly with fatigue and stress, and partly with what she was about to say. I helped bring him into this world, she thought again, and now I am about to witness his departure from it.

'I'm sorry.'

What do you mean, you're sorry? The fragile security Kara had built round her collapsed. Against the wall behind her the four men looked at the doctor.

'Jovan has appendicitis. If it hasn't burst already it's about to.'

'So?'

'We're a medical centre, not a hospital; there's nothing we can do about it here. The nearest place where Jovan could be treated is Tesanj. We do take patients there, but only at night.' In the hope of catching the snipers and gunners asleep. And on horseback, because there's no petrol for the cars. 'A group left with two people eight hours ago.' She checked her watch. It was three in the morning, going on four. 'Perhaps we can try tomorrow night.' If Jovan's still alive, which is unlikely, but we can only pray. And if there's somebody to take him, because even at night it's dangerous.

Not my little Jovan. Kara reached forward and held his hand, stroked his face. Not after all he's been through.

He was awake now, his eyes looking at her. The men behind her were getting up, Finn taking out a map and asking the doctor the route; Steve wrapping Jovan again and slipping him into Finn's bergen; Jim giving the doctor one of the food packs and telling her how it worked, telling her to use it herself, because everyone was hungry but she was the one they all relied on.

Kara realized what they were doing. 'I'm coming with you,' she told them.

'You'll slow us down.' Finn pulled the bergen on to his back and picked up his Heckler.

'I'm still coming with you.'

They left the basement, crouched in the doorway for the

next shell, then moved into the street, Maglaj cold and bleak and battered round them, green and stark and unreal in the PNGs. They moved quickly, keeping the height of the buildings between them and the incoming shells and mortars. In the hills it will be a frozen hell, she thought, on the road to Tesanj it would be like going to the Arctic Circle.

They cleared the town, climbing now, Steve in front again and Finn following, Kara tucked into the middle. At least she wasn't hungry, at least the stew had warmed her. The quarter segment of the moon was above them, the trees ghostly round them and the ground phantom-green with snow and ice. Behind them, and to their right, the sounds of the guns and mortars faded in the dark. At least the road to Tesanj was in the Maglaj–Tesanj pocket, she thought, at least they didn't have to go through the lines. Just pray that the gunners are asleep or happy on slivovic.

They had been going thirty minutes and she was tiring more than she could have imagined. Two kilometres gone, she told herself, perhaps three. Oh God, the night was running out, oh God, they weren't going to make it in time. She should have listened to them, shouldn't have insisted she go with them. Her lungs seared every time she breathed and there was no longer any feeling in her feet.

'You're slowing us down,' she was only half-aware what Finn was telling her. 'Steve and I will go ahead with Jovan, Ken and Jim will stay with you.'

She tried to reply but they had already left, the two of them running, bergens on their backs and guns held in front of them.

'Doing well,' Jim told her. 'Let's go.'

The cold was killing her. The road was undulating, dropping then climbing, occasionally they slipped off it and hid in the bushes when someone came the other way, just in case they were Chetniks. She was no longer thinking in terms of hours or minutes or seconds, was thinking only if Finn and Steve would make it to Tesanj in time, was thinking only in terms of putting one foot before the other, making herself go on, making herself stop crying with pain and desperation. Soon it would be getting light, soon they would have to stop because soon the Chetniks in the hills would be able to see them. She was on Ken's shoulders, not even aware how or when it had happened, Jim carrying Ken's bergen as well as his own, and the two men still moving quickly. Not running, but not walking, something between. One man moving and the other covering him, then the second moving and the first covering him. Guns at the ready, guns across the chest, and the butt in the shoulder position.

In the distance – not too far in the distance – she heard the sounds of the guns pounding Tesanj. Perhaps they had been there all night and she had been unable to hear them because of the pounding in her ears. Jim was carrying her now, the black gone, fading into grey, and the grey soon mixing into the cold sharp light of a winter morning. They took off the PNGs and came out of the trees, dropped into the edge of the town, Finn and Steve suddenly with them – she wasn't sure where they had come from. Finn lifted her from Jim's shoulders and ran with her into the cover of the buildings, took her into the basement of the hospital.

'Where's Jovan?' she asked.

'In the operating theatre.'

They sat on a bench in one of the corridors and waited.

The hospital was grey concrete and multistorey, though because of the shelling the top floors had been cleared. The corridor was dark and gloomy, the hospital running on an emergency generator, so lighting was restricted to key areas. A doctor hesitated by them, then passed on. In the town outside the streets were empty and the shells and mortars rained down on the buildings.

Another doctor stopped. He was old before his time, his shoulders drooped with fatigue and his eyes were haunted.

'You're Jovan's mother?'

'Yes.' She stood up, fists clenched in fear.

'Jovan's fine, he's going to be okay. He was lucky. Another half-hour and he wouldn't have made it.'

'Thank you.' It was all she could say. 'May I see him?'

'He's not come round yet, but of course you can.'

He led her along the corridor and into what now served as a ward. The beds were pushed tight together and the room was packed, a limited amount of lighting. She saw Jovan immediately, saw the others. Oh God, she almost wept. The children were wrapped in bandages, some had legs or parts of legs missing, some arms or parts of arms where their limbs had been blown off by shrapnel or snipers' bullets. Others had their faces and eyes covered, or their bodies or abdomens bandaged. Some were crying softly, others still frozen in pain or shock or fear. My poor dear Jovan, she thought, yet you were lucky. She knelt by his bedside and held his hand, sensed Finn crouching beside her.

'Thank you,' she said.

He shook his head and left her, walked along the rows of tightly-packed beds and looked at the other children. When she looked five minutes later he was still in the ward, still standing as if transfixed, still looking at a girl with the sweetest smile in the world and no legs.

For most of that morning she stayed with Jovan. At noon – sometime round noon, she could not be sure – she left the ward and sat hunched with the four men, shared their food with them and the other parents who sat equally anxiously in the corridor. Outside the ice was solid on the streets and the shells continued to fall. What about you, Adin – her husband was never far from her mind – where are you and how are you?

'Are the others okay?' she asked.

'Janner and Max should make it.' Finn was to her left, both of them sitting on the floor with their backs against the wall. The others were somewhere else in the hospital.

'What about the men who did the food drops?' Because I assume you're the same as they were, though I don't know what that means.

'They're all right. You interpreted for them?'

'Yes.'

They sat in silence.

'Remember me to them.'

'Of course.'

The conversation was almost formal. Any moment she'd offer him coffee, Kara thought, any moment she'd grind the beans and put the coffee on the stove to boil, any moment now she'd pour them each the creamy froth at the top, but still give him the first cup, in the local tradition, because he was her guest.

'What were you doing in Maglaj?' she asked. The question was unexpected. Because you weren't dropping aid – the implication was clear.

'There was a possibility of an air strike. We came in to locate the guns in the hills and direct the aircraft on to them.'

'I thought I heard planes.' Sometime yesterday afternoon, though yesterday was already a lifetime away. 'So the air strike was to stop the Chetniks shelling the people.' Perhaps there was hope after all, she remembered she had thought, perhaps there really was a ceasefire.

'Sort of.' Finn shifted slightly.

'But there weren't any air strikes.'

'No.'

'So there will be today?' Except there can't be, because you were supposed to locate the positions of the guns in the hills, and you're here in Tesanj, not Maglaj, even though Tesanj is also being shelled. Even though, officially at least, there's a ceasefire.

'No,' Finn told her. 'There won't be.'

'Why not, if it was to stop the Chetniks shelling the people? They're still doing it.'

Because it wasn't to stop the people being killed, Finn didn't know how to tell her. It was to save UN personnel, even though those personnel might have called in the air strike to save the town.

'Because the United Nations decided against it.' He stared at the far wall and thought of Jovan, of the girl with the smile and no legs. 'Don't ask me why.' He hadn't meant to say it. 'Because I don't know why.' All I know is that we were in position, the Jaguar came in, pulled out of the first run, then was told to abort.

'My country right or wrong?' she asked him.

'I'm just a soldier,' he told her.

Perhaps he felt guilt, perhaps not.

She left him and went back to Jovan.

It was mid-afternoon, the temperature falling again and the day losing its light. Again she sat hunched with Finn and the others in a corner of the corridor, the shells still falling outside.

You speak English, Finn almost said; so how did someone like you end up in a place like Maglaj?

My husband's job, she would have told him.

'Family?' he asked instead.

'Adin, my husband, is on the front line.' She couldn't remember whether or not she had told him. 'The rest of his and my families are missing. Perhaps they're dead, perhaps they're refugees.' The statement was a mix of accusation, anger and resignation. 'The only one I know is still alive is my mother's mother, my grandmother, who lives in Travnik.'

'Travnik is a mixed town.'

'Yes.' She turned her head slightly, so she was looking at him. 'She's a Croat.' Crazy world, she thought again, crazy war, crazy people. But only because someone else made us so.

She pulled herself up and went into the ward, knelt by Jovan's bed and stroked his face. 'Told you everything would be all right,' she whispered to him as he opened his eyes and tried to smile at her. 'Told you we'd be okay.'

Finn knelt beside her.

'When will the war end?' she asked him. 'You're a soldier, you should know. How are we going to win and how long will it take us?'

He stared at her, stared at her son, stared at the shattered limbs and bodies of the other children. At the bed of the girl five metres away a woman doctor pulled the sheet over the still white face and turned away so that the parents would not see her cry.

'You'll never win,' he told Kara. 'Even if the war ends, which it has to sometime and in some way, you and your people are going to lose.'

'What about the West and the United Nations?' she asked. 'They know we are in the right, they have already said so, so when will they help us, when will they intervene on our behalf?'

'The West will never intervene on your behalf.'

'But what about the Gulf? You intervened there. Waged war to save democracy in Kuwait.'

'Kuwait and the Gulf War wasn't about democracy. It was about protecting the West's oil.'

She looked at Jovan again, smiled at him again, watched as he slipped into sleep.

'But what about people like me, what about fighters like Adin?'

Even though he's not really a fighter, even though all he

does is lie in the mud and ice on the front line and wait to die and pray he's not going to.

Two beds away an orderly wrapped the body of the girl in a sheet and carried her gently away.

'People like you and Adin will never win,' Finn told Kara.

'Why not?'

He shrugged.

'What about people like you?' she asked.

'People like me win because we have power, because of who we are and what we do. So people are afraid of us. Therefore we can win.'

'What about if you don't win?'

'There's a saying,' he told her. Perhaps it was a poem, perhaps just a quotation – he couldn't remember. Why complicate things, he asked himself; why allow himself to be drawn into this maze? 'It isn't the critic who counts; it isn't the one who points out how the strong man stumbled or how the doer of deeds might have done them better. The credit belongs to the man who is actually in the arena. Who, if he wins, knows the triumph of achievement. And who, if he fails, at least fails while daring greatly.'

So that his place shall never be with those cold and timid souls who know neither victory nor defeat, he might have added.

So how do you win? she asked. What decides who wins?

His regiment had a motto, he told her.

What's that, she asked him.

Who Dares Wins.

They left the ward and sat against the wall. The gloom in the corridor was deeper, colder.

'So how can I win? The next time they bomb Maglaj or Tesanj or somewhere like it, and the West and the United Nations does nothing to stop it, what must I do and what must I have to make the West stop it?'

What can my people do, she meant, what must my people have?

'Power,' Finn told her again. 'The next time you must have something the West wants, or something which makes them afraid of you.'

Outside it was dark and the buildings were like ghosts. He opened a food pack and made them each a tea, broke open a pack and gave her the fruit biscuits inside. In the room to the left someone was sobbing.

'Why did you come back last night?' She wrapped her fingers round the mug and tried to massage some warmth back into them.

'Because I said I would.'

'That doesn't answer the question,' she told him. 'You were supposed to leave last night, so why didn't you? Why did you come to the house? Why did you save little Jovan?'

They went again into the ward, stood again by Jovan's bed and watched him sleeping, went back again to the corridor and joined the others.

'So now we're even,' Kara suggested. Because I saved yours and you saved mine.

In the shadows to the right Steve watched without speaking.

Yet you think you still owe – Kara looked at Finn. Because I saved two of yours and you only saved one of mine. But the one of mine was my only son, therefore I owe you more than you can ever imagine.

'We came back because you'd done something for us,' Finn told her. 'You helped us even though you didn't have to.'

Therefore we still owe.

'You're leaving?' she asked.

'Yes.' Because the United Nations have refused to sanction further air strikes. Because everyone else thinks we stayed behind to provide ground cover in case the opposition attacked as the chopper took Janner and Max out. Because we should have been out of here twelve hours ago. Because nobody else knows we're still here.

Perhaps the guilt was settling again, perhaps it hadn't lifted.

They went to the ward and stood by Jovan – Kara and the four men. Smiled at him and told him he was a good boy even though he was barely awake and would not have understood them anyway. Then they walked to the corridor and picked up their bergens.

'Thanks, Jim.' She shook each of their hands. 'Thanks, Ken.' Kissed each of them on the cheek as a sister would kiss them. 'Thanks, Steve.' Suddenly and spontaneously. 'On behalf of little Jovan.'

'Thanks, Kara,' they told her. 'On behalf of Janner and Max.'

She smiled, wiped away the tears.

'Thanks, Finn.'

'Thanks, Kara.'

'Ciao, Finn. See you again sometime.'

'Sure, Kara. See you again.'

# 4

London was bleak. No snow or ice, just the incessant drizzle which marked the capital at this time of year.

Langdon's schedule was even tighter than most days. Breakfast at six – full English, the way he liked to start each morning; briefings at the FCO, the Foreign and Commonwealth Office, then the flight to Brussels for the 10.00 AM meeting of European Foreign Secretaries. And after that the rush home for a full day squeezed into late afternoon and evening.

When his driver delivered him to Whitehall there was still an hour of darkness left. His advisers, some of whom would accompany him to Brussels, were waiting in the room outside his own office, the aroma of fresh coffee hanging in the air. He led them through, settled in his favourite chair, accepted a coffee and began the briefing.

'Bosnia.' Because Bosnia would top the Brussels agenda, especially with the peace negotiations in Vienna seeming to report some progress.

They went through the overnights, plus the way Langdon should play whatever else the other Foreign Ministers might bring up.

One: the so-called ceasefire, even though it was in name only, and even though the UN had sought to play down violations in case they interfered with the Vienna talks.

Two: the state of siege in the Maglaj–Tesanj pocket and the reason for the UN pulling out the air strike at the last minute.

Three: the reporting of the siege by the press, mainly based on radio messages from the two towns pleading for help.

Four: the presence of the SAS in the area, the deaths of two SAS men and the wounding of two others. Plus the follow-up on how the FCO should play it vis-à-vis the press.

Langdon was in his mid-fifties but fit and tall, with dark hair just beginning to show the first streaks of silver. His background was representative of the new guard elbowing its way to the top at Westminster: Eton, Oxford, the City, twenty years in politics, the last fifteen in government, the last ten in the Cabinet, and the last three as Foreign Secretary.

Balkan Games, he thought. The Serbs, the Croats and the Muslims in one game. The Serbs and the West in another. London, Washington, Moscow and Paris in a third. The United Nations and the governments comprising the Security Council in a fourth, even the games within the UN itself.

And somewhere in the middle the people whom the UN was supposed to help. But if you allowed yourself to think like that then you lost the game before it was even started.

He closed the meeting and was driven to Heathrow.

The night had been long and cold, even in the ward, the occasional shell or mortar falling on the town. Kara had sat by the bed and held Jovan's hands, told him his favourite stories as he drifted in and out of sleep.

It was seven o'clock in the morning. She was in the corridor, jerking in the half-world between sleep and fear.

'Hello, Kara.'

She woke and looked up. Was laughing and crying, holding her husband and hugging him. 'You made it,' she was asking Adin, telling Adin. 'You're alive. You got the note.'

'How's Jovan?' Adin held her tight, kissed her again and again. 'Where is he, can I see him?'

They stood by Jovan's bed, stayed an hour till the boy woke and saw his father, then they sat together in the corridor and shared the food, leaning against each other with their backs against the walls. It was going to be all right, she knew: Jovan had pulled through and Adin was alive.

'Tell me what happened,' Adin's arm was round her. 'Tell me how you got here.'

She told him, though her account at this stage was disjointed and apparently without logic. About how she had heard a scream in the night and thought it was him, how she helped the two injured men and how Finn and the others had come back. How they had carried Jovan to Tesanj and how they had given her their food when they had left.

The shells and mortars echoed outside.

The three of them would stay in Tesanj until Jovan recovered, they decided; then they would return to Maglaj but probably lock up the house, find a basement in the new town so they didn't have to cross the bridge to get to the food. A basement on the far edge of town where they would be marginally safer.

They left the corridor and went back into the ward, hunched together again by Jovan's bed and waited till he woke.

The shells and mortars were still falling.

Kara watched as Adin knelt by Jovan and talked and laughed with him, saw the moment Adin's eyes drifted to the children in the other beds and realized how lucky they were as a family, how others had suffered. Jovan's eyes closed again. They kissed him and began to return to the corridor. In the next bed a younger boy whimpered with pain; Kara stayed with him and held his hand, stroked his face and talked to him until his own mother came, then she went outside and sat with Adin.

The shells were still falling, sometimes far away, other times closer. Once you became accustomed to them, though, it was strange how you almost ignored them, almost lived with them.

'Tell me again about Jim and Steve and the others,' he said.

She had already told him once, now she went through it again in more detail. 'I love you.' She slipped her arm round him and kissed him. 'I wish Finn and the others could have met you.'

It was mid-morning; the shells and mortars were closer now, she thought, almost subconsciously.

The Brussels meeting broke at twelve-thirty for a buffet lunch in an adjoining room. Langdon chose smoked salmon and mineral water, then spent fifteen minutes talking with the French Foreign Minister.

'Update on Maglaj and Tesanj?' he asked Nicholls as the meeting reconvened.

'The situation in the Maglaj–Tesanj pocket remains at levels consistent with previous days,' Nicholls told him wryly.

Langdon understood the UN-speak, and to show that he understood he laughed.

The stomach pains were gripping her. Perhaps she shouldn't have eaten so much from the food packs, she thought, even though she had rationed it carefully; perhaps, because she was accustomed to the daily diet of beans and dry bread, she should have rationed it even more stringently. She heard the express train, then the sound as the shell landed. Even closer to the hospital this time, she thought.

The front line was bad, Adin told her, but the men were good and brave. They would definitely move to the new town, they decided, definitely find somewhere where they didn't have to cross the bridge to reach the food kitchen. Love you, she thought again, told him again. They went to the ward and sat again with Jovan; returned to the corridor and sat against the wall. He didn't know how afraid she had been when she and Jovan were alone and Jovan was falling ill, she told him; he didn't know how much safer she felt now he was with her.

She heard the noise again and felt the shuddering, the whole world deafening her and the vibrations shaking her, the express trains coming in and the mortars suddenly whining around them.

'Oh God.' She heard someone screaming.

'Oh no.' Another voice. 'They're shelling the hospital.'

Another express train came in, then another, the whine of a mortar. Someone beside her was lying on the floor, pressing himself down to protect himself from the bombs and the debris. Kara was ignoring the noise and the explosion, was on her feet and running, Adin at her side. The smoke and dust billowed from the door of the ward and the sounds of children screaming came from inside. Another shell was coming in. She ignored it, ignored everything, and pushed into the room. The ceiling had collapsed, there were holes in the walls, and the beds and the children in them were buried under a layer of concrete and brick and plaster. She pulled at the rubble, tried to reach Jovan, more people suddenly beside her and more people trying to dig their children out. Mothers and fathers, brothers and sisters, doctors and nurses.

'Stop.'

She heard Adin's voice and froze, almost involuntarily, still in shock.

They all stopped, all looked at him.

'We have to be organized.' His voice was calm. 'We have to do this methodically. That's the only way of saving the children.' He took the arms of the woman digging in the rubble next to Kara and helped her step back. The woman had been standing on the leg of a child, Kara realized. 'Doctors and nurses don't dig,' Adin ordered. Doctors and nurses are too important, because we can dig but we can't do what they can once we've got our children out. 'Three columns going in simultaneously. Make sure we don't make anything collapse, make sure we've got the children in the first beds out before we move to the second.'

The doctors and nurses fell back and the men and women took their place, Kara among them. 'Three lines behind the diggers to remove the rubble and pass the children out as we get them,' Adin ordered. 'Don't worry, my son's at the other end.'

The doctors and nurses were running, preparing the rooms which now passed as operating theatres, others hurrying from different parts of the hospital as the news spread. Adin took his place at the front of the line which would reach Jovan's bed and began to dig, carefully and methodically, began to remove the debris and pass it back, began to burrow his way in towards the child on whom the woman had been standing.

You're a good man, Adin, Kara thought again. You're a great man. Please be alive, Jovan, please be okay.

'Reached the first.' Adin passed the tortured piece of metal that had once been part of a bed to the man behind him, and burrowed a little deeper. 'She's okay.' His face was grimed with sweat and dust. 'Passing her down now.'

It's okay, Jovan, he told his son; I'm here, I'm coming for you. Your mother's waiting to take you in her arms again and the doctors and nurses are waiting to make you better.

Three places down the line a man edged forward and

looked at his daughter, followed the doctors and nurses as they rushed her away.

It's okay, Jovan, Kara willed her son. Your father's coming for you, your father's digging his way in to save you.

'Second coming out.' From the column on the left of the ward. 'Injured. Get a doctor.'

It's okay, Jovan – it was like a drum in Adin's head. Coming for you, Jovan. Coming to get you.

Perhaps the shells and mortars were still coming in, perhaps not. Nobody cared, even listened.

It's okay, Jovan. Your father's coming, your father will get to you.

'Third child.' They all knew by the tone of the voice, all watched as the broken remains were passed back.

Almost there, Jovan, almost reached you. Adin worked methodically, telling people what to do, telling them to be careful, telling them what pieces of debris to move and what to leave in place. Telling those digging to change but never leaving his place at the front of his line.

'Fourth child, okay.'

Fifth and sixth.

Hang on, Jovan, Kara willed her son. You're all right, you're bound to be all right. Your father's coming. Just hang on till he gets to you.

Seventh.

Soon be your turn, Jovan, soon Adin will get you out.

Adin was below the rubble, burrowing deeper, the top layer moving and someone shifting a beam, making sure it didn't collapse the delicate fretwork below.

'Eighth.'

Kara heard Adin's voice.

Okay now, my son. Your father's reached you as I told you he would, your father's saved you because he always would.

She could no longer hear the breathing of the diggers or the anxious whispers of the men and women around her, no longer heard anything.

It's all right now, Jovan. Your father's hands are picking you up now, your father is saving you now.

She saw Adin's head, saw his body, saw the thin little bundle he held in his arms.

Adin's face was fixed and grey, eyes staring straight ahead and jaw locked. Slowly he stood and turned, looked at her, looked at the bundle in his arms. His face dissolved and the tears streamed down his face. 'Sorry,' he said to the man behind him. 'Have to stop for a moment.' He walked past the next digger, crying and shaking, still muttering that he was sorry, still apologizing that he could no longer work. Kara stepped forward and stood beside him, looked at the bundle in his arms and stroked the boy's face, held Adin's arm and allowed him to carry their son from the ward. A doctor was suddenly with them, a nurse helping. Carefully they took Jovan from Adin and laid him on one of the beds they had placed in the corridor, began examining him, gently but firmly, searched for a pulse, for a flicker of breath. Tried to breathe life into him, tried to inject life into him. Tried to make his heart beat and his lungs breathe.

'Sorry.' The doctor stood, did not know what to do, held Adin by his arm and thanked him for what he had done that day. Said he was sorry again.

'There are others,' Kara told the doctor and the nurse. 'If you can no longer help Jovan, you can still help them.' She knelt and lifted Jovan in her arms, stroked his cheek again and kissed him. Wanted to hold him for ever but gave him instead to his father.

That afternoon they bathed him and laid him in a clean white sheet, placed him with the other children who had died that day, but did not leave him. Sat with him, as the other parents sat with their children, and talked with him for the last time, told him his favourite story and how the summer and the peace would soon come.

That evening, after the dark of night had taken over from the grey of day, offering at least a degree of protection, they walked with the other parents and the doctors and nurses to the cemetery on the hill. As they approached the men finished digging the holes in the rock-hard soil of the winter. Small little holes, Kara thought, small little children.

All so fast now, all so sudden.

Goodbye, my little Jovan – she looked at him again, kissed him again, watched as Adin kissed him then folded the cloth over his face, gave their son back to her for the last time.

They held him, lowered him into the grave, knelt in silence as the imam said the prayers they did not understand.

Nothing else could happen now, she knew; nothing more could be visited upon them.

They trickled the first soil on to the sheet and said goodbye. Then they returned to the hospital, sat in the corridor, and wept.

The grey was coming up and the air was pinched with ice. In the village in the hills to the east of Maglaj, where the surrounding Serb forces withdrew to take their rest and recuperation, the sniper Valeschov left his billet and began the trudge through the snow.

'Not today,' his commanding officer told him. 'You're needed somewhere else.'

'Where?' Valeschov asked.

'Tesanj.'

London was cold, but at least it had stopped drizzling.

So the Serbs had declared a ceasefire round the Maglaj–

Tesanj pocket and he himself had put one across on the Opposition – Langdon sat in the inner sanctum of his office, an adviser on either side, and watched the recording of the early evening news bulletin: the reports from Vienna, his own performance in Brussels that afternoon, plus the live transmission from the House during the bulletin itself.

The schedule that day had been even tighter than he had feared. Brussels had overrun, which had delayed his return to London, so that he had been unable to make his appearance in the House at the customary time. Which had meant that he had made his statement shortly after six. Eight minutes after, to be precise. Or bang in the middle of the BBC TV's early evening news. So they had gone live on it. Prompted, of course, by the right word in the right ear that the Foreign Secretary had something of interest to say.

So the Serbs had declared a ceasefire, he mused again. Notwithstanding that a ceasefire was already in place, of course. He reached for a sherry. But everything was *notwithstanding* nowadays.

He should be able to grab a day and a half off this weekend – the thought was in the back of his mind. Even get down to the family home in the West Country. Hilary and Rob and little Sammi were back from Berlin for a flying visit, and he and his wife saw too little of their daughter and granddaughter nowadays.

He sipped the sherry and watched the news bites from Vienna.

'I think we have a way forward,' the Bosnian-Serb spokesman told the TV cameras.

'The latest ceasefire might well give cause for optimism,' one of the West's negotiators told the press.

Quite nicely worded, one of Langdon's advisers commented. Almost gets round the problem of the ceasefire that wasn't. Almost but not quite.

'What about the UN refusal to launch an air strike at Maglaj?' one of the BBC team asked.

'You could say that the UN decision led to the situation we're able to report today.'

The report switched to Langdon leaving the Brussels meeting.

'If the UN and the West had taken firmer action earlier, perhaps the conflict might not have escalated to the present situation?'

'Perhaps yes, perhaps no,' he had replied. 'It's always easy to be wise, or at least wiser, with hindsight.'

'What about the reports of a hospital being shelled in Tesanj?'

Langdon had nodded, as if sharing the reporter's concern. 'We *have* received reports of this . . . At present we're still trying to get confirmation.'

Wrong time to say that first reports suggested that children had been among the dead, he and his advisers had decided. Wrong time also to take away from the impact of the surprise he had in store at Westminster.

Pity about the kids, of course, but kids were always the victims. And victims were an inevitable price of practically everything.

The bulletin went back to the studio, then live to the House. He leaned forward and paid closer attention.

The Speaker was calling him; he was rising from the front bench and taking his position at the dispatch box.

'There has been a breach of the original ceasefire, especially in the area of the Maglaj–Tesanj pocket.' He glanced at the advisers and nodded his approval of the wording they had chosen for him. 'The renegotiation of the ceasefire, however, is to be welcomed.'

Why not an air strike – the intervention from the Opposition front bench had been predictable. Why not more direct military intervention?

'The decision whether or not to launch an air strike is the sole prerogative of the United Nations.' His delivery emphasized the point. 'It is not the responsibility of Her Majesty's Government.'

He had held up his hand at this point, stopped the heckling from the other side of the House.

'What *is* the responsibility of Her Majesty's Government is not only to ensure that its commitment to the United Nations Protection Force is fulfilled, but also to ensure the safety of the British contingent in UNPROFOR.'

One British life is a life too many, the Opposition knew he was going to say, and prepared its response. Why not a more positive position on Bosnia, he knew they would throw at him.

'I have to tell the House . . .' his voice was sombre now '. . . and it is right and proper that the House is the first to know, that there have been a number of British casualties during an incident in the Maglaj–Tesanj pocket.'

Even now, even on television, he could sense the sudden tension, the moment the mood in the chamber swung in his favour.

'It is my sad duty this afternoon to inform the House that, in a reconnaissance operation ordered by UNPROFOR, and acting in their role as authorized military observers, two members of the Special Air Service have been killed in an incident near the town of Maglaj, and two others seriously injured. The injured men have been flown home and we are in negotiation to retrieve the bodies of the two others.'

Of course it wasn't quite news; of course the press had been sniffing at the rumour. But he had done what he always did: got his retaliation in first, so that it was the others, rather than himself, who were now on the defensive.

'I have nothing further to say.'

And then he had sat down. And no one, not even the

Opposition front bench, had moved even a finger to ask him another question.

Tesanj was spread below him.

Most people were still keeping away from the areas known to be exposed to rifle fire, those that didn't still darting furtively between doorways. A few hours of peace, then they'd come out, though.

Valeschov shifted his position slightly and studied the town, fixed in his mind the streets and the places they would be entering and leaving and where, therefore, they would be exposed to him. The food centres, of course, the radio station, the hospital.

All night, after they had returned from the graveyard on the hillside, Kara and Adin had slumped together in the corridor, occasionally talking, though not often, most of the time staring into the black and trying to struggle back from the abyss which engulfed them.

A nurse brought them tea, a mug each, made sure their hands were firmly gripping the handles, sat with them without speaking before she was needed elsewhere.

Perhaps they should have begun the journey back to Maglaj last night, after they had laid little Jovan to rest; perhaps it was right that they had delayed till this morning. There was, after all, a ceasefire, and the shells and mortars had stopped.

They finished the tea, fastened the backpack Adin had brought with him, and began to leave. Thanked the doctors and nurses who were on duty, and asked for their thanks to be passed to those who were resting. Then they left the hospital and stepped into the cold, shuffled rather than walked down the street.

An old couple leaving the hospital – Valeschov targeted them through the crosswires. At least a couple who looked old, but nowadays you couldn't tell. Range four hundred metres, wind speed not enough to worry about. He followed them, played with them, as they walked down the street. But played with them without them knowing, and that was the problem.

Interesting job, being a sniper, gave you such power. Plus the decision of life and death over them, almost like being God, really. Like being the emperor in the old Roman games, thumb up or thumb down. But for you to have that power people needed to at least know you were there. Only then were they afraid, and that was what gave you the power.

And that was the problem today.

The old couple, for example. Hadn't been his enemies before the conflict and wouldn't be after. But they weren't afraid of him, because they didn't know he was there. And that irked. He didn't need to kill them, perhaps didn't even want to kill them. This morning, anyway, because last night he'd eaten well and slept better than he'd done for days. But unless they knew he was there they weren't playing the game. Nobody was. And there was only one way people could be persuaded to play the game.

'You want to see Jovan before we leave?' Adin suggested. 'You want to say goodbye to him, tell him we'll be back?'

Because we *will* be back, because we'll never leave him.

They were tight together, holding and supporting each other.

'Yes,' Kara told him. 'I'd like to see Jovan before we leave.'

'Me, too.' Adin tried to smile.

The man or the woman, Valeschov wondered. It was like tossing a coin at the start of a football match, see who decided which way they'd play. Nothing personal, of course. Just part of the game. And the one thing he liked was the game. So after he'd killed them, or at least killed one of them, everybody would know he was there. And after that people would play the game again. He moved the rifle slightly, swung from the man to the woman then back to the man. The woman, he decided, and swung back again.

Kara heard the shout and turned. The doctor was standing in the doorway, his white coat flapping slightly and his hand raised to them. 'Good luck.'

The man – Valeschov changed his mind. He swung the Dragunov and squeezed the trigger.

'Thank you,' Kara began to say and heard the crack, flinched and turned. Adin was falling backwards slightly, his fingers clutched at his chest and the pain and fear and bewilderment frozen on his face.

No . . . she was screaming, no sound coming out. Please God, no.

Adin was already crumpled on the ground. She crouched beside him, held his head in one arm and the hands clutching his chest with the other.

The doctor ran – away from the safety of the door and down the street. Sniper, someone shouted at him and grabbed him into a doorway. 'It's all right,' Kara was whispering to Adin, to herself. 'The doctor's coming, soon you'll be okay.' He was trying to push her away, trying to tell her to seek shelter. She was pulling him, dragging him across the ice towards a doorway. Someone grabbed her and pulled her inside, someone else hauling Adin behind her and slamming the door shut as the sniper aimed again. The room was dark and cold, the people inside staring at her. The doctor came in through a door at the back and knelt down, pulled Adin's coat open and checked the entry area in the chest, then nodded to the others to move Kara from the room. She was screaming, protesting; they held her and dragged her out. Only then did the doctor turn Adin over and take off his pack. The back of the coat was shredded and oozing thick blood where the bullet had exited. Christ what a mess, someone whispered. Still a pulse – the doctor checked. 'Help me get him to the hospital.' Three of them lifted Adin, and squeezed through the door at the rear, ran through the side streets – two holding his arms and one his legs – and into a door at the side of the hospital.

Kara ran with them, followed them through the door and down the corridor, heard them shouting for people to get out of the way. They turned left then left again, into an operating theatre. The doctor was already giving instructions and a nurse was cutting through Adin's clothing, more doctors and nurses arriving. One of them took Kara by the shoulder and led her away, closed the door behind her and sat with her. Isn't this the man who led the digging for the children? another asked. Didn't he lose his son yesterday?

Stay alive, Kara prayed. The panic swept over her in waves: the cold and the fear and the sudden abyss.

Pulse, the first doctor pleaded; come on, where are you? Not much they could do about the wound anyway, they all knew, hardly anything they could do to counter the internal damage. Doesn't matter, the doctor whispered to himself. I can do it, we can do it. Come on, my friend, he urged Adin. For Chrissake come on. No pulse – he was still checking for it. Perhaps there hadn't been anyway, perhaps he'd felt it because he wanted to. Perhaps the pulse he'd felt was the last draining of Adin's blood from his body.

Don't leave me, my dear precious husband. Don't leave me ever, but don't leave me at the moment I need you the most.

Come on, the doctor was still saying, almost shouting. Don't die. You haven't died. You're okay, you're going to be okay. For Christ's sake don't give up, don't stop your heart beating or your lungs breathing. For God's sake help me to help you.

Not you, my wonderful Adin. Not you who was such a good father, such a great man. Not you who gave so much to so many. Who loved the flowers in spring and the snow in winter.

A nurse was still tying the lead surgeon's face mask, the man bent over Adin. Slowly he stepped back from the operating table, peeled off his gloves, and shook his head.

When they carried Adin Isak to the hillside that night the moon was barely rising over the trees, the dark was as cold as ever, and the hole was already dug. Thin and shallow, because the soil was frozen hard and the men had difficulty breaking it open. Perhaps there's always a hole, Kara thought; perhaps they're always ready because there are always bodies to bury.

'I'd like my husband to lie with his son,' she told the men who accompanied her. For some reason there was no imam. Perhaps he was elsewhere, perhaps he himself had been killed.

They nodded their understanding and carried the body to the place where she and Adin had knelt the night before, then they laid it down and began to remove the soil from the small grave on the crest of the hill. When they came to the shroud containing Jovan's body Kara lifted it out and held it while the men made the hole bigger. Then she kissed Adin goodbye and helped lay him in the hole, then Jovan, the father's arm round the boy, as if they were lying together in the summer fields and looking up at the cloudless blue of the sky.

The moon was above her now, and the night was colder.

She sprinkled the soil back in, carefully and gently, then stood back and waited till the men had filled the hole, placed the wooden memorial at the head, and left her.

The snow was falling again.

From a pocket she took a pencil, and added Adin's name to the one already on the wood.

Thirty-six hours ago she had everything to live for, she thought. She had a husband and a son, and Jovan was going to live and Adin was alive and well and at her side.

Perhaps she should take the road to Maglaj tonight, perhaps she should wait till morning as she and Adin had waited till morning. But then perhaps the sniper would be waiting for her. Not that it mattered any more or that she cared any longer.

'Goodbye, my husband. Goodbye, my son.'

She left the graveyard on the hillside and took the road to Maglaj. Her hands were frozen and she could no longer feel her feet. Sometime in the next hours she met a convoy coming the other way – men leading horses carrying wounded and injured to the hospital in Tesanj. Sometime, she was not sure when, she passed the turning and the track – hardly wide enough for goats – over the hill called Bandera. Sometime just after the light came up, she descended from the hills and entered Maglaj.

At ten, an hour before the food kitchen opened, she joined the line already forming outside; at eleven she shuffled in front of the vats containing the beans.

'I'm sorry, I've just come back from the hospital at Tesanj and I don't have a bowl.'

One of the women serving the beans shrugged, as if the problem was not hers.

'Did Adin find you?' another asked. 'Where's Jovan?'

'Adin and Jovan are dead.'

The second woman gave her her own bowl and poured the beans for her, broke the bread for her and led her to a corner where she might be warm. At least where she might be less cold. When she finished the soup Kara thanked the woman, returned the bowl to her, and went outside.

I saw you running across the bridge the other day – the Canadian MacFarlane remembered her, even though in some ways he barely recognized her now. Her face was ashen, her eyes were dead, and she crossed the bridge slowly, almost numbly, as if she was immune to the sniper who might be waiting for her in the hills; as if she was challenging him to shoot her.

The bridge was behind her. She walked in a trance through the rubble of what had once been the old town, and climbed the hill to the house. Stood still and looked at it. Began to cry.

The roof had been blown apart and the walls were sagging, the windows and doors gaping open and the snow falling in.

She went through the garden and pushed her way into what had once been the kitchen. At least she would be able to live here, she told herself, at least this part of the house would be secure.

The furniture was wrecked and ice hung from the ceiling, the holes gaping in it.

She was aware of the cold again now, not aware of her physical actions. Slowly she searched through the rubble, found the tin in which she and Adin kept any deutschmarks they had been able to save; found the photograph of Adin and Jovan which had stood on the dresser, found the remnants of one of the food packs Finn had left them.

She could go to the new town, find a space in a basement and sit there for the rest of the war, sit there for the rest of her life. Her thoughts were as numb and automatic as her movements. Or she could make her way to Travnik, seek out her mother's mother, her own grandmother, and stay with her. Except that Travnik was thirty kilometres from Zenica, and Zenica was nearly fifty kilometres from

Maglaj and two front lines away – one from the Muslim pocket of Maglaj–Tesanj into the surrounding Serb/Croat-controlled countryside, and the second back into the Muslim-held land to the south. But the front lines at the points where she would have to cross might not be active, might not be carefully guarded, might not be mined. Or they might be.

Not that it mattered. Not that anything mattered any more.

She packed the handful of items in a bag, left the house and walked down through the old town and back across the bridge. Either she had been doing things more slowly than she had imagined, or it was getting dark earlier.

The doctor was in the doorway of the medical centre. Sorry about Jovan and Adin, she said; where was Kara going, she asked. Travnik, Kara told her, I have a grandmother who lives there.

The town was a ghost, the doctor thought, Kara was a ghost. Already gone, already finished. Not on her way to join her grandmother in Travnik, because Travnik was eighty kilometres away through two sets of front lines. Kara was on her way to join her husband and her son.

Good luck, she told Kara. God go with you.

Kara thanked her, left Maglaj, and took the road back towards Tesanj. A quarter way along it, just after the light had faded and the night had closed in, she left the road and began the climb up through the snow and ice to the hill called Bandera and the first of the front lines.

# 5

The unmarked police Audi, two men in the front and one in the rear, was parked where it was always parked at this time of night: near one of the cab ranks on the edge of the Gare du Midi. Sometime tonight they'd score; sometime in the next hours the man in the rear would slip out, arrange to buy some dope – what sort didn't matter, but headquarters was heavy on crack at the moment – then they'd make the bust.

On the edge of the Gare du Nord, close to the predominantly immigrant quarter, the pimps and hookers went about their business.

On the other side of the city, in the *haute de la ville*, the Upper Town, the industrialists, the bankers, the diplomats and the Eurocrats attended their functions and passed the evening over cocktails and secret deals.

Brussels.

Eleven at night.

Rue Léopold, one of several named after the nineteenth-century Belgian king, appeared empty, and the night above was black. The road and pavements, with their occasional discreet but expensive boutiques, had just been swept, and the windows of the apartment blocks were curtained. In the past minutes snow had fallen – not heavily, but enough for the first white to have settled on the tarmac of the road and the grey of the pavements.

The lookout was sunk like a shadow in the recess of a

doorway fifty metres down the road in the direction from which the car would approach.

The car turned up the street, its Mercedes engine a low rumble – driver and one other in the front, and a third man in the back. The man in the doorway tensed slightly and swept the street. The Mercedes turned right, into the car park below the apartments, the three men glancing round as they descended the ramp. The sound now was different, almost hollow, and the lighting was subdued. The lift was in the far corner, on the left. The driver swung in a circle so that when he stopped by it the Mercedes was facing out, towards his exit point. The door of the lift opened and the next two men appeared. The front passenger and the man in the rear seat left the car and stepped into the lift.

'Secure,' the first man whispered in the motorola. The chip of the set had been replaced, the frequency pre-set to one not used in Belgium.

The second Mercedes slipped out of the night and up the street – same model, same colour, same registration number.

Everyone played their games, Abu Sharaf had long known. The Israelis, with their snatch teams or platter bombs or rocket launchers opposite flats or suites where they knew their enemies were plotting against them. The British and the French and the Americans. Plus those who were supposed to be on one's own side. Even the three men he would meet that night, though in the end they would agree. Because unless they had already decided to agree there would have been no meeting.

He left the car, stepped the two paces to the lift, and was whisked to the third floor.

The politician and the secret policeman were waiting, relaxed and comfortable in the soft luxury of the suite, both smiling and both smartly dressed Western-style. Only the holy man to come, Sharaf thought, but the holy men had kept the world waiting from the time the first man had thought of the first religion.

He shook their hands, accepted the sweet thick coffee an aide offered him, and sat down. The suite had been electronically swept for bugs, and when the meeting began the advisers and minders would leave the room.

'He'll be here soon.' The secret policeman was in his early fifties, the same age as the politician but some ten years older than Sharaf. His suit was smartly cut, and the fold of the lids gave his eyes a slightly hooded appearance.

'*Insh'allah.*' Sharaf sat down. 'God willing.'

The door opened and the holy man entered, the man Sharaf knew to be his closest adviser on his right, and his minder on his left. Two of the newcomers – the holy man and his adviser – were dressed traditionally, but the minder was wearing a suit.

The holy man was the same age as the politician and the secret policeman. He greeted them, nodded to the aide and minder to leave, then took his place in one of the chairs.

'The world is once again at an interesting time and place.' The holy man sat forward slightly and summed up the starting point of their previous discussions, the others allowing him the chairmanship, perhaps because it was his by right, perhaps because he represented the religious rather than the secular, and without the religious the secular which they represented could not develop, or not so easily.

Therefore they allowed him the moment: the politician who played the intrigues of the region with the experience of a juggler, the secret policeman who ruled it with a rod of fear, and the man whom the West would describe as the terrorist mastermind, the new Carlos, the new Abu Nidal.

Of course Sharaf had not always held such importance. Nor was his name generally known to the great public of the East and the West, though he was under no illusions that their intelligence services had him on their computers, and that when the time was right they would try to turn him, or take him out, depending on the secret dealings and hidden agendas of the Middle East. For that reason Sharaf was always careful, even when meeting those he considered his allies. Perhaps especially when meeting those who called themselves his friends.

'The fall of the Berlin Wall and the collapse of the Soviet empire . . . the agreement between Israel and the Palestinians . . . the Iran–Iraq conflict and the Gulf War.'

The holy man's eyes were small and sharp.

'The new situation in South Africa . . . the talk of peace in Northern Ireland . . . the decision by certain states to abandon a certain line of struggle.'

To cease support for what the West called terrorism.

So the world appeared to be at peace. Yet at the same time the world was closer to war than it had ever been.

He sat back and indicated with a wave of his right hand that perhaps it was the politician who would best lead the discussion from that point.

The politician talked for less than thirty seconds then passed the chairmanship to Sharaf. It was the way their meetings always progressed, wreathed in formalities and allusions, just as the smoke from their cigarettes was wreathed above the table.

'The armed struggle has seen a number of developments over the past decades.' Another couple of minutes and they would know whether they were in agreement, whether the forces they represented had concurred. 'In the sixties and seventies the struggle was global. In the eighties it was confined, in the main, to the Middle East.' Killings and kidnappings, and mainly against the West in the Lebanon.

Excluding the Irish, of course, but the Irish were a separate concern anyway. 'It was therefore agreed at our previous meetings that the time might now be approaching where we should prepare to make that struggle international again.'

He sat back.

The holy man stroked his beard, as if considering what had just been said. To his left the adviser waited, to his left the secret policeman said nothing. 'So what are you suggesting?' he asked at last.

'The setting up of a new organization, its members recruited and trained in line with the new criteria of the present and future.'

Which we all understand, but we also understand we have to endure the formalities.

'Why new members?' It was the secret policeman. 'Why new criteria?'

'Because other people are already planning using old members.' Bomb attacks in New York, the killing of Jews in Argentina and the bombing of Jewish targets in London. 'But they'll be using Muslims, so in future the West will be looking for Muslims. In future the West will be looking for people whom they think look and act like Muslims.'

'And where will you find Muslims who don't look and act in the manner the Great Satan thinks they should?' It was the holy man.

'And who have the same motivation of those who fought for us in the past?' It was the politician.

'Bosnia.' Sharaf looked at each of them in turn. 'Among the dispossessed who have been driven from their homes by ethnic cleansing. Among those who have lost everything and therefore have nothing more to lose and everything to fight for.'

'And this is in motion?'

'The plans are laid and the first steps taken.'

But that is all, because that was all I was required to do.

Because it was agreed that each of us should fulfil his task before the plan could be finalized. Again it was wrapped in formality and politeness.

'The religious leaders have agreed,' the holy man told the meeting. Not all the religious leaders, he had no need to say, simply those who would support the plan anyway.

'Our leaders as well.' The politician did not specify which leaders.

'My people are also prepared.' The secret policeman played with his Rolex as if it was a set of worry beads.

'Therefore we should proceed,' the holy man resumed the chair. '*Insh'allah*,' he added.

The politician leaned forward, lifted the handset of the telephone, punched the number, waited ten seconds, then spoke.

'The transfer of funds is approved. Do it now.'

The monies already held on deposit, now about to be transferred electronically to the accounts specified in Switzerland.

He terminated the call and handed the telephone to Sharaf.

He should have anticipated it, Sharaf thought; should have planned for it. But perhaps, on the other hand, it was a symbol of the moment, a sealing of their trust in each other, the first step on the road ahead. Even though such a call was a security risk. Never link one thing to another, he insisted to his aides and operatives; never do or leave anything which might connect one part of one section to another.

He took the telephone and keyed the number in Istanbul.

'You're on the morning flight,' he told Keefer.

When Wolfgang Keefer passed through immigration at Rome's Leonardo da Vinci Airport five hours later, the passport he carried was in the name of Mulhardt. When he left on the Croatia Airlines flight to Split six hours after that, the passport he used was in the name of Lacroix. Contained in the false lining of the Zenith briefcase which was his only luggage, and which he hand-carried on both flights, was the range of press, political and military accreditation which he might need in the weeks he would spend in the war zone of Bosnia-Herzegovina.

It was the way he had led the past fourteen of his thirty-nine years.

Wolfgang Keefer was the second son of a nurse and a lathe operator from the former East German city of Leipzig. Neither at school nor in the Free German Youth had Keefer distinguished himself. It was only during his national service in the Frontier Troops, manning what the East called the Anti-Fascist Barrier and the West referred to as the Berlin Wall, that he had appeared to find a vocation and an inner drive. He had been decorated three times and promoted twice, graduating with distinction at the GMK training school before being recruited into the MfS, the Ministry for State Security, also known as the Stasi. At the MfS headquarters on Normannenstrasse, and in other MfS establishments throughout both East Germany and the other satellite states of the then Communist bloc, he had fulfilled the promise he had demonstrated in the Frontier Troops, before making his final transfer to the unit dealing with the training and support of those whom the East called freedom fighters and the West termed terrorists.

By the time the Berlin Wall fell in November 1989, he had attained the rank of colonel. On the actual night the Wall was breached he had been in the Beqa'a valley in the Lebanon; the actual moment he had heard the news he had been squatting at a camp fire, Sharaf at his side. In the weeks that followed, while many of his contemporaries were looking east to the KGB in Moscow, to the people whom they had called the Brothers, Keefer had transferred his loyalty. Not for reasons of ideology or religion, especially not from political commitment, but for the simple reason that this was the life he had grown to love, that that life was now finished in East Germany, and that if a man found a job he liked and at which he excelled, then he should stick with it.

He had returned to his old haunts, of course – except that the city he loved was now called simply Berlin. Had made contact with old friends and colleagues, especially the people he and his new masters might need in the future. Occasionally the men and women from the front line, but more often the technicians, with their specialist skills and equipment.

The 737 dropped out of the cloud and he saw the lights of the airport at Split. The land was grey and washed with snow, and the night had already settled. The terminal was low and long, and the Air Croatia planes parked in front were outnumbered by the helicopters and transports painted with the stark black initials of the United Nations.

Bergmann was waiting for him in the terminal, two Nikons on his shoulder, a false press ID tag round his neck, and the word PRESS on the sides, bonnet and roof of the dilapidated Range Rover outside. Standard appearance for standard photographer in a war zone. To the right a TV crew loaded their silver metal boxes into an armour-plated jeep.

'Welcome to the war.' Bergmann shook his hand, tightened the hood of his anorak against the cold, and led Keefer to the Range Rover. 'Where you heading?' he asked one of the TV crew. Sarejevo or Travnik, the man replied, possibly Vitez. His face was pinched, either with cold or apprehension. 'Got some good stuff in Vitez couple of days ago,' Bergmann told him. 'We're back up tomorrow.'

Stasi training was always the best, Keefer thought. Best

covers in the world, best men. He slammed the door and Bergmann started the engine. As they left the airport two Sea King helicopters landed in the British army base five hundred yards away.

'How is it up-country?'

'Cold with the occasional hot spot.' Bergmann laughed.

They skirted Split, the hills to their left, the islands of Brac and Hvar on their right already lost in the night, and the snow and a UN convoy in front of them. Everywhere – Zagreb and Split – there seemed to be UN and UNPROFOR. War's business, Keefer had no need to remind himself.

'Any hassles?'

'Press are still getting some.'

'So it's better to go as UNPROFOR?'

Bergmann swerved to avoid a pothole. 'Probably. That way also explains the communication set-up we'll be carrying.'

'Any friends around, any Brothers?'

'Not that I've seen.'

The house was on the south side of Split, on the beach and looking west across the bay. The white long-wheelbase Toyota Landcruiser in the garage bore the markings and flags of the UN and UNPROFOR, and jerry cans of fuel, the satcom unit and the metal tins of self-heating food, plus other ration packs, were already loaded.

For an hour that evening, over stew and beer, and looking across the snow-flecked grey of the Adriatic, the two men ran through their itinerary and target areas. The map on the table was an HQ Britfor current situation map, dated the day before. The legend at the bottom showed the main supply routes, the international border of Bosnia-Herzegovina was marked in thick black, and areas of Serbian, Croatian and Muslim activity in red, black and green respectively.

'So where do we start?' Keefer asked, as he had asked the last time he had been here, when he and Bergmann had set up the safe house.

'Any special requirements?' Bergmann fetched two more beers from the fridge and placed them unopened on the table. 'You name it, it's there.'

'Somewhere where the Muj are involved.'

Because recruitment in areas where the Mujihadeen were fighting would please those in the Middle East who controlled the political and financial purse strings.

'In that case, Travnik.' Bergmann indicated the town on the map. 'There are some Muj in Zenica, but most of them are near Travnik.'

'And . . .'

'The fighting in Travnik's been heavy, Muslim against Croat. Now the town's quiet, but it's where we'll find the sort of people we're looking for.'

'Why?'

'The front's only a few kilometres away, men as well as women fighting there. Lot of mercenaries, most of them no good. Lot of Muj, some of them good, some not, but none of them liked by the locals. Refugee camps, hardly any food, so a thriving black market. Travnik's the end of the line.'

'What's dealing on the black market?'

'Fuel, cigarettes, cooking oil. Mainly food.'

'How's it coming in?' Keefer opened the beers.

'From the Serbian side. Place called Popovekuce, on the outskirts of Turbe, fifteen kilometres from Travnik. Each night the black marketeers make the walk, go through the front line, open up the mines, do the business, and come back over. Last man out puts the mines back in place.'

Some things never change, Keefer thought. 'What about Muslim pockets in the other areas?'

'Also in a bad way, in some cases worse. The problem with them is getting in.'

'So what time do we leave?'

It was already ten, closing on eleven.

'Two o'clock. Most of the aid convoys are on the road around midnight, trying to get to the border crossing first so they stand a chance of getting through early.'

When Keefer and Bergmann left it was ten minutes to two. Bergmann was dressed in French combat fatigues, with UNPROFOR accreditation, and Keefer's documentation identified him as a colonel in the French Parachute Regiment temporarily assigned to the European Commission's monitoring team. The snow had stopped but the temperature had dipped to seventeen degrees below. In Travnik it would be colder, Bergmann warned him.

The last articulated lorries of the aid convoys were already picking their way up the valley in the break in the hills which lined the coast, their engines thundering and their headlights like ghostly fingers. When they reached the checkpoint at the border between Croatia and Bosnia-Herzegovina the first lorries were tailed back, the Croat guards inspecting their documentation and the drivers resigning themselves to a long wait. Bergmann pulled the Toyota left, round the convoy, and drove to the checkpoint. The fields on either side were hard with snow and the arc lights swept down on the machine guns and barbed wire. A guard motioned them to pull in and a second stepped forward to inspect their identification. Bergmann slowed, held out his ID and slipped the miniature brandy to the other man. The corporal slid it into the sleeve of his greatcoat and shouted at a private to open the barrier.

Three hours later, on the supply route known as Triangle, they poured themselves cans of self-heating soup and waited patiently while engineers tried to move an Aid Scania which had overturned when the side of the road had collapsed. By the time they reached the valley head running into the town of Gornji Vakuf it was gone midday.

Two hours later they came to the junction on the Travnik–Vitez road. Right was Vitez, the Muslim enclave in the old town surrounded by Croats who were themselves being fired upon by Muslim forces in the front line in the hills, the fighting bitter and bloody. Left was Travnik, where the fighting had been equally ferocious. They turned left, still in Croat-held territory, and came to the cluster of houses which constituted the front line at this point. Some of the buildings were destroyed, others were merely peppered with holes, though only one side, the side facing the enemy. They slowed slightly, Bergmann blasting the horn to warn both sides they were United Nations, then accelerated through.

The light was going now and the landscape was changing slightly. They were in a shallow valley, hills either side and a small river running by the right of the road, the road itself curving as the valley narrowed.

In front of them, caught momentarily in the headlights, Keefer saw a woman. She was old, young – there was no way he could tell. Tucked into a bundle, bag tied like a pack on her back and walking with a set, determined motion. Eyes fixed ahead, body rigid, and arms moving slightly in an effort to keep herself going. Scarf over her head, and clothes sodden and lined with ice. In front of her a family appeared as if from nowhere – man, woman and two children, hauling a handcart with their belongings tied to it, another family in front.

The families were going to make it but the woman probably wasn't. The woman was spent, had to fight to put one foot in front of the other. Keefer glanced behind but she was already lost in the gloom.

'UN,' he told the soldiers at the road block. The men were old before their years, wrapped ineffectively against the cold, and aggressive. 'Seeing the colonel.'

They opened the barrier and let them through.

Bergmann drove on, round the bend, the fortifications of the old town on the hillside above and to his right, though he could not see it, and into the town. The streets were dark and empty, no lights because there had been no electricity for months. From the north came the sounds of battle.

* * *

She was going to die. From the cold or the fear or both.

Keep going because Adin and Jovan are waiting for you, the voice told her; keep going because unless you make it they won't be able to eat, won't be able to share the food you're carrying for them. Adin and Jovan are dead and the last of the food Finn had given her had been stolen in the camp in Zenica, the second voice came back at her. The snow was deep around her and the cold was in her bones and her limbs and her soul. Please God, don't let me die, she prayed; please God, take me gently and softly so I can be with my husband and my son.

She tried to follow the footprints along what was a path, and pulled the pack tighter on her back, tried to take the strain from her shoulders. She had been walking for six hours now, had been walking since before dawn. Knew she had another two hours of light left, three at most, before the next night closed in around her. Please God may I make Travnik before dark, because if I don't I won't make it at all.

Perhaps she should have stayed in Maglaj and tried to rebuild the house, or moved into the newer part of the town and found a space in a basement. Perhaps she should have stayed in the refugee camp in Zenica, because Zenica was not only a Muslim stronghold, it was away from the front line therefore away from any danger.

But Adin and Jovan were no longer in Maglaj, not even their bodies. And she had no family in Zenica, nothing to stay for or to hold on to. And Zenica was where someone had stolen the last of the food.

Therefore she was right in trying to get to Travnik, because her grandmother lived there. She remembered the small flat in the block on the side of the valley, the smell of cooking from the kitchen and the photographs of the family on the wall of the sitting room.

It had taken her three days to reach Zenica. On the first night – the night after she had left Maglaj – she had slept as best she could in a forester's hut somewhere in the hills, the cold biting into her and her clothes pulled tight around her. The second night, when she had been in Serb-held territory, she had risked everything and sheltered with a group of other refugees in a barn beside a farm, though she had no idea where they had come from or where they were going.

She had moved slowly and carefully, especially when she was crossing the front lines, picking her way between the gun positions. Twice she had stumbled into a minefield; once she had been following a line of footprints, then heard the explosion and knew that whoever she had been following had died in her place. On another occasion, when she had been crossing the thin neck of land held by the Serbs, she had thought a patrol had seen her. Even when she had been crossing back into Muslim-held land she had gone carefully, aware the forward patrols and lookout points might think she was a spy or an infiltrator, and shoot her or pull the trip wires to the mines.

In Zenica she had found a space in a tent in one of the refugee camps and almost decided to stay. Then she had turned away for just one moment and the food had gone from her pack. So at five that morning she had left, following one of the side roads and skirting north to avoid the Croat belt round the Muslim enclave in Stari Vitez.

And then, somewhere in the woods above Vitez, she had lost her way. Had left the road to avoid the Croats, picked up a path heading west, then the path had petered out and the panic had seized her. Had fallen in the snow and not got up, had lain in the warmth and the peace and known she was going home to meet Adin and Jovan. Then, without knowing how or why, she had been walking again, had picked up a path again. But now she was wet as well as cold, the seams of her boots were splitting and the scarf she had pulled over her head had slipped, so the snow was running down her neck.

The light was going and the winter dusk was about to take its place. She panicked again, knew that she wouldn't survive the night in the open. The path left the woods and she found herself on a ridge. There was a road three hundred metres to her left, along the foot of the ridge, and a cluster of houses at one point on it, all damaged and the sound of firing coming from them. The snow was falling again. Don't fall too hard or I'll lose the road, she prayed, and the road would get her to Travnik. As long as she didn't drop on to it too quickly, as long as she had the confidence and the will and the strength to stay on the high ground till she was clear of the Croats.

The light was going fast now. She walked another twenty minutes, till the sound of the small-arms fire was behind her. The snow cleared but the dark closed in and she could no longer see the road. She dropped across the fields towards where the road should be and came to a river.

The road was on the other side of the river, she told herself; she had seen the river from the ridge but had failed to register it in the mental map she had tried to draw.

She turned right and moved slowly along the bank. Five hundred metres later she found a footbridge, crossed it, and stepped on to the metalled surface of the Vitez–Travnik road.

She was walking quicker now, still bent and still shuffling. Almost there, she told herself, almost home. In front of her she saw the lights of a road block. Please God may she have been right, please God may the soldiers be Muslims not Croats. Please God may they let her through. In front of her a family appeared as if from nowhere – man and woman and two children, hauling a handcart with their belongings tied to it, another family in front of them.

A UN jeep passed her, two men in it.

She came to the steel drums and razor wire of the checkpoint. The soldiers were red-eyed and unshaven, their fingers cold on their Kalashnikovs. She shuffled after the family in front and showed them her ID.

'Name?' one of them asked.

'Kadira Isak.' A Muslim name.

Please God may the front lines not have changed again. Please God may she not be talking to the Croats.

The soldier shone a torch at her ID, checked the details, and nodded that she should pass.

Travnik was in darkness. She stopped and tried to remember the layout of the town and where her grandmother's flat was situated.

The road on which she entered continued on up the valley, skirting the main area of the town. To the right, and creeping up the hillsides, was an older section of houses. A hundred metres to the left another road also ran up the valley, houses and apartment blocks between the two. It was this road, more a street she now remembered, that was the main centre of the town, and along which most of the shops and cafés were situated. A hundred metres the other side was the river, which she had crossed for the second time after the checkpoint, a smaller road alongside it with more apartment blocks, and some buildings and apartment blocks rising up the hill to the other side. At the other end of the town were the hospital and factories, more apartment blocks beyond.

Further up the valley she heard the low rumble of the artillery.

She turned left and hurried through the town centre; the doors and windows were barred and the streets were dark and unlit. The wood on the bridge was icy and she almost slipped. In front of her the white of the tower blocks loomed like phantoms. Her body and mind were frozen now, and she tried to convince herself she no longer felt the cold. For one moment it was as if Adin and Jovan were with her, as if the country was not at war, as if they were coming as a family to visit the grandmother their son had never seen.

Third block – she remembered clearly – the one that was slightly lower than the others. Fifth floor, third apartment on the left, the windows facing on to the town. She pushed open the doors – wood blockboard instead of glass – went inside, and felt for the stairs in the dark. Shuffled forward and stumbled against the first stair, stepped on it, feeling her way with her hand against the wall. First floor, four to go. She felt her way round the corner and continued up the next flight. Almost there, Adin; almost home, little Jovan. In front of her she saw the flicker of a candle and heard the shuffle of someone else walking up. Something about the smell, she tried to shake off the unease; something about how the place felt. The person with the candle was still climbing. She came to the fifth floor, turned off the stairs and felt her way along the corridor till her fingers touched the third door. Knocked on the door and waited, knocked again.

The door opened a fraction.

'It's me . . .' she began to say. 'It's Kara . . .'

Something about the smell, the fear gripped her. Something about the feel. The door began to close. She put her hand up and pushed it open again, felt the force as someone resisted her.

'Who is it?' She heard the man's voice.

'It's me. Kadira Isak. My grandmother lives here.'

'Your grandmother was a Croat?' It was a woman, standing in the candlelight behind the man.

Yes, Kara tried to say, but why is that relevant? My husband and son and I have lost our home and have walked through the lines from Maglaj.

'The Croats moved out of Travnik six months ago, we've taken over now.'

The door slammed shut and she was in darkness. Kara lay on the floor, rolled into a ball, and pulled the cold wet of the coat around her.

The light from the window at the end of the corridor was cold and bleak, and the wind blew through where the glass had been broken and the boarding which had been nailed in its place had slipped. Kara did not know when the shaking had gripped her body, only knew that she had not slept all night. Her face was creased and she was crying. Feet echoed along the concrete of the corridor and stepped over her. She saw no faces, merely the plates the hands were gripping. She pulled herself up and walked with them, down the stairs and out of the building, not knowing where they were going or why.

The day was biting cold and she was weak with the shivering. There were people now, wrapped in black, scarves and hoods over their heads against the cold, the images stark against the snow.

They crossed the wooden bridge over the river and cut

through the apartment blocks to a square between the river and the main street. They're going for food, she realized she had been thinking, I'm going to eat.

The square had trees and grass in the middle, the trees now bare and the grass thin and worn; on the opposite side was a series of modern flats, five storeys high, a thin line of thin people trickling into the one nearest the square. On the side of the square closest to her was a two-storey building, painted off-white, the snow on its roof, its windows boarded and its front pockmarked and shell-damaged. The entrance was up a set of five steps at the other end, the name of the building – Ceotar – above. The line of people, all wrapped against the cold so she couldn't see their faces, was five deep and stretched out of the door, down the steps, along the front of the building and round the corner.

The sky was threatening more snow and icicles hung from the roof. She dragged herself round the corner and saw how far the queue for food stretched.

Perhaps she should give up now, perhaps she should go into the woods above Travnik, lie down in the snow and let herself begin the journey home. Go back to Adin and Jovan.

She was standing still, neither joining the queue nor leaving it. Someone jostled her but she hardly noticed.

Perhaps she should go now, while the day was still young. Lie in the snow so she would not have to face another night.

You're okay, Kara – it was as if someone was talking to her, guiding her, telling her what to do. Adin and Jovan still love you, the voice told her, Adin and Jovan want you to live. Adin and Jovan don't want you to die pointlessly and without reason, as they died. You're doing fine, Kara, you're doing well. You crossed the lines and made it to Travnik. But you're hungry and need to eat. So stand in the line with the others because this is where someone will give you food.

A man jostled her. She ignored him, joined the line, and shuffled forward.

Think it through, Kara – it was as if someone was talking to her again. The other people are carrying mugs and bowls. So to get food you also need a mug and a bowl.

Of course I need a mug and a bowl, just as I needed a saucepan to collect the food in the Red Cross station in Maglaj. God, how cold she was; God, how her feet hurt her. God, how all she wanted to do was die.

Don't think like that, Kara, the voice told her. Think the way you'd begun to think. Think positive. You'd begun to identify the problem, now just work out what you need and what you have to do to get it.

But what do I need? What do I have to do?

The queue was moving slowly. She eased with it, almost lost in it.

I need to eat, but I don't have a mug or a bowl. So I need a mug and a bowl.

More basic than that, Kara. Get right back to fundamentals. You're lost and alone, and you don't have food or anywhere to sleep, and in order to be alive tomorrow you need both.

Who are you and why are you helping me? she asked. Why are you telling me what to do? Of course it wasn't someone else, of course it was herself working out what to do. Except that the voice wasn't a woman's, it was a man's. Adin or Jovan. But it wasn't, because she would have recognized their voices instantly, would have cried and given up if they had talked to her.

It doesn't matter who I am or why I'm talking to you, Kara . . . the voice was calm and controlled, almost low-key. What matters is that you don't waste time, because in the state you're in you don't have any time to waste. So move it, Kara. Just work it out and do it.

Okay, to get food I need a bowl and a mug, but I also need a ration card like I had at Maglaj. And at the place where they give me the ration card they'll also give me a mug and bowl. And at that place they'll also tell me where I can sleep, where there'll be a camp like the one at Zenica.

Good girl, Kara. That's what you have to do. Now just do it.

She knew who the voice was. 'Where do I get a mug and bowl?' she asked a woman at her side. 'Where do I get a ration card?'

'There's an office in the block of flats on the other side of the square and another over the fire station.' The woman's face and eyes were blank, as if there was no life in her.

'Thank you,' she told the woman.

Thanks, Finn, she meant.

Even though she probably wasn't really hearing his voice. Even though it was probably her own brain telling her what she needed and what to do.

She left the queue and crossed the square. Forget that you're hungry, she ordered herself, forget that you're cold. Because soon you'll have food, soon you'll have somewhere to sleep. She couldn't rely on anyone else to help her, Finn had told her as they sat crouched against the wall in the corridor of the hospital in Tesanj. She and her own had to help themselves.

The queue at the foot of the block of flats wasn't moving. She left the square and asked someone for the fire station. It was as if she was walking and acting automatically, either because she was doing what Finn had told her, or because the cold and pain had drained everything else from her. There were people in the streets – cold and pinched and huddled. There were soldiers and an occasional lorry rumbling by, but she saw none of them. It was as if she saw only what she needed to see; as if what she saw was not even in black and white, but in the drab grey of a winter at war.

The fire station was white and two-storey, four large doors on the ground floor, offices above and a smaller door at the end. People waiting at it, but not so many. She shuffled forward for half an hour till she was inside.

'Name?'

'Kara Isak.'

The woman behind the desk nodded, wrote her details on a ration card, and gave the card to her. 'You get two meals a day. You get the card stamped each time.'

The office around them was chaos, people moving and children crying.

'Can I have a plate and mug?'

The woman fetched them from the room at the back.

'Where can I sleep?'

'The Gymnasium,' the woman told her. 'On the other side of the river.'

A large and imposing teaching college near the Music Conservatory – Kara remembered it from when she had visited her grandmother, even though she had never been inside. Three-storey round a central courtyard, the façade a light yellow, and a magnificent dome topping the centre of the front wall.

Someone was pushing from behind, anxious to take her place.

'Anything else?' Kara asked.

'If you find somewhere else we can give you a small stove, so you can collect wood from the hills.'

'Thank you.'

She left the fire station and went back outside.

It was already afternoon, getting colder and threatening dark, and a wind cutting through the streets. Return to the queue and she would get food, but by the time she did it might be dark and she might not find a good place in the Gymnasium. But go to the Gymnasium first and she might not get back to the food kitchen in time to eat that day. She would get somewhere to sleep first, she decided: if she didn't eat today she might be even hungrier in the morning, but if she didn't find somewhere to sleep she'd be dead.

She cut through the side streets to the river, then turned right and walked along the road which ran beside it. The river was ten metres wide and running hard, the ice solid on its edges. She crossed by the wooden bridge close to the Music Conservatory then walked along the path on the other bank. A hundred metres on she came to the Gymnasium. Even now, even though part of its façade was marked with bullet holes, it was as she remembered, large and imposing, strong and immoveable. Inside it will be warm, she told herself, inside it will be dry and friendly and welcoming. She walked up the steps beneath the dome, and went inside.

The reception area was on the left, an outer office with a window and door, and a smaller office somewhere inside. No electricity, but there wouldn't be; just the light from an oil lamp flickering in the gloom. There were people around – she was tired now, and couldn't see how many. Someone sliding back the window, inspecting her ration card and telling her to find a space somewhere, someone else giving her a blanket from a box marked FEED THE CHILDREN, and another person directing her along the corridor into the bowels of the building.

She went right, then left, followed the corridor. It was tall and dark and cold, people shuffling by her like ghosts, shoulders bent, and children crying somewhere, the noise echoing in the hollowness. There was no lighting, doors on the right shut and just the glimmer of candles from two doorways without doors on the left. She glanced in the first and realized it was the men's washroom, jerked back and went to the second. The walls were lime green and dirty, the toilets were open style in the floor, and the only water came from a tap in the wall. In the centre of the floor was a dustbin filled with water.

Outside the air had been cold, but at least it had smelt clean. Here the odour was of damp and human waste, the effect almost overpowering.

Please God no, she prayed. Please God, may this not be where you have decided I should sleep.

She came to the end of the corridor, lost and frightened. There was a blast of wind from the right, so she assumed that was an outer door, and turned left. The doors were closed, the corridors almost black now, adults as well as children crying and sobbing. She knocked on one door and pushed it open, peered inside. The room was large and packed with beds and mattresses and people.

'I'm looking for somewhere to sleep,' she began to say.

'Sorry,' someone told her. Not friendly, not unfriendly, just telling her. 'No room.'

Thank God, she thought, she couldn't sleep here, couldn't sleep in a room like that. She shut the door and went down the corridor, opening doors and asking for a space. The rooms were the same, all large and high-ceilinged, crammed with beds and mattresses and people, stoves in some belching smoke and fumes.

She climbed the first stairs, then the second. Perhaps went down again, perhaps not. She was too exhausted to notice now, too scared.

Sorry, a man was telling her as they had told her everywhere, no room. Only me, she was saying, not even Adin and Jovan. Little Jovan was killed when they shelled the hospital and Adin was shot by a sniper.

Room for one, a woman told her, showed her the place on a mattress on the floor, tucked between the beds in the far corner of the room. The bed on the right of the mattress was filled with children, an old man coughing up blood in the bed to the left. Some heat, though not much, coming from the stove in the corner, and the room smelt of damp and cold and poverty and desperation.

Thank you, Kara told the woman. She was still shivering, still shaking. She took off her wet coat and boots, sat on the mattress, the beds towering above her, and wrapped the charity blanket around her.

* * *

Yesterday afternoon Finn had attended the funeral service for Kev; last night he had stayed for the wake in the pub in the middle of the Forest which had been Kev's local, the men wearing black suits and the women in dark dresses, the doors closed to strangers and the logs roaring in the fire. The day before that he had attended a similar service for Geordie John. And the day before that he had stood to attention in front of the clock in the barracks at Hereford as their names were added to the list of members of the regiment who had died on operations.

He woke at seven, went for a run, then had breakfast in the small hotel on the edge of the Forest, and drove the ninety minutes to the CMH, the Cambridge Military Hospital, in Aldershot.

Max was in the intensive care unit. His left leg had been pinned and was in plaster, and his right was covered with a fretwork of external plates. His left arm was completely plastered, his right from the elbow down. Three electrodes were stuck to his chest, the lines connected to a heart monitor; there were suture lines across his abdomen and his head, which had been shaved. A blood pressure cuff was wrapped round his upper right arm, and a central line ran into his neck, three lumens from it for drugs, drip and blood. His face was white, his eyes were sunk and surrounded by black, and he was slipping between consciousness and unconsciousness.

'Back soon,' he tried to tell Finn.

Back with the regiment, back with the boys.

'Sure, Max. Keep your place open for you.'

He left intensive care and found his way to Janner's ward. The consultant was in the middle of his rounds, a staff nurse informed him. Perhaps he might care to wait in the corridor.

The bench was along the wall on the right; he sat and watched the activity at the nurses' station by the entrance to the ward.

The last time he'd been in a hospital corridor had been in Tesanj. The last time had been when he and the woman called Kara had sat on the floor in the half-light, had talked about Adin and Jovan, and Kara had thanked him and said they were square, that she'd saved his and he'd saved hers.

The nurse called him and he went through.

Janner was sitting up, the pillows stacked behind him. A drip ran into his right arm, and blood seeped through the dressings on his chest.

'No grapes,' Finn joked.

'Thanks for coming anyway.'

They talked about when and how the Bosnian teams had been pulled out, other teams taking their places. About what Finn was doing on leave, about the funerals and wakes he had attended and what duties the squadron had been assigned now all its members were back in England. About how Max would pull through but never make it back to the regiment. How the doctor had told Janner he would be out of hospital in three weeks; biff chit – medical slang for sick leave – after that; on light duties in three months; and operational again in six.

A nurse brought them a cup of tea each.

They talked about how they'd applied to join the regiment at the same time, how they'd done selection together, about the incidents which no one else would consider funny but they found hilarious.

'I thought she wasn't coming back, you know.'

'Who?' Finn asked.

'The woman in Maglaj. I thought she was going to leave me for dead, she'd already done too much getting Max out.'

'Just be thankful she did.' Time to be going, Finn told himself; time to bug out.

'What happened after you got me heli'd out?' Janner shifted slightly and winced with the pain.

'How'd you mean?'

'I don't remember much, especially after you gave me the morphine. But I do remember her asking you to help the kid.'

And this is the first time you and I have met since, and nobody else can tell me what happened because nobody else knows. All they can tell me is that you were supposed to come out that night and didn't.

'The kid's okay, we got him to hospital. No problems. Then we left Kara the rest of the food packs and pulled out.'

'I'm going back, you know.' Janner looked at him. 'When I'm fit and the Bosnian thing is over. See her, thank her. See if there's anything she and her family need.'

'Sure, Janner.'

Except you won't, and we both know it. Because everybody says they'll go back, sometime and somewhere, and they never do. We did the job. She helped us and we helped her. Finito, end of story.

Janner was looking at him. 'Fuck off, Finn.'

'Okay. We'll go back together, make a family holiday out of it. You and Jude and young Janner and Mary, me and Caz and the boys. Summer break in Maglaj.'

'Like I said, Finn. Fuck off.'

They sat in silence.

'What's up, Finn?'

'Nothing.'

By the time he reached the house on the outskirts of Hereford it was five in the afternoon and already dark. His wife was making tea and the boys were playing. It hadn't been long ago that they'd been the same age as Jovan – the thought crept up on him, caught him unawares. Thank Christ nothing had happened to them, but you made your own luck.

'Jude's coming round this evening,' his wife told him.

Caz worked three days a week as a remedial teacher and Jude was an agency nurse, the part-time work suiting both of them because of the ages of the children.

'That's good.' Because Jude would need someone to talk to, work out her anxieties about Janner. Wives had it tough, wives supported each other.

'It's you she wants to see, not me.'

What is this, he thought, a bloody conspiracy? Janner this morning, now Janner's wife.

'What is it, Finn?'

'You're the second person to ask me that today.'

Jude came at seven; Caz took the children upstairs to play together, then came down again. Finn opened a bottle of wine and they sat round the fire in the lounge.

'Saw Janner this morning,' he told them both. 'He's doing well, be up and running soon.'

'What happened, Finn?' Jude's face was white and her eyes stared slightly.

'How'd you mean, what happened?' Because Janner would have told you all he could, and you know we don't discuss the details of that sort of thing.

'Janner's talking about going back.'

Jude had been biting her nails, Finn could see; Jude had been smoking. He topped up their glasses.

'So what happened?' It was his own wife this time. Okay to pour a drink, okay to relax the atmosphere. But now stop frigging around, now tell Jude what she needs to know.

He thought it through.

'We went in to prepare the ground for an air strike.' Which everybody knew, because the bloody Foreign Secretary had given the game away in the House of Commons. 'No air strike, but Janner's team were targeted. Kev and Geordie John were killed immediately. Janner and Max were wounded, Max very badly. Janner carried him out.' Even though he himself was shot to pieces, he didn't need to say. 'They got to a rendezvous point, which is where we picked them up.'

'How did they get to the RV?' Jude gulped down the wine. 'Janner said someone helped him. Max and him, but him especially. That's why he wants to go back.'

Caz was staring at him.

'When I said Janner carried Max out, it's not quite correct. Janner was a hero that night, Jude; even though he himself was in a bad way he brought Max out.' He was getting too far into it, but was already too far down the line to pull back. So what is it, Finn, what the hell is your problem? 'Janner started carrying Max, then dragging him, didn't leave him even though it was probably going to cost him his own life.' He stalled, tried to pull back. 'Janner doesn't know it, and don't say anything, but he's got the MC for what he did that night.'

'So how did he get Max to the RV?' Jude refused to be diverted.

'He didn't. Somebody else did.'

'But there was no one else.'

Finn laughed. 'There was a woman.'

Caz opened another bottle and poured them each another glass, stared at him till he continued.

'The RV was near a house. The woman lived there. For some reason she heard Janner and Max, and came out for them.' Actually, he said, she thought it was her husband. 'She tried to get both of them back to the house, but couldn't, so Janner told her to take Max and come back for him. He didn't think she would.'

'Why not?' It was almost inaudible.

'They were under fire.' He hesitated again. 'They were also in a minefield.' He downed the glass, offered the bottle to them, and poured himself another.

'When we got there they were inside the house. We got Janner and Max heli'd out, covered the LZ because it was a hot extraction, as you know, and walked out ourselves the next night.' He looked at Jude. 'That's why Janner wants to go back, to thank the woman who saved his life.'

You're lying – he sensed it in his wife's stare. Not lying. You just haven't told us the whole truth.

'Thanks, Finn.' There was relief on Jude's face. 'Anything I can do for the woman?' she suddenly asked. 'Anything I can do for her family?'

'She's okay. The family are okay.' And there you should leave it.

'What was her name?'

Finn shook his head. 'No names, Jude. You know the game.'

It was ten in the evening; Jude had gone, and the boys were asleep.

'So what happened after you got Janner and Max out, Finn?' Caz sat opposite him, the door closed.

Because you've told us what happened up to that point, but not what happened after. You know. Jim and Ken and Steve know because they were with you. Janner and Max know, or suspect. But nobody's saying. Not to us, not to the debriefers, not even to the regiment. Because after you got Janner and Max out you broke the rules, didn't you? After that you did something you weren't supposed to do. Okay, so in the regiment you're paid to break the rules, that's what it's all about. But this time you went too far. This time you did something that only those who were there are allowed to know.

He shrugged.

'What's up, Finn?' Caz stared at him again. 'What's eating you that you won't admit?'

He leaned back in the chair and looked at the ceiling, looked back at her. 'The woman didn't just get Janner and Max out, she saved their lives.'

So . . .

'She was by herself. Husband on the front line; local stuff, two days on, one day off. She also had a son. About four.' He waved his hand dismissively. 'Younger than the boys.'

She waited.

'Jovan,' he said, as if Caz had asked.

She still waited.

'The boy was ill, because she was by herself she couldn't do anything. I told her that because she'd saved Janner and Max, we owed. When we took them to the chopper she asked us to take her son.'

Which is what I would have done, Caz thought. What I would have fought tooth and nail for. Done anything to save my child, especially after what I'd done for you and yours.

'I told her I couldn't. I said I'd be back. Which is why we didn't get out that night.'

But to cover it they'd told Hereford it was a hot extraction, Caz began to understand. Which it probably was. And to cover themselves they'd told everyone they had to stay to protect the LZ, to make sure Janner and Max got out okay.

'What happened?' she asked.

'We took the kid to the local medical centre, but they couldn't do anything, didn't have any operating facilities. Said he had appendicitis, and that they'd try to get him to a hospital with better facilities the following night.'

'So why didn't you pull out then?'

'They said it was about to burst, if it hadn't already, and that he wouldn't last till the next night.'

'So you and the others took him to the other hospital. That's what you can't tell anyone.'

'Yes.'

Caz stared at the glass in her hand and thought of the other woman, the other mother.

'Were you in time?'

'Just about. It was touch and go, only just made it.'

'And she's okay now? Her son's okay now?'

There was a silence.

'What's up, Finn, what's wrong?'

'You know the TV report of a hospital being shelled and kids being killed?'

'Yes.'

'That was the hospital we took her son to.'

The night was long and dark. Sometimes it was as if he was back in Maglaj. In the house in the old town, crossing the bridge, seeing the shake of the doctor's head as she told them she couldn't operate on little Jovan. Running through the night with Jovan on his back. Sitting with Kara in the corridor and imagining what it must have been like when the shells came in.

No longer his responsibility, though. He and the boys had done their bit, repaid their debt. Broken all the rules on the way. Invented some cock and bull story to explain why they hadn't exfiltrated that night. So the kid wasn't his problem any more. Neither the kid nor the woman.

Bollocks, Finn. The woman risked everything for you and your people. All you and the boys did was a quick night run through the woods, no danger to yourselves.

Plenty of danger to them. Okay, not physical. But if anyone had found out they'd have been RTU'd – returned to unit – faster than their feet would have touched the ground.

Crap, Finn, and you know it. The woman saved Janner and Max, therefore the regiment would have understood, therefore you could have choppered Kara and the boy out, because you should have done. And if you had then the kid wouldn't have been in Tesanj hospital when the bastards shelled it.

But you don't know he's dead. And if you hadn't taken him there he'd probably be dead anyway, so what the hell.

Come off it, Finn, stop fucking around. We owe, you told Kara, I owe. Anything you want you get. Any time, any place.

Okay, but what can you do about it? You're in Hereford, first leave for as long as you can remember, you and Caz talking about using the ten days before you're back on duty, even having a week's holiday in the sun. And Kara and Adin and Jovan are in Bosnia. Not just in Bosnia. Stuck in a Muslim pocket surrounded by the Serbs and Croats, no way out and no way in.

Plenty of ways in and out if he really wanted. Okay, it would mean breaking the rules again, so he couldn't tell anyone, couldn't make it official. And if they found out then he'd be in it right up to his neck. Easy, though, if he really wanted to do it. Quick call in the morning to the company in London, set up and run by ex-regiment people now supplying a lot of training overseas, as well as support and technical staff to people like the UN and UNPROFOR in Bosnia. Second phone call to the UNHCR office in Zenica. Cover job and false ID to get him there, plus transport in-country. Commercial flight out to Zagreb and down the coast to Split, or one of the RAF flights direct from Brize Norton. No questions asked, either in London or Zenica, and if there were, then Mike and Nick would sort everything out.

Up to you, Finn. Depending on whether or not you meant what you said.

No choice – he knew what Janner would have said. Either that or ask the bastards to hold up the war for six months till I can go myself.

# 6

In one of the beds above the mattress the old man rolled and coughed, and the old woman who shared the bed with him told him it would be all right in the morning. In the other the children sobbed with hunger and fear.

Kara clutched the blanket and tried to tell herself that she wasn't cold.

In the darkness she heard someone getting out of bed, feeling their way then lighting a candle. It was six o'clock. Some of the people were already going for food, already going for their places in the queue. Her shoes and coat were still wet. She folded the blanket, placed it at the top of the mattress, left the mattress in place to preserve her section of the floor, picked up her mug, plate and ration card, and went outside.

Even though the morning was still pitch black the queue at the food kitchen was four deep and stretched back to the corner. Overnight it had snowed again; the road was packed hard with ice and a wind cut from the east. She joined the queue, tried to secure a position on the inside, close to the wall so that she might be sheltered a little from the wind, and edged forward.

Half an hour later – sooner than she had feared – she came to the five steps at the door of the building. Ten minutes later she was inside. The thin bean soup was in cauldrons on the left, hard brown bread beside them. She shuffled forward, showed her ration card, had it stamped, received her portion, and followed the line through the internal door at the other end.

The room was filled with tables and the tables were packed with people bent over their bowls and drinking the soup. The room was cold, but not as cold as outside. She found a seat, sat down and began to eat. Made herself eat slowly, partly because she told herself it was better to eat that way, not having eaten for three days, and partly so that she could stay in the comparative warmth. To her left a woman fed a baby, to her right a young boy helped an old man spoon the thin soup into his toothless mouth. More people were standing at the door and looking for spaces at the tables. She made the food last as long as she could, then returned to the Gymnasium.

Now it was light she could see the room properly. The walls were an indistinguishable merge of yellow and grey, the bulbs were missing from the electric lights on the walls, which was of no consequence because there was no electricity anyway. Damp seeped from the corner nearest the outside wall and smoke belched from the makeshift flue which ran from the stove through a hole in the window. The floor was jammed with beds and mattresses, and the walls were hung with clothes, some neat and clean, but most wet and worn, plus pictures and photographs of places which had once been home.

After the cold outside the room smelt of bodies.

The old man on the bed above her mattress had rolled on his side, pulling the bedclothes off, so that he lay exposed and shivering. She helped him back in place and tucked the blanket round him, then she put the plate and mug in the bag at the head of her mattress and went outside again.

The metal of the bridge over the river was laced with ice, and the road which ran along the Gymnasium side was rutted with snow. To the left was a single-storey building, its concrete splattered with bullet marks and its windows shattered. Beyond it was a square, lined with wooden shacks which served as shops, the hill rising behind them. Three trees stood on the river bank, next to the bridge; beyond them was a footbridge over the river, a small park on the other side.

The road and the square were crammed with people selling things, some at stalls, old and torn polythene pulled over them, others with their wares spread on the ground in front of them. Those buying moved slowly, looking and haggling over prices, many of them carrying household items they were trying to barter. The last time she had been here it had been summer and the market and the people had been full of colour; today Kara saw it only in shades of grey.

The wet was already seeping through her coat and shoes. She turned left and drifted into the market area. Ahead of her was a woman carrying a television set. She followed the woman, watched mesmerized as she tried to exchange the set at each of the stalls and trailed after her to the next.

Somebody under the trees was smoking. How could anyone smoke – afford to smoke – when there wasn't even food to eat?

She walked on, looked at what was available and listened as the black marketeers told the people their prices. Flour fifteen deutschmarks a kilo; sugar thirty and cooking oil twenty; coffee a hundred marks a kilo, cigarettes five for a packet of twelve, a can of beer fifteen and a bottle of whisky seventy. A litre of diesel twenty-five and a litre of petrol thirty-five.

In the old days the seventy marks she'd carried from Maglaj would buy the world; now they were worth almost nothing. She turned away and crossed the footbridge to the main town. The windows and doors were boarded, the ice on the roads was a dirty grey, and the few figures moved like wraiths, everyone else inside because of the terrible cold. A convoy of lorries came through. Aid, someone said, though not as if they were certain. Going the wrong way, Kara thought: going towards the front line.

She speeded up, trying to warm herself and counting the hours till she could sit again in the room at the food kitchen, went back to her mattress in the Gymnasium. It was one o'clock – God, it seemed to have taken an eternity to get to this time. She went back to the food kitchen and began to queue. At three they opened the doors, at four-thirty she sat again in the room and tried to make the soup and bread last as long as she could. By six she was wrapped in the blanket on the floor of the room in the Gymnasium, the candles flickering in the corner near the stove, and the women around it cooking something they'd bought on the black market that morning.

Finn left Hereford at two and was in Aldershot by five.

Janner was improving fast but Max was still wired to every machine imaginable, even though he was saying he would be back with the regiment by the end of the year. Perhaps in the intelligence unit, Finn began to think, perhaps in planning. Not operational though.

'You go in the day after tomorrow,' Janner confirmed.

Finn was sitting on one side of Max's bed and Janner the other.

'UN flight direct to Split. Zenica by the evening and try for Maglaj the day after.'

'Something for her, Finn.' Max spoke in a whisper, and then only with difficulty. 'Something personal from Janner and me.' He gave Finn the bottle of perfume. 'Just make sure she gets it.'

When Kara left the Gymnasium it was shortly after four; when she sat down to eat in the dining area of the food kitchen it was six and she had forgotten when she had last felt her feet. God how she was hungry, how she measured time not in hours and minutes, how she no longer thought of days of the week or months of the year. How she simply measured and thought of everything in terms of cold and hunger.

No way of changing the situation – she spent as long as she could over the food – no way of making life better.

The next morning, even though she arrived at the soup kitchen earlier than usual, the queue seemed deeper and she had to wait longer even to get inside, then even longer to find a space at a table. All the night before the old man above her had coughed up his blood and the children had cried in fear and hunger.

There was a way, of course.

The soup in the bowl was finished. She used the last of the bread to wipe the bowl, then sucked the bread and wiped the bowl again. Then she left the food kitchen, took her bowl and mug back to the Gymnasium, and walked the streets, prayed for the time when she could queue for food again.

Of course she couldn't because it was illegal, immoral . . .

It was one o'clock. Not quite, but she told herself it was. She drifted back to the Gymnasium, sat for forty minutes, then left again for the food kitchen and stood in the queue.

Of course she couldn't because she didn't know how much things cost . . .

She was inside now, holding out her bowl then shuffling forward and searching for a place at a table.

Look at you – it was as if the voice was speaking to her again. Look at how you are. Your shoulders are hunched, your body is bent, and you shuffle along as if you're eighty years old. You're acting as if you have nothing to remember and nothing to fight for. So get it together, Kara. Get yourself some food, get yourself out of the Gymnasium. Because unless you do, you may as well give up now.

She saw a place and darted for it before someone else took it.

Keefer returned from the front lines at seven in the morning. The night before he had huddled by the fire, talking to the three people he had talent spotted, the winter around them, the occasional shell landing near them, and nobody else knowing who he was or what they were talking about.

Bergmann was waiting in the room on the outskirts of the holding village four miles back from the front which they had rented for two hundred and fifty marks a week, plus a pack of self-heating foods. The village was on a hillside, surrounded by pines; the track through it was a sea of mud and the handful of villagers who remained lived in perpetual fear. The area itself was used mainly by Bosnian government forces, but also by the group of foreign mercenaries who had been drawn, for whatever reasons, to the conflict in Bosnia, as well as by the Mujihadeen. Later, as their numbers grew and the nature of the war changed, the Mujihadeen would establish their own bases, heavily fortified and mined. Even in the holding village, however, they operated as a group, living together in two houses slightly separate from the others, and prowling the grounds with suspicion in their eyes and Kalashnikovs in their hands.

'How's the front?' Bergmann passed Keefer a mug of steaming coffee, heavily sweetened.

The room was small: camp cots folded during the day, a stove and washbasin with no running water; a table and two chairs, a Tilley lamp on the table and the windows shuttered, the glass broken long ago and replaced now by polythene sheets they had brought from Split.

'Plenty of soldiers, lot of them good, not enough weapons.' Keefer dumped his parka by the door and wrapped his fingers round the mug. 'If I was choosing sides it wouldn't be this one.'

Bergmann made breakfast – beans and stew. The poor bastards on the front would kill for this, Keefer thought. 'Three recruits,' he told Bergmann between mouthfuls. 'Two men, one woman. I told them to check out their friends, see if anyone else might come through. Gave them some food and told them I'd pick them up in a couple of days.'

'As long as they're not dead.'

'*Insh'allah*,' Keefer said. 'How about here?'

'Two possibles.'

'Local?'

'Yeah. No one we could use among the mercs, and the Muj are tight as hell and look the part even if some of them aren't.'

'How so?' Keefer nodded as Bergmann poured him another mug of coffee.

'Some of them are good. Afghan veterans, a few from the Lebanon.' He sniffed. 'Others are the sons of well-off Arabs doing their thing for the cause before they scuttle back to Europe for the birds and the booze.'

It was the same in any war, Keefer supposed. 'How's Akram?' he asked.

Akram was the Mujihadeen leader in the area.

'Happy like he always is.' It was said cuttingly. 'Loves the foreigners more each day and looking for conspiracies everywhere. Thinks the Great Satan is behind every tree.'

'In other words, watch our backs.'

'Watch everything. So what now?'

'You keep going here, I'll start looking in Travnik. You've got transport?'

'If you have deutschmarks and food here you can get anything.'

They cleared the breakfast, tidied the room and left.

The mercenary called Walton was crouched under a polythene sheet strung between the branches of a pine tree, the recruits in a circle round him.

Keefer started the Toyota, let the engine run, and watched to see what Walton was doing and how he was doing it.

Walton was in his early thirties, six feet three inches tall and well-built, head shaved almost bare. He had been in Bosnia two months though he had not seen action at the front. The emblem of the Parachute Regiment was sewn on one sleeve of his combat jacket, the distinctive wings on his chest, and the emblem of Delta Force was on the other, sergeant's stripes below it. Plus the wings and scuba mask of the US Force Recon.

Hell of a collection, Keefer thought. Except no one would be in both the British Paras and the US Delta teams unless they'd been on secondment, which he supposed was possible. And except for the fact that no matter how good the guys in it had been, Force Recon was a relic from the Vietnam War.

The Kalashnikov was in pieces on the ground in front of Walton. 'Blindfold on and assemble it,' he told one of the recruits. The soldier was eighteen, thin and shabbily dressed, and his fingers were stiff with cold. Bolt slides down, he tried to remember, and felt for the pieces. Spring round bolt, so you push the spring down and clip it into place. Except the clip was hard at the best of times, and now his fingers were stiff, his stomach felt empty, and the blindfold was over his eyes. He put the bolt in place and tried to push the spring down, tried to clip the spring in place.

The spring flew out and fell on the ground.

'Get it right.' Walton jerked the blindfold from the boy's eyes and hit him hard round the ears. 'Next time you get it wrong it might cost you your life.' He pulled off his combat jacket and rolled up the left sleeve of the jersey. The tattoo was on the forearm: the curve of the wings round the dagger and the motto beneath, though the lines were raggedly drawn and the words slightly smudged. 'Who Dares Wins,' he told the boy. 'SAS. If you want to train with me you got to be the best.'

Poor bastards being trained by a prick like that, Keefer thought; no wonder they're losing. He pushed the Toyota into gear and left.

Eight kilometres down the road he pulled into Travnik, parked near the food kitchen, and crossed the bridge. The Gymnasium was to his left, the exterior walls a faded yellow, and some of the windows boarded. He ignored the front and went through the side entrance, pushed open a door and looked in. The room was packed with beds and mattresses and the human wastage of war. Nothing in the eyes of the people staring at him, he thought: no warmth or passion or fire or anger. Even after the war is over these people would still be here, even after the war most of these people would still be the same.

Therefore nobody here he wanted, nobody here he could use. Not even the place to start looking. He left the Gymnasium and walked the fifty metres to the market, moving slowly now, looking and listening. People hassling and haggling, a woman carrying a television set on her shoulders and trying to sell it.

There were a few vegetables, a farmer or perhaps a gardener selling potatoes; some people selling what the West would call consumer goods, but most people were at the stalls or polythene sheets on the ground where the black marketeers were selling their wares. All the same eyes, though, all dead.

The man was in his mid-twenties and arguing over the price of flour. At least he was arguing, Keefer thought, at least he was showing some spirit. He was also educated –

Keefer could tell by the way he was talking, even though he couldn't understand the torrent of language between the seller and potential buyer. The crowd had gathered round, partly because it broke the monotony, and partly to see if the man could get a good price which they themselves could exploit.

You won't do it, Kara thought. You won't get the man with the packets of flour to come down even one mark. Because at the end of the day he's got something you want. So you may as well quit haggling and pay up, because it's already eleven in the morning and most of the black market food that was here earlier has gone, so unless you buy soon you'll end up with nothing, and the man with the flour knows that.

God she was hungry, God she was cold. God she couldn't face another night in the Gymnasium, but the Gymnasium was all there was. No way round it, no way of changing things. One way, the seventy marks she'd saved in the tin in the house at Maglaj.

Her shoulders were hunched, her body was bent, and the winter cut so deep into her that it felt as if it had taken her over. Look at you – she heard the voice again. You're acting as if you have nothing to remember and nothing to fight for. So get it together, Kara. Because unless you do, you may as well give up now.

The man on her left was still arguing about the prices, the crowd still watching. Mine or not mine, Keefer wondered. His eyes left the man and drifted over the faces in the crowd.

So if she decided to spend some of the money, what should she buy? Some flour or some sugar, but if she bought flour she'd need cooking oil. And if she bought flour and sugar and cooking oil that would come to sixty-five deutschmarks and she'd only have five left. The wind whipped the snow from the branches of the trees above them. She turned her head and protected her face from the steel of the ice.

No one he wanted, Keefer decided – same faces and eyes, all dead. Some young, some old, some with their bodies and shoulders bent like the woman three from the man who'd been arguing, even though he couldn't see her face.

Kara left the market and walked back to the Gymnasium, sat hunched on the mattress for ninety minutes then joined the queue already forming outside the food kitchen. By the time she was inside it was five o'clock and already dark.

There were even fewer beans in the soup than there had been that morning, and the water was almost tasteless. You couldn't blame the people who manned the kitchen, she reminded herself: they did their best, and even they looked hungry.

She should have bought some food, could at least have bought some flour. What was the use of money in her pocket if she died of cold or starvation? Perhaps some vegetables, or a can of corned beef to add to the bean soup. That would cost ten marks given the scarcity of everything. Plus some flour to make bread, which was what most people were living on now. That would be another fifteen, so she'd still have forty-five marks.

The food kitchen was emptying.

But even if she spent twenty-five marks, that would only last her a couple of days. And then she'd only have forty-five left. And if she spent that she'd only keep going another week. But if she didn't spend it she'd be dead anyway.

She wiped the bread round the bowl. Okay, she decided. She couldn't go on like this, so tomorrow she'd take a risk, tomorrow she'd spend some of her precious d'marks. Tomorrow she'd do it.

She slipped her right hand in her coat pocket. The cloth was wet and sodden, and her fingers went through the hole in the bottom. Oh Christ, the shock hit her. Oh God, where was the money? The panic seized her and the blood thumped through her. She stood up and dug her fingers deep into the pocket and through the hole; held the coat with her left hand while she searched for the money with her right.

Closing now, someone was saying, time to go.

Okay, she was nodding. She took off the coat and felt in the pocket again, turned it inside out. Purse or tin or loose, she was no longer sure, no longer certain.

You're the last one, someone was telling her, we have to close now.

She was still nodding, panicking even more. Sorry, she said, I've lost something.

Calm it, the voice told her. Slow down and think it through. You're sure the money was in your coat pocket? What was it in – a purse or a tin or a roll?

'Sorry,' she turned to the woman. 'I had some money. I think I've lost it.'

The woman nodded. 'Don't be too long.'

'Thank you.'

So what do I do now, Finn?

Just keep calm and be methodical, she told herself. You've tried the right pocket, now try the left.

Of course – she felt the relief. Of course the money's in the left, not the right where it normally is and where I always hold it. She felt in the left, felt the despair grip her again.

Okay, so what about any other pockets? Go through them, check them.

She checked. Knew she had lost.

What about your knickers, Kara; that's where you girls sometimes keep your money.

No Finn, not my knickers. Felt anyway just in case.

So check one more time – it was her voice now, perhaps it always had been. You know the money was in the coat's right pocket, so check slowly and carefully.

She laid the coat on the table and felt every crease of the cloth. Turned the coat upside down and examined the lining. There was a tear at the bottom, she opened it a little more and felt up. She was quiet now, checking slowly and carefully and hearing nothing, as if there was a calm upon her.

Her fingers touched it, small and wet and almost lost at the bottom of the lining near the hole. Got it, she felt the elation, got her money. Thanks, Finn. Oh thank you. Seventy deutschmarks. So tomorrow she wouldn't waste it, tomorrow she would use it, buy some food.

She pulled it out.

Ten deutschmarks . . . Where was the rest, what had happened to the other sixty?

The woman from the kitchen asked if she'd found anything and told her she had to go.

Okay, Kara nodded. Thanks for letting me stay so long.

If there was one note in the lining there might be more, but if there was it might fall out. She pushed the ten-mark note down the front of her pants, wrapped the coat in a tight bundle and went outside, left hand holding the coat and right gripped firmly over the hole in the lining, and returned to the Gymnasium.

One of the families in the room was feeding the stove with wood they had collected from the trees above the town, and making bread. Kara wrapped the blanket round her, found a space on the floor as close as she could get to the stove they were using, and examined the coat again and again. Even after the others had finished eating she squatted on her mattress and continued the search. Only when the last candle flickered out did she stop looking.

Finn left Hereford shortly after four, Caz half-asleep in the passenger seat. By six they were at the RAF station at Brize

Norton. He kissed her goodbye, watched her drive away, confirmed the flight to Split and checked in.

'Marshall, ODA?' The clerk called up Finn's name and details on the passenger list. ODA – Overseas Development Administration.

'Yes,' Finn confirmed, and shuffled through.

In his bergen he carried food packs, chocolate, thermals, and warm gloves and socks. Plus a small assortment of gifts from his, Janner's and Max's wives. Copies of *Vogue*, *Tatler* and *Cosmopolitan* for the girls in the UNHCR office in Zenica, and that week's *Spectator* for Nick.

Something wrong – he knew the moment the civilians came into the waiting area. United Nations staff en route to a conference in Split, he was informed fifteen minutes later, and UN staff took priority over everything and everybody. Therefore there were no longer seats available.

Bastards, he thought, and considered the options:

London–Rome–Sarajevo, except Sarajevo was closed at the moment. Air Croatia to Zagreb then the local hop down the coast, which was probably better than risking his luck on the next RAF flight, except the Zagreb service wasn't daily, but neither were those from Brize Norton.

The Zagreb flight, he decided, and if that was full he'd fly to Italy and get a ferry across to Split. As long as the ferries were running. And if they weren't he'd drive.

Keefer and Bergmann hunched over the table in the room in the village, the dawn breaking and the coffee and beans hot. Keefer had been up since six and Bergmann had just returned from his early morning prowl round the camp.

'The Brit mercenary . . .' Bergmann ladled the beans on to the plates.

'What about him?' Keefer cut the bread.

'Apparently he's playing the hard man and hitting the recruits.'

'So?' Because that sounded like any NCO in any army.

'One of the guys he knocked about shows every sign of converting to Islamic fundamentalism, therefore the Muj are looking for blood.'

'How's that affect us?'

'Walton's not a fundamentalist, we're not fundamentalists, even though Akram knows where we've come from.' More or less. No details, though, nothing that would be of any use to whoever the opposition was. 'Therefore we're the same as Walton.'

'Keep your eye on it,' Keefer told him and left for Travnik.

The town was already busy, but only in the manner of a town under siege in winter: shadowy figures, occasional army lorries, snow and ice everywhere. The woman with the television was still trying to sell it at the marketplace. He lost himself in the jumble of people and looked for eyes that weren't dead.

Kara picked her way between the stalls and checked the prices. The soup had been thicker that morning, she told herself, therefore she didn't have to spend the ten marks. The soup was as thin as the day before, and she knew it. Buy and you survived, don't buy and you didn't. Depending how you defined survival. She couldn't buy much with ten marks though, not even the kilo of flour she'd been thinking about yesterday.

The woman with the television set passed her and asked if she wanted to buy it. She shook her head and stood beneath the trees. Ten marks would get her some potatoes and a can of meat, and at least that would get her through to tomorrow, perhaps the day after. She left the trees and pushed her way to the man selling potatoes.

'How much?'

'Eight marks,' he told her.

Which was more than she had anticipated and wouldn't leave enough for the corned beef.

'Last there is,' he told her.

'Okay.'

Think about it, Kara – she heard Finn's voice. Think about the ten marks and what they really mean. Okay, they'll help you survive a few more days, but after that it's the thin bean soup again, and after that you're dead or as good as.

What do you mean, Finn? Because I thought we'd talked it through, thought we'd agreed.

Sure we talked it through, Kara, sure we agreed. But that was when you had more than just ten marks. But ten marks aren't ten marks, are they? Ten marks are actually a hundred and fifty. Only if you have the will, though; only if you have the need to survive like Janner and Max had the will to live.

What the hell do you mean, Finn? What the hell are you talking about? How the hell are ten deutschmarks really a hundred and fifty?

Because flour is selling here for fifteen marks a kilo, but the people who are selling it are buying it for one mark. The same with sugar and cooking oil and everything else. Therefore your ten marks will actually buy you enough food to sell for a hundred and fifty. But only if you make the run to the place called Popovekuce, because everyone knows that's where they're buying the stuff. Only if you're prepared to risk getting beaten up at the road blocks, or shot or blown up when you cross the front line. Because that's what the black marketeers face. Only if you're prepared to move the mines to the side of the road at the crossing point, and put them back after, because that's what the black marketeers do. Because Popovekuce is the other side of the front line, Popovekuce is in land held by the Chetniks. So think about it, Kara, think about how much you want to live and how much you want to die.

Why are you pushing me like this, Finn? Why do I think it's your voice I hear? Why do I think I hear a voice?

'Take it or leave it,' the man with the potatoes said.

Waste away on the soup they give you in the food kitchen, Kara; lie awake each night in the awfulness which is the Gymnasium. Okay, most people will survive it, but think what they're like now and how they'll be when it's over, if it's ever over. Think of what you would do for Adin and Jovan, therefore think of what you must do for yourself. Who Dares Wins, Kara, and winning means surviving by your terms and your conditions. So think of the money you've got in your pants, because the way you're going and the way you're looking nobody will want whatever else is there.

Sod you, Finn, she laughed. 'Leave it,' she told the man. So what the hell do I do now, she thought.

The woman selling flour at the edge of the shack twenty metres away seemed friendlier than most.

'How'd you get through the military checkpoint at Kralgevice?' Kara asked her.

Kralgevice was midway between Travnik and Turbe, and Popovekuce was the other side of the front to the west of Turbe.

'You use the side road in the hills to the east.'

'How do I get on to the side road?'

Not that she was going to do it, of course. So why was she asking if she wasn't?

Not many people risked crossing the line, the woman understood, therefore one more wouldn't make any difference. 'Several ways, the easiest is up the hill of the old town. It links with the one you want.'

'Thanks.'

She left the market and went back to the room in the

Gymnasium, pulled the blanket round her and thought it through.

She would rest up till around two, then start queuing for food, because she needed to eat again before she started. She would set off as soon as she could after, which would probably be five o'clock. But it would be dark by then, so most of the black marketeers would probably be on the road already.

She had ten deutschmarks, so she would split what she bought – say six kilos of flour and two of sugar, because people probably wanted flour more than sugar, but sugar cost twice as much, so she could make the same profit and carry half the amount. Which would come to ten marks. Then she'd sell for one hundred and fifty. But she still wouldn't have food for herself.

Okay, she'd keep one kilo of flour, and buy some other food with some of the other money . . .

Forget what you'll do tomorrow, Finn told her. Just concentrate on what you have to do tonight.

It was two o'clock. She tidied the mattress, picked up the thin blue nylon bag, left the Gymnasium and stood in the queue already winding its way round the food kitchen. By the time she was inside it was four-thirty. She was excited but calm, as if she was acting automatically, as if the nerves weren't tightening in her stomach and twisting in her body.

By the time she had finished and returned her bowl and plate to the Gymnasium it was grey, fast going black. She crossed the main street, then the road on which she had entered Travnik the first evening, and climbed the street between the older houses on the other side. The hill was steep and icy, and she was already breathing heavily. She paused, hands on hips and bag slung over her back, then straightened and began walking again.

The temperature was plummeting and the sky was clear

and speckled with stars, just the occasional shadowy image of a person. The road left the houses, still climbing, then curved and flattened slightly, ran through some trees, then picked up an undulating line along the side of the valley heading north. The hedges and ground on either side were eerie white, and the packed snow on the road itself showed footmarks. In front of her she saw a shape, moving slowly and deliberately, a child's sledge on a rope behind. Kara fell in behind and settled into the pace.

The lights of the military checkpoint between Travnik and Turbe were to her left and slightly below them, the tiniest flicker of flame in the dark. The adrenalin had worn off now and she was cold. The shape in front was still moving steadily, but she was having trouble keeping up, and had lost count of how long she had been walking.

They were dropping now, were at a junction with a main road and turning right, the surface riddled with the deep grooves of military vehicles.

They were an hour past the checkpoint, in the dark she saw someone coming the other way. As they passed, head down and trudging, she saw the pack on their back. Fifteen minutes later a man and woman passed, pulling a pram together. To the right she sensed rather than saw the town of Turbe. She had been walking another fifteen minutes, the figure she had been following now swallowed in the dark and more figures passing her, on their way back to Travnik, someone occasionally overtaking her because she was walking so slowly.

She heard the click of a gun. I'm here, she thought, I'm at the front line. The rolls of razor wire were pulled back slightly, allowing access. She stepped through, aware of the eyes watching her and the guns on her. The road was even icier, even more slippery. She looked down and saw the black shapes moved to the right and left. Oh God, she realized, it's true. The first black marketeer across moves the mines and the last puts them back. She froze. Go on, she told herself; because if you don't Adin and Jovan won't eat, if you don't Adin and Jovan will starve. She walked on, passed through the second barrier of wire into the Serb-held area of the former Yugoslavia. Ten minutes later she came to the four houses and garage at Popovekuce.

The fires roared in the dustbins in front of the garage, and the vans were pulled in a rough semicircle, tails in towards the fires, the backs open and the dealers lounging against them, the cluster of black marketeers from Travnik flitting between them. Somewhere along the front line there was exchange of machine-gun fire.

The Fat Man's van was white, the back down, and the bags of flour were stacked on the tailboard. He was tall, wearing a Cossack hat and sheepskin coat, heavy jowled face and smoking long thin cheroots. Ignore him, she decided, he would rip her off. Deal with a woman, except there were no women among the sellers, and a woman was as likely to drive as hard a bargain and be as untrustworthy as a man.

She shuffled between the vans and listened in to the deals, saw the money and food change hands. Some vans were selling just one thing, others a mix, the prices the same at each of them, even at The Fat Man's. The heat from the fires was blistering; she settled by one and tried to bring the warmth to her body. Time to do it, she told herself; Christ, she thought, the ten-mark note was still in her pants. She left the fires and stood outside the circle of light they cast, undid her coat and took out the note.

Three or four kilo bags of flour, two of sugar, and the other two deutschmarks on canned meat, she had thought in Travnik. The nerves were in her stomach and her throat was tight.

'Five kilos,' she told The Fat Man.

His eyes were small and his face was red with the heat

of the fires. Do me a favour – it was in the way he looked at her, the way he didn't even take the cheroot from his mouth. Nobody comes this far just for five kilos.

You just walked from Travnik – he read the challenge in her face. You just crossed the front line, took your chance through the mines?

'Five kilos.' He took the bags from the stack, put them on the tailboard, and held out his hand for payment.

She gave him the note. 'You here tomorrow night?'

'Here every night.'

He lifted the bottom of the jacket and reached into his trouser pocket. The roll of notes was thicker than his wrist and bound by an elastic band. 'Five marks.' He took her note, slid off the band, placed the note in the roll, then thumbed through for a five-mark note.

'Give me singles,' Kara told him.

He stopped and looked at her. Took the cheroot from his mouth, flicked the ash from the end, and put it back in. 'Five marks,' he confirmed; he held the notes in his left and gave them to Kara one by one, snapping each between the thumb and second finger of his right.

She counted each of the notes, even though she knew the amount was accurate, rolled them together, and put the flour in her bag.

'See you tomorrow,' The Fat Man said.

She nodded at him and went to one of the vans selling sugar. 'Give me two.' She flicked the notes between her fingers as The Fat Man had done. She had one mark left. She crossed through the fires to the van selling cans of beef, even though the mark-up wasn't as good as with flour and sugar. 'I'll take one,' she told the man, and flicked the last note into his palm. 'Plus a packet of cigarettes.'

The heat of the fires was inviting. Don't be the last to cross back, she reminded herself, don't ever be the one who has to touch the mines. Fifteen minutes later she crossed the front line, an hour after that she saw the flicker of light from the military checkpoint below and to her right.

She was tired now, her body stiff with cold and the bag heavy on her back, but she was going to eat.

Thanks, Finn.

Keefer saw Walton immediately, though Walton did not register him. The British mercenary was by the bridge over the river to the Gymnasium and the market. It was eight-thirty in the morning, the sky a dark threatening grey. He watched as Walton turned back, assuming correctly he was going to the café on the main street where combatants on R and R from the front tended to gather. Only when Walton had disappeared did Keefer cross the bridge to the market. In front of him he saw the woman with the television set on her shoulder.

If she sold the items by ten she could make the morning soup kitchen, Kara thought, even though she might not need it. She had reached Travnik at four, exhausted and frozen, had curled up on the mattress in the Gymnasium and tried to warm herself in the charity blanket. Had never let the bag out of her sight or reach. By seven she had been in the market, found herself a place on the right, just past the trees, and huddled in a crouch, the bag on the hard snow and the flour and sugar on it. By seven-thirty she had sold one kilo of flour, by eight the area was filled with refugees and locals, checking the prices and going away then returning, checking and haggling.

'How much?' The man and woman had stopped ten minutes.

'Flour fifteen marks, sugar thirty.'

Behind them Kara saw the woman with the television on her shoulder. God, she hadn't thawed out from last night. God, she hadn't been warm since last summer. The woman with the TV would never sell it, but at least she was warm – warm being a comparative term. At least her coat looked thick and her boots seemed watertight.

'Someone down there's asking ten for flour.' It was the man, the collar of his coat pulled high and the scarf wrapped round his head.

Don't fall for it, she told herself, don't give in. Because it wasn't them who made the run to Popovekuce last night.

'Buy from them, then.'

'What about two kilos?'

'Twenty-five.' Because she was cold and hungry and wanted to leave the street and sit in the room at the food kitchen.

'What about the sugar?'

'Thirty.'

'I mean two.'

The woman with the TV was still turning, looking round as she always seemed to be doing for someone who might buy the set.

Fifty-five, Kara began to say. 'Here,' she shouted. The woman with the television turned and the hope drifted across the dead of her eyes. 'Colour,' she said anxiously. 'Get all the channels.'

God she was wet and cold – the thought drummed through Kara's mind. God how she wished the wet didn't seep through the shoulders of her coat and the snow through the worn leather of her shoes. 'I don't want the TV.' She saw the way the woman's face and eyes and soul dropped. 'A kilo of flour for your coat and boots.'

The woman was lost, confused. 'I can't,' she began to say. 'They're all I have . . .'

'I don't want you to go cold. I'll give you mine, plus the flour.'

The woman knelt on the ground and began playing with the controls of the set, telling Kara how many channels it could receive and how she could operate the remote control.

'My coat plus two kilos of flour,' Kara told her.

A small crowd had gathered, the woman looking at their faces as if she wanted them to decide for her.

'You have a family?' Kara asked.

'Husband and mother.'

'Okay.' Kara put two kilos of flour and a kilo of sugar on the top of the TV set, took off her coat and handed it to the woman. 'Give me yours.' Okay, the woman agreed; she took off her coat, pulled a string bag from one of the pockets, and put on Kara's coat. Kara put the woman's coat on and pulled off her shoes, gave them to the woman. 'Your socks as well.' Two kilos of flour *and* the sugar, the woman asked. Yes, Kara said. The woman took off her boots and socks and Kara put them on.

The woman put the flour and sugar in the bag, lifted the TV set on her shoulder, and drifted again into the crowd.

There were two kilos of flour and one of sugar left on the bag. 'Fifty-five,' Kara told the man.

'Okay.' He reached down to take the bags.

'Money first.'

He grunted, took a purse from his pocket, and gave her five ten-mark notes and five singles. 'Good deal,' she told him, 'come back tomorrow.' She added the notes to those she had received earlier, rolled them up, picked up the bag, and headed through the crowd to the other side of the market.

'Four potatoes, an onion and two carrots,' she told the man at the side of the shack. 'Worth three marks, but I'll pay in cigarettes.' Which were worth five but which had cost her one.

'Done.' The man dropped the vegetables into her bag and took the packet.

'If I need some more tomorrow, what do you want?'

'Some cooking oil.'

'We've got a deal.'

She left the market and went to the food kitchen. An hour later she was back in the room in the Gymnasium. She scrubbed two potatoes and the carrots, and cut them and the onion into sections. At the stove a woman was preparing bread. 'Two potatoes for the loan of a saucepan and the stove,' Kara told her. Because even though the stove was free the wood which fuelled it either had to be bought or collected from the hillsides above the town. The woman nodded. Kara tipped the bean soup from the food kitchen into the saucepan, and added the potatoes, carrots and onion. When the stew was ready she poured half of it into her bowl, opened the tin of corned beef, and added half of that.

'The rest of the meat for some fresh bread?' she suggested to the woman.

'It'll be ready this afternoon.'

The woman with the TV set was still in the marketplace – Keefer watched, lost in the crowd. The woman with the TV set on her shoulder was always there. It was only later, when he was back in the room in the village off the hill road between Travnik and Turbe, that he realized . . . The woman was carrying a string bag, the bag was filled with food, and she was wearing a different coat and shoes.

It was four-thirty, the light outside turning a dark grey. Kara heated the rest of the stew, thanked the woman for the bread, then sat at the table and ate slowly and deliberately. Begin to plan now, she told herself; work out what she would buy at Popovekuce that night and how much she could carry back. She had seventy deutschmarks, so she could be coming back with around fifty kilos of food, so that by this time tomorrow the seventy marks could be around seven hundred. And the night after the seven hundred could be . . .

Easy, Kara – she heard the voice. Okay to plan ahead, okay to know what you're doing. But don't lose sight of where you started from; don't ever forget why you're doing it.

Okay, Finn.

When she left the Gymnasium it was just gone five and the temperature was already dipping. Good time to set out, she told herself; get a good rest in the afternoon so she could be back in time to snatch at least some sleep that night, but not so early that she was the first one to cross the lines.

The snow swirled in flurries and there was a crash of artillery fire somewhere to the right. She skirted Turbe and sensed the moment she was approaching the first barbed wire, walked through it and along the road to the second layers, then passed to the Serb side.

'Thought you'd be back,' The Fat Man told her. She checked the other prices, then bought five kilos of flour from him, plus three kilos of sugar which he hadn't been selling the night before, and two litres of cooking oil from a dealer on the other side of the fires, plus cigarettes and corned beef.

Cigarettes might not be a bad buy, she began to think. Cigarettes cost one mark here and five on the black market in Travnik. The mark-up wouldn't be as good as with flour and sugar, but cigarettes were lighter and she could carry more, therefore make more. Coffee was the same. Not yet, she decided; for the time being she would deal with those items she knew she could move quickly. Thirty thousand people lived in Travnik, someone had told her, and now there were just as many refugees. Most with deutschmarks and all needing food. So she'd have no problem shifting anything.

She nodded at The Fat Man and began the journey back.

At seven she was in position in the road along the river by the Gymnasium.

Keefer was in the market by eight. There was no woman with a television set over her shoulder. He should have spotted it and acted on it yesterday, he reprimanded himself. Because someone had done a deal with her, someone had bought her waterproof coat and boots for the two kilos of flour and kilo of sugar she'd had in the bag. So someone was being smart, someone might be different. Possibly one of the black market dealers buying for his wife or girlfriend, but hopefully not, because the woman with the TV set was wearing a woman's coat, so the chances were that whoever had done the deal was a woman. But the only person who knew who it was was the woman with the TV, and she wasn't here.

By ten Kara had sold all she wished to sell, the notes wrapped tightly round the roll from the previous day. She left the plot under the trees and bought some vegetables from the man at the side of the shack, from whom she'd bought the day before, paying him in corned beef. Cooking oil tomorrow, she told him. But only when she had somewhere to store the amount of potatoes and carrots and onions a litre of cooking oil would buy. She was hungry now, the pangs gripping her stomach. She returned to the room in the Gymnasium and made stew, using the saucepan the woman had loaned her the morning before and paying her in potatoes. By the time she ate it was almost midday and the tiredness was seeping into her.

'You have a purse?' she asked the woman.

The woman showed her.

'How much?'

They agreed a price, then Kara tied it on a cord round her neck, left the Gymnasium, crossed through the town, and made her way up the street to the hill road to Turbe. Most of the houses were old and solid, though some were new, men and women flitting between and past them like shadows.

'I'm looking for a room,' Kara began asking. 'I can pay.'

Fifty deutschmarks a week, one man told her. He led her up a side street and showed her a room under the eaves of his house. It was small and cold, and the roof leaked so that the water was frozen on the inner walls.

By two o'clock she'd forgotten how many people she asked, had been offered two more rooms, only to find that what was meant was a share with other refugees. It was three o'clock, time running out. Almost time to be on the road to Popovekuce, and she hadn't rested.

She needed a room and she would pay in food, she told a woman as she headed down the hill. How much food, a man behind the woman asked. Depends, Kara told him. He led her back up the hill, then along one of the side streets to the right, and opened a set of doors. The basement inside was dry, no windows and no proper floor, and appeared to be a work room. No thanks, she told him, anything else? Time to go, she was thinking; time to gather what remained of her mental and physical strength for the run to Popovekuce.

There was one other, he began to say, except his wife's sister was using it.

'Like I said, I can pay in food.'

He took her to the front entrance of the house and they went inside. The room was through a door to the right. It was clean and tidy and dry, not large but not small, a table and chair, plus a slightly battered armchair; a single bed against one wall and a carpet on the wooden floor. A second door led to a small porch and a set of steps at the side of the house.

'How much?' she asked.

He fetched his wife. 'Sorry,' she told Kara. 'As my husband says, my sister's using it.'

'Fine,' Kara kept the delivery flat, as if to say it was a pity but she understood. 'If you know anyone else with a room and who'd like to be paid in food . . .'

'What sort?' The woman looked at the bag on the floor.

'A kilo of flour and a kilo of sugar.' Which would cost forty-five marks on the black market, and rooms were going for fifty a week. 'Plus a litre of cooking oil.' Which brought it up to sixty-five. 'Something different if you wanted it.'

'A week?' the woman asked.

'A week,' Kara confirmed.

'When do you want the room?'

'Now.'

'And you can pay now?'

Kara took the flour, sugar and oil from her bag and placed them on the table. 'You're a carpenter?' she asked the husband.

He remembered the tools in the basement. 'Not professionally, but yes.'

'I need a stove in here, so I can cook. Not one of the small ones from the Refugee Centre. Plus a large pram, wheels off and replaced with runners.' For the run to and from Popovekuce. 'But the wheels able to be put back on.' For when the ice and snow melt. 'I'll pay in food.' Because I think in the prices I pay at Popovekuce, and you think in the prices you'd have to pay on the Travnik black market, so we both think we're getting a bargain.

'When do you want them?'

'Tomorrow.'

They shook hands on it.

'You smoke?' she asked.

'Used to.'

She reached in her pocket and gave him a packet of cigarettes. 'Down payment. Is there a key to the side door?'

By the time she returned to the Gymnasium it was almost

five. She warmed and ate the remains of the stew, then gathered the few personal belongings she had retained, plus the charity blanket, and left. The woman at the house was waiting with the key, and there was a candle on the table in the room. Kara took the photograph of Adin and Jovan which she had salvaged from the house in Maglaj and placed it in the centre of the table. Then she left the house, locking the side door, and began the climb up the hill.

When she returned it was two in the morning, the sky was clear and the steps at the side were slippery with ice. The night had gone well; she'd cleared no man's land without problems, even joked with The Fat Man and the other dealers. She unlocked the porch, then the second door, and went inside. Put the bag on the floor, felt across the room and lit the candle on the table, then sat on the bed and looked round.

It was good to have made it, good to have things that other people wanted and would pay for, good to be able to sit here and work out how she'd started with ten deutschmarks and now had the equivalent of over two hundred, and that was after paying for a room and setting aside what it would cost her for a stove and a pram.

It was good to have people recognize that – dealers like The Fat Man, even the woman from whom she'd rented the room. Good to have another woman take off her warm coat and boots and sell them to you because you had something she needed.

Careful, Kara – she heard the voice.

Okay, Finn, she told him. Give me a break. Who the hell's just made the run to Popovekuce, who's just slogged through the ice and snow half the goddamn night?

She sat in the armchair, kicked off the boots and lit a cigarette, even though she did not smoke. Only after she had sat for half an hour more did she go to bed.

When she woke it was with the same sense of freedom.

Christ how good it was to wake and not to have to crawl over the rest of mankind, not to have to queue for the thin tasteless soup at the food kitchen along with everybody else. Of course she felt hungry now, but today it didn't matter. Because tonight she would have what she wanted.

She dressed, left the room, taking a strange satisfaction in locking the doors after her, crossed the town and reached the marketplace in time to secure what she already considered her regular place near the trees by the river. Already there were people hoping for early bargains; by eight she had sold two kilos of flour, one of sugar, and a litre of cooking oil; by nine the area was packed and business was brisk.

'How much is the flour?' The man was thin and stooped.

'Fifteen marks a kilo.'

'It's a lot.' He grimaced.

'That's the price.' She shrugged her shoulders.

Keefer had been in the marketplace two hours when he saw the woman with the TV set. It was ten in the morning, the sky brilliant blue and the day freezing cold.

'Not sold the set yet.' He smiled at her.

She turned, slightly startled. 'A hundred deutschmarks,' she said optimistically. 'It's colour, really good reception.'

'Someone bought your coat and boots.'

The woman knew he didn't want the set and began to turn away.

'Man or woman?' Keefer asked. Probably a man, but it was a long shot, and whoever had bought it might be one of those he was looking for.

'Woman.'

'Fifty marks if you find her for me.'

The woman looked at him in amazement, then nodded and held out her hand.

'Ten now,' Keefer told her. 'The rest when we find her.'

'Okay.' The woman nodded, suddenly anxious. 'She's always by the trees.'

'Show me.'

The woman turned and began to push her way through the crowd. Don't rush, Keefer told her, plenty of time. So it had been a woman who'd bought the coat and boots, so his instinct might be right. No need to hurry, he told the woman again. Don't say anything to her, just point her out to me. And don't screw me, he didn't have to say. Don't think you can get by with just pointing out anyone, because if you do I'll know and you won't get your money.

They came to the trees. The road was crowded, the refugees packed tight and looking at the items for sale.

'She's not here.' The woman's voice was almost panicky. No woman and no deutschmarks, no marks no food. 'She's here, she's always here. This is where she was when I sold her the coat.'

There was an empty space – half an empty space – between plots but already filling.

'Who you looking for?' The man was in his mid-twenties, half-crouched on the ground with a dozen packets of cigarettes on top of a battered leather briefcase.

'Woman selling flour and sugar. I sold her my coat.'

'I remember. She's finished, sold up and left twenty minutes ago.'

I tried – Keefer read it in the woman's face. I really did tell the truth.

'Ten marks now as I promised,' he told her. Give someone nothing and they might not come back; give them a down payment and they certainly would. 'The other forty when we find her. Eight o'clock tomorrow morning, at the other side of the footbridge, but don't bring the TV set.'

Keefer led the woman away. 'How much did I say?'

'Fifty. Ten now, forty when we found her.'

'Let's make it twenty now, thirty later.'

He counted out two ten-mark notes. 'No need to mention it to anyone.' Especially not the woman. 'Between you and me, no one else. Might be some more work sometime.' Even though you don't know who I am and what I'm doing. Because to you it doesn't matter. And you'll keep quiet about it, won't breathe a whisper to anyone. Because you need the money and you think there might be more to come. Because everyone has not just their price, but their *type* of price. And what I've just told you is more effective than threatening you, even cutting your throat. 'Where do you live?' She told him. 'I'll be in touch.' She nodded. 'I'll be waiting.'

The Air Croatia flight from Zagreb to Split landed on time and the Gurkha was waiting, civilian clothes.

'Mr Marshall?'

It was strange going into somewhere without back-up, Finn thought; without the satellite links and secure communications; without people like Jim and Ken and Steve beside him and the likes of Janner and his patrol somewhere around.

'Yes,' he said.

An hour later they passed through the checkpoint from Croatia into Bosnia-Herzegovina, the Gurkha driver swinging past the line of aid trucks held up at the border. Three hours after that, delayed slightly by road conditions in the mountains, they joined a line of lorries waiting for the Warrior escorts to conduct them through the fire zone of Gornji Vacuf. Two hours after that, having suffered further though minor delays, they reached the UNHCR base in Zenica.

The Boss was due but not back yet, he was told – trouble on an aid run to Sarajevo. He gave the girls the magazines, accepted a coffee, and settled in Nick Stacey's office.

Stacey returned at nine. He was tall and bearded.

'Problems?' Finn asked.

'The Serbs shot up an aid convoy, one of the volunteers was killed.' Stacey poured them each a large Black Label. 'Good-looking girl. Twenty-three and due home next week to get married.' He knocked the drink back in one and poured them each another. 'Okay, my friend. Maglaj. Tell me what you want.'

When Kara returned to the room in the old town the stove was in position, the flue going through a hole in the board covering the window, and a stack of wood at the side and in the porch. She knelt down and lit it, listened to the crackling of the wood and felt the first warmth. The stove was old but efficient, ten minutes later the iron was hot and the warmth was beginning to radiate through the room. She took off her coat and boots and placed the items she had bought at the market that morning on the table: pans and plates, sheets for the bed, and polythene and rope for the pram. Then she made a pot of coffee – black and sweet, no milk – fried some potatoes and corned beef, ate her first meal of the day, and lay on the bed, not using the sheets yet, because she hadn't washed properly. When she woke it was three in the afternoon and the pram was ready. She thanked and paid the husband of the household, then removed the mattress, lining and hood of the pram, so that only the shell remained. When she was satisfied she made more coffee and finished the remnants of the meal she had cooked that morning, then she sat in the armchair and dozed again till the light began to fade. Tomorrow she would get herself organized, she told herself, but today was already good.

It was four-thirty. She damped down the stove and left, locking the doors and pulling the pram up the street. Tobacco Road – she remembered Adin singing the words of the song, and hummed them. Uphill the pram was heavy to push; she tied the rope round the handles and pulled it backwards. Once she reached the flatter section of the hill road, however, it moved quickly and easily on its runners. The moon was slightly fuller tonight and she walked calmly and rhythmically, not fast but overtaking an occasional straggler, and reaching Popovekuce earlier than she had calculated.

'Wondered how long it would take you to get transport,' The Fat Man told her. She half-loaded the pram with flour, then spent more of her funds on sugar, corned beef, cigarettes, soap and washing powder. Not much of the last two, because they were personal. When the load was level with the top of the pram she stopped buying, even though she had thirty marks left.

'Expanding,' The Fat Man joked as she left.

'Capitalism,' she joked back.

The return trip to Tobacco Road took slightly over an hour longer than the outward leg, and the steps to the porch were sheeted with ice. She positioned the pram at the bottom of the steps, unlocked the outer door, placed a candle at the top of the steps, and carried the load into the porch. When she was finished she shut the porch door and began carrying the load into the inner room.

The photograph of Adin and Jovan was on the table. She moved it to the dresser and placed the sugar and flour and other items on the table, then she hauled the pram up the steps, shut it in the porch, and locked the doors.

She was breathing heavily, almost sweating with the work. She took off her coat and boots, made herself some coffee, settled back in the chair, and looked at the table. The candle was flickering. Even though the day had been long and hard she felt good, felt full of energy. She boiled a bowl of water, and stripped and washed; then she sprinkled some powder in the bowl, washed one set of clothes plus the sheets, and hung them across the room.

It was three now, almost three-thirty, and the tiredness was beginning to overtake her. Tomorrow night she'd wash the other clothes, tomorrow she'd wash herself again, take her time over it and enjoy it, go to sleep between clean sheets.

Thank God she was no longer in the Gymnasium, she'd thought the night before; pity the poor bastards who were still there. But perhaps the problem with people like those in the Gymnasium and the food kitchen wasn't just to do with the fact that they didn't know how to take care of themselves – the thought drifted in the night. Perhaps it was simply that in life, as in everything else, there were winners and there were losers.

Keefer saw her at nine. Under a square of polythene stretched beneath the branches, so that the snow or wet wouldn't fall on either her or her goods. Sitting on a box behind a pram fitted with runners and loaded with sugar and flour and cooking oil. Most of the other dealers in the market – except for the big boys at the top end – squatting with their items on the ground.

It was snowing, though not heavily. He moved away slightly, drifted in the crowd near the target.

Her face was thin, her eyes were sunken and dark and she was exhausted though she herself didn't recognize it. She was a good operator though – he watched the way she dealt with customers: laughed and joked or threatened or shrugged. Must be an operator to have that amount of black market food in front of her, if she was making the nightly run to Popovekuce. Unless she was just a front.

He drifted away – never too far away so he would miss her if she left. Drifted back again, observed her again.

She was on the edge, at least close to it. Running on adrenalin but at least she was running. Eyes glancing. And that was it, that was what he'd been looking for, what made her different from the others whom he and Bergmann had so far recruited. The eyes. Sore and tired and slightly red, but alive. Darting and alert.

The sheets she'd washed probably wouldn't be dry for tonight, Kara thought, though some of the clothes would be. Tonight at Popovekuce she'd pile the pram a little higher, see how much she could pull without killing herself. Pity she couldn't use two prams, there were so many people looking for food that she could have sold twice the amount she'd brought back last night. She took the polythene down from the tree, folded it, placed it into the pram, put the box on top, and pushed her way through the market to the vegetable man on the far side. Then she loaded up with the items she needed, paying in food or cigarettes, and made her way back to the room on what she already thought of as Tobacco Road.

So who are you – Keefer watched from the hill. What are you? Who's with you and who's not with you? Where have you come from and where might you let me take you? If you're the one. But you are. And I know it.

# 7

The UNHCR convoy left Zenica at first light, three Land-cruisers packed with medical supplies; Finn, Stacey and a woman interpreter in the lead vehicle; Stacey and the woman in front, and Finn in the back. An hour later they came to the front line, the pine-covered sides of the valley rising on either side, the snowdrifts deep and the barbed wire and machine-gun emplacements in front of them. In the still of the morning they heard the roll of the guns and the chatter of small-arms fire.

The command bunker was sunk into the ground to their right. Stacey wound down his window and nodded at the soldiers who emerged.

'United Nations High Commission for Refugees,' he told the corporal through the interpreter.

Where were they going, the corporal asked. The soldiers looked badly equipped and ragged, Finn thought. And cold.

'Maglaj and Tesanj.'

'What are you carrying?'

'Medical supplies.'

'But you're going into territory held by the Chetniks.'

'I have to in order to reach Maglaj,' Stacey said patiently. The corporal returned to the bunker.

'What now?' Finn asked.

'We wait.'

'How long?'

'How long's a piece of string?'

Two hours later a jeep carrying a captain arrived, half an hour after that one carrying a major, the conversation repeated each time. Three hours after they had reached the checkpoint the corporal ordered his men to roll back the barbed wire from the road.

The mines were on the road in front of them – twenty, scattered randomly.

'You or me?' Finn asked.

'Both of us.' Stacey left the driver's seat and the interpreter took his place.

Finn climbed out of the passenger door and pulled his jacket tight. 'She insured to drive?' Bad joke, but one of them would make it.

The mines were Russian anti-tank, disc-shaped and olive green, with small handles on the side. When there was time they would drive a small stake next to one, run a piece of string from the mine, round the stake and back to where they were crouching, then pull the mine to the side in case there was an anti-lift device beneath it. When there was time ... Today was a wing and a prayer. They agreed which mines had to be moved, then Stacey knelt by the first and Finn by the second. This is crazy, he thought. This isn't crazy, this is bloody stupid. This is what Nick does every day he's in Bosnia, just to get the aid through, just to help a few refugees. He tried to relax and eased the mine from the ice. One down, one to go. When a track had been cleared, just wide enough for the vehicle wheels, they returned to the convoy. Stacey took over the driving and Finn walked in front, guiding him through.

Half a kilometre on they stopped at the next set of dark shapes in the road, the barbed wire and the machine-gun nests of the Serb and Croat forces. Stacey flashed his lights, then stepped out.

'Want me to come?' Finn asked.

'Better for you to stay here.'

Finn climbed into the driving seat, shut the door, and watched as the UNHCR man and the interpreter walked slowly and carefully between the mines and stopped at the barbed wire. The soldiers appeared from the bunkers on the other side, then escorted them through the wire and into the woods. Into a command post, Finn hoped. The interpreter was slim, a Muslim, and eighteen years old. Amazing woman, Finn thought, a lot more like her in this place.

Half an hour later they reappeared.

'We wait,' Stacey told him. The interpreter broke open a coffee pack and they sat drinking. It was midday, time slipping away. An hour later Stacey and the interpreter made their way to the barbed wire again, disappeared for half an hour, then came back. An hour after that they repeated the process.

'No go.' Stacey climbed back into the Landcruiser. It was gone three, almost four, and the light was fading fast. 'Try again tomorrow.'

Kara left the house at five.

The black market was a strange world, Keefer thought as he watched. Everyone knew what the woman pulling the pram up the hill was doing and everyone accepted it. Anyone could do it but in the end few did. He collected the Landcruiser and parked it halfway down a street opposite, in a position from which he could observe both the door at the front of the house and the one at the top of the steps at the side, which the target had used. Five hours later he saw her coming back down the hill. Since he had last seen her no one had entered or left the house by either door, therefore she was doing it alone. Unless there was someone inside, a child or a sick husband, but he'd know that when he'd been inside himself. And he'd go inside once he knew her timetable.

The coffee she'd placed on the stove when she'd first arrived was bubbling and the room was warm. Kara flopped back in the chair, spooned some sugar into the mug, and drank the hot sweet liquid. She'd done well, managed with the pram loaded three layers of bags above the top, the polythene wrapped over and tied down. She stood up, searched among the bags on the table, found the chocolate, and sat back in the chair munching it.

She felt good, the electricity still pulsing through her. Enjoy it, she told herself, because she'd worked for it. And because she'd worked for it she'd give herself a treat. She put the water on the stove, and felt the washing she had hung up the morning before. Even the sheets were dry. She folded one set and made the bed with the other, then she opened the bottle of whisky she'd bought at Popovekuce, cracked the seal, and poured herself a glass. The towel was warming by the stove. She undressed and washed herself, enjoying the smell of the soap and sipping the whisky.

The marks from the rope were red raw across her shoulders. Plan it, she told herself, organize it, look to the future. She was bringing back as much as she could haul every night, but in the market the following morning she could sell two, three times what she'd brought back. So if she brought back more, she could increase her profit.

Adin's face and eyes stared at her from the photograph on the dresser. Still love you, she told him; still respect and honour and cherish you. But the world's changed. I want to survive, you'd want me to survive, and this is the way I have to do it.

She rinsed the soap off, poured another whisky, and began to dry herself.

So she could shift twice as much every day without a problem. Which meant she would have to bring back twice as much. Which in turn meant she would need a helper. Or two. Because she couldn't just shift twice the amount she was shifting every day now, she could sell three times what she was moving in the market near the Gymnasium. So if she was making five hundred deutschmarks a load, she could be making a thousand with one helper and fifteen hundred with two. Fifteen hundred d'marks a night and she'd started with ten.

Okay, Finn, she admitted. It was as if she'd heard the voice. I know I'm pushing it. But it's not just the survival, it's not just the fact that I have food and warmth. It's also the edge which comes with what I'm doing – with what you told me to do. Which you should understand, because that's why you do what you do. It's the adrenalin of making the run to Popovekuce; the thrill that comes with the risks and the rewards; the exhilaration which comes with running the system rather than the system running me.

Different world now, Finn; different me. But what do you expect me to do, why the hell are you questioning?

Adin was still staring at her. She looked again at the photograph, looked at the eyes. Felt the excitement and the resolution and the determination dissolve. As if someone had reached up and switched off the electricity.

I'm sorry – she told Adin, told Finn. You're right, I'm wrong.

She poured the whisky back in the bottle, wrapped a blanket round herself, and sank into the chair.

Keefer saw the door open at six. He watched as the target lowered the pram down the steps then loaded it with the items she had unloaded six hours before, watched as she manhandled it down the road. He knew her approximate routine at the market, therefore he would wait in the street in case anyone else showed at the house. And when he knew both routines, he would take it on a stage, find out the next things about her.

Kara was at her place in the market by seven. By seven-thirty the boy who normally sold cigarettes in the next plot hadn't appeared and his place had been taken by a woman selling what were left of her household items. Perhaps there was no longer a demand for cigarettes, perhaps something had happened to him on the run to or from Popovekuce.

The goods weren't moving as fast this morning. She was still concerned about Adin, still guilty about the way his face and eyes had accused her from the photograph, still worried about Finn. Therefore she wasn't herself, wasn't the wheeler dealer people loved to haggle with, wasn't full of the life and energy that attracted people to her. By eleven she still had a fifth of the sugar and flour. She packed up and drifted into the market, unsure what to do. A man was offering her wood, a woman – young and attractive – was trying to persuade her to buy some clothes. Nice dressing gown, she told Kara. How much, Kara asked. Fifty marks, the woman told her. Two kilos of flour, Kara haggled. But without conviction. Make it sugar – the woman saw the opening. Okay, Kara told her, even though the sugar was worth ten marks more than the woman had asked, and what she had asked was just the starting price and she would have dropped by half.

She stuffed the dressing gown in the pram and trudged through the crowd. You're shuffling, the voice would have told her; your shoulders are bent and you're throwing away your will and your strength. So what, she would have replied. It was time to go back to the room, time to eat and rest before the run to Popovekuce. Except there was suddenly no point. Because Popovekuce wasn't about surviving. Okay, it started that way, but even after the first run it was something else. Take that something else away and the whole reason was gone.

Somewhere to her right a man was arguing with another black marketeer selling flour and sugar, people gathering as they always gathered. Fifteen deutschmarks for flour, the dealer was saying, thirty for sugar. He couldn't afford it, the buyer was protesting; his coat was thin and his face was haggard, his cheeks and eyes sunk.

She drifted a little closer.

'How much?' the man in the thin coat asked again.

'Fifteen and thirty.'

'I need to eat, my wife and children need to eat. But I only have ten.'

The dealer shrugged, the spectators getting bored and moving away. Something about the man, Kara sensed; something about what he was going to do. 'How much?' the man in the thin coat asked again. He moved slightly, slid his right hand into his coat pocket. 'Fifteen,' the dealer was impatient now. 'Take it or leave it.' The gun was in the man's hand before anyone realized. His eyes were staring and his lips were still moving. In the split second before he died the dealer registered fear, then the man pulled the trigger and the single shot entered the dealer's skull slightly above and to the right of the bridge of his nose.

'Now how much is fifteen deutschmarks worth to you?' The man with the thin coat put the gun back in the coat, walked away, and disappeared into the crowd as if he had never existed.

Winners and losers – Kara stared at the body.

It could have been her the man with the gun stopped at, could be her on the ground now. Her time would come sometime, probably sooner rather than later the way she was living, but at least she was living, not eking out some miserable sub-existence. At least she was playing her game her way. She was snapping her fingers, the life and the energy and the urgency were zipping back through her body. The way she was going and the risks she was taking she was going to die. But she was going to die anyway, because everyone did. What mattered was what you did before. What had Finn told her in the hospital in Tesanj? It's not the critic who counts; the credit belongs to the man who is actually in the arena . . . So no problems now, Finn. I'm fine. I know what I'm doing.

Do you, Kara? Do you know what you're doing any more, do you know why?

Back off, Finn. It was you who told me to start, remember. You who told me what to do. Winners and losers, and nothing and no one in between.

The crowd was still gathered round the body and the blood was running towards the bags of flour. 'Take what you want,' Kara told one of the women; she was old and could barely stand, the child in her arms was crying and the shopping bag she carried was empty. 'It's been paid for.'

She left the market and returned to Tobacco Road, made coffee. Crossed the room and picked up the photograph of Adin and Jovan. Sorry, my husband and my son. Love you both and always will. But you and I were a different time and a different place. Perhaps another in the future, but not now. She placed the photograph in the drawer, and closed it. Then she poured two capfuls of whisky into the coffee and sat in front of the stove.

Places to go and things to do – she was snapping her fingers again. Enjoy it because you've worked hard for it. Get back what you put in, and if something comes your way then try it, whatever it is. See if you like it and if you do then try it again; if not, look for something else. So when whoever it is pulls the gun on you, you can laugh in their face and tell them to fuck off before they squeeze the trigger.

Keefer waited two hours after the target had left, then approached the house and went up the steps at the side.

The locks were no problem, though he had not expected them to be.

So who are you, what are you?

He switched on the torch and began the routine. She was organized – the impression was overwhelming. Bed neatly made with blankets and sheets. Carpet on floor and bags of flour and sugar she hadn't sold that day stacked neatly at the side of the dresser. Candles in place ready to be lit, dressing gown and other washing hanging to dry. Scented soap, even hair shampoo. Water ready to heat by the stove and pan of stew simmering on it for her return. Place already laid at table: plate and knife and fork, and freshly made bread. Bottle of whisky in centre of table with glass.

One place at the table; one knife and fork, one glass. The woman, whoever she was, lived alone.

Photograph of man and boy in the top left drawer. Interesting that. Why should anyone keep a photograph but not have it on display where they could see it? Nothing behind the dresser, nothing hidden in or under the bed, no floorboards concealing a hiding place.

Stew smells good; not a bad whisky either. Tomorrow he'd make first contact, see her up close. He checked that the room was as he had found it and left.

The room was welcoming and the smell of the stew wafted in the air. The run that evening had gone well, even though she was tired she'd made the return trip twenty minutes faster than before. Kara stacked the bags against the dresser, locked the pram in the porch, and shut herself off from the world. The stew was good and the whisky was strong; she added a dash of water and ate, enjoying herself and planning the next day. Perhaps she'd get an oil lamp, the light would be better. Perhaps she'd drop her prices slightly tomorrow, offload the surplus and finish at the market earlier, except the prices were in units of five and therefore easy for people to handle.

She finished the meal, cleaned the dishes, then washed and put on clean bra and pants, and the dressing gown she'd bought the morning before. Then she poured another whisky and sat in the armchair by the fire. No cigarettes, she decided; she didn't like them, so there was no point smoking again.

The war won't last for ever – the thought drifted across her mind. And when it ends so will the black market. So make the most of it, maximize her profits so that when peace came, she'd be in a position to move on to something else. Because when the end did come there'd be food and consumer items again but no one would have the money to buy because everyone would have spent their deutschmarks surviving.

The glass was empty. She refilled it, again with a dash of water.

Therefore she'd see how much she really could unload. No point having money in a roll in the purse round her neck, because one mark in your pocket remained one mark, but every mark she spent in Popovekuce turned into ten in Travnik the following morning.

Christ, how life was wonderful if you worked it out. Christ, how she was getting through the whisky. She laughed at herself and poured another glass.

But she was already bringing back as much as she could in one pram, so perhaps she should bring back two – it was a repetition of her thoughts the previous night. But to do that she'd need somebody else. Somebody she could trust; somebody young and strong; somebody who was afraid to go through the lines but who needed the food. And she'd pay in kind, because that way she'd be paying Popovekuce prices. Because then the other person wouldn't screw her. Because they themselves would make a couple of marks on each bag of flour or sugar she paid them, therefore wouldn't want to kill the proverbial golden goose. Therefore she'd start on it in the morning.

She checked the stove and went to bed, stretched out her legs and relaxed. She was still wearing her bra and pants. Don't need them on, she thought, because there's nobody here. Wouldn't need them on if there *was* someone here, of course. Christ, she really was drunk, but what the hell. Winners and losers. Try everything once. Because one day *she'd* be the one on the ground in the market. The bullet in *her* head and *her* blood running down *her* face.

The three Landcruisers left Zenica thirty minutes before first light; an hour later they passed through the Muslim section of the first front line. Two hours later, having waited patiently at the Serb-Croat section, they passed into the land held by the people whom the Muslims called the Chetniks.

It was mid-morning, the land frozen and the air bitterly cold. They passed through two tunnels, one long and one short, neither lit and both rutted. Ahead of them, bleak and cold, was the grey metal structure of a bridge.

'Half an hour to the next cross point.' Stacey looked back at Finn and took the mug of coffee the interpreter passed him.

'Stop . . .' Finn pushed past the interpreter and grabbed the wheel, Stacey braking hard. Land mine, he thought; why the hell had he looked back, why had the interpreter passed the mug? They were halfway over the bridge, the other Landcruisers braking and sliding on the ice. 'Close,' he said.

The section of bridge in front of them had been blasted away.

He wound down the window, motioned to the other drivers to reverse, and pulled back slowly till they were on the approach road to the bridge. The road itself was built up slightly, the bank on either side gradual then dropping more sharply to the fields. Hope to hell there are no mines. Almost certain to be, he knew. 'Tracks to the left,' Finn told him. 'Someone's been through ahead of us.' Therefore they'd either be confronted with a mangled vehicle, or the detour would be safe. Stacey flicked the vehicle into four-wheel low and eased down the slope. The main river was beneath the section of the bridge which still appeared intact. They splashed through the river bed, jerking to avoid the rocks and boulders, and pulled up the steep slope on the other side. Five minutes later they were back on the remainder of the bridge. Thirty minutes after that they saw the barbed wire and road mines of the Serb-Croat sector of the front line round the Maglaj–Tesanj pocket.

Kara had been in the market an hour when Keefer arrived. The first light was streaking the sky, the queue at the food kitchen already wound round three sides of the building, and the marketplace was beginning to fill with the human shadows of the new day.

Give it an hour, he decided, perhaps two; but watch her, see how she was operating today, make sure no one was helping her. Then make the first contact. He left the marketplace, did the trawl of the Gymnasium and the food kitchen, as well as the other places a talent spotter might look, then began to return to the market.

As he passed the boarded-up shop in the main street where the men from the front line sometimes stopped to be fed the mercenary called Walton came out. He was looking cold, but everyone was, stubble on his face and his parka pulled tight. Haven't seen you for a couple of days – Keefer watched as Walton went down the street. Wonder what you've been up to and how you've been rubbing up Akram and the rest of the Muj. Stupid bastard:

pretending he was one of the hard men from the front, making people get off the pavement for him.

He waited till Walton was out of sight, then cut right, crossed the bridge by the Gymnasium, and melted into the crowd in the market.

The target was doing well – he was positioned so he could see her, moving location occasionally, apparently drifting with the crowd and not conspicuous in the fatigues he was wearing because there were other men similarly dressed.

Time to do it, he thought.

What the hell was Walton doing?

The mercenary was bundling through the crowd. Keefer slid away and waited for the idiot to clear the area. Don't stop at her plot; don't do anything to fuck it up for me.

'How much?' Walton's Serbo-Croat was poor and Kara didn't understand.

'How much?' Walton asked, this time in English. 'How much?' he asked again, louder, as if it would help.

Move on, Keefer willed him, don't hang around.

'How much for what?' Kara asked.

'You speak English?' The smile spread across Walton's face.

Keefer was close enough to hear. She's alone, she's organized, she's got something in her past about two people whose photograph she doesn't look at, she's working the black market, and now she speaks English.

It was a scam, a come-on. Someone was setting him up just as he'd set up so many in Berlin in the old days. Except he'd stumbled on her by chance, had to go looking for her, and the day he'd gone looking she hadn't been there. Which was the way he himself would have set it up, what he'd done so well and so often in the past.

'You speak English?' Walton asked.

Kara shook her head as if she barely understood. Good girl, Keefer almost whispered. Because you speak it much better than you're pretending, because you've seen through Walton and want him off your back.

'English,' Walton told Kara, speaking slowly and loudly. Keefer knew what Walton was going to do next, because it was what he always did. Walton took off his parka, rolled up his right sleeve, and pointed to the tattoo on his forearm. 'SAS,' he said. 'Special Air Service.' He flung his hand to the sky, as if to indicate that the cold did not bother him. Clasped his right hand into a ball and jerked his right lower arm up. 'Hard.'

Kara shook her head again, as if she still did not understand. Good girl, Keefer thought a second time. Walton sniffed, pulled on the parka, and pushed back through the crowd.

There was another man in combat gear looking at her, Kara was aware. Glancing at the first man as he moved away then back at her, shaking his head in disbelief then seeing she was looking at him. First contact, Keefer thought. Not the way he had been going to do it, but it had been so natural, so easy. Too good to miss. The target was looking at him. He shook his head and laughed, as if sharing the joke. Kara understood and laughed back. That's life – Keefer's shrug said it all. He turned away, still laughing and shaking his head, and moved deeper into the market.

Kara left an hour later. She'd moved everything, including the surplus from yesterday, and could have shifted double the amount. When she returned to Tobacco Road it was late morning and she could hear the family from whom she rented the room. She pulled off her coat and boots, sank into the armchair by the stove, and rested for half an hour. Then she put the bags of sugar and flour, the plastic bottle of cooking oil and some coffee on the table, and knocked on the door separating her room from the main house.

The door was bolted on the other side; she heard the scrabbling, then the wife opened the door and stood back a little.

'Thought I ought to pay you for next week,' Kara told her. 'I also thought you might like some coffee.'

'Thank you.' The woman took the items. 'Come through,' she suddenly said, 'share the coffee with us.' She led Kara through.

'Stove working well?' the husband asked.

'Couldn't be better. Thanks again for all you did.' Are you the ones? Not you, of course, because you're both too old. But are you the ones who know the person I'm looking for? 'The pram works a treat.'

The husband laughed and the wife placed the cups on the table and poured them each a coffee. 'By yourself?' she asked.

'My family are all dead.' Kara raised the cup. 'Which is why I do what I do. The only way to eat.'

They nodded as if they understood. Keep building, Kara told herself. Don't simply wait for the opening to come, engineer it yourself. 'If there's anything you want that I could help with,' she suggested.

They nodded their thanks. Because there are a lot of things – it was in the furrows on their faces and the worry in their eyes.

'You have a family?' Kara asked. 'Apart from your sister.'

'A daughter.' The wife nodded. 'Nineteen years old with a little girl. It's harder for them than it is for us.'

'Her husband's at the front?'

'He was wounded. Not badly, but enough to send him home. Waiting till they send him back and hoping they won't.'

It's opening up for you, Kara; but when you're winning everything runs your way. So don't screw it, don't lose it. 'As you said, it must be hard for them.'

'Very.'

'Better go.' Kara pushed the chair back. 'As I said, if there's anything you or they want.' She stood to leave. 'Actually . . .' They were going for it, she knew. 'Actually . . . Why doesn't your son-in-law help me?'

She sat down again. 'It's hard bringing the stuff back. Even with your pram.' She laughed and made them laugh back. 'He wouldn't have to work in the market, of course. He could just help me carry the stuff.'

I'd pay him, she was going to say next, deutschmarks if he wanted, but I'm sure he and your daughter would prefer food.

'He wouldn't go near the front.' It was the husband.

The wife was making more coffee, Kara noted; the deal was already done. 'He wouldn't have to.' Because I wouldn't want him to, because if he came with me to Popovekuce he would see how easy it really is. 'We'd go together; he'll never have to go by himself.' She changed the verb tense. 'He'll wait this side of the border, I'll go through and buy the stuff and bring it back through the lines, then he'll help me haul it back here.'

'And you'll pay him?'

'A kilo of flour and a kilo of sugar every trip. Or the equivalent.' In cooking oil or coffee or whatever you and he want. 'Plus . . .' She made them wait. 'Plus he can sell what I don't sell in the market, and take a commission on it.'

'How much commission?'

'For flour, sugar and cooking oil . . . say three marks.'

'Six.' Because they had to negotiate.

'Four.'

'Five.'

They shook hands on it.

'You need to check with him?' Kara asked.

'He'll do it,' the woman told her. 'What time do you want him tonight?'

'Four o'clock, to meet and talk it through. We'll leave at four-thirty.'

'Anything else?' the husband asked.

'How about another pram, then he could haul one and I could haul the other.'

'Tomorrow afternoon,' the husband nodded, then glanced at his wife. What are you thinking? Because I'm thinking the same. 'Actually our son-in-law has a brother. Big boy. Very strong.'

Say the son-in-law pulled fifty kilos a night and she pulled thirty – the figures were already twirling in her head. Averaging a mark-up of fifteen marks per item for the items she sold, and ten for those he sold, that would make her almost a thousand marks a night. And fifty kilos was less than an average body weight, so the boy could probably haul a lot more. Give it a week, then bring in his brother. And three pulling together could haul far more than three hauling individually. Hell, she could be a millionaire by Christmas.

'I think one is enough for the moment.'

It was always better to leave people wanting a little more.

The light was fading and they had been waiting three hours, the Serb barbed wire and land mines were still in front of them and the Muslim barbed wire and mines somewhere beyond.

Time to turn back, Finn began to think. Except there was a front line ahead of them, another behind, and themselves in the middle.

'Shouldn't be long now.' Stacey accepted a mug and settled in the seat. He and the interpreter had left the vehicle twice, talked and argued with the officers in charge, then shared a cigarette and a slivovic with them, argued with them again.

Nick was a good man, Finn thought, a good operator. And the interpreter was a saint. 'How'd you mean?'

Stacey's shrug said it. Been here, seen it, done it.

'You hope.'

Stacey laughed.

The afternoon light was long gone. Keefer turned into the village and drove up the track to the cluster of houses where he and Bergmann shared a room. There was something wrong: either too many Muj hanging round the corners, or too few. From the house on the edge of the woods to the right he heard someone scream. He picked up the Heckler and went to the room.

Bergmann was inside, cooking supper from one of the self-heat packs, his AK on the table.

'What's up?' Keefer asked.

'One of the sections of the front that the Muj were manning took a hammering last night. Akram lost some of his best guys. Now he wants blood.'

'Whose?' Keefer knew whose.

'Walton's.'

He could do with a coffee, Keefer thought. 'Ours as well?'

'Probably. But I thought it best to wait till there were two of us.'

'Better sort Akram out, then.'

They left the room, locked the door, and crossed the darkness to the torture house. There were three Mujihadeen on the door, each armed with a Kalashnikov. Keefer ignored them and pushed his way inside. The room they were using was on the ground floor to the right. Akram himself was standing impassively, watching without any reaction.

Round him were a circle of ten more Mujihadeen. In the centre, naked and strapped to a chair, was the mercenary called Walton. His face, his body and his genitals were scarred with cigarette burns and his mouth was twisted where his jaw had been broken.

Bit primitive, Keefer thought, probably effective with someone like Walton, though.

Akram saw them enter and waited for either Keefer or Bergmann to react. Save me, Keefer saw the pleading in Walton's eyes; you're white, you're a Christian, save me from these bastards. Akram nodded and one of the men applied the cigarette butt again.

'Who did you lose last night?' Keefer asked.

Akram told him.

'Good men. They should not be forgotten.' Keefer was deliberately formal.

It was not the reaction Akram expected. '*Shukran*,' he told Keefer. Thank you.

'*La shukr ala wajeb*,' Keefer replied. No thanks are necessary where it is my duty.

Walton was squirming, twisting, trying to avoid the next pain. Any moment now Walton would start talking – Keefer looked at him. And when he started talking Walton would say anything to stop the pain. Anything Akram wanted to hear, whether or not it was the truth. Probably something about Keefer and Bergmann, which wasn't good news; almost certainly something about the guys he'd met and the people he'd spoken to that day.

Walton would say he'd spoken to a woman in the market who spoke English.

'Untie him,' Keefer told one of the Mujihadeen.

The fingers moved on the guns. Akram looked at Keefer, studied his face and his eyes, the men in the room waiting for his orders. Akram nodded and one of them undid the rope binding Walton to the chair.

Thanks – it was in Walton's eyes, in his body language. Now let's get the fuck out of here.

So what's this about – it was in Akram's eyes. What are you going to do now?

'Tie his feet,' Keefer ordered. 'Hands behind his back.'

Walton's eyes were rolling and his face was contorted with a combination of hope and fresh fear.

'Outside,' Keefer ordered.

Two of the Mujihadeen lifted Walton from the chair and dragged him across the floor and out of the house.

'Rope?' Keefer asked. He tied one end round Walton's ankles and threw the other over the branch of a tree. Up – he indicated with a wave of his hand. 'You want a *dhabiha*?' he asked Akram.

Walton was hanging head down, his body swaying gently and his arms at a grotesque angle because his hands were tied behind his back.

Keefer wouldn't do it, Akram knew. No way Keefer would give him a *dhabiha*. 'Yes,' he said. He turned to the man on his immediate right and motioned with a sweep of his hand. The Mujihadeen reached in his battledress and took out the Brusletto, wooden handle, razor-edge single-sided blade, the manufacturer's name stamped on the polished metal.

No way Keefer would do it, Akram still knew. No way Keefer would give him a sacrificial lamb.

Keefer took the Brusletto, stood behind Walton so that the blood would spurt away from him, pulled Walton's head back with his left hand, and cut his throat with his right.

The torch flickered in the gloom, then the soldiers rolled back the wire and waved them through. Finn and Stacey left the lead vehicle and went ahead, Stacey holding the lamp and Finn moving the mines. Bastards, Finn thought.

Held us up till dusk. Light going fast, so the Muslims half a kilometre ahead won't know who we are. Won't have any reason to believe we're not the opposition, so will blast the hell out of us.

They walked back, climbed in, and drove on. Slowly, headlights flashing, hazard warning lights blinking, and horn blasting a regular pattern. 'There it is.' Stacey turned the Landcruiser sideways across the road, so that the soldiers concealed in the dark could see the white bodywork and the UN lettering. Then he switched the headlights off, leaving on the sidelights and hazard lights, got out, and walked slowly towards the wire, his arms held out from his sides.

'United Nations,' he shouted. 'Medicine for Maglaj.'

Twenty minutes later they entered the town. The streets were in darkness and the shells were coming in. The gunners on the hills ordered to give them a little reception, Finn assumed. So a few more houses would be destroyed and a few more people would die, and all because he'd asked Stacey to get him here. The Red Cross centre was in front of them. They pulled into the shelter of a narrow street next to it, and ran inside.

The Popovekuce run had gone well.

Nedim, the son-in-law, had arrived early. He was in his early twenties, strong build and black hair, and walked with a limp. Outside the town, though, both on the outward journey and the way back, he walked better, no sign of a limp at all. He'd done his bit for his people, Kara thought, so perhaps she couldn't blame him.

Half a kilometre from the front line they had found a place where he could wait and she had gone on alone. At Popovekuce she had loaded the pram heavier than normal, laughed at The Fat Man when he asked her whether or not she would make it back, and made the haul back to where Nedim was waiting. After that he had taken the strain, pulling harder than she could have, often hauling the pram by himself but not minding.

When they reached Travnik it was not quite eleven-thirty. 'Fastest run so far,' she told him. They carried the load up the steps, then she gave him the night's pay of a kilo of flour, plus one of sugar. 'One more thing.' She split the load into two – three-quarters for herself to sell in the marketplace the next morning, and one quarter for him to try to sell among his contacts. 'See how you get on tomorrow. If you shift it you can have more.'

They moved his quarter through the connecting door to his in-laws' house.

'Thanks,' he told her. 'See you tomorrow, four-thirty.'

She told him to wait, went back to her room, pulled two hundred deutschmarks off the roll she carried in the purse round her neck, then went back and gave them to him. 'Roll them up and make sure people see them. Looks good, makes them think you know what you're doing, therefore they'll want to buy from you. Make a show of them. Pay me back when you can.'

Which would be tomorrow or the day after, the following day at the latest. Because Nedim was hers, to do with as she wanted. Because she'd opened the golden door and allowed Nedim to peep inside, and Nedim had liked what he had seen.

She bolted the door, poured herself a whisky, then ate and heated the water. When she had finished she undressed, poured herself another whisky, and washed, slower than last night and smelling the fragrance of the soap.

Winners and losers. Try everything once, if she liked it try it again, if not then move on to something else.

Try what?

The glass was empty already. She poured herself another and sipped it, began to put on a clean bra and pants, and dressing gown. Kept the dressing gown on but slipped off the bra and pants, and slid into bed. Knew what she'd been thinking, because she'd been thinking it all day.

The food queue was wound round the Red Cross kitchen and the first shells had landed on the town.

'How long will you be?' Stacey asked.

'One hour, two max.'

Finn left the basement and made his way to the bridge. No sniper, he prayed, and ran over. The streets of the old town were lined with rubble, a dog sniffed its way past him, and an old man pushing a wheelbarrow slipped down a side street. He made his way up the hill, remembering the details and the last time he had been here, and anticipating the surprise on Kara's face, seeing little Jovan's excitement when he held his present and Adin's pride when Finn told him what his wife had done.

Might have to wait, he reminded himself; Kara or Adin might be at the food kitchen. Should have checked. He turned the corner.

Even since Kara had left, the shell of the house had deteriorated. The side walls had collapsed further, and the little that remained of the lowest floor was totally covered in charred and shattered beams and masonry. He took off the bergen and examined the wreckage, tried to work out how and when it had happened, whether there was any indication of survivors. Kara wouldn't die like this, he tried to tell himself. Kara wouldn't let Adin or Jovan die like this. Kara would make sure they were okay. Perhaps Jovan was still in hospital, perhaps they'd decided to stay in Tesanj rather than risk the run back to Maglaj.

He pulled the bergen on his back, went back down the hill, crossed the bridge, and made his way to the basement.

'Problems?' Stacey asked.

'The house has been hit by a shell, no indication whether they're dead or alive.'

'What do you want to do?'

'Check with the hospital in Tesanj.'

'We've saved some supplies for there anyway.'

'Thanks, Nick.'

Second contact, Keefer thought; the target in position and everything normal, no Walton to worry about this morning. It was nine-thirty and she was doing well, had sold more than half the items in her pram and looked like moving the rest quickly.

'How much is the flour?' he asked in Serbo-Croat. He had drifted into the front row of people, now he stood relaxed and confident. Not over-relaxed, not over-confident, simply not threatening.

'Fifteen deutschmarks. How's your friend?'

'Sorry?' Perhaps he didn't understand, perhaps it was a ploy. Either way it was friendly, the gentlest shake of the head that he didn't understand. Not loud or spoken slowly, though, not hostile or condescending.

'How's your friend?' Kara asked in English this time.

Soldier's clothes but not a soldier, she thought, though she was unsure why. Probably the way he stood, as if he was confident and disciplined but not regimented. Strange how she had taken so much of him in already.

'Not my friend.' Keefer laughed. 'Shouldn't think he'll worry you again, though.'

Because he'd dealt with him – she felt a frisson. Because somehow and somewhere, the man in front of her had taken the other aside and talked to him, told him not to pester her again. More than that, she realized, because the other man wouldn't have listened to just a talking-to.

'Thanks.' She looked him in the eyes.

He'd gone too far too fast, Keefer thought; had said

something which sounded simple and she'd picked him up on it. Amazing eyes, red with fatigue and circled with black, but so alert, so alive. Christ, it was as though she was making contact with him rather than the other way round. He shook his head as if to dismiss her thanks or deny there was a reason. She's stretched out, he thought, she's so stretched out she doesn't know where she is. She's on the wire and running on self destruct, but she's got a room together, and a nice little black market set-up.

'What about the sugar?' He was still staring at her. Wrong thing to do and wrong time to do it, he reprimanded himself.

'Thirty.' She realized she was still staring at him. What is it, Kara, what are you telling him and why?

'A kilo of each.' What are you thinking, Keefer. You know what you're thinking, and you also know you shouldn't be thinking it.

'Forty-five marks.' Stop thinking it, Kara, because it's what you were thinking in bed last night.

She gave him the bags and he gave her the money.

'Whisky?' he asked.

You're in bed with her already, he told himself, and that's not why you're here. Okay, so that's one way of recruiting, the old way back in the old days. But this situation is different.

'Seventy deutschmarks a bottle.'

Stop thinking it, Kara. Christ this is crazy. Because he's thinking it as well.

'I'll have two.'

Someone pushed in and asked for flour, said he wanted five kilos and asked for a special price. She dealt with him briskly and efficiently, arguing and laughing.

'I don't have any whisky today,' she told Keefer.

On the edge, she told herself; try anything once and if she liked it then try it again. One day it could be *her* lying in the snow, the bullet in *her* head and the blood trickling down *her* cheek.

'How about tomorrow?' You're playing this wrong, Keefer. But it's working. This one will go anywhere and do anything, this one will take on the world and win. More than that. This one is so tired and worn, but so cold and controlled, that she scares you witless.

'Pay me now,' she told him. 'That's one hundred and forty marks, and I can't afford to carry it if you don't come back,' she explained.

'I'll be back.'

'Okay, pay me tomorrow.'

An hour after leaving Maglaj they were in the doctor's room in the hospital in Tesanj. The snow and wind tore through the tarpaulin which covered the hole of what had once been the children's ward, and the patients and operating rooms had been crammed into the basement areas.

'I was here a few weeks back. Brought in a kid from Maglaj suffering from appendicitis.'

'Jovan?'

Why should someone remember one boy, Finn wondered. What had happened to make the doctor remember?

'Yes, Jovan. You operated on him, saved his life.'

'He's dead.' Perhaps the doctor was so accustomed to death he no longer felt a reaction. Perhaps he had learned that if he was to survive, and especially if he was to survive in order to help others, reaction and feelings were things he could no longer afford. 'He was killed when the shells hit the children's ward. He's buried on the hill.'

The makeshift cemetery on the hill, because the old one was full and exposed to sniper fire.

'Thanks.'

Borrow the motor, he asked Stacey.

''Course. You want company?'

'No.'

He drove through the town and up the hill, found the wooden headpiece among the many, knelt by the snow-covered mound and wiped the ice from the wood. Saw the two names on it.

Adin Isak. 1962–1994.

Jovan Isak. 1990–1994.

Not Adin as well – his mind and body were numb. The doctor had said the son was dead, but not the father. So what did you do then – he knew Janner would ask. He pulled down the hood of the parka, came to attention, and stood stiff in the cold and the snow. Not the Lord's Prayer, he decided, because he didn't know what religion Adin and Jovan were, because Kara herself had been unclear. Instead he said the words of the poem. Not aloud, to anyone else. But aloud anyway. To the wind and the snow and to the black gathered round him. The verse of the poem written fifty years before, which Caz had found in a book and given to him.

Thank you, God, for moments free from pain.
Thank you for thy warmth of sun – and cooling rain.
Thank you for the faith and strength to bear
The weight of those who need our loving care.
And when we falter, helpless, tired and weak,
Hold out your hand. Give us the grace we seek.

The third verse of a poem found on a scrap of a paper in the women's concentration camp at Ravensbrück.

What about the regiment – Janner would also ask. Finn was still at attention, still bareheaded in the winter snow.

O Lord, who didst call on thy disciples to venture all to win all men to thee, grant that we, the chosen members of the Special Air Service Regiment, may by our works and our ways dare all to win all . . .

Where are you, Kara? How are you? How can I find you, help you?

The next grave was that of a woman. Asra Salko. Funny the details you remembered, he would think later, but that was part of the training. Notice the little things, because sometime a little thing might be important.

What else did you do, he knew Janner would also ask. He took the hip flask from his pocket, and raised it above the grave. 'Janner and Max and me and the boys,' he said aloud. Then he sipped from it, screwed the top back on and drove back to the hospital. Found the doctor and asked about the death of Adin Isak.

'Sorry.' The doctor was white-faced with fatigue. 'I should have told you, I forgot.'

'You're busy,' Finn told him. 'You can't deal with everything.'

'Thanks anyway.'

By the time Kara returned from Popovekuce it was one in the morning. The run that night had taken longer, but only because it had gone according to plan. The husband from the house had delivered the second pram, Nedim had been early, and they had reached what she termed the pick-up point, half a kilometre from the front line, an hour and a half after dark. She had gone in with one pram, loaded it as high as she could, and hauled it back to Nedim; then she had shared a bar of chocolate with him and gone back with the second pram, filled it with slightly less.

'Expanding?' The Fat Man had joked.

'Got to,' she had replied.

'Back tomorrow night?'

'Of course.'

'Build in an extra fifteen minutes this end. Somebody might want to make you an offer.'

The room was warm and the items sorted: her load to sell in the market, Nedim's to sell wherever and however he wanted, the payment to her, minus his commission, the following night.

'Your brother. Is he as good as you?'

'He's okay.'

'Will he cross the front line?'

'No.'

'Okay. Two prams between the three of us, that way we can really load up mine. The same commission as you. Unless you want to sub-contract.' Divide and rule, she thought.

'Same commission as me.'

'See you both tomorrow.'

How she enjoyed it, how she savoured the risks, how she feasted on the edge. She bolted the door and heated the food and water. So what did The Fat Man mean, what was someone going to offer her? Except that wasn't what the nerves in her stomach were about.

The whisky was hot and strong, and her head was swimming slightly now. She ate and washed, then sat in the armchair with the dressing gown loose around her, her stomach knotted and her fingers slightly trembling. Made herself wait. Only after another glass of whisky did she rise, cross the room, and slide into the bed. Christ, she felt good, felt on the edge. She stretched her hands above her head, enjoying the tension in her arms, and stretched her legs. Made herself wait again. The man in the marketplace was above her, around her, inside her and all over her – she could see him, feel him. Light as a feather and hard as a rod. She was wide open, body moving round her fingers and her fingers moving inside her. Do it to me, she was telling him. Any way you want. Long and hard and not stopping.

*

The hospital was quiet. Finn sat against the corridor wall and stared into the black.

Why the guilt, Finn?

Because I killed Jovan and Adin.

How? Kara asked him. What do you mean?

Because if I hadn't brought Jovan here he wouldn't have been in the ward when the shell hit.

But if you hadn't brought Jovan here he would have died the next day. You didn't kill him, you saved his life. Something else killed him, someone else.

I still killed him, Kara.

You didn't, Finn.

What about Adin? If I hadn't brought Jovan here, Adin wouldn't have come here, therefore I killed Adin as well.

You didn't, Finn, you didn't kill Adin. What is it, Finn? What are you really thinking?

You want to know? You really want to know?

Yes, Finn. I really want to know.

I'm thinking about the cas-evac. I'm thinking about the night we got Janner and Max out by chopper. You asked if I could take Jovan, and I said I couldn't. But I could have. And if I had then he and Adin would both be alive. So that's why I say I killed them both.

'You okay?' Stacey came down the corridor and sat beside him.

'Probably.'

'What do you want to do next?'

'Go back to Maglaj and ask if anyone knows what happened to her.'

Which he should have done in the first place.

Don't show yet, Kara almost told him, because the waiting is part of the game. Don't make the contact too early, Keefer reminded himself, because that way you spoil the play.

It was nine, the morning not quite as cold as the previous day but still eight below. It was nine-thirty, nine forty-five, people pushing and haggling and eventually buying because they knew they had to.

'Get my whisky?'

'Of course.' She reached into the pram and gave him the two bottles.

'One-forty.' He counted the notes and gave them to her.

She began serving someone else, Keefer hanging on the side of the plot as they both knew he would.

'What are you doing here?' he asked.

'Surviving.'

'Doing more than surviving.' He looked at the items in the pram.

'Depends how you define it,' she came back at him.

The conversation was in segments, interrupted by people pushing and jostling and hoping for a bargain.

'What about you?' she asked. 'What are you doing here?'

'This and that.'

'Front line?'

'I'm not a soldier.'

'So what are you doing here?'

'Like I said, this and that.'

The market was still crowded, locals and refugees and what the international agencies called displaced persons.

'Where did you learn English?' Keefer slid the question in.

'At university, I used to be a teacher. I also speak German.' Because you're German and that, for some reason, was what you wanted to know.

'Family?' He deliberately kept the question to one word.

'No family.'

'No husband?' Because someone like you must be married, someone as good-looking as you must have guys lining up.

'He's dead,' she told him.

Probably a son as well, he realized; the father and son in the photograph she'd hidden in the drawer of the dresser. Except there was no other sign of the son in the room.

Why tell him, she asked herself, why talk with him. 'You?' she asked.

'Divorced.'

'Children?'

'One,' he said. 'Somewhere,' he added. Why, Keefer? Why say that even though it's true. Why give away a personal detail when that's the sort of thing you're supposed to be getting from her. Because she was also cross-examining him; because she knew the conversation wasn't accidental and wanted to know why.

'Somewhere?' She came back at him.

'Doesn't matter.' Because when the Wall came down my wife went West with my son and I never saw them again. Christ, Keefer; what the hell are you doing, what are you playing at? She's going to come at you now, he told himself, so get ready, be prepared for it.

'So why are you buying from me?'

'How'd you mean?'

'I've seen you in the market before. Watching someone arguing over prices.'

'Arguing about flour.'

She sold some more flour, more sugar, the pram almost empty now.

'The woman with the TV set,' Keefer told her.

'What about her?'

'I wanted to see who'd bought her coat and boots.'

A woman to his left bought the last cooking oil. Kara took down the polythene from the tree and packed it in the pram.

'Ciao,' she told him.

'What time shall I see you tonight?'

'I don't get back from Popovekuce till eleven.'

'I'll see you then. I'll bring some food. I'm in the mountains, the people there aren't exactly pleasant.'

'I'll show you where I live.'

They crossed the town, climbed Tobacco Road, and came to the house with the side steps to the room.

'I might be earlier, might be slightly later,' she told him. 'I'll be with a couple of helpers, wait till they've gone.'

'You haven't asked why?' He pushed it one stage further.

'This and that.' She threw the words back at him.

'I'll bring some whisky.'

'Don't worry, I already have some.'

The women who cooked the Red Cross food in the small basement kitchen beneath Radio Maglaj were in the break between the morning and afternoon sessions. The cellar was dark and dank, and a rat scuttled in a corner.

'Kara Isak,' Stacey's interpreter asked. 'Used to live in the old town. Her husband and little boy were both killed. Any idea where she is now?'

'No,' they were told.

'Kara Isak,' the interpreter asked the women in the distribution centre. 'Do you know her, do you see her at all?'

'Used to see her,' they told her. 'Not any more.'

'Kara Isak,' the interpreter asked the woman who ran the medical centre. 'Little boy called Jovan. Had appendicitis and was taken to the hospital in Tesanj. Any idea what happened to her after?'

'Sorry,' the doctor told them, 'no idea.'

Because I see so many here, have so many patients.

They began to leave.

'Kara Isak,' the doctor said, looked at Finn. I know you, because you and the others brought Jovan in and left me some food. I know Jovan, because I helped him into this world. Except so much has happened since, and Jovan is just one of the many things I have tried to wipe from my mind, because otherwise I could not keep going. 'Little Jovan was killed when the Chetniks shelled the hospital. Husband killed by a sniper.'

'Yes,' Finn told her. 'How'd you know?' he asked.

'Kara told me before she left.'

'Where did she say she was going?'

The doctor struggled to remember. 'Travnik, I think.'

Because she has a grandmother there – Finn remembered. Though Christ knows how she'd have made it, because Travnik is across two sets of front lines.

Nedim and his brother were at the pick-up point, and The Fat Man was waiting. The flames shot from the dustbins and the halo of light hung over the four houses and garage which constituted Popovekuce. Kara loaded the first pram high, crossed to the pick-up point and returned with the second. The Fat Man nodded for her to join him at the side of his van. She left the pram where she could see it and followed him. This is where they take me out, she suddenly thought; this is where they rape me and rob me and leave me for dead. Except The Fat Man wouldn't do that, because The Fat Man meant it when he told her someone wanted to make her an offer.

The second man was smaller and thinner, with dark eyes.

'You seem to be doing well.' He shook her hand.

'Doing okay.' She waited.

'My friend . . .' he indicated The Fat Man '. . . my friend suggested that you might be able to help me.'

'Your friend said you wanted to make me an offer.'

'I may as well come to the point.'

'Yes.'

'I'm buying, not selling.' He lit a cigarette and waited to see how she would respond.

'What exactly?'

'Medical supplies.'

'What exactly?' she asked again.

'Whatever you can get. Syringes, dressings, suture packs. Morphine and pethidine. Any fluids. Saline etc. Haemaccel.'

You can't, Finn's voice told her. These people are the enemy, you can't sell to them. You can't because the stuff he's asking for is for the front line, and you know it.

But I'm already buying from them, the logic came back at her. So what's the difference. 'Price?' she asked.

'Depends what you can get.'

'I'll think about it.' Because all I can think about at the moment is the man in the marketplace at Travnik. 'Let you know tomorrow night.'

She piled the pram and crossed back across the front line. Two hours later they reached Travnik, Nedim and his brother pulling the loads and her stomach churning. The white Landcruiser was parked in the street opposite.

'Good night's work,' she told the boys as they broke up the load. 'Need a flash roll?' she asked Nedim's brother when they had finished.

'Got one. Nedim's seen me all right.'

She poured herself a whisky, pulled off her coat and boots, put the water on to heat, and heard the knock on the door. Keefer was sitting on the pram, a food pack in his left hand.

'Good to see you.' He looked round as if he had not seen the room before.

'You too.' She poured him a whisky.

He took off his parka and boots and laid them by hers. 'You're cold.' He felt her cheek.

'It's not summer.'

They ate, the self-heating food on the plates and the candle flickering, most of the conversation unimportant and inconsequential, something important slipped in but only occasionally.

'Where are you from?'

'Doesn't matter.'

'Where are you going?'

A laugh. 'No idea.'

'When did you last go to bed with someone?' Keefer poured them each another whisky.

'Another lifetime ago.'

'How do you like to make love?'

'Any way you want.'

'Any way?'

'Any.'

When they finished it was gone three, almost four.

'You okay?' he asked.

'Yes.'

'Want some coffee?'

'Prefer whisky.'

'Enjoy it?' He gave her the glass. 'Like it all? What about when it hurt?'

'What do you think?'

'Do it again?'

'Why not?'

They lay back.

'What about you?' she asked. 'Like it?'

'You have to be joking,' he told her. 'Tomorrow night?' he asked.

'Why not?'

'I'd like someone else to come as well.'

'Why?'

'To see how far you'll go and what you're like when you get there.'

'You mean how I am with two men?'

'Yes.'

'Why?'

Okay, so partly the sex. Partly because he wanted to know how far she would really go psychologically as well as physically, and what she'd be like when she got there. Whether she kept or lost control. But okay, sexually as well. What she'd be like and how far she'd go, how far she'd make him want to go. You're pushing it, he told himself. Why not stop now. Why risk everything?

On the edge, she reminded herself. Winners and losers. Risk as much as you can and try as much as you can before it's your turn. See if you like it and if you do then have some more. In a couple of hours she'd begin making her way to the market, she thought. She finished the glass and poured them each another.

Finn and Stacey's interpreter left Zenica at eight, skirting the Croat ring around Vitez and clearing the Muslim road block outside Travnik by nine. For the next seven hours they scoured the food kitchens, the Gymnasium, and the market area next to it. At four they returned to the food kitchen and checked again.

'UNHCR,' the interpreter told the woman doing the paperwork. 'We're looking for someone. Any ideas how we might find her?' She offered the woman a cigarette and left the packet on the table.

'Local?'

'No, displaced person.'

'So she'd be using this kitchen?'

'Presumably.'

'In that case she'd be on the list.'

'What list?'

'There's a list of refugees, displaced persons and others who've been issued with ration cards. It's to make sure they're not collecting food at more than one centre.'

'Any chance of checking if she's on it?'

'Give me her name and call back tomorrow.'

# 8

The Mercedes was the third car to arrive, Abu Sharaf tucked low in the right rear seat. Rue Léopold was quiet. Tonight would be a good night. Tonight was already a good night. Because tonight the first of the recruits Keefer had spirited out of Bosnia would slip into the secret training camp in Afghanistan.

Sharaf walked the two paces to the lift and was escorted to the third floor.

The financier and the politician were waiting, relaxed and comfortable in the armchairs, the sweet black coffee on the low glass-topped table between them and the cigarette smoke curling above them. As he entered they rose.

'Bosnia went well?' the financier asked.

'Very well,' Abu Sharaf confirmed. 'The first shipment comes in tonight.' Even in situations like the present he slipped into metaphors.

The other two understood and nodded. 'Excellent.'

The aide Kamir poured them each another coffee and left the room.

The holy man arrived two minutes later; after three hours the meeting ended and the four participants returned to their apparently separate worlds. Ninety-six hours after that Kamir took his customary coffee with the Englishman called Burton.

They were seated in a salon off the Street called Straight in Damascus, the pavements outside dusted with snow and the windows running with condensation.

It was the way both Burton and the system he represented operated. Sometimes you were lucky, accessed those with hard intelligence, though this was not Burton's brief. Occasionally you infiltrated the organizations in which you had a present or future interest. That again was not Burton's task, though it came close to what he had done on occasions in the past, albeit that had been in Northern Ireland, rather than the Middle East. Often you spent your time trawling, picking up the rag-ends of rumour, gossip and innuendo on which the analysts in London thrived, and which he and they referred to as Soukh News. Often, therefore, you spent what appeared to be your leisure time with people like Kamir – an aide to a more important aide. People who enjoyed the company of an Englishman who spoke their language and who himself enjoyed their company. Because even so late in the twentieth century, there was an affinity and a bond between them.

For the first thirty minutes, therefore, they nodded over the latest rumours and intrigues, mainly political but also social, both men contributing and Kamir enjoying the information Burton had somehow acquired from other such meetings. For the next thirty they discussed developments in Iraq, the future of Saddam Hussein, the continued lack of democracy in Kuwait, and the first indications of Islamic fundamentalism in Saudi Arabia. For the hour after that they played *tawli*, still laughing their way through the maze of political, financial and military gossip drifting in the circles each occupied. For the twenty minutes after that, in the time before they each departed, they again discussed the problems posed by Saddam and the effect the UN sanctions were having on Iraq, and whether they were strengthening or weakening his grip on that country.

Sometime in the middle mention was made of Kamir's trip to Brussels; sometime towards the end mention was also made of the late night meeting in the apartment on

Rue Léopold and the identities of those who had attended, with the exception of the third man to arrive that night, whose face Kamir knew, but about whom the financier said nothing. Nothing serious, of course, just a mention in passing of how business had gone and how the schedule had almost prevented them from eating well. Almost not a mention, really.

Three hours after that the Englishman called Burton filed his report to the place in London he called Riverside and the organization he still referred to as Box.

Fiona Marchant was at her desk by eight. The open-plan office was on the sixth floor of the new building and in the north-east corner, so that she could see Westminster half a mile down the Thames.

Fiona Marchant was twenty-eight years old, tall, slim, good-looking and unmarried, though for the past three years she had shared her life, plus a flat in the Barnsbury area of Islington, with a partner, Geoff, who was a lawyer in the City. She had been educated at Manchester High and Somerville College, Oxford, where she had gained an upper second and where the attention of the talent spotters had first been directed towards her. She had taken the year after Oxford off, travelling mainly in America and the Far East, though only after informing her future employers and confirming that her travel would not affect her prospects with them. When anyone asked what she now did, she replied simply that she worked for the Foreign Office, which was technically correct.

The winter sun glinted through the glass and a barge pulled up the river below her. The office was already busy, though in the quiet, detached way to which she had become accustomed and in which she did her best work, the other analysts crouched over their screens. She poured herself a coffee from the percolator near the door and settled at the overnights. An hour later she came to the Burton report.

Most of it was Middle East desk, and almost all of it Soukh News. Nothing of interest on Saddam, but the Iraq boys would have covered that anyway. A few apparently specious rumours about who was screwing who, which might not seem of interest but which she or someone else might be able to use at some future date. She entered the names on the file she used for such purposes, ran a quick cross-check, and came to the sixth item.

The report of the meeting in the apartment on Rue Léopold.

Probably nothing more than Soukh News to whoever had sourced the material. The source probably not even aware of the significance of those present. One such meeting might be coincidence. Except for those involved. Two and you might be on to something.

She had almost missed it last time. Because it had been tucked away in the rest of the gossip, because none of the names rang the proverbial bell. Because there was a flap on for an item which the JIC, the Joint Intelligence Committee, wanted to include in the Red Book, the weekly intelligence assessment for ministers.

Perhaps it had been her mathematics background, or the training she had received after she had joined Box, or her natural instinct. But that evening she had sat alone – alone being a relative term, because there had been others in the room, but isolated in a mental rather than a physical sense – and gone through the report again, run the cross-checks. Picked up on the intelligence backgrounds on three of those present at the Rue Léopold meeting. Not the fourth, because the informant had been unable to supply a name for the fourth.

Had seen the potential connections. So thin, so silky, that they were almost invisible. Like the skeins of a spider's web, the mesh you hardly ever saw, unless it was in autumn, when the morning dew had not cleared, or winter, when the frosted webs hung like decorations in places where you had never seen them before.

Nothing hard on any of the participants, of course, because you wouldn't expect it with the likes of them. Just the odd whisper from a source far removed from them; the tiniest hint of a connection with another party with a connection with . . . Therefore she had logged the meeting, had waited for the next time any details of it, or reference to it or any of those involved in it, showed in any of the reports emanating from the region.

Now she sat down again and read through the details of the second meeting. The second meeting she knew about – she corrected herself. Because there might have been others before what she called the first. Same names, she noted. Three names, plus a reference to a fourth person as yet unidentified. She extrapolated the details, fed them into the file she had created on the item, and cross-checked against the material already there.

The holy man.

The politician cum financier.

The secret policeman.

All with legitimate fronts and even more legitimate reasons to be in Brussels. All associated, however tenuously, with the terrorist business. Her business. Because anti-terrorism was the department in which she worked at Riverside.

Interesting addendum – she noted the remaining detail of what she already referred to as the Léopold Group. A connection with Bosnia, and a reference to shipments. Possibly interesting, possibly not. People like the Léopold Group would have links with the Mujihadeen, and the Mujihadeen already had a significant presence in Bosnia. Therefore logical rather than interesting.

*

Langdon's timetable began at five on the Friday morning and was scheduled to end at two the following afternoon, when the official Rover would deposit him at the door of the house in the Wiltshire countryside outside Salisbury, and he would relax with his family for thirty-six precious hours. In the event, and with the exception of six hours in Wiltshire, the Foreign Secretary's timetable would stretch into Wednesday of the following week, during which a myriad of minor appointments and functions would be cancelled, and at the end of which the world, or at least his part of it, would be a slightly different place.

The crossroad was in New York, late Friday afternoon Eastern Seaboard Time, in a break during a United Nations debate on the continuing crisis in Bosnia and the apparent inability of the international negotiators in Geneva to secure a breakthrough. He and the American Secretary of State were relaxed over coffee, the two men momentarily alone amidst the flurry of aides and officials.

Thought we were on the verge of a breakthrough this morning, they agreed, whispers that the Croats wanted to change sides. At the beginning of the Bosnian conflict the Croats had sided with the Muslims against the Serbs; a year ago, however, they had switched to support the Serbs. Both the US and the United Kingdom getting the same signals, the British and the Americans agreed, and if the forces realigned, then there was at least movement, and movement might mean solution. Whether in a week, a month, a year. And a year was a short time in the Balkans. So what went wrong – the conversation was relaxed but focused, always changing, always going forward. And what could they do to resurrect the possibility?

An hour later Langdon took coffee with the Russian Foreign Minister, their interpreters dismissed because the Russian spoke English, and the meeting was, after all, not a meeting but relaxation over coffee. Shame about Bosnia

– the conversation was informal, almost casual. Shame about the lack of progress. Because unless they sorted it out fast it might escalate and drag them all in even more than they were now. Whispers that the Croats were about to change sides, they agreed, some sort of federation with the Muslims. Wouldn't that be a problem for Moscow, Langdon asked, because Moscow was a traditional supporter of the Serbs. Among the extremists and nationalists, the Russian agreed, but separate the Croats from the Serbs, then you could begin to pressure the Belgrade Serbs to separate from the Bosnian Serbs. And if you did that . . .

Fifteen minutes later Langdon instructed an aide to cancel his overnight flight back to London. By the time he had returned to Heathrow, briefed the Prime Minister personally and been driven to the house west of Salisbury, it was late Sunday morning. The trees were bare and bleak, the overnight frost still clung to the lawns, and his family were gathering to greet him. He kissed his wife, then his daughter and granddaughter, and shook hands with his son-in-law.

'How's Berlin?' he asked.

His son-in-law ran the computer section of a major American bank, and was now stationed in Berlin, his wife and daughter with him.

'Berlin's fine.' A week before they had moved into an apartment in a side street off the Kurfürstendamm. 'How's the world?'

'Perhaps we'll know in a few days.'

After lunch Langdon and his daughter and granddaughter walked in the grounds, huddled in coats and scarves against the cold.

'So what will we know in a few days?' His daughter slid her hand through his arm. In front of them Sammi fed the ducks. 'What have you been up to?'

He shrugged.

'Tell me.'

Because you and I are close. Because you and I think the same. Because you're proud to have me as a daughter, and I'm proud to have you as a father. Which is why I kept the family name when I married. Why I prefer to be known as Hilary Langdon Carpenter and why I have continued that tradition with my daughter.

'We might have some movement on Bosnia-Herzegovina.'

Sammi was ahead of them, the river beyond.

'Movement or solution?'

'Movement first, perhaps a solution from it.'

'What precisely?'

'The Croats might change sides again, form a federation with the Muslims.'

Their breath formed clouds in the air.

'Why might they do that?'

'Because the Americans have agreed to bankroll it.'

They were further from the house now and closing on the river, Sammi running ahead again.

'And what will the Serbs do when the Croats switch sides?'

Ahead of them she could hear the river.

'Probably shell a few towns, kill and maim a few people. Usual thing.'

In front of them a swan skimmed across the river. On the bank Sammi jumped in excitement. The water in front of her was grey and running strong, the surface specked with snow.

'Is that a political statement or a fact of life?'

Sammi bent over and stretched towards the water. Langdon broke into a run, grabbed her coat, and pulled her back.

Something was nibbling at a corner of her mind. Had been since she'd read the latest Burton report. Interesting addendum – even now Fiona Marchant remembered the detail of what she already referred to as the Léopold Group.

A connection with Bosnia, and a reference to shipments. Possibly interesting, she had mused, possibly not. People like the Léopold Group would have links with the Mujihadeen, and the Mujihadeen already had a significant presence in Bosnia. Therefore the addendum was logical rather than interesting.

It was just after midnight, she and Geoff making love.

The addendum had referred to Bosnia, and to shipments *coming in*. Everyone knew the Bosnian Muslims were short of weapons, and that certain Middle East states and organizations were trying to ship arms and ammunition in to them. Therefore she had assumed that the reference to shipments meant items going in, which was logical, but put it outside her sphere of interest. Therefore she had binned it.

Except . . .

The report had been sourced in the Middle East, therefore the Bosnian item should have referred to items *going* in, not *coming* in.

*Coming in* might be taken to mean coming into the Middle East, which would imply something leaving Bosnia. Except what could the Bosnian Muslims have that anyone else wanted?

* * *

The clouds skidded across the moon and the runners of the prams slid easily across the ice. The first dealers were coming the other way, passing them in the night. She dropped Nedim and his brother at the pick-up point and took the first pram through the front line. Winners and losers, either you liked it or you didn't.

The Fat Man and the contact were waiting.

'I'll need time to make contact with the right people at the hospital,' Kara told them. 'I'll also see who's delivering the stuff and if I can do anything with them.' The flames from the dustbins lit the sky and an artillery barrage echoed in the hills. 'I'm not sure I can use my people to deliver the goods here, so you might have to collect them from a point near Travnik.'

'No problems. We can get people across. Even get a van over if you need it.'

And the van could bring food – Kara was already thinking, planning. Might have to be a private deal, of course, and The Fat Man would want his cut, but she was on to a killing.

'Sounds good. I'll get it together fast. We can work out the prices when I know what I can get.'

The contact pulled the hip flask from his pocket, poured a capful of slivovic, and gave it to her.

'To a good partnership,' she toasted him.

'A profitable future,' he toasted her back.

'Just hope the war doesn't end too quickly,' she joked.

'No worry about that.'

When they returned to Travnik it was still not midnight and the Landcruiser was parked in the street opposite.

'How much can you two move tomorrow?' she asked Nedim and his brother.

'As much as you can give us.'

'Take most of it. I can't make the market tomorrow.' Because she'd be making the first moves for the medical supplies. She kept what she considered she would need to offer as the first inducement, then they carried the rest through to the house. 'See you tomorrow, same time. And well done tonight.'

She bolted the door, took off her coat and boots, and

laid three places at the table: the plates and the knives and forks and the whisky glasses. Her body and hands were shaking now. She poured herself a drink and sat in the chair, tried to focus on what she would do tomorrow and how she would decide the person at the hospital to whom she would make her first approach. Jumped slightly when she heard the knock on the door even though she was waiting for it.

The two men were in the porch.

'Come in,' she told Keefer.

They came inside, took off their outer coats.

'This is Pieter.'

'Hello, Pieter.'

The candles she'd placed round the room flickered slightly.

'Drink?' she asked.

Malt, Keefer said, and gave her the bottle, watched as she broke the seal and poured them each a glass.

'*Salud.*' She raised the glass and sipped the liquid.

They sat and ate, emptying the bottle and opening another, hardly talking. They finished eating and she cleared the plates, told them to sit down. Keefer on the bed and Pieter in the armchair. The candles were almost dead; she lit another set, poured a bowl of water and undressed.

Keefer began to unbutton his shirt, began to get up.

'Not yet,' she told him. She trickled the water over her body and soaped herself, knew they were looking at her but appeared not to look at them. Glanced at the erections bursting in their trousers but appeared to ignore them as if they were not there. Rinsed the soap off and dried herself, still not looking at them. Poured herself another malt and let them pour their own.

'There's more hot water.' She sat slightly curled on the bed as they undressed. Good bodies – she looked at them now, made sure they saw her looking. Hard and fit, their erections like scimitars.

She was good, Keefer thought, she was playing the game. He soaped his chest, soaped his torso, soaped his erection.

The figures of the men were almost surreal, as if they were no more than shadows in a painting, the light flickering on their bodies and their bodies almost lost in the candlelight. Thank Christ they'd got back early tonight, thank God she had more time. Thank God she didn't have to get up early for the market. Thank Christ she didn't have to wait much longer.

They were wiping themselves, drying themselves. Pouring themselves another drink. Were close to her now and filling her glass. Christ how big they seemed together, how they appeared to fill the room, how the power seemed to exude from them as they towered over and around and above her.

Keefer was kissing her, softly and gently, his lips almost like feathers on her. Bergmann's fingers trailing along her, touching her, fingernails dragging along her.

Keefer was still bent over her, still kissing her. She stood and draped her arms round his neck, bodies hardly touching, kissed his mouth, lips like snowflakes.

She left him and turned to Bergmann, felt down with her hands. Dipped her head slightly and bit his nipples, drew her fingernails up his thighs and across his stomach. Half-turned him so she was slightly behind him, kissed his shoulders and his back then slid her hands round him and almost touched him, began to withdraw then held him, felt the way his entire body stiffened. Moved between them and held the two of them. Felt her head fall back as their hands came over her, as Bergmann kissed her throat and her breasts and her front and Keefer ran his tongue and his teeth round her neck and her shoulders and her buttocks.

She was shuddering now, the bodies of the two men also

shaking. Keefer was oiling her, Bergmann's fingers and hands feeling for her and opening her.

'Ready?' Keefer laid her on the bed.

'Ready,' she told him.

It was four in the morning. Bergmann had been gone an hour.

'How was it?' Keefer was in the armchair, the stove still warm and the malt on the floor at the side.

You know how it was – Kara was on the bed, the dressing gown loose around her. You know you and Pieter took me places I couldn't have dreamed existed.

What are you thinking, he wondered. Why haven't you answered my question?

She offered him a cigarette and lit one for herself.

'So what was that really all about?' she asked him.

'You're good,' he told her. 'You know that. You could be the best.'

'The best at what?' she said. 'What's going on? What have the past days really been about?'

'Last night – and tonight – was good.' The oil still glistened on Keefer's body. 'I wanted it and you wanted it, and we both knew that.'

'But . . .'

'I also wanted to see how far over the edge of what most people would call normality you would go. I wanted to see how you would react when you got there.'

She sipped the malt and drew on the cigarette, held him with her eyes. 'I know that. What I want to know is why.'

'I'm recruiting,' Keefer told her.

Silence.

'There are people who feel that it's time that certain courses of action which have been followed in the past but which have been laid aside should be resurrected.'

Still silence, still the stare.

'The people concerned are Islamic fundamentalists. They wish to recruit Muslims, but specifically Bosnian Muslims.'

Still the stare, still the eyes held by hers.

'I'm recruiting fighters.'

Still the eyes held by hers, still the tension between them.

'I'm recruiting freedom fighters.'

'You're recruiting terrorists.'

'Yes. I'm recruiting what the West calls terrorists.'

She moved slightly. 'Why Bosnian Muslims?' she asked.

'Because most Muslims look like Muslims, therefore the West will be looking for them.'

'And Bosnian Muslims look like Europeans.'

'Precisely.'

'What's in it for my country?'

'Possibly nothing, possibly a lot. Nobody's helped you so far, the West have betrayed you totally.'

'And what's in it for me?'

A shrug. Who knows? 'You could be the best. I could make you the best.' And after that it's up to you. To decide what you do and how far you go.

To lie on the ground with the bullet in my face and my blood trickling down my skin. But in the moment before the bastards pull the trigger on me to look them in the eye and know I'd been to the edge and gone over it. To know that the end didn't matter, that what did matter was the manner of getting there. Winners and losers. Try everything once and see if you like it.

'How long do I have to decide?'

'I leave tomorrow.'

She was still looking at him. 'The English mercenary with the tattoo on his arm,' she asked. 'You said he wouldn't bother me again?'

'When I got back to the camp that night the Mujihadeen were torturing him. I thought he would start making up stories, start naming people. I thought he might say he'd spoken to you. So I cut his throat.'

'Why?'

'Why did I cut his throat?'

'No. Why did you tell me the detail when all you had to say was that you killed him?'

'Because that's the world I'm recruiting into.'

'What happens to me if I say no?'

She really was the best, he thought. She was still in control, still covering every angle.

'You don't know enough about me, who I am or where I came from or where I'm going.'

Which wasn't an answer.

'You want some coffee before you go?' she asked.

'No.'

Finn and the interpreter were at the food kitchen by eight-thirty.

'She's on the list,' the woman told them. 'She's registered as having her food here.'

'Found her,' the interpreter looked up at Finn.

'Ask if she's already eaten today,' he instructed her.

'Sorry,' the woman told them. 'We don't keep a record of whether or not those on the list have eaten.'

But at least she's here, at least he was in the right place. So all he had to do was wait at the kitchen until she showed, because she was bound to, because that was the only way she could eat.

'Could you give this lady my thanks and ask her to accept something from me.' Finn gave the interpreter a food pack in a plastic bag. 'Not official, just from me.'

For the next hour and a half he waited, till the morning session was finished and the kitchen was shutting. The Gymnasium or the marketplace, he decided, except there was no list at the Gymnasium and little hope of spotting her at the market. One other place there would be a list though, even though she was probably not there.

They left the food kitchen and asked their way to the hospital.

The knock on the door was quiet, almost apologetic.

Keefer didn't knock like that, Kara knew.

It was ten in the morning, seven hours since the man she called Pieter had left, five and a half since the other had made his offer. So Keefer, or The Fat Man and the black market contact? Winners and losers, and she'd win whichever she chose. So which to go for? A lot of very fast bucks, or something totally different? Which edge? Great sex if she decided to go with Keefer, great nights with the two of them. Plus whatever else and whatever other edges they were offering. A lot of money if she went for the other. And there were plenty more men. Probably not as good as the two last night, but she could always look.

It was time to go, time to check the hospital.

She heard the knock again. Crossed the room, went into the porch, and opened the outer door.

The woman and child stood on the top step, the snowflakes drifting on to them and the despair and wet seeping deep into them.

'I'm sorry.' The woman's face was tight with hunger and fear. 'My son hasn't eaten for three days.'

Seen it before, heard it before, Kara thought. Give to one and they'd be back the next day. Either that or they'd tell their friends and the next thing you knew the whole bloody world was queuing at your door.

'What?' she asked.

'I'm sorry, but my son hasn't eaten for three days and he's not well.' . . .

*

. . . Back off, Finn, she heard her own voice before she heard his. I told you not to come again, told you I didn't want to listen to you. So sod off now before you say a word.

Why, Kara? What are you afraid of? Why are you hesitating? Why haven't you told the woman and the boy to go?

Back off, Finn, like I told you. Because you're wrong. I know where I am and what I'm seeing. I'm not back in Maglaj, Finn, I'm not seeing a woman like this one tending her son and carrying him down the street through the snow and the ice and the shells and mortars and telling him everything will be okay once they've eaten. So sod off, Finn. Don't tell me who I am or what I'm seeing or thinking.

Why not, Kara, somebody has to.

Okay, Finn, but make it fast. Because I've got things to do and places to see. Money to make and people to screw.

You want to know it, Kara? You *really* want to know it?

Yeah, Finn. I really want to know it.

You're thinking everybody's fucked you, Kara, and you're right. The UN and NATO fucked you and your people because they didn't stop the war in Bosnia when they could have, didn't even send in the air strikes to help Maglaj when they should have done.

I fucked you because I didn't take Jovan out in the chopper. Because I took him to the hospital in Tesanj, and he and Adin were killed because of it.

Keefer fucked you. Every which way. Then came back with the one called Pieter and double fucked you every way you and they could think of, fucked every cavity of your body and every crevice of your soul.

But you're also doing the fucking, Kara.

You fucked Keefer and Pieter as long and as hard as they fucked you. You're fucking the people who buy from you on the black market. Worse than that. You're fucking the men and the women and the children in the hospital because you're about to sell the medical supplies which are meant for them to the enemy. *The fucking enemy, Kara.*

So stop feeling sorry for yourself. Stop telling me the whole world is fucking you, because you're fucking it just as much.

Tell me something I don't know, Finn. Because there's something you should know. I actually like what I do. I actually enjoy the black market and the screwing and the fucking. I love it. More than that, I'm good at it. And I could be equally good at what Keefer wants me to do. Because Keefer's right when he says he can make me the best. So tell me something I don't know. Tell me what the hell you mean and what you're really getting at.

He told her.

Hell, Finn, you really mean that? You know what you're telling me to do?

Yes, Kara, I really mean it. Your decision, of course. But it always has been . . .

. . . 'Come in,' she said to the woman.

The woman and boy stepped into the warmth.

'It's yours,' Kara told them.

She took the money from the purse round her neck and gave it to them. 'I work the black market. I cross each night to a place called Popovekuce. Two boys help me. They're due here at four-thirty. They're afraid to cross the front line; it's easy but don't tell them that. Deal with a fat man, but don't tell him I sent you. That's if you want to. If you don't, there's enough food and money to keep you going.'

The woman was still staring at her. Give me two minutes, Kara told her. She led the woman and the boy to the porch and closed the door. The room was warm and the food on the stove was bubbling. She went to the dresser, took out the photograph of Adin and Jovan, and kissed them both. There were some things to leave for ever, others to come back for. She took out the drawer, taped the photograph to the bottom of the section above it, where no one would ever find it, and slid the drawer back in. Then she burned her ID and ration card in the stove, checked no personal detail remained – either on her or in the room – and went to the porch.

The woman and boy were halfway down the steps, as if they did not believe what had happened or what she had told them.

'It's yours.' Kara gave the woman the keys. 'Good luck.'

The white Landcruiser was in the street opposite, Keefer waiting at the wheel. He watched as she came down the road. Coat and boots but no bag, he noted; she was carrying nothing. No money, food or personal items. As if nothing now existed of whoever or whatever she had once been.

She opened the door. 'One condition,' she told him.

'What?'

'Neither you nor Pieter or whatever his real name is ever touch me again.'

'Agreed.'

'Okay,' she told Keefer. 'Let's do it.'

# Book Two

*seven months later . . .*
*late August/early September 1994*

# 9

The sun was setting to the west, the wash of a river boat sparkled white on the Thames, and the distinctive stonework of Westminster and the Houses of Parliament looked mellow to the east. London, late summer; the weather warm and the evening outside the glass cocoon of Riverside friendly and relaxing.

Fiona Marchant settled at the computer and flicked through the updates.

There had been nothing from Burton for the past months, by which she meant nothing of specific interest to her. No fresh meetings in the apartment on Rue Léopold in Brussels, and nothing significant on the shadows who had attended the previous two. Every day she checked, just in case; every day she cross-referenced with other sources and ran the names through Turing.

Alan Turing was the mathematician and founding father of artificial intelligence who, during World War Two, had worked for MI6 and cracked the German Enigma code. It was appropriate, Marchant considered, that the Prolog-based system the department was now using was named after him.

The system itself analysed reports to make connections and predict possible logical outcomes. A human analyst would then alter search strategies to explore personal hunches, technically known as heuristics, if he or she thought the machine was missing a point or not behaving intelligently. The machine, however, could use its own heuristics to make a more human-like analysis, and employ a technology such as Case-Based-Reason to predict outcomes. Plus it could utilize machine-learning technologies, such as Genetic Algorithms and/or Neural Networks, to improve its own predictive powers by learning from its own experiences.

Which was where the problem – at least in the department, and at least at the present time – began. Because although so-called Expert Systems had been around for some time, much of the technology was quite recent and, in the case of Neural Networks, still a research topic. Despite this, some fuzz-head with a PhD had persuaded Riverside to run Turing using a Neural Network. And sometimes it went wrong. And when it did the problems were indescribable. And then analysts like her were back to the Stone Age.

At least it was Thursday, she reminded herself. And when she finished work tomorrow she and Geoff would be out of London as fast as they could, get a mid-evening ferry across the Channel, and hit the motorways. Overnight in some plastic motel and make Kandersteg by Saturday afternoon. The mountains all round them, the wooden chalets, the handful of shops and hotels, and the glorious invigorating clean Swiss air. And hardly any tourists, because the valley was a dead end so there was no through traffic except for the railway tunnel to Goppenstein. Meet up with Mike and Mel in the Victoria, where they'd stayed on a short cross-country skiing holiday last winter. Mike worked with Geoff; Melanie, his wife, was a solicitor with a firm specializing in civil matters. Even among her friends Fiona Marchant was careful.

Nothing from Burton, she confirmed, and nothing on the Léopold Group. She hopped files, glancing at the material that had come in that afternoon, then pressed a number on the console and spoke to Kilpatrick. 'Got five minutes?'

Kilpatrick was late thirties, public school and, she assumed, Oxbridge. Typical background, she'd originally thought, typical way in. Irish, of course – the slightest accent occasionally confirming what was suggested by the name, though only, she thought, when he chose to allow it. Probably ex-military, though she wasn't sure why she had gained that impression. And good – at putting things together, at suggesting the links which no one else might consider, at pulling apart those links which others had made and exposing their weaknesses.

'Make it now.' Because I've been here since six this morning and am about to go home.

Not home in the New Forest; wife and kids and ponies and dinghies on the Solent, because that was for weekends. Home midweek was a flat near Queensway.

Forty seconds later she sat in his office. The Sanctum, he occasionally called it. The windows were shuttered, and the desk and other furniture were functional rather than decorative, which was interesting given the architectural flamboyance of the exterior of the building.

'Item from the Cousins.' She quoted the report reference. 'Guerrilla training camp in Afghanistan.' The report was from Langley and the source and chain of communication were obvious. The CIA had supported and supplied the various groups which had opposed the Soviet-backed government in Kabul in the seventies and eighties, now the CIA was keeping its eyes and ears open even though the Soviets had pulled out and Kabul had fallen years ago. Some of the locals probably still on the payroll and trying to keep their previous paymasters happy. 'Just wondered if there was any satellite back-up?'

Because the report is bare-bones, the local equivalent of Soukh News, but even so it might be interesting, because intelligence was a jigsaw, multi-layered and multi-dimensional. The pieces from somebody else's occasionally fitting yours, even though you didn't know what picture you were going for.

'Any particular reason?' Kilpatrick had looked after her back a couple of times, made sure she'd got the credit when it was her due.

'Nothing specific, but the wording is interesting. The report refers to a training camp, but there have been no such camps in the past and no reason for there to be one now.'

'Plus?'

There was nothing in the room to suggest a personal connection, no family photographs, no souvenirs or mementoes from a previous existence, no photographs of rugby teams or Kilpatrick meeting foreign dignitaries or visiting spooks.

'Most of the training camps have been in the Beqa'a, the Sudan, or North Yemen.'

'But those were for international terrorists.'

'Agreed, but the Afghans don't need to train their own people, because they already know what to do.'

'So where does that leave us?' Kilpatrick asked.

'I'm not sure.' Except this is what you pay me for.

'I'll check.'

By the time she reached the flat in Barnsbury it was seven, and there was a message from Geoff on the answerphone that he'd be late. She made a light supper of meats and salad, and had almost finished packing when he arrived. The following morning she was at her desk by eight.

'Nothing on the satellite front,' Kilpatrick told her at eleven. 'Afghanistan's low priority at the moment.' Because Saddam was making threatening noises again and every item of intelligence gathering was directed at the Middle

East. 'If you want a special overfly I could push it upstairs.' Except that would mean calling in a favour, so make sure you have something before you even ask.

'Not worth it, but thanks anyway.'

Because unless she had something solid it wasn't worth building any debts. And because tonight she was on two weeks' leave, so if something came of it she wouldn't be around to take the credit. Rules and games, and unless you understood the rules there was no point playing the game.

The newspapers were on the table in the kitchen of the safe house, and the date was on the newspapers.

In three weeks Jovan would be five and she and Adin would hold a small party for him and his little friends; in three weeks they would give Jovan a present and watch his face as he opened it. Except that today Jovan was in his father's arms on a hillside above Tesanj, and she was someone else and somewhere else.

Kara tried to ignore the thoughts and picked up the newspapers, forced herself to read them.

Bosnia was breaking down again. The Serbs were pressuring Sarajevo and the United Nations were threatening to bomb the Muslims unless they stopped reacting. The Serbs were encircling towns like Srebrenica and Zepa and Gorazde and Bihac, just as they had encircled Maglaj and Tesanj. The Serbs were stopping the aid convoys getting in and soon the Serbs would start the shelling again. And when they did the UN and NATO would wring their hands and continue to do nothing.

She left the kitchen, went to the lounge, and sat in one of the armchairs against the windows overlooking the street.

The flat was on the second floor, the stairs sweeping up from the entrance hall; a doorway off the landing, bedrooms, bathroom and kitchen off the hallway, and lounge at the end. Most of the other buildings in the area were the same: converted into apartments and bed-sits, comfortable and quiet.

Just the place to put a safe house.

It was six weeks since she had left the training camp in Afghanistan. Sometimes, especially at the beginning, she had thought she would never survive, never live through the cold of winter and the furnace of summer. But the cold of Afghanistan wasn't the cold of Bosnia, because in Afghanistan she had a reason and a purpose; because, even though the training was hard and frequently brutal, she and the others were well-fed. And gradually she had learned. More than that. Gradually she had become what Keefer said she would become. Gradually she had emerged as the best. Not always on the surface, because on the surface Keefer had taught her the things which had made the Stasi so effective. So on the surface she could be charming and provocative. On the surface she could smile and laugh, and make anybody – but especially men – believe what she wished them to believe. And underneath she was cold and calculating and strong as steel. So that the night Keefer tested her, the night he engineered the situation whereby the two Mujihadeen had found her by herself and tried to rape her, it had been their throats that were cut and not hers. So that it had come as no surprise when she had been appointed leader of one of the four teams Keefer had first sent out from the camp.

The flat was quiet, only the ticking of a clock. The others had been out since eight and were not due back till late that evening. Please may nobody find the photograph of Adin and Jovan she had taped in the dresser in the room off Tobacco Road, please may it still be there when she returned to Travnik. Because it was all she had of them, all that was left of them.

She collected the travel bag from the bedroom, pulled on a coat and left.

The usual cars were in the usual places in the street – the check was automatic. Nothing and no one out of place, but there wouldn't be if the Eyes were looking for her. Kara walked three blocks, doubled back on herself, then caught a cab to the station. The train left at 12.09. Nine hours later she left the compartment, taking the travel bag with her, and locked herself in the toilet. The wig, tinted contact lenses and cheek padders were in a plastic container. Simple things were always the best, Keefer had taught her. Plus a reversible coat, different colours inside and out, and two travel bags, each able to be folded into the other. An hour after that the train pulled in to Zurich. She allowed other passengers to take the first cabs, chose the fifth, and asked for the Hotel zum Störchen.

The appointment the following morning was at ten. She ordered a cab for nine, checked out of the hotel, left the travel bag in a locker at the station, then took another cab to a side street in the banking quarter of the city, arriving five minutes early. Even though the morning was warm she was dressed in business clothes – smartly cut suit, silk blouse, nylons – because men always preferred them – and high-heeled shoes.

No briefcase – the commissionaire who opened the door for her noted. But many of the bank's clients didn't need briefcases. Most of them, after all, carried the important things in their heads. She smiled at him and stepped into the bank. The foyer was well-furnished, with subtle lighting and tinted windows, and the receptionist was multilingual.

'Good morning.' Kara spoke in German. 'I have an appointment with Herr Satri at ten.'

No name, the receptionist noted, but most clients never used names anyway. 'Of course,' she said. 'Coffee?' she asked.

'No, thank you.'

Thirty seconds later a secretary collected her from the private waiting room.

Banks were security risks, Keefer had told her. Banks check on any large payments of money into them, in case it's drugs money and they might be accused of laundering. A private bank in a discreet street in Switzerland, however . . .

An emergency fund sitting in a bank account in Geneva, Keefer had also told her, given her the code for it. Not to be touched under normal circumstances. For emergencies only. And then she should check with him if possible.

The office was on the first floor. The secretary knocked once, opened the door for her, allowed her to step inside, then closed the door behind her. The office was like the bank – discreet. Not opulent, just stylish yet comfortable, not even the computer seeming out of place.

'Frau Schullenberg.' Satri stood to greet her. He was large – well-fed was the word which came immediately to her mind; early forties, and of Middle Eastern origin. But a lot of people in banking were, Keefer had told her. He shook her hand, offered her a seat in one of the armchairs, smiling slightly and waiting till she sat, then sitting himself and waiting.

'I wish to open an account.'

'Of course.' Why else would you be here – the smile again.

'An initial deposit of two hundred and fifty thousand US dollars,' she smiled back at him.

'There are, of course, certain formalities.' Classy legs, he thought, and classy legs were always encased in nylons. 'Certain checks to be made.'

'Of course.' Her right leg was crossed over her left. 'The deposit to be made this morning.' She shifted her weight slightly, and crossed her left leg over her right.

'May I ask how it will be paid?' Because cash is a

problem – not a big one, but still a problem until we've checked that we can accept you as a client.

'Electronic transfer.'

'Aah.' Because that's different. Unless you've simply paid cash into a bank somewhere. But even that's not such a problem once we've run our client checks.

'From one of your own branches.'

*Aah* again, but different this time. Because everything's okay now, because if you already have an account with us, then the checks have already been done.

She gave him the code number of the account in Geneva.

Kandersteg was like it always was: the mountains rising on either side of the valley, the paragliders circling in the thermals close to the cliff face of the Almenalp, and hardly any tourists.

On Sunday, Fiona Marchant, Geoff and the others did a gentle warm-up walk to the Doldenhorn, lunch of bread and goulash soup at the Swiss Alpine Club hut looking down on the blue waters of the lake at Oeschinensee. On the Monday they did the Gellihorn, overlooking Kandersteg from the south; on Tuesday Birre, looming to the east; on Wednesday the glacier at the head of the Gasterntal, five hours up and four back, break at the cluster of houses at Selden on both sections.

The weather was warm and settled, the peacefulness of early September in the daytime but the first chill of autumn as dusk closed in.

On Thursday they did the Balmhorn, informing the hotel they wouldn't be back till Saturday, leaving late and reaching the mountain hut at two, dumping their backpacks and climbing gear in the mattresslaagen – a room off the side, with long wooden beds in tiers and the mattresses side by side on each. Then they ate the bread and cheese they'd brought with them and lay in the sun for the rest of the afternoon. The fresh air was getting to her, she knew.

The night was cold. At three they woke, dressed, and made themselves tea and muesli. By four they were on the mountain, the Petzl lamps picking out the path and the snow glistening ghostly above them. At five they stopped and watched the sunrise, the sky and the mountains and the snow reflecting the red she always remembered. By six they were on the ice, crampons on and roped together. At seven-thirty they hauled the last metres to the summit.

Nobody who hadn't done it, hadn't been here, could even imagine what it was like, she thought. Okay it wasn't Everest, and a lot of people had been here a lot of times, but this morning the Balmhorn was theirs and nobody else's.

Mel glanced across at her. It was interesting how, even in the mountains, even at a moment like this, Fiona appeared to think clearly and calmly, almost coldly; how she could automatically remove herself from the situation. Sometimes Mel wondered what Fiona Marchant really did; at least, what her real job was within the corridors of the Foreign and Commonwealth Office.

By ten they were back at the hut and the guide had left them. They dropped their backpacks, walked the ten minutes to the point where the water cascaded off the cliff into a small lagoon, then stripped to their pants, covered themselves with high factor cream, and lay in the sun.

'What are you thinking?' Mel asked.

'Nothing,' Fiona Marchant replied honestly.

Great day to be here, she thought. Wonder whether anything more's come in from Burton; it was as if Mel's question had logged her in to the computer at Riverside. Wonder what's happening in the Gulf. Wonder if the Cousins have run a satellite check over Afghanistan ... The sun was hot and all she could hear was the sound of the water. The Bosnia shipment has arrived safely ...

That afternoon they dropped back into the valley, walked up to Selden, then climbed east towards the Lötschenpass, overnighting in an SAC hut then crossing into the Lötschental, taking the post bus to Goppenstein and the train back through the tunnel to Kandersteg. Above them the greens and reds and yellows of the paragliders drifted in the blue. On the slope of the Almenalp she saw the sun glinting on the purple and orange of a paraglider taking off.

The next morning she left the hotel, walked to the station, and picked up copies of the previous day's *Times* and *Guardian* from the kiosk. The paragliders were drifting above the valley like eagles. She walked up the path along the river, and stood watching.

The landing zone was a meadow, the cliff face of the Almenalp – where the paragliders were taking off – towering above it. A row of trees stood on the left, as she looked at the cliff, a small tree-covered hillock to the right, and power cables drooping between the meadow and the cliff, a red-roofed cowshed beneath them. Further to the left, the wires of a cable car swept in a tight curve to the Almenalp three thousand feet above them. The cross, indicating the target of the landing zone, was at the end of the meadow closest to the river. In the left corner was a small hut, a handful of friends and families watching, and an instructor talking beginners down on a radio set. As she watched, a paraglider drifted in, circled right then left to lose height, and dropped three metres from the target. That's incredible – she felt the thrill and the fear. That's absolutely amazing.

She stood for another fifteen minutes, then walked to the cable car, bought a ticket, and took the next car to the Almenalp. The ride was gentle at first, then suddenly they were climbing almost vertically, the wires taut above them and the drop of the cliff face sheer in front of her. Two thousand feet up the cliff ended, and the mountain sloped back and up, through trees, then to meadows above, the mountains ringed around them. The cable car station was close to a farm, a small café at the side. Three hundred feet above, and to the side, the chutes were spread like butterflies.

So how do you tell yourself to do it; what do you think when you're in the air; how is it when you go over the cliff and see nothing below you? Because that's what it's all about, isn't it? What's it like deciding whether you're going to the edge? What sort of person do you need to be to actually do it?

She bought a Coke, climbed the slope to the take-off point, and sat watching.

A girl was preparing to take off, the concentration on her face as she ran through the last checks. Harness done up. Chute laid out properly and lines not tangling. Wind right and harness done up properly. The harness was the first and last check. Hands holding the lines. Check wind and hands up, above head, bringing the chute off the ground, the chute suddenly open in the air. Glance up and begin running, pull down slightly and check again, still running. The slope giving way and the girl suddenly airborne.

Incredible, Fiona Marchant thought. She returned to the cable car station and took the next car down, looking up at the cliff as they descended, then stood again at the landing zone.

'Lesson starting tomorrow,' the instructor told her.

'Perhaps.'

When she returned to the hotel the others were sitting in the garden, drinking beer and discussing the climbs for the following week. She settled in a chair and flicked through the two newspapers, picked up on the items from Bosnia.

Sarajevo was again feeling the effect of the encirclement by Serbian forces, the Serbs had stopped aid convoys and UN flights coming in, as well as cutting off power and water. There were also suggestions that Muslim towns exposed and isolated in Serb-held areas were under increasing pressure.

Some things never changed, she thought, though it was too good a day to be cynical. She called to the waiter for four more beers and turned to the other Bosnian item.

A Westminster MP was demanding an investigation into allegations that a British mercenary fighting in Bosnia had been murdered by Mujihadeen guerrillas. The dead man, Brian Walton, had gone to Bosnia to fight with Muslim forces against the Serbs and Croats. In January he had been on the front near the town of Travnik, based at a camp also occupied by Mujihadeen. The Mujihadeen had believed him to be a spy, and had tortured then executed him.

Possibly interesting, she thought. Not today, though. She rolled off the chair and slid into the pool.

Kara waved down a cab, gave a street name five blocks from the address she wanted, and checked the road behind her as the cab pulled away. In fourteen days' time Jovan would be five. She pushed the thought to the back of her mind and checked behind her again, told the driver to stop even though it was not the street name she had given him. She paid him, walked through the department store, out by another door, then along a street at the rear, doubling back on herself in case there was a tail. Which there shouldn't be, but you never knew. She was wearing the wig, contact lenses and cheek padders she had worn in Zurich, but different clothes. Today she wore a light jacket, light wool sweater, jeans, and shoes she could move fast in. She walked for another ten minutes and came to the street she wanted.

The office was at the side of a travel agency, the agency itself slightly upmarket – judging by the destinations advertised in the window – as were most of the shops and boutiques in the area. She spent ten minutes checking for anything resembling a stake-out vehicle – not someone spying on her, but on the person she was about to visit. Then another ten minutes looking for the back way out, the emergency exits or fire escapes. The street was beginning to get busy. She checked it again, then rang the bell on the right side of the door.

'Yes . . .' the voice was metallic.

'I have a meeting with Rolf.'

She heard the buzz as the door was unlocked, and went in. The stairs were on the left, another door – locked – on the right. Window halfway up the stairs, she noted, but bars across it. The stairs turned at a right angle, up another flight, then a right angle again to a landing. The area was neatly carpeted and the walls were tastefully painted. The door was on the right, another security system on it. She pressed the buzzer and was allowed in. The office was larger than she had expected: leather-topped executive desk, comfortable chairs, paintings on the walls, three telephones, a fax machine and a computer. Nothing ostentatious, though; no symbols of newly-acquired affluence as she might have expected from someone from the East now making it in the West. Just the aroma of coffee from the percolator in one corner, the fridge beneath it concealed in a walnut cabinet, and the faintest hint of a cigar.

'Coffee?' The contact was in his mid-forties and smartly dressed.

'Black, no sugar.'

There was no other exit from the room, unless it was

concealed behind the bookshelf, and the windows were barred again, but they were on the third floor so the window was out anyway. Probably.

The contact poured them both a cup then settled behind the desk. 'How may I help you?' He was polite, almost formal.

'You have airport contacts?'

'Depends who gave you my name and address.'

'The fact that I have your name and address should be enough.' Because whoever gave it to me would not wish to have his name used, just as you would not wish to have yours disclosed. Because you and Keefer are both ex-Stasi – East German secret police before the Wall came down. And you and I both know it.

The contact smiled for the first time. 'Which airport?'

'Berlin Tegel.'

'What exactly do you want?'

'Nothing big. Just a switch. One briefcase for another.'

'What sort of briefcase?'

'The sort pilots carry. Black, slightly square, stiff leather. They sometimes call them navigation bags.'

'Coming in or going out?' Because most people want stuff brought in, especially given the various trades with the former Eastern bloc: anything from icons to diamonds to military items. Therefore most people wanted it after customs.

'Airside. Going out.' The departure lounge, the other side of immigration and the security checks.

'When?'

'I'll give you the case itself within the next five days. The switch will be in the ten days after that, though I can't be specific at this stage. I'll be able to give you at least two days' notice.'

The contact nodded. 'Ten thousand dollars.' Cash. 'Five now, five when you make the switch.'

'Two and half now, two and a half when I give you the case. Five when we make the switch.'

'Agreed. Anything else?'

'I'll also need you to arrange for some airline ticket counterfoils to be lost.'

Two days later she kept her next appointment.

The streets on either side of the canal were cobbled, and the shop windows facing on to them were filled with women. Amsterdam's Oude Kerke, the city's red light district. A group of American sailors were arguing with someone over prices, and a tourist boat was passing along the canal, someone with a baseball cap facing backwards and videoing the shops with a small camcorder. Instinctively Kara turned away, the movement casual enough to avoid any suggestion she did not want her face to be seen. Then she crossed the footbridge to the other side, checked the street map, and turned down one of the streets running off the canal. Two blocks away the clubs and sex bars gave way to antique shops and expensive restaurants.

The contact address was three doors down and, judging by the window, appeared to specialize in Eastern European art. She walked past it, confirmed the number, then spent fifteen minutes looking for rear exits and surveillance positions. Only when she was as satisfied as she could be did she enter the shop.

The inside was filled with furniture, most of it well displayed, plus paintings, mainly watercolours. Good as a cover, she thought, though judging by the dust and the general feel of the place business wasn't exactly brisk.

'I'm looking for Frank,' she told the proprietor.

He was like a mole, she thought, nose twitching and hair brushed back. Yellow coat and extravagant bow tie.

'Who shall I say wants him?'

'Elsa.' The name had been agreed when the meeting had been arranged.

'I'm Frank.'

The telephone was on a desk to the side, and the desk itself was littered with magazines. He locked the door, switched on the answerphone, and led her through a door at the rear and up a flight of slightly rickety stairs. No back door, she noted; the windows heavily barred as the windows in such places always were. They came to a landing, the stairs continuing. Possible way out across the roof, she thought; waited as he unlocked the door and went in. Door wooden, but strengthened from the way it swung. Frank was obviously careful.

The room was a cross between a photographer's studio and a laboratory: cameras and lights, plus computers, printers, and a bench of other apparatus she assumed he required for his profession. Frank was good, Keefer had said; Frank was the best. Frank was also reliable, which counted in this world.

'What exactly do you want?'

Frank sat on a swivel chair next to one of the computers, Kara on a slightly lower chair opposite him. Downstairs the shop had appeared chaotic and the contact had appeared disorganized. Upstairs everything was clinically clean and the contact was sharp as a razor.

'Eight passports. Four male, four female. Genuine, not fakes. By which I mean actual official documents stolen from the printing works or purchased from a bent official, not second-rate replicas run up in some backstreet graphics factory. But that's why I've come to you.'

And that's why I know I'll have to pay.

'When?'

'Next week. I'll bring the photos and details then. Phone in advance to confirm that you have them.'

'Six grand each,' he told her. 'US dollars, used notes and a mix of denominations.'

'Four.'

'Five. Half now, half on collection.'

The price was higher than she had anticipated. Inflation, she supposed. But she was in a hurry and Frank, after all, was the best. She counted out the dollars, watched as he counted the notes again, then left, walked three blocks, and picked up a cab.

The forger watched as she left, locked the door, and made the call. Forty grand was good, forty grand was over the odds, especially when business wasn't like it had been in the old days. Too many doing it now, too many cowboys. Forty wouldn't cover his debts, however – perhaps gambling came with the patch. But forty thousand dollars would go some way towards it, plus it would get the gorillas off his back. And if the woman had forty grand to burn, then she had a lot more somewhere. And that *would* put the heavies back on the leash. Winners and losers. Shame really, but the last thing he wanted was his legs broken and the shop torched.

He lifted the telephone and punched the number.

* * *

The storm clouds were gathering over the Gellihorn and the sky was blackening from the west. As they left Kandersteg, shortly after seven on the Saturday morning, the first rain was sheeting across the valley; when they reached London the following afternoon the weather was warm and pleasant. By eight the next morning Fiona Marchant was at her desk at Riverside.

Three other analysts were already in, and Kilpatrick was in The Sanctum. She knocked on his door, waited till the voice said to come in, and sat comfortably opposite him.

'Welcome back.' He closed the file and laid it to one side. 'Good break?' Because you look as if it was. Because you look different.

'Great break.'

'Switzerland, wasn't it?'

'Small place called Kandersteg. Good walking and climbing; almost did some paragliding.'

'You should have done.'

'You've been?' She sat forward slightly.

'Not paragliding, but I've done a few jumps.' Another time and place, and a part of my life we don't talk about. 'Try it next time.'

Perhaps she might, she agreed. Anything happening? she asked. Nothing, he told her. Everyone and everything shut for summer, and still waiting to re-open.

Turing was down again, he also told her, almost in passing. So it was back to the Stone Age. She left his office, went to her desk, logged on, and began trawling through the reports channelled to the department since she had been away.

The source code-named Burton had filed again, though most of it was Soukh News. Another meeting scheduled for the apartment on Rue Léopold in Brussels, she noted. She cross-checked against the names of previous known participants, then closed the file and continued elsewhere. Something on the British mercenary executed by the Muj in Bosnia – she'd read about it in Switzerland – but nothing of use to her . . . A lot on the Gulf . . . Something about a training camp in Afghanistan.

The other analysts were leaving their desks, collecting their coffee and making for the conference room. Eleven o'clock – she checked the time.

Training camp in Afghanistan. Been there – the thought was almost subliminal. Seen it, done it. Before she went on leave. She logged out, helped herself to a coffee and followed the others through.

The Tank was in the centre of the building, no exterior windows, the lighting recessed into the ceiling. The conference table was rectangular, and the chairs around it were executive-style. Two walls were bare and painted a pastel primrose, the front wall was sectioned and contained a screen for the overhead projector, and the remaining side wall was wood-panelled, with display boards for charts and maps behind.

The session was routine – regular time and regular format. Kilpatrick briefing them on what Upstairs had briefed him an hour earlier, then discussing the strands they had identified previously, throwing ideas at them and expecting them to throw them back, goading them to think laterally, to make the connections nobody else would imagine. The session concluding, as always, with Kilpatrick sitting back and allowing them to throw up what they wanted and what might be on their minds.

Marchant sat quietly, listening but not contributing, taking in the details and thoughts and hypotheses of what had happened in her two-week absence. Kilpatrick was right: next time she really should try paragliding. Next time she should go over the edge. So Kilpatrick had been military, otherwise why would he have done some jumps? Interesting guy, Kilpatrick.

Training camp – the thought came at her. Not hard, not strong; just a breeze in the morning.

Training camp in Afghanistan – the same report she'd seen before she went on leave. Except it wasn't. Because the first had been CIA and this was FSK.

FSK – the Federal Counter-Intelligence Service, the new name for the KGB in Russia after the collapse of the Soviet Union. In the other republics the KGB had been renamed the KNB.

Ten years ago Moscow was the Evil Empire; now Moscow, London and Washington were exchanging security and intelligence reports on a regular basis. There would be a reason, of course; Moscow was still Moscow. So perhaps the data was unimportant, perhaps someone was trawling, or perhaps it was still part of a double-game. She made a note to check anyway, and focused on the meeting.

By the time she ran the Moscow summary it was twenty minutes past twelve. She noted the reference and called up the main report. The document was from the Counter-Terrorism Directorate of the FSK, and the Afghan source was unnamed but presumably local, recruited by the KGB during the Soviet Union's occupation of Afghanistan and kept on the payroll after the Soviet pull-out, his allegiance shifted to the FSK in Moscow, presumably because the unit to which he belonged, or his controller, was Moscow-based.

*Guerrilla training camp reported in Afghanistan* – she summarized the information. *Location and training details.* Worth cross-checking the location with the CIA report. Probably the same, too much of a coincidence if it wasn't. *Trainees believed to number sixteen.* Everything was too accurate, too specific, to be local. If the local Mujihadeen were running a camp, and there was no reason why they should be, they wouldn't be training up just sixteen. *Trainees believed to be European, and include women.* Therefore not the Muj, except if it was in Afghanistan it had to be.

She read the details again, cross-referenced them against the Langley report, and called Kilpatrick.

'Got five minutes?'

'Three this afternoon?'

'Fine.'

At three exactly she sat in The Sanctum. The door was closed, as the door was always closed with Kilpatrick. Nothing personal in the room which might give any clue to his background, she thought as she always thought: no photographs or souvenirs or memorabilia.

Sandhurst and Irish Guards, he would have told her. The usual tours in Northern Ireland he might have conceded. The last two assigned to 14 Int as liaison with the boys with no faces. Undercover work down on the border and a couple of tight runs, more than a couple if he cared to remember. After the second tour with 14 Int he'd volunteered for, and passed, selection for the outfit with the paper bags over their heads. And then the bastard had got him; then one afternoon, just after he'd passed selection for Hereford, he'd been out running and some drunk had driven over him. And though he'd recovered, the medics said he would never be able to parachute again, so he'd had a drink in the mess and moved to the organization he now called Riverside. The bastard had got off, of course, because of the usual connections. Although six months later he'd been found with his BMW wrapped round a tree; broken neck, so he was DOA – dead on arrival – at the local emergency unit, and three times over the limit. Whether by the hand of Fate, God, or Michael Kilpatrick was never made clear.

'The CIA report of a training camp in Afghanistan two weeks ago.' The printouts of the CIA and FSK reports were on Marchant's lap.

'No satellite overfly because everyone was looking at the Gulf.' Kilpatrick showed he remembered.

'Correct.'

He leaned back in his chair and waited. She was different – it crept up on him. She was suddenly turned on, and in so being, she was turning him on. And they knew it.

'There's a second report of a camp in Afghanistan.'

'Langley again?' Because if so they might have some Sat Int – satellite intelligence. Might have done some homework.

'Moscow.'

Kilpatrick took the reports she passed him and read each

carefully, concentrating on the information she had highlighted. 'So . . .'

'Only a first guess,' she warned him.

'Understood.'

'Perhaps someone's building up a team.'

'Why?'

'No idea.'

'Why Afghanistan?'

'Probably because it's safe. Probably because a lot of the traditional areas – Syria, Sudan, Libya – are closed down or their governments are playing the good guy.'

'What about Iran or Iraq, what about the Empty Quarter in North Yemen?'

She shrugged. 'Perhaps there are too many political strings in those places.'

'Or because whoever's putting this together knows Afghanistan and has worked there,' Kilpatrick suggested.

'Mujihadeen?'

'Not if they're training Europeans.'

'Afghani?' Marchant used the Russian slang for Soviet veterans of the Afghan campaign. 'Special Forces or Alpha Group?'

'Possibly.' But said with a slight shake of the head.

'Maybe someone who was with the Soviets in Afghanistan,' he suggested. 'Someone already involved in training terrorists. Who did the Soviets use as trainers?' The question was rhetorical. 'Mainly they used East Germans.' Kilpatrick sat back in his chair. 'The East Germans were everywhere.'

'What about the reference to Europeans?'

'Could be anyone.'

Which they both knew.

The secretary brought them coffee.

'So where do we go from here?' Marchant asked.

'Circulate the connection.' Under the new international

liaison scheme. 'See if anyone has any leads.' Because if Riverside had picked up a cross-reference, someone else should have, especially something so obvious. Unless not everyone was getting both CIA and FSK reports.

'How about Sat Int?' she asked. Because now we have reason to request it from Langley.

'I'll run it Upstairs and see what they say.'

An hour later Kilpatrick called her in. The request for more data had gone to Langley and Moscow fifteen minutes ago, Riverside asking for additional data plus map references. If the references tied in Riverside would ask DC for a satellite overfly. Which would mean taking the game up a notch, which would also mean interrupting the priority surveillance over the Gulf, and which would cost. But which would also mean money in the bank, because Langley wouldn't be thinking of it as a Brit debt; Langley would be panicking and wondering what they'd missed.

And if the references didn't match there'd be no request for an overfly and they'd look somewhere else. But Riverside would still be ahead of the game, the department would still be leading within Riverside and she would be ahead in the department.

'What time do we expect an answer?' Marchant asked. Because it was four in the afternoon in London, eleven in the morning in DC, but seven in the evening in Moscow. And because she and Geoff had tickets for the Royal Court plus dinner after.

'How long is a piece of string? You have something on?'

'No.'

She left The Sanctum, returned to her desk, telephoned Geoff's office and left a message that she had to work late and therefore had to cancel that evening. Then she fetched a coffee, switched on the terminal, and began trawling. So why lie about this evening; why not say she had something on but could cancel it? The sun was going down and the sky outside was fading purple. The office was deserted, only the desk in Kilpatrick's room still occupied. She picked up the phone on the first ring.

'You'd better come in,' Kilpatrick told her.

She picked up a notepad and went through.

'Drink?' he asked.

'What's on offer?' It ties, she sensed. Washington and Moscow have come up with map references, and the references match.

'Black Bush do?'

'Black Bush sounds fine.'

Kilpatrick opened the cocktail cabinet concealed in the wall to his right, and poured them each a glass, a handful of ice in each. 'First time.' He gave her the glass. 'Enjoy.' He raised his glass and tapped it against hers. 'Good luck.'

'First time for what?'

'First time on the line. It's the same camp. The request for a satellite overfly went to Washington fifteen minutes ago.'

They sat sipping the whisky and talking through it, then she went back to her desk and tried to occupy herself. Okay, so it was low key; so it was only the first move and the game might not go anywhere. But it was her first time on the line, as Kilpatrick had put it; the first time somebody had made a play and invited her in. The first time she'd moved into another game. Strange, the feeling. The excitement. Like looking at the paragliders coming over the cliff in Kandersteg; like standing on the Almenalp and wondering if she could go over the edge too.

'Langley's agreed.' She hadn't heard Kilpatrick behind her. 'They're dropping a KH-12 tomorrow morning local time. We're due at Grosvenor Square at eleven. Seeing the Russians after.'

Got to make your first play with the Big Boys sometime, Kilpatrick might have said. Got to get your name known among those who count, got to get your feet under the table. Because that's the name of the game, and a lot of others are playing it. Even though the meeting's low level, almost informal; a coffee with old friends. Show you off to them, he might have said; show them off to you.

'Thanks,' she told him. 'I appreciate it.'

'Supper?' Kilpatrick suggested.

Kilpatrick was fast lane, Kilpatrick was international terrorism, and international terrorism and narcotics were the buzz words. Therefore Kilpatrick was destined for the top, and people going that high that fast worked out early who they could trust and who they would take with them.

'Why not?'

The street was on the edge of the university campus, the evening was getting dark, and she had already checked the area twice. In eleven days Jovan would be five. Kara sat in the car and waited. A couple walked past, early twenties and laughing.

For one moment she wasn't in the street. For one moment she was back in the training camp in Afghanistan. Further back than that. Back in Travnik, in the room on Tobacco Road. Hearing the knock and opening the door. Seeing the woman and the boy standing outside, the snowflakes drifting on to them and the wet seeping into them. The woman thin and stooped and badly dressed, and the boy white with cold . . .

. . . Back off, Finn, she heard her own voice before she heard his. I told you not to come again, told you I didn't want to listen to you. So sod off now before you say a word.

Why, Kara? What are you afraid of? Why are you hesitating? Why haven't you told the woman and the boy to go?

Back off, Finn, like I told you. Because you're wrong,

Finn. I know where I am and what I'm seeing. So sod off, Finn. Don't tell me who I am or what I'm seeing or thinking.

Why not, Kara? Because somebody has to.

Okay, Finn, but make it fast. Because I've got things to do and places to see. Money to make and people to screw.

You're thinking everyone's fucked you, Kara, and you're right. The UN and NATO fucked you. I fucked you because I didn't take Jovan out on the chopper. Keefer fucked you, every which way. Then came back with Pieter and double fucked you.

But you're also doing the fucking, Kara. So stop feeling sorry for yourself, stop telling me the whole world is fucking you, because you're fucking it just as much.

Except the world hasn't stopped fucking you, because Keefer is about to fuck you again. Not your pussy and your mouth and your ass this time. Worse than that, Kara. Because through you they're going to fuck your people, going to fuck the Karas and the Adins and the little Jovans who haven't yet been born. You know what they're playing at, Kara; they told you who they're working for. They're recruiting for the fundamentalists. Nothing wrong with the fundamentalists, but everything wrong with the politicos and the extremists and the madmen who suck on their blood. So they're recruiting Bosnian Muslims because they say it will help Bosnia, but that's fuck, Kara, and you know it. Because the Bosnians aren't Muslims, but the extremists are trying to make them so, trying to use Bosnia to spread their form of religious politics into Europe. Because once they've recruited Bosnians, and once you die as a terrorist and the world knows you were a Bosnian, then everyone in Bosnia will be termed a terrorist and you and your people will lose. And the West, who've fucked you like there's no tomorrow, will say they were right because look, you're a Bosnian and a Muslim and a terrorist. And the extremists in the Middle East will rub their hands and say look how the West has abandoned you, so come to us . . .

. . . She was back in the car, back in the street. The evening was darker and the couple were disappearing round the corner. Kara left the car and walked the two streets to the address.

The apartment was on the second floor. She rang the bell and stepped back, sensed rather than saw the moment the person inside peered through the security grille. 'Frederick,' she said. 'I'm Eva.'

The man was in his early thirties, with short hair and stylish spectacles. He stood back and indicated she should enter. 'Coffee?' he asked. He was slightly nervous, she thought, as if he was more at home with his computers than with people.

'Coffee would be good.' She was wearing the wig, contact lenses and cheek fillers, plus gloves.

The room was small and interesting. Some would have called it jumbled: the computer on the desk, the bookshelves lined with technical journals, other books open on chairs or on the floor. Except there was a pattern, as if the hacker knew exactly where everything was, as if he had been working on something before she arrived.

He came back in, gave her the mug, and sat down at the computer.

'So what do you want?' When he drank the coffee he took off his glasses, put them back on again each time he stopped drinking.

'Four viruses.' Kara gave him the list of the systems into which they should be introduced. Three of them were covers, the range of organizations further disguising her target, and one was the system she wished to disrupt.

'Okay.' He was nervous in a different way this time. Suddenly full of nervous energy, she thought. 'You're not talking about viruses, because viruses do one thing, and what you're talking about is something different.'

She waited for him to explain.

'What we're talking about is accessing certain systems, then inserting our own programs, so that the systems will do things they're not supposed to do.'

They went through the four targets, then went back to the beginning and focused on each in detail. Came to the third.

'Let's assume the airline has a fully integrated system.' He was totally engrossed in the problem and the mechanics of solving it. 'Fully integrated systems cover everything: passenger ticket information, crew assignments, aircraft maintenance history. Anything and everything.'

Passenger boarding lists, she thought.

'Might even be using the system devised by American Airlines.' It was half to her and half to himself. 'Probably find that the system is written in C++. No problem once we know what system they're using, but I can probably get that by trawling round the Internet. Then I write and insert the program, the program itself to be fired when a specified event occurs.'

The passenger boarding list to be wiped when an airline official keyed in the information that the flight in question had taken off.

They moved on to the fourth target – the third cover – then agreed that she would phone in seven days, plus the codes which would confirm that the programs had been inserted.

'I'll be back,' she also told him, even though she wouldn't be. Make them commit to you, Keefer had said; make them think it's not a one-off. That way they'll be loyal to you. As far as loyalty went in this business. She gave him the envelope. 'I know we agreed five thousand.' And I know you would have done it just for the challenge. 'But I've put an extra thousand in as down payment for next time.'

*

When Kilpatrick and Marchant left Riverside the following morning it was ten-thirty, the drizzle settling slightly and the soundproof screen shutting them off from the driver. The unmarked Vauxhall Senator slid unnoticed across Vauxhall Bridge and along Millbank, the Thames on their right.

'Ed Lessons is HoS.' Kilpatrick was seated to the left. HoS – Head of Station. 'He'll be trying to score points. US Marines before he joined CIA, married with two girls. Good operator and on the way up.'

So watch him because he'll be watching us, because sometime he'll be sitting at The Big Table. And when he is I don't want to be anywhere else. And I assume you don't want to be either.

'Leonid Brizinski is head of FSK station. Good connections in Moscow, London's a stepping stone for him as it is for Lessons. Married, three kids, wife back home and a bit of a lady's man. Careful, of course; if he fancied you he'd ask, but only if he knew you'd say yes and it wouldn't do him any harm.'

Kilpatrick looked straight at her.

So now we know the ground rules, she thought. Good operator, Kilpatrick, good negotiator. Make you an offer and leave you both with the back door out as if the offer had never been made . . .

The Senator cut through Victoria towards Buckingham Palace.

Good operator, Fiona Marchant – there was no need for Kilpatrick to even glance at her. Suit well cut enough to show off her legs and figure, but stopped plenty short of the line which said she was on offer. Power dresser to say she knew what she was talking about, but way short of the line which said she was a threat . . .

They circled Hyde Park Corner, headed north up Park Lane, turned right, then right again into the underground car park beneath the grey structure of the US embassy.

Lessons was waiting in his office. He was shorter than Marchant had anticipated: five six and squat, blond hair now receding slightly but still crew cut; sharp features and alert eyes. There were pictures of presidents on the walls, photographs of family on the desk, the Stars and Stripes and the Agency flag behind, and two aides in attendance. The bird's already flown and he knows the results, she thought. But Kilpatrick had both understood and expected it.

'Ed, good to see you again.' Kilpatrick shook Lessons's hand. 'May I introduce Fiona Marchant. Fiona, Ed Lessons, London HoS.'

Lessons introduced them to the others, then they sat down and accepted coffee.

'So what news, Ed?' Kilpatrick was relaxed, almost informal.

'The good news or the bad?' Lessons spread his hands and shrugged.

'You know me, Ed.' Kilpatrick nodded as one of the aides handed him coffee, and shook his head at the offer of cream and sugar.

Lessons indicated that the other aide should begin the briefing.

'The good news is that there is a camp.' The aide spoke with a brisk East Coast accent. 'Still in operation. Instructors and trainees present.' He paused, allowed enough time for Kilpatrick to ask about the bad.

'Actually . . .' Kilpatrick leaned forward slightly. 'Perhaps I will take cream after all.' The first aide offered him the silver jug; Kilpatrick nodded his thanks, poured a little into his coffee, handed it back, and waited, not drinking.

'The bad news is that there aren't sixteen trainees, there are six. They aren't European, and there are no women among them.'

So what now, Marchant thought.

'You'll let us have copies, plus the analysis?' Kilpatrick still hadn't drunk his coffee.

'Of course.' Lessons smiled. Good operator, Marchant thought; even though this morning he was under orders to screw them. 'Anything else?' Lessons asked.

'Fiona?' Kilpatrick turned to her.

Two questions, she almost said but didn't. Because if he'd wanted her to speak he would have told her before the meeting. 'No.'

'The Langley report indicating the existence of a training camp.' Kilpatrick addressed the aide. 'Who or what was the source?'

'I'm afraid I can't disclose that.'

Out of order, she thought. Shouldn't have answered. Should have deferred to Lessons, because he and Kilpatrick are playing games with us this morning. And now you've stepped out of line, and Lessons is going to let you hang yourself.

Of course – it was in Kilpatrick's shrug. Pity you can't tell us, because we *are* supposed to be on the same side. 'The original Langley report.' It was almost an afterthought, as if it was of no importance. 'When was it sourced?'

You had it coming – Lessons waited for the aide to answer.

The aide checked the date on the file. 'August 25th.'

'Fiona?' Kilpatrick glanced at Marchant again.

'No,' she told the aide. 'Not the date Langley circulated the report.' Because we all know that date, because it's on the piece of paper in front of us, and even I can read joined-up writing. 'The date on which your source said he or she observed the training camp.' Because we're talking about different dates, aren't we? Because we need to know how long ago your source said he saw things happening.

Because the longer the time between them and the satellite overfly, the greater the chance of things changing.

'I don't know.' The aide was flustered.

'You'll find out,' she said.

Welcome to the club, Lessons thought. Not The Big Table, because not even Kilpatrick and I are there yet. But at least you're through the front door. 'Yeah,' he said. 'We'll find out.'

Thirty minutes later Kilpatrick introduced her to Leonid Brizinski.

'So the Americans say there are no Europeans in the camp?' Brizinski leaned forward.

'Apparently.' Kilpatrick seemed impassive.

They were seated in a semicircle of armchairs round the fireplace, though the fire was not lit. Brizinski on one side, flanked by aides, Kilpatrick and Marchant on the other. The conversation being recorded, she assumed, but so had the discussion in Grosvenor Square been.

'And no women?'

'No.'

She remembered Kilpatrick's run-down on the Russian and waited for Brizinski's response.

'So what do you want?' Brizinski sat back and waited, virgin of virgins and innocent of innocents.

'Fiona?' Kilpatrick turned slightly.

'Sixteen trainees,' she asked. 'All European, five women.'

'Yes.'

'Who else?'

What does she mean, who else ... Brizinski turned to Kilpatrick but Kilpatrick was still looking at Marchant. 'What do you mean, who else?' Brizinski asked at last.

'I mean we need a name.' Kilpatrick now. No pissing about with saying there were trainers, all that crap. Because we all know something's going down and we're playing games and not getting anywhere. And unless we do we're all in the brown stuff when it hits the fan.

'Actually there were two.' The statement was almost a throwaway, as if they were discussing the time of day or the result of a horse race. 'East Germans, ex-Stasi. Used to work with us in what you British call the Good Old Days.' Brizinski smiled again and allowed them time to appreciate the joke. 'On file if you really need the material.' Though not everything, of course, even post-glasnost, Euroterrorism co-operation and all that. 'Photographs as well if you think they might help.'

'Names?' Marchant asked.

'One was called Bergmann.'

'And Bergmann's boss?' Kilpatrick this time. Because we're still playing games, Leonid, and you won't give me what I want until I've sung for my supper.

'His name's Keefer.'

# 10

The sun was hot and the water of the swimming pool shimmered blue. Langdon swung in the hammock between the palms, laughed at the others splashing in the pool, and accepted the glass of orange juice – iced and freshly squeezed – the maid brought him.

Langdon loved it here. Partly because there were few tourists, and especially no British, therefore he could relax untroubled. Get away from it, even though there needed to be something to get away from: unless there was, the game wasn't worth playing. Partly because of the more traditional connections: Cadiz, where Drake had come in with guns blazing and disappeared almost as quickly on a freak change of wind; Cape Trafalgar, which would have been a relatively uninspiring promontory except for Nelson. And the English had even married into the sherry families who dominated the region's economy and politics.

Therefore Langdon and his wife came to this part of south-west Spain at least once a year, stayed in the villa outside the town. Before, when he had simply been a back-bencher, even when he'd been rewarded with a junior ministerial post, he'd made it for *feria*, the local celebrations after Easter. But now things were different, now there was no time. Family the same, really. This summer Hilary had brought Sammi down from Berlin, though Rob was tied up and had only managed a weekend.

There was the occasional visit from a politician or

statesman, of course, but that was to be expected. Plus the red boxes, which arrived daily.

Bosnia was blowing up again; problems with the Serbs and the Contact Group, and the Russian nationalists were applying their own form of pressure. Every sign that the Serbs were going to take it out on another Muslim safe haven. More innocents suffering, he supposed, but in war there was always a price to pay, therefore someone had to pay it. Plus some nonsense now about a British mercenary getting his throat cut, and his local MP demanding the Foreign Office do something about it. Just when he didn't need it, but that was how backbenchers kept their names in their local papers.

The mobile buzzed. The Nicholls's visit was almost at an end, one of the Osborne family PAs informed him.

Langdon had dropped Nicholls and his wife and daughter off two hours earlier – special tour of the bodega, including personal greeting by one of the Osborne family. Langdon was, after all, the British Foreign Secretary, even though he was also a family friend and rented one of the family's villas overlooking Cadiz bay to the north of Puerto de Santa María. Not many were invited, of course: either to stay in the villa, or as guests of Langdon when he was in residence. And Nicholls understood that. Not in an obsequious manner – Nicholls was, after all, both a Balliol man and a Civil Service high flyer; but he and his wife showed it anyway.

'Time to go,' Langdon shouted to the others.

They dried and dressed, then picked up the Nicholls family and headed south. The sky was a cloudless blue and the restaurant – off the main road midway between Cadiz and Tarifa, on the Atlantic coast of Spain – was white-walled and red-roofed.

'Only locals, of course,' Langdon informed Nicholls as they went inside. He greeted the head waiter as an old friend, and allowed him to escort them to one of the tables on the upper floor. 'If I may I suggest the gazpacho,' he addressed the Nichollses. 'It really is the best you'll ever taste.' He snapped his fingers. 'Gazpacho to start,' he told the waiter. 'Little snifter to begin with,' he suggested.

'Has to be fino,' Nicholls was relaxed but aware.

'As long as it's Osborne,' Sammi told them.

Correct pronunciation, Langdon noted. The emphasis on the second o, but the e at the end also pronounced in the Spanish fashion, even the Andalucian accent correct. Which was no more than he expected.

'Of course,' he told his granddaughter.

The following morning he and Nicholls caught the first flight to London. At nine minutes past two that afternoon the Rover whisked him from the Foreign and Commonwealth Office, down Whitehall and through Carriage Gates into the Houses of Parliament. His PPS was waiting in the area behind the Speaker's chair. Langdon conferred with him for four minutes, then took his place on the front bench for question time, his junior ministers with him. At two-thirty the Speaker called for the first question. Questions were tabled in advance, supplementaries not. Three minutes later the Opposition spokesman asked the supplementary Langdon understood was inevitable.

'The Foreign Secretary will no doubt be aware of the latest report from Bosnia. Is it not time for the Foreign Secretary to insist that the United Nations take a more positive role?'

Langdon rose and walked the two paces to the dispatch box.

'I share the honourable member's concern for Bosnia-Herzegovina. But he, even more than others, should be aware that the actions of UN personnel are governed by the mandate under which the United Nations is present in the first place. UN troops are in Bosnia-Herzegovina as part of UNPROFOR, the United Nations Protection Force. The task of UNPROFOR is to protect UN personnel, plus others. It is not to take one side or the other.'

There would be more questions. Most of them would be the same, and all of them would be answered with ease. He sat down and waited confidently for the next. At three-thirty he bowed to the Speaker and left the chamber.

Nicholls was waiting. 'The Israeli ambassador's on his way,' he informed Langdon. 'Sounds serious.'

It was five in the afternoon. Marchant fed in the key-words she and Kilpatrick had acquired from the Russian Brizinski and waited to see what the databases came up with. Turing was still down and showing no sign of returning to anything approaching the computer version of Life. Bit of a race now – she felt the slight thumping in her head. Washington and Moscow now knew about the Afghan camp and its significance, so the CIA and the FSK, and every agency in Europe, as well as everyone in Six, plus sections of Five, would be running hard and trying to be first to make the next connection. The file names flashed on the screen; she called up each and began the trawl through. Somebody else is doing this in DC and Moscow and Paris and Bonn and Rome and everywhere she could possibly think of, she was aware. There were no connections, at least none she could see. She tried to shake the fuzziness from her brain and started again.

'Conference, now,' Kilpatrick's PA told them.

Marchant logged off and made her way to The Tank. Most of the others were already round the table. Kilpatrick came in, a cup of coffee in one hand and a file under his arm. 'You're late,' he told the man behind him. 'Close the door.' Funny how Kilpatrick always liked the door closed, Marchant thought, even in the middle of the building housing Riverside.

'The Israelis just shouted wolf.' There was no preamble. 'General warning, nothing specific.' But that was how things started. And the last time the Israelis had shouted wolf it had been about attacks on Jews in Argentina and Mexico and Britain. And two months later the attacks had taken place. And the time before that, the warning had been about an extremist attack in New York, and six weeks later someone had bombed Manhattan. 'Attacks on four locations: London, Moscow, Paris and Washington. Any ideas?'

There were half a dozen, none of them specific and none of them, at this stage, particularly well-informed. Any chance this connects with the Afghan camp, he asked Marchant. The bastards have scored, she thought; either Lessons or Brizinski had held something back and now they were ahead of the game. She'd been through everything and come up with nothing, she admitted. Don't worry about it, Kilpatrick told her, Ed and Leonid hadn't come up with anything either.

It was almost six.

'Downing Street wants a first analysis by nine this evening.' Kilpatrick closed the session. 'Everything else goes by the board. We'll meet again at seven, again at eight.'

The evening was drifting on, suddenly not drifting, time suddenly spinning away. They were running cross-checks like they were going out of fashion, scanning the computer files for the slightest hint of the slightest connection, talking with each other then going back to their terminals, calling up Sat Int and Elec Int and Hum Int and every other classification of Int anybody had ever dreamed up. FSK in Moscow, DST in Paris, and CIA in DC doing the same thing. The lines between them hot with activity and everybody screaming at Tel Aviv for more details.

Marchant reached for her mug and drank the coffee even

though it was cold, swung in her seat and talked it through with the analyst next to her. Suggested something, picked up on something, and swung back again, ran another check, and came up with another dead end.

They went through to the seven o'clock meeting, most people contributing but Kilpatrick keeping it tight then sending them back to their desks.

They filed through for the eight o'clock meeting.

'So what have we got?' Kilpatrick asked.

They summarized the lines suggested during the two meetings. Not good, they understood, but with such short notice no one else was likely to come up with anything better. No points gained, but none lost.

'Good try,' Kilpatrick told them. 'See what we come up with tomorrow.'

The cross-check still wasn't getting her anywhere. She tapped in the key-word again and waited as it accessed the databases. This is crazy, she knew: run a check with Israel as the single key-word and the screen would scroll for ever. She cancelled the request, then tapped in the key-words Israel, guerrilla, terrorist, Afghanistan, Keefer and Bergmann, and re-ran the program. There were no files or reports in which all the key-words appeared. Therefore the search was too specific, too ambitious. She keyed the words Afghanistan, Keefer and Bergmann and tried again.

It was four o'clock in the morning and she was having a nightmare, Fiona Marchant told herself. The night was dark around her and Geoff was sleeping heavily beside her. She slid out of bed, wrapped a dressing gown round her, went to the kitchen and made herself a coffee. At least it was gone four now, almost five, at least she would soon be at Riverside. Outside it was getting light. She sat for another half-hour, then showered, dressed, made herself toast, took Geoff a coffee, and left. By seven she was at her terminal, by seven-thirty everyone else was in.

Why include Keefer and Bergmann as key-words in the cross-checks? Because Brizinski had named them as being at the Afghan training camp ... What's the connection between the Israeli shout and Afghanistan? Not sure, except that at this stage there was nothing else ...

She tapped in the key-words Israel, Afghanistan, guerrilla, terrorist, Keefer and Bergmann and ran the check. Already done this – the thought floated through the cavern of her brain. Except that was in her sleep and now it was for real.

The Israelis have shouted wolf, Kilpatrick had said the previous afternoon. Attacks on four locations: London, Moscow, Paris and Washington. Keefer and Bergmann were both ex-Stasi, Brizinski had said. You've got it – she wasn't sure where the feeling came from. It's there and it's yours, but you can't bloody well see it.

The farm was fifteen kilometres from the town. Three minutes before she estimated she would reach the turning to it, Kara pulled the BMW off the road, unscrewed the number plates, replaced them with a set she had bought earlier, and concealed the correct plates in a plastic bag in the ditch. Just in case the contacts tried to trace her through the vehicle. Just in case they searched the vehicle while she was inside the building.

She was wearing what she always wore when she made contact: wig, cheek pads and tinted lenses. Gloves so she wouldn't leave any fingerprints, and shoes she could move fast in.

Next week Jovan would be five – the thought lingered as always at the back of her mind. And in the time between now and then someone would try and take her out – the new thought crept up on her. Because of the people with whom she was dealing, and the money they would know she had to be carrying. Therefore sometime in the next days there would be the one man she was expecting sitting at a desk in front of her, but another lurking unseen behind her.

It was ten in the morning and she wasn't due till eleven. Specify a time then arrive early, Keefer had told her. That way you take them by surprise, see how they react. That way you see if they're setting you up, and set them up instead.

Bosnia was on the cross – she had watched the television pictures that morning. Bihac was about to be crucified.

She checked the map, confirmed the other ways out – cross-country if she had to – then eased back on to the side road. One and a half kilometres later she turned left, up the gravel track, and through the trees. The farmhouse was large and two-storey, the barns and sheds around it were modern, and there was a security camera tucked discreetly in the hedge. Not too many cows, she noted, but there wouldn't be. She swung the BMW into the yard. No manure, she noted, no mud. No other vehicles. She parked facing out and knocked on the door.

The man who answered was big – tall and broad-shouldered – but not a farmer. You're not alone, she thought, and you've seen me coming, because the camera in the hedge isn't the only security you've got.

'I'm here about the crates,' she told him the first line of the code. Followed him inside, along a corridor and into the room at the end. Security locks on the doors and windows, she noted, some of the furnishings comfortable but most of them functional. An empty feel about the place, as if it was an office or a warehouse rather than a farm. Computers and filing cabinets and security monitors.

'Coffee?' The man had large hands and thick muscular fingers.

'Black, no sugar.'

'What sort of crates?' Male voice. From behind her.

'I have to move some machine parts.' The second section of the code.

'What sort?'

'Small engineering stuff. Drills, that sort of thing.' The last line of the code.

The first man gave her the coffee and settled behind the desk.

'You said on the phone how you knew about us.' The voice from behind her again, moving slightly now.

The door was to her left, but she sensed there was a third man outside it. 'Like you said, I told you on the phone.' Through the go-between who calls himself Mickey. And Mickey's a fixer, a wheeler-dealer. Mickey knows who's who and who's got what. Which we all know. And Mickey is a contact of Keefer's, which I know but you don't.

'Cash up front.' Because we don't take plastic in this business. It was the man at the desk, the man in front of her.

'Of course.' The alarm bells were ringing. Don't blow it, she told herself; keep it under control. 'A small order to start with. Sub-machine guns, machine pistols, handguns.'

'Specific models?' Because this is a man's business and we don't exactly cater for women here.

'What are you carrying?' Kara asked him.

'M70k,' he told her.

'Manufactured by Zavodi Crvena Zastava of Belgrade,' she came back at him.

Fine – he shrugged. Except anyone could get that sort of information from any weapons magazine.

'Nine-millimetre short cartridge. Weight empty 720 grams, muzzle velocity 260 metres per second.' She leaned forward and held out her hand. The dealer opened his coat, took out the M70, removed the magazine and passed the weapon to her. Something about the way she handled it – the unease crept on the second man. Something about how she was sitting now, something about the gun. Not just the fact that she had held out her hand for the magazine and clipped it back in, or that she had placed the gun on the desk rather than give it back. He realized . . . that she had handled the M70 as if it was second nature; that she had moved her chair slightly so that she was sitting sideways and could see both of them; that she had placed the gun on the desk so that she rather than the man behind the desk could reach it. BMW outside parked facing out in case she had to leave quickly – he thought it through; probably false plates, and in any case she'd have another motor ten kliks away, transfer the load and torch the first.

He stepped in front of her, nodded at her, and sat down. 'So what do you want?'

'Five handguns, M70ks will do. Sub-machine guns: Zastava M85s and/or Socimi 821s; 7.65mm Model 84 Scorpio machine pistols. Ammunition and grenades.' The sub-machine guns between six and eight hundred dollars each, the pistols between two and four hundred, and the ammunition at fifty dollars for a thousand rounds. 'You can help me?' By which I mean: we can do the business?

'Yes.'

'You have a place I can test them?'

'Of course.'

It was twenty minutes to the next session in The Tank. Five have come up with a lead, someone to her left was whispering; Langley think they have an angle. Marchant fetched another coffee and settled again at the screen. It was there, hanging in the air in front of her – she couldn't shake off the feeling.

They filed into The Tank.

'Ideas,' Kilpatrick asked immediately.

They were talking, discussing, throwing ideas around and aware they were getting nowhere.

'You've got something?' Kilpatrick turned to her.

'Perhaps,' she said. 'Just can't grasp it.'

'Afghanistan?'

'Possibly.'

'Go lateral on it.' Kilpatrick relaxed. Made her relax. 'Go as far off the wall as you like.'

'Okay,' she nodded. It was there, she reminded herself; all she needed to do was reach out and grasp it. 'Okay,' she said again. 'Try this. Four cities being targeted, the Israelis said yesterday . . .'

Yes – a nod from Kilpatrick.

'Four cities, four teams . . .'

Yes, again. So – he nodded at her. Take it forward. Take me on.

She reached out and grasped it. 'Afghan training camp, sixteen trainees . . .'

'Washington, London, Paris and Moscow.' It was Michaels, another section head, seated two to her right. The words spoken with a snap of the fingers as he realized what she was saying and where it might lead. 'Four targets. Four teams of four.'

'Go on,' Kilpatrick told Marchant.

'Look at the targets.' She sat forward, suddenly alive, suddenly electric. 'Look at what they have in common.' Because they're all players in one major game.

'I understand,' Kilpatrick told her. 'Ideas?' He looked round the table. 'Contributions?'

'Look at the trainees in Afghanistan.' It was Michaels. 'All Europeans.'

'But Muslims.' Someone else. 'Otherwise the Muj wouldn't be training them or allowing them to be trained.'

'Exactly.' Michaels again. As if the breakthrough had been his.

'So what's the key?' Kilpatrick asked, drew the strands together, even though he already knew. 'Where are we talking about?' He looked to Marchant. Because you started it, you made the connection. Because you and I are playing our own little game.

'Bosnia.'

Oh hell . . .

Because Bosnia was already a quagmire, Bosnia had already sucked in the East and the West and was leading them inexorably along the road to Armageddon.

'The Muj, or some new terrorist grouping, recruits from Bosnia.' Marchant knew Michaels was going to summarize and made sure she spoke before him. 'Targets London, Washington, Moscow and Paris because Britain, the US, Russia and France are the four major external powers in the Bosnian crisis.'

'So we might have a goer.' Kilpatrick sat forward slightly. 'Connections? Links on to the next stage?' He looked at Marchant again. 'Keefer in the Afghan camp . . . Might that be the way?'

'Possibly.'

Kilpatrick straightened the file in front of him and summed up. 'We think there's a Bosnian involvement.'

'Yes.'

'And that Keefer's the link to it?'

'Perhaps.'

'But you haven't given me that link yet.'

Okay, the nods round the table said. Understood. Let's go.

'One other thing,' Kilpatrick pulled them back. 'How do we explain the satellite report? How do we explain the fact that the camp is now virtually empty?

'Because the main teams have finished training and left

Afghanistan.' He answered his own question. 'Because they're already in place.'

* * *

The house was on the outskirts of the village of Emirgân, almost lost among the eucalyptus trees on the hillside on the European side of the Bosphorus and some two and a half miles outside the main sprawl of Istanbul. It was two-storey, with white walls and red tiled roof, surrounded by lawns and a whitewashed perimeter wall, a satellite TV dish positioned discreetly at the rear. Similar houses were scattered round it, the minaret of a mosque rose two hundred metres away, and its position, on the east of the hill, allowed it a panoramic view over the Bosphorus to the fishing village of Kanlica on the Asian shore, the spans of the Faith Bridge to the right. The neighbourhood was discreet, and its occupants prosperous without being ostentatious. For five years, since the fall of the Berlin Wall, Keefer had used it as a base and a safe house.

His meeting with the terrorist organizer Sharaf was the following day. Three days earlier Keefer and Bergmann had returned from the training camp in Afghanistan. Now they spent two hours working through the details. At one they broke for a light lunch; at three one of the two bodyguards drove Keefer to the airport.

When Keefer checked in, the passport he used was in the name of Schilling. When flight IB 6969 departed Istanbul's Ataturk Airport at fifteen minutes to five, its destination was Madrid, rather than Rome, where the meeting with Sharaf was scheduled. Keefer had always been careful.

The motorway was behind them and the perimeter fence of the RAF station flashed alongside them.

'Inform Lyneham we are one minute out,' Finn told

Hereford on the secure radio. 'Inform Lyneham thirty seconds out.'

The exercise was routine for teams going on to anti-terrorist duty. Three weeks' work-up with the outgoing squadron – run through the standard procedures, plus anything new the squadron they were replacing might have come up with. Continuous rehearsals on buses, aircraft and trains. Fast-roping and specialist driving. Specialist courses, including what the military called MOE – Method of Entry – but which others might have called lock-picking. Plus the reconnaissance visits: the familiarization checks, the discussions with police and the detailed analysis of layouts and procedures. Liaison with other services, including the RAF for fast transport to other parts of the country. And hour after hour of shooting practice: on the range or in the Killing House at Hereford, the team practising its entry into hostage or terrorist situations; each man working to a specific pattern so that if they did it for real each would know where the others were and what they were doing.

The Range Rovers were fully operational – when you were on the team you never went anywhere unless you were ready to react – and the services upon whom you might call were also being trained or re-trained. This afternoon, therefore, they would fly to Arbroath, touch down, then fly back. Tomorrow it might be Gatwick, the week after Heathrow.

The barriers at the main gate were open and the Hercules was waiting on the tarmac, engines winding up and tail ramp down. The two Range Rovers screeched through the gate, past the office buildings and on to the runway. The engines of the Hercules were screaming. The Range Rovers slowed, ran up the ramp into the body of the plane, the ramp began to come up, and the Hercules trundled down the runway.

When Finn returned home that night it was almost ten

o'clock, the boys were in bed and Caz was sitting in front of the television. Her fists were clenched and her eyes fixed.

'What's wrong?' He put the travel bag down and sat beside her. When you were on the team you even brought some of your kit home with you. 'What's wrong?' he asked again.

ITV News at Ten was just beginning.

'Bosnia,' she told him. 'They've started to shell Bihac.'

A police launch moved along the river below, and the night sky above was smudged by the glare of London. It was mid-evening, closer to late evening, and the department was still working, though slower now, the tiredness setting in. Take-aways were being opened and feet were up on desks.

Marchant felt tired. Still full of adrenalin, but suddenly and inexplicably drained. There were plenty of connections, most of them branching out from her start point, but no leads and no indication which way to go from here. Three desks to her left the analyst called Michaels leaned back, stretched, fetched himself a coffee, and settled again.

The phone rang. She leaned forward and picked it up.

'A word,' Kilpatrick said.

She left her desk and went to his office.

'Close the door,' he told her.

She closed the door and sat opposite him.

'Good day today. If we crack it the credit's yours.'

'And if we screw it?'

He laughed and poured them each a Black Bush, handful of ice. 'Any luck with the Keefer connection yet?'

'Not so far.' Christ, she thought, she hadn't phoned Geoff and told him she would be late.

'Problems?' Kilpatrick asked.

'Can I use your phone?'

He waited while she made the call. 'Husband?' he asked.

Even though he knew, she thought. 'Partner,' she explained. 'I imagine your wife and family are used to it.' Ground rules time. Establish the parameters. Move the game on a stage.

'Probably.' And . . . 'They're in the country. I have a small place for when I have to stay in town.'

So now we both know.

When she returned home it was shortly after midnight and Geoff was asleep; when she woke Geoff was downstairs, the smell of fresh coffee seeping up the stairs. She pulled on a dressing gown, collected a cup, then showered and dressed.

'Sorry about last night. Something came up and I forgot to call.'

'No problem. We're still okay for the weekend?' Because tomorrow was Friday, and this Saturday and Sunday they were helping Mike and Mel with a cottage they'd just bought in the Fens.

Is it Friday already? she thought. 'Of course,' she told him.

By the time she reached Riverside it was almost nine; at ten they assembled for the first session in The Tank, by ten-thirty she was back at her desk. Bosnia was breaking down again – it hung like a shadow over all of them. And if Bosnia was breaking down and the terrorist threat was connected with Bosnia . . . Why the hell wasn't Turing up and running? Why the hell had the fuzz-heads not been able to sort it out? Because if they had, then the computers could have been doing the nuts and bolts stuff, and she and the others needn't be wasting their time.

Change the key-words, she decided, run them in different combinations. Make it simple, go right back to basics.

Afghan and Bosnia. Afghan and Keefer. Afghan and German. Afghan and Stasi.

Bosnia and Keefer. Bosnia and German. Bosnia and Stasi.

She activated the search and left her desk, went for a coffee and talked to the other analysts. When she returned the list of hits was on her screen. She scrolled through them, discarding those thrown up by previous searches.

Afghan and Bosnia ... there was nothing she hadn't checked before, the same with Afghan and Keefer. Afghan and German, and Afghan and Stasi ... there were mountains of references, most of them applicable to the period of Soviet occupation of Afghanistan.

Bosnia and Keefer ... which she'd already checked, but which she'd now check again. Bosnia and German ... mountains of hits again, most of them with a political context but one referring to British mercenaries. Bosnia and Stasi ... there wasn't much.

She selected the hits she didn't recognize and went through them in detail.

Bosnia and German ... She cruised through the political material and almost went for another coffee. Bosnia, German, British mercenary ... British mercenary killed in Bosnia earlier in the year ... demands for an enquiry by his local MP.

Why a reference to a British mercenary if the search she'd ordered referred to Bosnia and German? Bosnia, okay. But why German? She remembered the newspaper report when she'd been in Switzerland and the file when she'd returned from leave. No connection, she thought. No reason for a connection, she meant. Interesting though. She was thinking automatically now, almost subconsciously.

Walton, Brian – she read the details. Age thirty-one, medical discharge from the British army. No connections with British Intelligence, and no indications of links with any other intelligence service. Bosnia as mercenary with Muslim government forces, though little front line action.

Based as instructor near Travnik, Central Bosnia, at camp shared with Mujihadeen. Suspected by Mujihadeen of spying. Taken from billet for interrogation by Mujihadeen, found hanging upside down from tree following morning with throat cut. Others present at camp at time: French, Belgian and British mercenaries, Mujihadeen, Bosnian Muslim conscripts, two East Germans. Intelligence dated January and sourced other British mercenaries in camp.

She ran a printout, highlighted the key sections, and grabbed Kilpatrick the moment he returned from Upstairs.

'Keefer.'

'Yes.' He accepted the coffee his PA brought him and asked if Marchant wanted one. 'What about Keefer?'

'It's possible I might have something.' She gave him the printout, accepted the coffee the PA brought, and watched as he read the Walton report.

'Two East Germans in Afghanistan, two in Bosnia, might cross-match.' He finished reading. 'Names of East Germans in Bosnia?'

'No names.'

Kilpatrick skimmed the report again. 'Get Keefer's photograph from Brizinski, Bergmann's as well.' It was as if he was thinking aloud. 'Show them to the British mercenaries who were in Travnik with Walton and who reported his death. See if they recognize either of our two.'

He picked up the phone and began the call. As she went out, Michaels went in.

'Keefer,' she heard him say. 'Might have a Bosnian connection. British mercenary called Walton . . .'

The lookout was sunk like a shadow in the shop doorway.

The car turned up the street, its Mercedes engine a low rumble – driver and one man in the front, and a third man in the back. The man in the doorway swept the street carefully. The Mercedes turned into the parking area below the apartments and the man in the rear hurried inside.

Rome.

Keefer had arrived thirty minutes before. Now he sat patiently while Sharaf's minders ran their normal routine. Clear, the man next to him whispered in his radio. Secure, the lookout whispered in his motorola. The second Mercedes slid up the road.

The meeting between Keefer and Sharaf lasted ten minutes under three hours. Only when Sharaf was satisfied with Keefer's arrangements did he open a bottle of champagne and they began to relax.

'The first teams are in place and ready to go?' Sharaf asked again.

'In place and ready to go,' Keefer confirmed.

* * *

The Serbs were pressuring Sarajevo, and there were reports, as yet unconfirmed, that the UN safe haven of Bihac had been shelled again. Fiona Marchant logged off and went to the first session of the day in The Tank.

'There are no more details from the Israelis,' Kilpatrick told the meeting. 'London, Moscow, Washington and Paris continue to take the threat seriously. They've taken on board our hypothesis of a Bosnian connection and want anything else we come up with.' So well done. 'Thoughts,' he asked.

Something she'd missed – it crept up on her like a fog. Something she'd forgotten.

The photographs arrived at four that afternoon. So you're Keefer, Marchant thought, you're the man I'm after. You're Bergmann, she looked at the other, you're either at Keefer's side or the one who might lead us to him. If you were the ones in Travnik at the time Walton was murdered, if the two of you really were recruiting in Bosnia.

Something she'd missed – it crept up on her again.

The weekend.

She phoned Geoff at the office and caught him as he was leaving.

'You're not going to believe this. The job I'm working on is overrunning. I can't make it tonight. Why don't you leave me the car, travel down with Mike and Mel, and I'll drive down first thing in the morning.'

'Okay,' he replied, as if he had been expecting it.

'Thanks for understanding.' She meant it.

'It really is okay.'

The next session in The Tank was at seven.

'Three of the four British mercenaries believed to have been in Travnik at the time Walton was murdered have been traced,' Kilpatrick informed them. 'One is on a North Sea oil platform and the second is somewhere in Edinburgh. The third is working for a security company in the Gulf.'

'What about the fourth?'

'The fourth is believed to have joined the Foreign Legion.'

'So when will we know?' Something she'd missed – the thought still nagged at her. Something she'd forgotten. Not the weekend.

'Local Special Branch are chasing the first two now. Our embassy people are making arrangements for the third, and we can't do anything about the last until we know what name he might have used when he signed on. If he did, in fact, sign on for the Legion.' Or unless he was using it as cover to go walkabout.

Aberdeen Special Branch are flying out to contact number one on the first chopper tomorrow morning, Kilpatrick told them at eight. Dubai embassy have an address for contact three and are calling on him now, he updated them at nine. Even though it was one in the morning local time. Edinburgh contact has been traced but left Bosnia before Walton arrived, he briefed them at ten. Dubai contact was never in Bosnia, but has provided the name with which the fourth contact signed on for the Foreign Legion, he told them at eleven.

Time to call it a day, he also told them. Get a rest and start fresh in the morning. Even though the morning was Saturday.

The television was in the corner of the hotel room.

Kara packed the black leather navigator's bag – all the pistols except one, shoulder holsters and ammunition, sub-machine guns broken down so they would fit in, plus machine pistols. The bag was heavy, but manageable, and the weapons fitted. The remaining pistol she zipped into her coat pocket.

It was seven-thirty, Saturday morning.

She locked the case, tidied the room, and sat on the bed looking at the television news: the images of Bosnia which she remembered from last January. Different place, of course, different weather, but the story the same. No emotion, she told herself. The time for emotion has gone. Now is the time to do something about it. She left the room and checked out of the hotel.

Three hours later she sat in the office above the travel agent's. The room was the same as last time, she thought; the former Stasi fixer also the same. So perhaps she was wrong, perhaps no one was going to take her out. She gave him the navigation bag, plus an envelope containing two and a half thousand dollars, and told him the probable date.

'I can't be certain of the time.' Because she was reliant on flight times, and flights were sometimes delayed. 'Assume the morning, but I'll confirm on the day. Once I've confirmed, the mule should go by the airport clocks.' Because the timing would be crucial and there was no chance of synchronizing watches.

'Where?' the fixer asked.

'Is the mule male or female?'

'Female.'

'The women's toilets in the departure lounge. The switch itself at the washbasins.'

'Put your case on the floor,' the fixer told her. 'Money in an envelope by the basin. The carrier will pick up the money, check it in a cubicle, then make the switch.'

'What about losing the ticket counterfoils?'

'Already arranged. Another two and a half thousand dollars.' He gave her the number of a public phone in the Europa Centre. 'Telephone me with the flight and boarding details when you've made the bag switch.'

An hour later Kara telephoned the passport forger in Amsterdam. The call was from a pay phone and the codes each used confirmed that the passports were ready, only the last details and photographs to be added.

'Tomorrow morning, eleven o'clock,' she told him.

Tomorrow morning, eleven o'clock, Frank confirmed. He held down the rest, lifted it, waited for the dialling tone, and made the call.

'Tomorrow morning, eleven o'clock,' he told the collector.

Pity really. But thank Christ he'd thought of it, because the gambling debt was growing daily with the interest they charged, and he'd only just been able to persuade them that the woman who was coming the next day might have access to enough money to meet the debt.

Eleven o'clock tomorrow morning, the collector told the gorillas. You know where Frank lives. Be there at five to, but don't let her see you.

Marchant checked whether Turing was running, was not surprised when it was not, and called up the overnight reports. At nine they assembled in The Tank.

'The Foreign Legion contact has been traced to an exercise in Angola,' Kilpatrick informed them. 'Someone's already on his way to show him the photographs.' Someone who was ex-SAS and working for a defence company run by ex-Regiment people and operating highly successfully, though low profile. 'Nothing else so far.'

They returned to their desks. Bosnia/politics; Bosnia/military; Bosnia/general. The list was endless, Marchant thought. The Tank again, Kilpatrick's PA told them at ten. They filed in and waited.

'Brownie points time.' Kilpatrick stood at the end of the table. 'Aberdeen Special Branch have just come through. The contact on the oil rig has seen the photos and confirms that the two East Germans in Travnik were Keefer and Bergmann.' Ninety minutes later he updated them again. 'The Legion contact in Angola has confirmed that our men were in Bosnia in January.' He allowed them time to congratulate themselves. 'So where do we go from here?'

They began again. CIA at Langley would be pissed off that it had been Riverside who'd made the first confirmation – the excitement hung in the air; FSK Moscow would be reading the riot act because it was London who'd stood it up. DST in Paris wasn't even opening its mouth.

The morning drifted into afternoon, and the afternoon was about to drift into evening. Back to basics, Marchant was aware she'd decided, run a search using just one keyword, but the search seemed to have called up every bloody file Riverside had ever put on the databases.

Oh hell – she remembered, and phoned the number in Norfolk. 'Sorry,' she told Geoff when Mel called him to the phone. 'Can't make it tonight.'

'Why not?'

Because there are four terrorist teams on the hoof, and

one of them is in London, and Christ only knows what's going to happen if we don't get the bastards before they get us. Because Kilpatrick's staying the weekend and you're out of town.

'One of the computers has gone down. Thrown everything into chaos.'

'Okay.'

'Thanks.'

That morning the boys had helped prepare the food for the barbecue; that afternoon Caz and Finn had gone mountain-biking with them – a couple of hours, not too hard. By the time they returned it was almost five.

'Help your dad start the barbecue,' Caz told the boys.

The television set was in the lounge. Both Caz and Finn had refused to have one in the kitchen. 'In Bosnia the town of Bihac has come under artillery fire for the third time in two days . . .' She stared at the pictures: the image of the town in the distance, the soldiers and artillery in the foreground and the caption *Serbian Television* superimposed over the bottom. Nine months ago this was Maglaj – the thought had been in her mind since the shelling had started again. And still the UN and the West was doing nothing. So the rules of the game made it difficult for the UN to intervene; so the UN wasn't there to take one side or the other. But the UN would have done the same in Germany and Austria and Czechoslovakia in 1938 and 1939.

The item ended. She poured Finn and herself a beer each, lemonade for the boys, and took the drinks to the garden.

'You all right?' Finn asked.

''Course,' she told him. 'Why shouldn't I be?'

The other families arrived at six – most of them from the regiment, though a few were friends from school. By seven the light was beginning to fade, at eight they lit the home-made torches, the children playing and the parents relaxed.

'Can I ask you something?' Caz asked.

'About what's troubling you?' he suggested. They were on the edge of the party, half-lost in the dark.

She moved slightly closer to him. 'In a way.'

He waited.

'They've shelled Bihac again, you know.'

'Yes, I know.' So that's why you watched the news, why you watch every news bulletin now.

'You ever think of Maglaj?' Caz asked him. 'Ever think of the woman there?' She took his glass, went to the table where they'd put the bottles, poured another drink for each of them, and came back. 'I mean . . . I know you think of what happened. What I mean is: how much do you think of it?' Which isn't what I really want to ask, but I've never asked before, so I probably won't now.

'Say it,' Finn told her.

She thought it through.

'I never ask about what you do. The specifics, I mean. Sometimes I want to know where you are, because I think that's my right. And if you can, you tell me. But sometimes I wonder what's in your mind, what you're thinking. And I never know, because you never tell me.' She paused. 'So what I'd like to know is this. What would happen if the government told you to do something you didn't want to do, something you didn't approve of. What would happen, for example, if the UN and the West change sides over Bosnia. Not now, but in a couple of years' time. What if the British decided, at some time, to support the Serbs and sent you back, but on the side of the Serbs.'

'Impossible,' Finn told her.

'But what if it did happen? What if they sent you against Maglaj, or somewhere like Maglaj?'

'They wouldn't,' he said simply.

'But what if they did?'

'My country right or wrong,' he half-laughed.

'Don't laugh at me, Finn. I'm serious.'

'I'm sorry,' he told her. 'The situation wouldn't arise,' he repeated.

One of the boys asked if they could have some more drinks.

So what was that all about – Caz watched as Finn went into the house. Of course it was about Finn, about what he did and what he was required to do. But perhaps it was also about herself, perhaps it was also about guilt. Of course it was about Bosnia, and Maglaj and Bihac, and all the other places in the world where the people were dying. But it was also about feeling helpless; about witnessing something – even on a television set – and feeling absolutely bloody useless and powerless to stop it, or do anything about it.

She heard the noise behind her and turned. Finn making the noise deliberately, she was aware, because Finn never made a noise. 'You all right?' he asked.

'Fine,' she told him. *Sort of* . . . the tone of voice gave it away.

You're still thinking about Bosnia, Finn almost said. You're thinking about a poor bloody town last January and another poor bloody town now. And it's beginning to crucify you.

'I was just thinking about the boys,' she told him.

He hadn't given her an answer, she reminded him. What if he was ordered to do something he disagreed with. And no more back door by saying it wouldn't happen.

'It doesn't happen, because when you're doing something, you don't have time to think. You might have time after, though not often. And some people have left the regiment because of it. Not because they disagreed with the politics of what they did in a specific situation, but because they had moral problems about it.'

'About killing, you mean?' Because we both know who we're talking about, and the man's still a great man, and is now a great priest.

'Yes.'

So what else . . . she allowed him the time.

'Like I said. You don't have time to think, because the moment you think you have that time, you allow yourself to relax, and that's the moment you're finished.'

Finished . . . she might have asked.

That's the moment to leave the regiment, he might have told her. Because that's the moment you're dead.

The light outside had faded and only half a dozen of them remained. Why was there a reference to Bosnia in one of the Burton reports, Marchant thought Bosnia was Europe and Burton was Middle East.

Kilpatrick came out of The Sanctum, a clutch of whisky glasses in each hand and a bottle of Black Bush under his right arm. 'The Tank, someone bring the ice.' They followed him through, closed the door, and sat round the table.

Good week, he told them. Even though, in a way, they were no further forward. Because they didn't have the next lead, didn't have whatever it was that might take them to the next stage, lead them to the four terrorist teams.

So why the hell had the search thrown up one of the Burton reports? The Burton report was history, the Burton report was dated last February, and what she was looking for would be up-to-date and present tense.

'Cheers, Boss.' Michaels raised his glass.

*Bosnian package arrived safely.* She remembered the reference but not the context; remembered that she hadn't thought it logical. *Bosnia shipment arrived* implied something entering Bosnia, but the intelligence had been sourced outside Bosnia, and that was why *arrived* had seemed the wrong word. So think it through, she told herself, work out what it might mean. Go lateral, as Kilpatrick might have told her.

Keefer and Bergmann enter Bosnia. Keefer and Bergmann recruit in Bosnia. Keefer and Bergmann leave Bosnia and those they have recruited come out, perhaps with them, perhaps not. Hence *Bosnia package arrived safely*. Keefer's and Bergmann's recruits out of the country and on their way to, or already at, the training camp in Afghanistan. Why Burton, though? What was the context in which Burton had reported it?

'Bosnian package arrived safely.' She turned to Michaels. 'Remember it?'

'Burton report,' he told her. 'Soukh News about a meeting in Brussels.'

'Hell,' she swore.

'Shit.' Michaels's face drained of colour.

'What?' Kilpatrick asked.

'The link,' Marchant kept her voice calm. 'Keefer and Bergmann slip into Bosnia, recruit, slip out again. The trainees they've chosen come out, head for Afghanistan. Hence *Bosnian package arrived safely*.'

'Except . . .' Kilpatrick asked. Because there was an *except*. Because the *except* was the key.

'Except the message that the team were out of Bosnia was on an intelligence report before we knew about Afghanistan and Keefer and Bergmann, and before Israel shouted wolf.'

The Tank was suddenly alive.

'Specifically?' Even Kilpatrick was suddenly on edge.

'The message, or at least the words, were on a report from Burton. They came from a meeting in Brussels.'

'When was that meeting?'

'I'm not sure. We can check.'

'But who was at it?'

Your turn – Marchant turned to Michaels.

He gave them the names and the details: the politician/financier, the secret policeman and the holy man. The covers and the hidden agendas. Plus the fourth person who had not been identified.

'Pull the Burton reports,' Kilpatrick told Marchant and Michaels. 'Confirm the details and see what else you can get from them, location of meeting, whether it was a one-off or a regular rendezvous point.' It was gone eight, creeping towards nine. 'Start cross-checking the databases, see if the location figures anywhere else,' he told two of the others. 'Run checks on Keefer and Bergmann and those known to have been at the Brussels meeting,' he told the last two. 'See if they have any form together. If not, start looking for other connections.'

He glanced at his watch. 'Briefing at ten, see what we've come up with. Then we'll call it a day, sleep on it, and see what we think when we're fresh in the morning.' Even though the morning was the day on which even God had rested.

At ten they met again, confirmed the Brussels meeting as the source of the code, confirmed that other Burton reports had also included references to meetings in Brussels, confirmed that the location was always the same. Confirmed that there had been four men present at each, only three of whom had been identified, and that none of these had links with Keefer and Bergmann. At least on file.

'One other thing,' Marchant said.

'What?'

'The latest Burton report suggested that another meeting is scheduled.'

'When?' Kilpatrick asked.

'Next Tuesday.'

Good work, he told them. Tomorrow's the Sabbath,

so sleep late. Don't bother to come in till nine.

Only the two of them were left: Marchant clearing her files and Kilpatrick locking the security cabinets in The Sanctum. She placed her chair neatly against the desk and drifted to his office.

'Care for a drink?' he suggested.

She was in the cable car to Almenalp. The chute in the pack on her back, the cliff towering above her, and the thought of how it would be to go over the edge in her mind. 'Shouldn't you be getting home?' she asked.

'I don't go home if I work this late. I have a flat.'

Big boys' games, they were both aware. Big girls' rules.

'Prefer something to eat,' she answered his original question.

'Won't Geoff wonder where you are?'

'Geoff's in Norfolk.'

'In that case perhaps I could knock together something.'

'Perhaps you could.'

The flat was on the second floor.

So who are you – she watched as Kilpatrick unlocked the door. Where are you from? He switched on the light. The room was twenty feet by twenty feet, a kitchen and breakfast bar to the left, and the area to the right serving as a lounge. A door off it leading, she assumed, to the bedroom and bathroom. The furniture was modern and the apartment immaculately kept, which she would have expected. A bookcase against one wall and paintings on another, blinds across the windows.

'White wine,' Kilpatrick suggested.

She was back in Kandersteg, the paragliders like eagles in the sky and the cliff of the Almenalp towering above her. So who are you, she wondered again, where have you come from? 'White wine would be good.' She kicked off her shoes and looked at the books and the paintings. Was riding the cable car up the mountain, the cliff rising frighteningly above her and the blue of the sky above the cliff, the red and yellow of a paraglider soaring in it.

'An Haut-Gardère.' He gave her the glass – slim and long-stemmed and delicate. Haven't heard of it, she might have said. Not many people have, he would have told her; I get it from the château myself.

She was leaving the cable car and making her way up the slope to the start point, unpacking the chute and laying it on the ground. Her heart was thumping now, because she still did not know whether she would do it, and the nerves swept in waves over her. She held the stem and swirled the wine gently in the glass, breathed in the bouquet and tilted the glass against her lips, felt the first drops. Felt him behind her as he undid her blouse and unzipped her skirt. Allowed it to fall and stepped out of it. The valley was silent below her and the mountains were silent around and above her. She checked the chute, checked the lines, checked and stepped into the harness. Did the harness up.

'That's exquisite.' She breathed in the fragrance again and sipped the wine again – no more than a sip. Allowed it to float in her mouth, allowed him to slide off her blouse and unhook her bra, slide it off her shoulders, so that the only thing she now wore was her pants.

The wind was gentle in her face and the sun was hot on her neck. She stood like a crucifix, hands held out and the lines to the chute in her fingers, the chute rustling gently behind her and the nerves and the fear and the doubt suddenly gone.

He kissed the nape of her neck and rolled her nipples between his fingers. 'Don't move,' he told her. She waited, was aware of him going away, then coming back.

The calm and cold were upon her, the wind still gentle in her face and the sun on her body. She stepped forward one pace, raised her hands above her head and lifted the chute off the ground, checked that it was open and full above her and began to run. Down the slope, the green beneath her feet, the blue above her, and the space in front of her.

He was naked now. She felt his erection hard against her, felt the trickle as he poured the oil down her back – the faintest aroma in it, or perhaps it was the taste of the wine lingering in her mouth. 'That's also exquisite,' she told him. She was still running down the slope of the Almenalp, the sensations of the room and the mountain merging into one now, the sky above her, the void still in front of her, and Kilpatrick against her. He touched her, almost lifted her. She felt her body rise and realized she was in the air, realized she was flying, the ground slipping away beneath her and the sky and the void and the blue suddenly around her.

Still time to pull out, she was aware, still time before she was so close to the edge she would never come back. Still time to go back inside her computer screen, still time to step away from the real world. His shaft was like a pillar against her. She was moving now, allowing him to hold her, feel her, open her. That's *exquisite* exquisite, she was aware she was mumbling. She was over the edge long ago. Over the cliff, over the valley. Free in the air, the thermals buffeting her and the blue round her.

She hooked her thumbs in her pants and slid them down, stepped out of them. Felt back and held him hard. 'Come into me,' she told him.

The streets on either side of the canal were crowded, though at this time on a Sunday morning most were tourists. A few pimps touting for business, though, a few women in windows, disappearing as a customer nodded. Kara crossed the bridge and turned away from the red light area. Almost there, she thought, almost ready. Just the passports to deal with. And Frank had said they were ready, that all they needed were the final details and the photographs.

The boutiques were busy and the antique shops were open, a few traders working from stalls, and tables on the pavement outside a café on the corner.

Eleven o'clock, she'd told Frank. Now it was nine-thirty. Turn up early, Keefer had told her; arrive before the person you were seeing was expecting you and check how they reacted. Not Frank though. If somebody had been going to take her out it would have been the arms dealers or the Stasi fixer with the airport contact.

The morning was warm, the sun was relaxing, and there was plenty of time before she was due at the forger's. She checked her watch, sat at one of the tables outside the café, and ordered coffee and a croissant.

She was almost there and everything was almost in place, so perhaps it was good to relax, perhaps it was the time to relax. Not for long, just for a few minutes: remember the good moments, because there had been no time to remember them for so long, and there would be no time in the future.

The waiter brought the coffee and pastry. She thanked him and sat back. Thought about the old days and was pleased that she could think about them. Tinged with sadness, of course, but at least she had good things to hold on to; at least, today, the sun warming her face and the danger removed for the time being, she could close her eyes and remember the smile in Adin's eyes and the laugh on Jovan's face.

It was ten o'clock. She paid, left a good tip – not because she should do so, but because she wanted to – and walked the two blocks to the antique shop. Ran the usual checks, even though they weren't necessary, and went inside.

'Hello, Frank.'

'You're early.' He pushed the chair back and tried to

fold the newspaper. 'Wasn't expecting you till eleven.'

'Couldn't sleep.'

'No problem.' The newspaper was still in his hand. 'Let's go upstairs.'

She nodded and began to follow him.

'Quick phone call,' he told her. 'Have to cancel something.' The sunlight from the window played on the dust on the furniture and the room smelt of must and polish. He lifted the phone and punched the number. 'A customer just called.' He held the phone close to his mouth. 'I'm afraid I'm not going to be able to make our meeting.' He smiled at her again and led her up the stairs at the rear and into the studio above, settled at the chair by the work bench. 'The passports . . .'

She's arrived early, the collector told the gorillas on the mobile. They were three streets away, they told him, be there yesterday.

'No problems, I hope?' Kara asked the forger.

'No problems. The genuine article.' He leaned to his right and began to open the lock on the security cabinet.

The gorillas started the motor, pulled out without bothering to check, and screamed away.

What's wrong, Frank? Why are your fingers trembling? . . . She was back in time. Back on the street and entering the shop. After the sun outside the shop seemed gloomy, Frank sitting behind the desk against the wall and reading a newspaper . . . 'You're early.' The forger was pushing the chair back and trying to fold the newspaper. 'Wasn't expecting you till eleven' . . . 'Couldn't sleep,' she was smiling at him . . . What's wrong, Frank? Why are you looking like a startled rabbit?

The gorillas turned down the street, checked for police, and stopped two doors away.

'Quick phone call,' the forger was telling her. 'Have to cancel something.' Wrong, Frank. Because you knew I was coming, therefore you wouldn't have arranged another meeting.

The gorillas locked the car and walked down the pavement.

What about the door to the shop, Frank? Last time you locked it, but this time you're leaving it open.

The gorillas entered the shop, held the bell on the door so it wouldn't ring, closed and locked the door, and hung the CLOSED sign on it.

Her nerves were tingling and her senses were on edge. I relaxed, allowed myself to think about something else. Not for long. Just for a fragment of time. And I almost blew it. Because I was right in the first place. Because someone was going to take me out. But it wasn't the Stasi fixer or the arms dealers. It was you, Frank. You bastard.

Get out now, she told herself. Because the opposition wasn't here yet, because Frank's call was to tell them to come. So the opposition probably wasn't the security services or the police, because if it had been there would have been no need for the telephone call, because they'd have had the place bugged and staked out. But there was still an opposition. So she should get out. Except she needed the passports. Because at the moment she and the team only had one set, supplied by Keefer, and they needed others.

The forger was bent over the table, the passports in front of him. She closed the door of the studio and crossed the room. No rope or string, she noted. Duck tape by one of the cameras. Plenty of inflammable items and more than enough photographic chemicals.

She picked up the duck tape and walked behind the forger. Jerked his head back and put the M70k in his mouth. 'Who's coming, Frank? Who did you phone?'

He was stiff, jerking with fear and gasping for breath. Shaking his head and trying to tell her he didn't know what she was talking about. She took the gun from his mouth, hit him, and folded him on the floor. Turned him over and taped his mouth, taped his hands behind his back and his ankles together, taped his hands to his ankles, then wound a loop of tape round his neck and ran it to his ankles, so his back was arched and if he tried to move he would strangle himself.

'Okay, Frank.' Her voice was cold. You or him, Finn would have told her. You or them. Only one side is getting out of this, so make sure it's you. 'You'll tell me the truth, Frank, won't you?'

His eyes were bulging and he was trying to nod.

'You've set me up, Frank.'

The gun was against his temple. He shook his head, tried to hold on to the last grain of hope. She lowered the gun and pressed the muzzle hard against his testicles.

'The truth, Frank.'

There was the slightest movement of the head, the slightest nod.

'I'm going to take the tape off your mouth, Frank. But no noise. Understand that.' Or I'll blow your balls off.

You're running out of time, she warned herself. You still don't know who's coming, or when they're going to get here. The gun was in her right hand. She held the tape in her left and ripped it back so it hung from his cheek.

'Who's coming, Frank?'

'Gambling debt . . .'

'Not the authorities?'

'No.'

She knew he was telling her the truth.

'How many?'

'One,' he told her.

Out of time, she warned herself. 'You don't move, Frank. You do nothing to warn them.' She taped the strip back across his mouth and pulled him behind a chair. No sound suppressor on the M70 – she was still acting and thinking automatically. Cushion which she could use to deaden at least part of the sound, though. She made sure Frank was out of sight and waited behind the door, so that as the door opened it would conceal her.

Footsteps on stairboards, she told herself. Door opening, one person entering. Would shut door if he was alone. Not shutting door, so there was a second person. Two men in room, second closing the door, the first turning and seeing her.

'Don't move.' The gun was pointed at him. 'Step back. Lie on the floor. Face down.'

Gorillas, she thought; big and heavy, but not trained. Beat the shit out of you if they could, but not knowing how to react now. She hoped.

'Tape his hands,' she told the second man. 'Behind his back.' She stepped back, gave herself more space in case they came at her. The cushion was to her left.

'Lie down beside him.'

So what now, Kara? What are you going to do? Them or you, Kara. Because there are still three of them, including Frank. Only one thing to do, Kara. Because you have to give Frank the names for the passports. And while you could trust Frank, that was okay. But now it's not. But you still need the passports. Which was why you risked staying. Only one solution when you go in on this sort of job, Kara. That's what the training was about.

She wrapped the cushion round the pistol and shot the man who was not taped in the head, shot the second in the head. Surprisingly little noise, she thought; might just get away with it. She crossed the room, pulled Frank upright, and cut off the tape.

'The passports,' she told him.

He was calm now, almost detached, as if the fear had isolated him. 'Okay,' he said.

Twenty minutes later she left the shop.

*

Bihac starving, just as Maglaj had starved. Bihac being crucified just as Maglaj and Tesanj and Sarajevo had been nailed to the cross. So time to let the world know, time to make the people sit up and take notice. Time to tell the United Nations that it could no longer let her people down . . .

. . . The woman and the child stood on the top step outside the room in Travnik, the snowflakes drifting on to them and the despair and wet seeping into them.

What are you afraid of, Kara, why haven't you told the woman and boy to go?

Back off, Finn. Because I know where I'm going and what I'm doing.

Stop feeling sorry for yourself, Kara. Stop telling me the whole world is fucking you, because you're fucking it just as much.

Except the world hasn't stopped fucking you, because Keefer is about to fuck you again. Because through you they're going to fuck your people, going to fuck the Adins and the little Jovans who haven't yet been born. You know what they're playing at, Kara; they told you who they're working for. They're recruiting for the fundamentalists. Nothing wrong with the fundamentalists, but everything wrong with the politicos and the extremists and the madmen who suck on their blood. So they're recruiting Bosnian Muslims because they say it will help Bosnia, but that's fuck, Kara, and you know it. Because once they've recruited Bosnians, and once you die as a terrorist and the world knows you were a Bosnian, then everyone in Bosnia will be termed a Muslim extremist, and you and your people will lose. And the West, who've fucked you like there's no tomorrow, will say they were right because look, you're a Bosnian and you're a terrorist and an extremist. And the extremists in the Middle East will rub their hands and say look how the West has abandoned you, so come to us.

So what do I do, Finn? I'm a slut and a crook and a whore. I'm so far down I can never pull myself back up.

You remember the hospital in Tesanj, Kara? You remember what I told you? That the only way the West would help you was if you had something the West wanted; that the only way you would succeed was if people were afraid of you like they're afraid of me. So you have to be ready, Kara. For the next time the Chetniks bomb the hospitals and the West stands back and wrings its hands and does fuck all, and most of the TV crews say how awful it is then sod off to the next disaster.

What are you saying, Finn?

What I'm saying is that when I told you those things there was no chance of you ever achieving them. Now there is. Because you've been down the cesspit with people like Keefer and me. So use it, Kara, as long as you can see the light and as long as you know what you're doing and why.

How, Finn?

Easy, Kara. You use the guys who fucked you last night just as they're trying to use you now. Go along with them, learn what they have to teach you. Learn whatever terrible things it is you have to know. So that when the time comes, you can do whatever it is that you have to do.

Time to change things, Kara. Time to change everything. Time to turn the world on its head.

Kara's Rules. Kara's Game.

Thanks, Finn . . .

At eleven fifty-five Kara left Amsterdam by train, reaching Ostend at six minutes to four and catching the jetfoil to Ramsgate an hour later. At forty-three minutes to nine – twenty-four minutes later than scheduled because of a signals failure – she was in London. Three-quarters of an hour after that she was in what she referred to as the safe house off the Edgware Road.

# 11

The intelligence and security services were on overload, and Scotland Yard Special Branch and Anti-Terrorist departments were working round the clock, Langdon informed the Prime Minister over breakfast at Downing Street. The eavesdroppers at GCHQ were sifting everything that came their way, but as yet no one had turned up the next lead to the terrorist team in London.

The first Riverside briefing of the day was at nine: jobs allocated and areas of investigation defined. Checks and cross-checks on the address in Brussels, including ownership, architectural plans, neighbours, and communications – telephone, fax and telex. Updates on the backgrounds of the three known members of what was already referred to as the Léopold Group, plus their travel movements and business schedules when the previous meetings took place, in an attempt to pinpoint the times at which such meetings were held, as well as covers they may have used and which they might use again. The material to be sent Upstairs only, not for dissemination to overseas agencies. London keeping this one close to its chest.

At noon the second briefing of the day had little to report: preliminary checks and enquiries were under way, first contacts and requests for basic information like telephone records had already been made. The problem, as Michaels pointed out, was that it was Sunday, therefore everywhere was closed down and they had to tread carefully to avoid creating suspicion. Thank God for computers, though, at least computers didn't take a day off.

Pity your partner's back this evening – Kilpatrick looked across the conference table at Marchant; pity you can't come back, even for a couple of hours. Last night was incredible, Marchant couldn't stop thinking. Until last night she'd lived essentially through her computer, almost as if she herself was a figure or a statistic; but last night she'd come off the screen, last night she'd come alive. And today she and Kilpatrick were behaving normally, as if he was locked in The Sanctum and she was back on the screen. Which was part of the game.

At four, when they assembled in The Tank, the framework had begun to come together. Details of the apartment, individual timetables, updates from Burton, plus re-examination of his previous reports, and confirmation of a Brussels meeting the following Tuesday. The possibility of accessing the apartment in Rue Léopold and installing electronic surveillance inside – discarded at this point because the apartment would almost certainly be swept before any such meeting. Details of the immediate area, plus information on buildings opposite and adjacent in which surveillance teams could be positioned.

'Still nothing on Number Four?' Kilpatrick asked. Because Number Four was the key, either directly or through Keefer, to the four terrorist teams, but especially to the bastards sitting in London.

'Nothing.'

It was almost time to call it a day, the late shift already in and being briefed by Kilpatrick in The Tank, Marchant and Michaels being called to join them and to help in the briefing.

'Telephone records are through,' Kilpatrick's PA informed him.

They filed from The Tank, Kilpatrick allowing the others to leave first, and Marchant hanging back slightly.

Kilpatrick's hand running down her lower spine as she passed him and Marchant's fingers brushing against the upper front of his thigh.

The day shift began to leave. Time to let the others build up the data then hit it fresh in the morning, Kilpatrick told them. It was coming together; one more link, one more connection, and they'd have it.

'See you tomorrow,' Marchant told Kilpatrick as she left.

'Yeah, see you in the morning.'

The pictures were on the early evening television news – the men round the guns, the guns shuddering slightly, then the puff of smoke in the town in the valley. Kara locked herself in a mind set of her own, threw up the walls around herself, and watched. Bihac on the rack just as Maglaj and Tesanj had been on the rack. Except this time it was different; this time she wouldn't let the UN get away with doing nothing; this time she wouldn't let the world forget.

This is how it started last January – Caz sat and stared. The boys were upstairs and Finn was in the kitchen. This is the way everybody sat back and allowed it to happen. Last January Kev and Geordie John were killed, and Janner and Max only just made it. Last January a woman who saved Janner's and Max's lives lost her husband and her son.

So what is it – she asked herself. What are you feeling?

I'm feeling that I don't know what I'm feeling. I'm feeling sad, and angry. And I'm feeling frustrated. And that's what forms part of the anger. Because we've all seen this before, and we all know what's going to happen. And nobody's doing anything about it. And all I, as a woman and a mother, can do, is to sit and watch it on the bloody television.

Kilpatrick phoned his wife, spoke to her then to the children, then left The Sanctum and walked round the department, stopping to talk and check, and wondering whether he should call another briefing before he went to the flat off Queensway.

'Anything?' he asked one of the analysts dealing with the telephone listings.

The routine was systematic and logical. Confirm the dates and times of the Léopold Group meetings, then run them against the telephone billings and see if any calls were made during or either side of the meetings. Then isolate those numbers and see if there was a pattern. And if there was, check if any of the numbers or addresses called cross-referenced with numbers and addresses associated with terrorism.

'Not yet,' the analyst told him.

Kilpatrick's back was beginning to stiffen. He rubbed his eyes and looked over the analyst's shoulder.

The numbers were broken down into three columns, one for each of the target dates. There was a total of seventy-three calls during or close to the meetings of the Léopold Group, twenty-three related to the first meeting on record, twenty-eight to the second, and twenty-two to the third. Fourteen numbers appeared on each date, and eleven appeared twice or more. With one exception, all were international calls, the destinations identified through the dialling codes.

'You'll get there,' Kilpatrick told the man, and returned to The Sanctum. An hour later he left his desk and drifted round the department again. It was time to leave, he told himself; he himself had reached diminishing marginal returns hours ago. Anything look interesting, he asked each of the analysts. Not yet – most of them gave him the standard line. Possibly, the one he'd talked to earlier informed him.

Kilpatrick waited.

'Most of the calls would seem to be business-related. By which I mean they were to numbers connected with banks or financial institutions. Therefore I've ruled them out.' Unless whoever or whatever they were looking for was using that as cover. 'Twelve of the calls were to five private numbers; we have the cities and addresses.'

'Any sort of pattern?' Because patterns were what they drummed into you – in training, in the real world. Establish a pattern and you might find a key. Find a key and it might unlock where you wanted to go.

'Two of the twelve private calls feature on the billing for each of the three meetings we know about, and two appear on two.' Which is why I said I might have something, because that might give us the pattern we're looking for. Or might at least be a step to it.

'That's two numbers called three times, and two twice,' Kilpatrick confirmed.

'Yes.'

'Which is ten calls.'

'Yes.'

'What about the other two?' You said there were twelve calls to private numbers.

'The other two were made to different numbers, the numbers don't appear anywhere else, and the calls were of short duration.' Therefore there's no pattern, therefore I've put them on the back burner.

'Cross-check the numbers where there might be a pattern.' Kilpatrick was fresh again. 'Get the names and details of companies, organizations or individuals associated with the numbers concerned. See if any of those details come up anywhere else. Get the addresses and run them through the databases, see if they're anywhere near any significant address or location.'

He waited for a printout, took it back to The Sanctum, poured himself a coffee, and settled again at his desk.

Geoff, Mike and Mel arrived at eight, telling her she'd missed a good weekend and sympathizing with her about computers going down.

'Missed you,' Geoff told her when the others left. They were in the hallway, Geoff had turned her, so she was against the wall, his arms round her waist and hers round his neck. 'Didn't sleep last night.'

'I didn't sleep either.' The truth was always the best line, as long as you were economical with it.

'You want to make love?' Geoff asked. He was already unbuttoning her dress and sliding it off, slipping off her bra and pants. Unzipping his trousers and moving against her.

She was smelling him, smelling Kilpatrick. Feeling and tasting and devouring Kilpatrick. 'Try and stop me.'

One last run through the telephone numbers then he *would* leave, Kilpatrick told himself. He thought about another coffee, poured himself a Black Bush instead, and tried to focus on the list.

Of the two numbers called at or around each of the three meetings on record, one was in Damascus and the other was in Amman. Of the two called at two of the meetings, one was in Riyadh and the other was in Teheran. The two numbers called only once were in Khartoum and Istanbul.

Damascus and Teheran might seem the front runners, because of Syria's and Iraq's traditional connection with terrorism. But Damascus was supposed to be playing a different tune nowadays, and you never knew which game Teheran was playing anyway. Amman, in Jordan, and

Riyadh, in Saudi Arabia, seemed less obvious. But when something was less obvious there was sometimes a reason.

It was probably worth considering surveillance on all four addresses in question, he began to think. He was tired, he told himself, and that's when mistakes happen, that's when people don't see things. Therefore he'd go through it again in the morning, therefore he'd talk to Marchant and Michaels before he made a decision.

He finished his drink, locked the security cabinets, left the department and walked along the corridor to the lifts. The building was silent, two lift doors in front of him and two behind. He pressed the down button and waited. There *was* a pattern though, and the pattern *was* regular ... he acknowledged that his brain hadn't switched off yet and told himself it soon would. One of the lifts arrived. He stepped in and pressed the button for the ground floor.

Most of the calls were between two and five minutes' duration ... The shortest was two minutes three seconds and the longest four minutes fifty-eight seconds ... Except the two calls made only once ...

The lift was silent. The only indication that it was moving was the slight sensation of descent, and that barely discernible.

Patterns: yes. What they were looking for: yes. Except the telephone calls were such an arrogant breach of security. And why risk your security even though you assumed nobody knew about you ... The lift door opened and he stepped out. Except the calls in question fell into patterns, and patterns were what they trained you to look for ...

Damascus and Amman, Riyadh and Teheran ... There was nothing pulsing in him, no reaction, no surge of adrenalin. No instinct. He smiled at the night security people and signed out, acknowledged the fact that his brain had switched to the two calls which didn't fit the patterns.

Khartoum and Istanbul ... Late night ... January meeting . . . Duration of first: five seconds, duration of second: six . . . A message on an answerphone machine or a fax sent down the same line as the telephone . . . Except there was a separate fax number in the apartment . . .

No reason for the duration of the calls, no explanation, therefore no pattern. He crossed the floor. No pattern, okay. But one reason, one explanation. He felt the shock.

Pushing it a bit, of course, but at this stage of the game you had to.

He turned back to the lift. So play it safe and go by the book, or risk it and follow his instinct? The lift stopped. He stepped out, turned right, walked along the corridor and punched in the security code to access the department. Go with his instinct, he told himself. Just as he'd done in South Armagh and Crossmaglen and the other places where the book said to do one thing and he'd done the other. Which was why he was still here.

Thought you'd gone, someone was saying to him. Later, his wave of the hand said.

Surveillance in, of course. But when? And when to request it? Because it was nine-fifteen on a Sunday evening, and the world either had its feet up, or should have. Except there were four terrorist teams on the hoof and one of them was sitting in London. Therefore the surveillance request in tonight: Watchers plus SAS minders in case things got funny, SAS also providing eyes. Riverside people in the nearest embassy working overnight to set things up, so that if he needed authorization in the morning everything would be ready.

It was 9.21 PM, according to the log Kilpatrick kept from this point on. He sat quietly for another three minutes, then he lifted the telephone and began the chain. At 9.24 he spoke to his immediate superior. At 9.35 his request, and the reasoning behind it, was passed to the Chief; by five minutes to ten both the chairman of the Joint Intelligence

Committee and the Foreign Secretary had been informed and approval given.

The television images were those they had seen on the early evening news. The guns and the men loading the shells and smiling at the camera, the sniper with the bandana tied round his head as if he was in a Western movie.

That afternoon Janner and Jude had taken the children swimming; now the children were in bed and the two of them sat and relaxed over a beer.

The lead item had been Bosnia, the pictures of Sarajevo again without electricity and water, the men and women running in fear of the snipers. Then the pictures from the forces surrounding Bihac.

Just like Maglaj last January; just like when he and Finn had taken their teams into the Maglaj–Tesanj pocket. Just like the place where it had almost been his turn.

'You ever think about her?' Jude asked him.

'Sometimes,' Janner admitted.

'I never stop thinking about her,' his wife told him.

The phone rang.

It was 10.35 PM.

'Yes.' Janner never identified his name or number.

'Fancy a drink?' the squadron commander asked him. The code that he was on call.

'When?' Janner was conscious of Jude looking at him.

'Now.'

Kara left the address at seven-thirty. Bihac was being shelled again – she had seen it on the early-morning news bulletins. London was quiet around her and the early-morning streets were still empty.

Marchant arrived at Riverside at three minutes to eight, Michaels two minutes later. Kilpatrick was already in. 'The Tank in five minutes,' he told them. 'You two. Nobody else.' They fetched coffee and went through. Kilpatrick came in, coffee in one hand and file under an arm, kicked the door shut behind him and sat down at the head of the conference table.

'The Israeli shout. There's a possible development.' Kilpatrick always came straight to the point. 'Based on the telephone records, the late shift have come up with a number of Middle Eastern addresses which might be connected to the Léopold Group. They may be what we're looking for, they may not.' He sipped the coffee. 'One address has been targeted. The JIC has been informed and the PM has been briefed. The Watchers are already out, SAS back-up will be in place late this morning.'

Christ, Marchant thought. 'So what do you want from us?'

'A cross-check. See if I've got it right or wrong. See if I've missed anything.' Which was why he hadn't told them where the Watchers were already in place.

'How much time do we have?'

'An hour. I'm due Upstairs at ten.' And Upstairs is briefing Downing Street at ten-fifteen.

'What about Washington and Moscow?' Michaels asking this time.

'We're keeping it in-house at the moment.'

Marchant returned to her desk and began, occasionally conferring with Michaels, then shutting herself off again. Checking the time and talking to him again at five past nine.

Perhaps he should have covered his bet, Kilpatrick thought; perhaps he should have sent teams into the other places. Except that would have cost, which in turn would have raised more questions and slowed everything down.

'We're ready,' Marchant told him on the phone. It was twenty minutes past nine, still forty minutes to the briefing.

Marchant and Michaels giving him extra time before he went Upstairs. They went through to The Tank and closed the door. No coffee now, because there was no time.

'An informed guess, not a prediction,' Marchant told Kilpatrick.

'Which one?' he asked.

'Istanbul. The others are a pattern, and what we're looking for on this one isn't going to run like that.'

'Why not Khartoum?' Why not the other single call?

'Too many connections with the terrorist business. Keefer would avoid it like the plague.'

'But why make the Istanbul call when they should have known it was a security risk?'

'Try this.' Marchant didn't need to look at her notes. 'Israel shouts wolf, CIA and FSK come up with a training camp in Afghanistan. Keefer recruits in Bosnia and Léopold Group meets.' Christ she could do with a coffee.

'The Léopold Group meets. Financier/politician, secret policeman, holy man, plus whoever our Fourth Friend is. We don't know who our Fourth Friend is. His identity, I mean. But we can assume he's the organizer, because there's no other reason for him to be there, because they have everything covered: the religion, the financial backing, and the intelligence support.

'They confirm the political decision, then all they have to do is activate it. The first part is financial – the funding for the operation. They wouldn't have got this far without funds being available and on standby. So the financier makes his call, gives his man the green light for the transfer to an account set up by Number Four.'

'The Khartoum call?'

'Yes.'

'Why Khartoum?'

'Because a considerable part of the funding for a range of Islamic militant groups is channelled through a certain businessman there. So the first call says green light, release the money.'

Time running out, Kilpatrick thought. 'And the Istanbul call?' he asked.

'Try this,' Marchant said again. 'The organizer is sitting in Brussels and Keefer is waiting in Istanbul. The Léopold Group have made the political decision to go ahead, and have ordered the transfer of funds. All that's left is to activate the programme, for our Fourth Friend to tell Keefer it's go, and to start recruiting.'

'But why risk such a call from such an address?'

'It's what the Middle East is all about; what some might call Face. They've made the political decision, made the financial call. Then they turn to our faceless friend and say: Okay, the ball's in your court. And he has no option. He picks up the phone, or they give it to him, and he calls the number and says do it. Ten seconds, less, nearer five. He knows he's wrong, but he has to make the call. And nobody's going to know because nobody knows about the meeting or about Keefer or about Bosnia.'

And now Bosnia's winding up again. Now Sarajevo's under pressure and Bihac is under attack, and everything is beginning to look like it did last January, when the meeting took place and the calls were made. And one of the teams Keefer recruited in Bosnia last winter has been through the camp in Afghanistan and is now sitting and waiting in London.

'So where are the Watchers?' she asked.

'Istanbul,' Kilpatrick told them.

Kensington High Street was busy with shoppers.

Kara left the underground station, turned left, and threaded her way through the people on the pavement. So much money – the thought was involuntary; so many people spending so much on such inconsequential things.

At an address off the High Street she passed through security, hired a safe deposit box, and left in it three false passports plus $25,000 in cash for the other members of the team. Then she returned to the underground station and took the District and Piccadilly lines to Knightsbridge.

Next time the UN lets your people down you must have something the world wants, he'd told her. Next time she had to make the world afraid of her.

Got it, Finn. About to do it.

No emotion though, because emotion cost. And no relaxing, because relaxing cost even more. You or them. Thus, when the Amsterdam fire brigade had put out the blaze in the antique shop two blocks from the red light district of the Oude Kerke, they had found three bodies. Because Frank might have remembered a detail or a name from the false passports. And Frank had betrayed her once, so Frank would have betrayed her again.

She left the tube station, walked three hundred yards to a street off Brompton Road, cleared the uniformed security people at the door, and left a passport for herself, plus $100,000 in used notes, in a safe deposit box.

Got it all set up, Finn. Got my back door. If I get this far.

Kilpatrick returned at eleven-fifteen. Fourteen minutes later he called them into The Sanctum.

'First eyeball in Istanbul.' He stirred the coffee. 'Male, mid-thirties. Not one of ours.'

'European?' Marchant asked.

'Yes.'

'Could be a minder.'

'Could be.'

But at least it was a European; at least they were in with a chance. Kilpatrick went Upstairs again and Marchant and Michaels returned to their desks.

The street map of Istanbul was on the wall of The Tank, the location marked. Marchant left the main office and stared at it. So how does it look? How does it feel? What's it like, does it have a connecting garage? What are the chances of someone getting in and out without the Watchers and the SAS boys being seen?

Turing coming on in an hour's time, they were informed; being tested now. Upstairs are happy so far, Kilpatrick told the department when he returned. Turing's still down, something wrong with the tests.

It was 11.45. 'In, now,' Kilpatrick's PA told Marchant and Michaels. They hurried through and shut the door.

'Istanbul coming through again.' Kilpatrick listened as the message was relayed to him. 'Second man, again not the target.'

Two minders, Marchant and Michaels agreed. Either that or the gardener and odd-job man.

* * *

Finn and the team reached Heathrow at eleven-fifteen. They locked the Range Rover in the security compound at the police station just outside the tunnel leading into Heathrow, then spent thirty minutes over coffee with the head of Special Branch, plus the former RAF officer who was director of security.

Today they would begin the first recce. The remote holding points, where the ground controllers would order planes they wished to have out of the spotlight. The storm drainage ducts and other means of access under certain positions on the runways, taxiways and stands which might allow them to approach a plane unseen. Where they would establish a holding position – a room where the AT teams would wait – in the event of an emergency at Heathrow. Where they would establish an operations room. How they would do these things without the press and the public being aware.

Tomorrow they would return and begin to run through the various elements in fine detail. Test for radio dead spots, train up as refuellers and ground staff, so that in the event of a hijack they would be able to approach an aircraft and gather their own intelligence. Work out the sniper positions.

And next week, or the week after, when the airport was quiet – quiet being a relative term at Heathrow – they would run an exercise. Softly softly and low-key. See if their procedures worked. Then they would move on to Gatwick and after that they would train on buses and trains and apartment blocks.

And sometime, when they weren't expecting it, the powers-that-be would hit them with an exercise: a hijacked plane full of real passengers, police and civilian negotiators also being tested, and Downing Street and Cobra involved. No one knowing the outcome; whether the hijackers would give in or whether they would kill a hostage and throw his or her body – or a tailor's dummy filled with blood and offal – from the plane. Everything real, even to the sounds of the passengers being tortured on the plane. Everyone being tested, everyone under scrutiny. Even down to the fact that the ammunition and grenades the assault teams would use were live. Because unless it was for real it didn't actually prepare you.

The morning was sliding into afternoon, the other analysts still running the databases. Marchant and Michaels as well, but only to pass the time now, only to take their minds from the waiting. SAS in position in Istanbul, Kilpatrick told them. Keefer and Bergmann now assigned code names: Keefer Orange, Bergmann Lemon.

Kilpatrick was summoned Upstairs again. The tension

was winding, the fear that the London team was going to hit the city before Riverside hit them. Washington, Paris and Moscow as well, of course. But they were Riverside, and Riverside was London. When Kilpatrick came back he checked with them on developments then sat with them in The Tank – all of them this time – and began throwing ideas around. Picked up the phone almost before it rang.

'Istanbul,' he told them, still listening. Satellite communication into Riverside on a secure frequency, the message computer-encrypted and decrypted each end. 'One man.' He cupped his hand over the mouthpiece. 'Getting car out of garage.'

'European.'

'Not ours.'

But at least European, at least they weren't wrong yet.

'Passenger getting in. Not one of those eyeballed before. Car driving away.'

He listened to the remaining five seconds of the message then put the phone down. 'They can't be sure, didn't get a good view or shot of him . . .'

'But?'

'They think the second man is Bergmann.'

Christ, they thought. Please may it be. Please may they have got it right.

'They're following him?'

'No, they don't have the resources.' And without the resources and the planning and the back-up they'd blow it.

'But no Keefer?'

'No.'

'So Keefer might not be in the house? Keefer might be elsewhere?'

The excitement evaporated.

'Who knows?' Kilpatrick said. 'Thoughts?' he asked.

'Why a car?' Marchant threw it at them. 'Why Bergmann

plus one other? Why one staying in the house?'

Because Bergmann wouldn't be leaving unless there was a reason.

'Pulling out perhaps?'

So perhaps they should risk everything, tell the Watchers to tail him. Perhaps they should lift Bergmann now. Except Bergmann might not know what Keefer knew, and if he didn't they would have blown it.

'Baggage?' Marchant asked Kilpatrick.

'The eyes didn't say so.' And if there had been they would have done, because it might have been significant.

'So perhaps he's picking someone up.' It was Michaels.

And if he was then it might be Keefer. Except that would be too much to hope for. But they'd got this far, so why not? Check the airline guide – Marchant broke off and told one of the other analysts. See if there are any flights due into Istanbul in the next hour.

The streets and shops were even busier. So much money, Kara thought again, so much food and so many expensive clothes. She took the underground to St James's Park, walked to the National Map Centre in Caxton Street, and bought an Ordnance Survey Pathfinder map, reference number 1174, two and a half inches to the mile scale, for Staines and Heathrow Airport. Then she walked back through Parliament Square, up Whitehall and across Trafalgar Square, to the reference library behind the National Portrait Gallery and the official publications section on the ground floor. The library was quiet; people bent over desks, the counter on the left, and a coin-operated photocopying machine at one side. She found an empty desk and left her coat on the chair, though not her bag.

'ABC flight guides,' she smiled at the librarian. The guide gave flight departure details, including times, destinations and aircraft details, from every airport in the world.

'The shelves on the right of the door.'
'Thanks.'
She found the guide, photocopied the page containing details of flights from Amsterdam to London Heathrow, returned the guide to the shelf and left.

Istanbul coming through, Kilpatrick was informed, car returning. He called for Marchant and Michaels.
'Driver and two men getting out.' The report was patched through to speakers the technical people had installed in his office.
Two men out, three back, they were all thinking. Hell, this was it. Hell, it was going down.
'Driver getting out. Not target.'
'First passenger getting out. It's Lemon.' Bergmann. So at least Bergmann wasn't doing a flyer. At least they still had him.
'Second passenger getting out. Is out. Walking to house. It's Orange. Repeat. It's Orange.'
They'd found him – the news swept through the department. They'd found Keefer. They'd bloody well found the way in to the terrorist groups.

The cabinet committee had been in session ninety minutes, Langdon in the chair. At four he would wind up the meeting, walk the fifty yards to the Foreign Office, and attend a think tank on Southern Africa. The knock on the door to the right, leading to the hallway beyond, was polite but firm. One of the secretaries from the Cabinet Office entered the room, walked quickly behind the chairs, and handed him a folded note.
'Excuse me.' He leaned back and unfolded it.

> Riverside on line and holding. The Chief requests priority meeting.

Only one thing was running at the moment, Langdon thought: the terrorist scare activated by the Israeli warning, the surveillance request he had approved the previous evening, and the threat of a bunch of madmen somewhere in London.

'My office, fifteen minutes.'

He placed the note in one of the files in front of him, and waited till the secretary left the room. 'I'm afraid we have to break early.' He summarized the discussions that afternoon, the agreements reached and the areas still to be discussed. 'Thank you for your contributions, and again, my apologies for concluding this meeting prematurely.' He closed the files, left the cabinet room, and returned to the Foreign Office.

'The JIC file on the Israeli warning,' he told Pemberton. 'Nicholls here now.'

'Coffee for five,' he told Edgars. Himself and two advisers, plus the Chief and whoever Gilman would bring with him.

Pemberton laid the file in front of him. Langdon sat forward, adjusted his glasses slightly, opened it, and read the first page. The summary was clear and concise, classic British civil service analysis. Israeli warning of terrorist attacks on named cities, SIS interpretation of intelligence, possible links with as yet unnamed grouping, and potential connections with the Bosnia problem.

Nicholls entered as he was reading; Langdon waved at him to sit down and continued, skimming through the detail but spending no more time on the report than was necessary.

'Sir Ian's on his way from Riverside. Probably about the Israeli warning.' He closed the file, placed it to the right of the desk, and looked at them. 'Thoughts?'

'Sir Ian himself?' Nicholls asked.

'Yes.' Langdon handed him the note delivered to him in the cabinet room.

One of the telephones rang. 'JIC request a priority meeting in one hour,' Pemberton told him. JIC – the Joint Intelligence Committee running out of Downing Street. 'You were scheduled to fly to Brussels this evening. I'll warn them you might cancel.'

'Check where the PM is at the moment,' Langdon told him. 'Plus his timetable for the rest of the afternoon.' He turned to Nicholls and waited for his assessment.

'The Israeli warning specified the UK, the USA, Russia and France.' Nicholls's approach was as concise as the summary in the file on the desk. 'London is obviously our primary concern, but the meeting with Sir Ian might involve those countries.'

'Therefore?'

'Therefore you might be talking to Washington, Moscow and Paris.'

'Sir Ian plus one on his way up,' Edgars came through.

'US, Russian and French ambassadors,' Langdon told Pemberton. 'Find where they are and what they're doing but don't create any ripples.'

There was a knock on the door and Edgars showed Gilman and Kilpatrick in.

'Sir Ian.' Langdon crossed the room.

'Foreign Secretary.' Gilman shook Langdon's hand. 'May I introduce Michael Kilpatrick.'

They shook hands and settled at the chairs beneath the bookcase, allowed Edgars to pour them each a coffee and waited till he left and shut the door behind him. Everything so English, Langdon would think later, everything the way it should be.

'The Israeli warning.' Gilman had been stirring his coffee. Now he stopped. 'There has been a major development. A report has gone to the Joint Intelligence Committee, but in case a rapid response was considered I thought you should be informed immediately.'

'Understood.'

Gilman nodded at Kilpatrick to brief the meeting.

'As you are aware, the situation until last night comprised a number of factors. One: the Israelis had warned of a terrorist attack on London, Washington, Moscow and Paris. The naming of the four target cities suggested, albeit tenuously, a connection with Bosnia. Two: Riverside had identified a potential new terrorist grouping, plus its leadership, and established that that leadership had held meetings in Brussels. Three: intelligence identified a camp in Afghanistan where Europeans were allegedly being trained. Four: the Russians also named two ex-Stasi officers, Keefer and Bergmann, as being involved at that camp. Five: intelligence on the murder of a British mercenary, Walton, placed Keefer and Bergmann in Bosnia at the time recruitment of the Europeans being trained in Afghanistan might have taken place. Six: the possible presence of Bosnian Muslims at the training camp provides some degree of confirmation that the four targets named by the Israelis might have a connection with the conflict in Bosnia-Herzegovina. Seven: the concern of Riverside that one of the terrorist teams was now in place in London.'

All of which you are aware of – Kilpatrick looked at Langdon. Because the last thing you did before this meeting was to update yourselves from the relevant file.

Langdon nodded.

'As of one hour ago, Riverside has established a connection between the leadership caucus, referred to in the reports as the Léopold Group, and the former Stasi operatives Keefer and Bergmann . . .

'As of one hour ago, Riverside has also established the current whereabouts of Keefer and Bergmann.'

'You mean where they're located in general terms. Or where they themselves are, physically, at this specific moment in time?'

Kilpatrick waited for Gilman to answer.

'Where they are, physically, at this moment in time.'

Well done – Langdon's body language conveyed his thoughts. The way he nodded, taking his time to do so. The way, having nodded, he leaned back in his chair and appeared – only appeared – to relax. The way he cupped the back of his head in his hands then glanced at Kilpatrick, nodded at him, then looked back at Gilman.

'How was this done?' he asked. Just in case that's why you're here. Just in case you broke the rules, the balloon's about to go up, and you're lobbying my protection.

Gilman nodded at Kilpatrick to continue.

'The surveillance you approved last night.'

Good move, Gilman thought: allow the Foreign Secretary to share in the credit.

'Well done.' Langdon sipped his coffee. Not just for getting there, but for getting there first, before the Russians and the Americans and the French. 'So where do we go from here?' Because the Joint Intelligence Committee meets in an hour, and you want a course of action agreed and under way by then. Because at the end of the day you want to make sure it's your names on the top and not someone else's.

'It seems to me that we do one of two things.' Gilman spoke even more carefully now. 'Either we continue in the intelligence mode, use what we have to develop more intelligence. Use the people we've spotted to lead us to other groups and other conspiracies . . .'

'Except . . .' Langdon said it for him.

'There are four terrorist teams sitting in place, every indication is they're about to be activated, and one of those teams is in London.'

'So the second option is?'

'We action it.' Gilman's words were short and sharply delivered. 'We've identified the threat, so we remove it.'

'How?'

They went into the details.

Fifteen minutes later Langdon briefed the Prime Minister. Five minutes after that he and Gilman attended the emergency meeting of the Joint Intelligence Committee. Five minutes after the meeting ended he again briefed the Prime Minister, this time on an encryptor to the Prime Minister's car, emphasizing that the discussions he would hold with the ambassadors were conditional upon the PM's approval, and that no course of action would be considered unless it was in line with the PM's thinking.

It was twenty minutes to six. Caz made sure the boys were eating, then turned on the ITN early evening news. School had been good that day; it could have been better, some of the kids had taken the proverbial one step forward and two back, but you couldn't win them all.

'Bihac still being shelled . . .' the newscaster read the headlines. 'Radio message says they have no food, and the hospital is running out of drugs. United Nations says a ceasefire might be imminent.'

She watched the bulletin, switched channels, and watched the BBC Six O'Clock News. The reports and the pictures were similar: the guns pounding in the hills; someone – she wasn't sure who – tuning a radio set and picking up the words from Bihac. The phone began to ring and the picture changed.

The new image was of a woman, around sixty years old, holding a placard outside the United Nations building in New York. The woman seemed to be dressed in striped pyjamas. The stripes were vertical, black and white, and there were badges of some sort on her sleeves. 'In New York . . .' the correspondent began to say.

Caz crossed the room, picked up the phone, and glanced back at the television.

'Yes.'

'Hello, love. It's me. I'll be back around seven.'

She was listening to Finn and trying to listen to the report and the interview with the woman. 'Thanks for letting me know.' She put down the phone and turned back to the television.

The phone rang again. 'It's Jude.'

Something wrong, Caz understood; something in Jude's voice. 'You all right?'

'Sure I'm all right.' Which means I'm not. Because Janner's away. Because he was called out last night, and I don't know where he is. Because it's the first time since he was almost killed in Maglaj, and I don't know what to do or which way to turn. 'Wondered if you fancied coming round for a drink tonight?'

'Finn's back at seven, which means eight. I'll be round as soon as he's home.'

'Thanks.'

The news bulletin had moved on to something else. Caz switched off the set and went back to the boys. The woman in New York wasn't wearing pyjamas, she realized. The woman outside the UN building was wearing the uniform of a prisoner in Hitler's concentration camps.

Langdon's meeting with the ambassadors of the American, French and Russian governments began at six, in Langdon's room at the Foreign and Commonwealth Office. The four men were seated at the mahogany conference table which ran along one wall; two either side, Langdon deliberately not taking what others might have assumed was his rightful place at the head of the table.

'Thank you for interrupting your schedules at such short notice.' Langdon prided himself on his ability to read the mood of a meeting. 'You all know why I've asked you to come.' Because Riverside has been in touch with your intelligence people, and they in turn have started the alarm bells with you. 'You will each already have been in contact with your own government, and will presumably remain in constant communication with them.'

The portraits looked down on them from the walls and a chandelier was suspended from the ceiling. A great many issues have been decided in this room – the atmosphere settled upon them: fates of men and futures of nations.

'So what precisely do you have?' The US ambassador was ex-military, haircut and bearing to match.

'Riverside has established the details of the organization which appears to be the basis of the Israeli warning . . .' Langdon paused briefly. 'Leadership. Locations of leadership meetings. Identities of key organizers . . .' He paused again. You name it, we've got it, the silence said. 'Where the man running the terrorist teams is at this precise moment in time . . .'

Christ – it was almost audible. But he's difficult to access – the thought pierced the air. And that's why you've called us in.

'For the past three hours he's been under constant surveillance . . .' Plus . . . 'We have an SAS team in position a hundred metres from him.'

He gave them the details. Tea, he suggested. Tea, they agreed. Everything a game, and all of them players in it.

'So what does the British government recommend?' The French ambassador was slim but an ex-rugby player, his nose slightly bent.

They waited while the tea was brought in and poured.

'There are a number of alternatives.' Langdon was deliberately careful.

'But which does your government recommend?' It was the Russian. Yeltsin build and Savile Row suit.

'Two committees,' Langdon slipped into committee mode. Which was not what they either wanted or expected at this stage, but which established the foundation from which he could move them to the next. 'Both running from London. The first comprising ourselves, plus advisers when necessary, making the political recommendations and passing them to our respective governments. The second an intelligence committee, comprising the Heads of Station of the CIA and the FSK in London, someone from Riverside, plus someone from the DST.' People who already know each other, people who have talked together about this one. 'The second committee drawing on whatever resources it needs, then reporting direct to the first.' No intermediaries, it was understood. No pen-pushers or bureaucrats, no prevaricators to get in the way.

Then . . .

'We've identified the threat.' Langdon used Gilman's words. 'Therefore we remove it.' Because otherwise we'll have bodies on our streets and blood on our hands.

'The head or the body?' the American asked.

The head – the three named and one unnamed members of the Léopold Group. The body – Keefer and Bergmann and the teams they've recruited. Plus the training camp as well.

'Remove the head and you still have the body.' Which is messy, and you still have four teams of hoods running round the world. You still have terrorist groups sitting and waiting in each of our capital cities. 'Remove the body and you still have the head.' And the head can start again, recruit more teams and send them back into Washington, Moscow, Paris and London.

'So?' The American ambassador.

'You remove both the head and the body.' The Russian.

'Except we don't know where all the body is.' The Frenchman again.

'But we could find out.' Langdon.

'Through Keefer.' The American took a cigar case from his inside jacket pocket, selected a Havana, rolled it between the thumb and second finger of his right hand, snipped the end off and lit it.

'Precisely.'

'What time frame are we talking about?' The Russian this time, his English with a slight East Coast American accent.

'We have thirty hours to put it together. For approximately two hours at the end of that time the organizing committee will be in session, therefore we will know where everyone is and can access them. Then the window's gone.'

'Then we lose the chance of wrapping it up in one?' The American.

'Then the window's closed,' Langdon confirmed.

'Rules of the game?' The American sat forward, elbows on the table and cigar held in his teeth.

'The intelligence team advises us, and we make our recommendations to our respective governments based on that.'

'Thirty hours ain't a lot of time.' The American was deliberately homespun.

It was like no other committee any of them had sat on: no prevarication, amendments or procedural irrelevancies. Bare-bones time, because unless they moved on it the terrorists would move on them.

'Therefore we begin now.' The clock was ticking in the background. Absolutely on cue, Langdon thought. 'Agreed?' he asked.

'Agreed.'

The co-ordinating committee code-named Strike, their aides would decide in the next two hours: the Strategic International Co-ordinating Executive. Rather dramatic, they would concede, but time was too precious to waste devising a more suitable acronym. Strike One, the political committee, Strike Two the intelligence. Special facilities in the Cobra rooms below Downing Street and access restricted to need-to-know.

The gin and tonic was on the coffee table, and Jude was sitting white-faced on the sofa. Caz poured herself a drink and sat beside her.

'Kids okay?' she asked.

Jude nodded.

'Where's Janner?'

'Away.'

'When did he go?'

'Last night.' Jude sat forward and took hold of the glass. 'He phoned just before midnight, as they were on the way out. Postcard job.' Our code – she looked at Caz and tried to smile. I suppose you have the same system, because all the old hands do. 'Overseas. Straightforward job, just an observation. Nothing more.'

'But?'

'It's still his first job since Maglaj.' Which is why I'm glad you're here now.

They talked about school and the kids and Christmas presents and birthdays which were coming up. Stayed clear of Bosnia, the United Nations and Bihac. At nine o'clock they turned on the BBC television news. The shelling of Bihac was the third item, and the woman in New York was the fourth.

She was thinner than she had first seemed – now Caz had time she could see the details. Her face was lined, and her eyes were troubled. The placard she carried said simply SAVE BIHAC. Her hair was a fuzzy grey, her arms were thin, and the badge on the sleeve of the black and white striped clothing she wore was the Star of David.

'My name is Helen Rabin.' Her voice was low, almost without emotion or feeling, and she stared straight at the camera rather than at the reporter who had asked her a question. 'My mother and my father and my grandparents and my brothers and my sisters perished in Auschwitz.' She rolled up her sleeve and showed the number tattooed on her forearm. 'I was the only member of my family to survive.' She rolled down the sleeve, as if she was cold, and grasped the handle of the placard again. 'I know how the United Nations will react, but somebody must say this to them. Save Bihac.'

Like you didn't save me and mine fifty years ago. Like you didn't save my mother and my father and . . .

'And you think your protest will influence the politicians, will stop the killing in Bosnia.'

'No.' The woman's face was as bleak and thin as her voice. 'I do not expect my action to change a single thing.'

'So why . . .' the reporter began to ask.

'Someone must tell the politicians and the governments that they're wrong, mustn't they.' The last words were a challenge rather than a question. 'Somebody must say what we all think.'

Strike reconvened at nine-thirty, in the Cobra room below Downing Street: the ambassadors along one side of the conference table, the four representatives of the intelligence communities along the other, and Langdon at the head. Jackets hanging on the backs of the chairs and the smell of cigarettes, cigars and coffee in the air.

The room itself was quietly furnished, mineral water and coffee, plus ashtrays, on the table, and telephones to the side.

The first ten minutes were taken with terms of reference and ground rules, each ambassador reporting that his country agreed to the committee on the understanding that its existence should never be disclosed, and on the further, and overriding, condition that each country exercised an individual sanction over final approval.

'Recommendations.' Langdon invited them to move to the next stage.

'As you are aware, Strike Two has been in session all evening.'

It was the American HoS Lessons who acted as spokesperson for the intelligence section. Interesting move on Kilpatrick's part, Langdon thought. Good politics though, especially as Langdon was in overall charge. If Lessons chaired Strike Two then the Americans would be more inclined to go along with whatever was decided.

'There have been no developments since mid-afternoon. Keefer and Bergmann are still in place in Istanbul, and the Tuesday meet in Brussels has been confirmed.'

Lessons lit a cigar and indicated that Kilpatrick would continue.

'There are two sets of targets.' Kilpatrick spoke succinctly, as if from notes. 'The first set comprises the individual locations in Istanbul, Brussels and Afghanistan. The second set comprises the cities specified by the Israeli warning: Washington, Paris, Moscow and London.'

The Russian ambassador raised his hand. 'Afghanistan will be a political problem for us.' Because we were involved there and eventually withdrew, which was one of the events which sparked the collapse of the Soviet Union. Therefore it would be politically inconvenient, to say the least, if it was ever known that the Russians were back in Afghanistan.

Already considered, Kilpatrick told him. As he assumed – the Russian nodded and allowed Kilpatrick to continue.

'The plan is straightforward. We lift Keefer, obtain from him the details of the terrorist teams, and deal with the teams. Simultaneously we deal with the Léopold Group in Brussels and the training camp in Afghanistan.

'As a preliminary to this, we have squads on standby in each of the cities targeted, those squads provided by the country affected. SAS on standby in Istanbul to lift Keefer. Belgian Special Forces on standby in Brussels, with SAS observers, to deal with the Léopold Group. SAS dealing with the training camp in Afghanistan via Alpha.'

Alpha – the anti-terrorist unit of the former KGB, operational in Afghanistan during the Soviet presence there, now fighting organized crime in the new Moscow.

'If it's agreed that the SAS handle the sharp end, I'd like your permission to invite the Brigadier, Special Forces, to join us,' Langdon suggested.

Agreed, the ambassadors nodded. Langdon lifted a telephone and asked an aide to bring the brigadier in. The newcomer was in his late forties, and wearing a suit. Kilpatrick waited for the introductions to be made, then poured himself a glass of water and continued.

'Keefer is the key to the terrorist teams on the street, but we can't access Keefer until we confirm that the Léopold Group is in session. Therefore . . .

'We confirm the Léopold Group is in session and lift Keefer. Preferably in the house, because that way we might get Bergmann as well. Interrogators standing by, but the assumption is that Keefer won't talk, at least for a long time, and we'll need to make him talk before anyone realizes we've got him, which might be minutes. Therefore we also have interrogators plus a medic and a caseful of sodium pentothal. Immediately we have Keefer, we deal with the leadership meeting in Brussels and the training camp in Afghanistan. Immediately Keefer starts giving us the details of the terrorist teams in London, Washington, Paris and Moscow we deal with them.'

The State Department will never buy this, the American ambassador was aware he was thinking. State will go apeshit. But if the Pentagon and the CIA and NSC tell the president that he goes along with it or sees half of Washington go up in a puff of blue smoke, then the president will tell State and State will think it's a great idea.

'Structure . . .' Kilpatrick moved to the next stage.

'One SAS team is already in Istanbul; the teams for Brussels and Afghanistan leave tonight. Afghanistan team fly to Moscow and are met by Alpha, who take them on via Kazakhstan and Uzbekistan.' And no problems with the KNB there – he was addressing the Russian ambassador now. Because former KGB colleagues maintained close contact, and a KNB delegation had only just left London after a liaison meeting on terrorism with New Scotland Yard. 'Alpha then fly them in by chopper. SAS team walk in for last part. Either walk out or exfiltrate by chopper, depending on reactions to their attack on the camp.

'Communications . . . The Operations Centre is here. Secure communication with our teams in the field, plus anything you want for communication to your embassies or governments. Which you may wish to set up yourselves, of course.'

Which they would definitely wish to set up themselves.

'On the night . . . Each field team confirms that its target is in position. We don't move unless Keefer is in position in Istanbul and the Léopold Group are in position in Brussels. If they aren't, we abort.

'Once we have confirmation, Istanbul team goes in first, lifts Keefer, plus Bergmann if possible.'

Why not simultaneous, he knew one of the diplomats was bound to ask.

'We know that the fourth man at the Brussels target knows where Keefer is, so if anything went wrong he might just have time to warn him. It seems unlikely, however, that

Keefer knows where the organizing committee is meeting, therefore he won't be in a position to alert them.'

The men on the other side of the table nodded.

'Istanbul signals once they have Keefer, Operations signals Brussels and Afghanistan. The Brussels team terminate the organizing committee and the Afghan team deals with the training camp.'

'How will the Brussels team deal with the committee?' It was the French ambassador.

'Rocket and grenade attack from across the street, straight into the apartment.'

Fast and basic and brutal. A few innocents might suffer, but that was inevitable, a cost of war. And that was the way the Israelis or the Arabs would do it, because that was one of the ways both had done it in the past. Therefore the source of the attack would be concealed.

The cardinal rule of the game: plausible deniability.

'Interrogators obtain identities and locations of terrorist teams from Keefer, and pass them to the Operations Centre. The Ops Centre then passes the details to our teams on standby in Washington, Moscow, Paris and London.'

He concluded the first part of the briefing and sat back.

'Questions?' Lessons addressed the politicians opposite him. 'Because we have one for you.'

'What?'

'Keefer. Do you want to keep him?'

'What are your recommendations?' The diplomats threw the question back at the intelligence committee.

'The Istanbul team will be moving fast. Plus they'll be taking care of the interrogators, who won't be used to this sort of thing. Trying to bring Keefer and/or Bergmann out with them will present additional problems, even though we'd obviously like to. Basically, it's a balance between long-term intelligence and getting out of this one and nobody knowing we've been there. Our recommendation, therefore, is that we don't bring him out.'

'Agreed.'

# 12

Tuesday morning was chilly. Not the cold of Bosnia at this time of year, though; certainly not the awful biting soul-destroying cold of Maglaj or Travnik in winter. Faraway places – Kara sat motionless in the chair and stared at the television pictures – faraway lives.

The gunners were loading the artillery. In the distance she could see the roofs of the houses. The gun shuddered, a puff of smoke appeared in the town, and the men laughed. Another house destroyed – she was tight with anger, another family killed. The sniper with the bandana round his head was taking aim, firing, then standing back and posing for the camera in triumph. He's just shot Adin – the thought swept over her. Adin or someone like him. Adin or someone else's father or husband or son.

She sat still, looking at the other pictures: the diplomats in Geneva, a reporter talking about the possibility of a ceasefire; someone somewhere else – she didn't know who – talking about the possibility of an air strike. I have been through this – the thread in her mind tightened slowly. I have been here, suffered like these people are suffering now. I have cowered in the ruins and buried my husband and my son.

She left what she mentally referred to as the safe house, walked to the underground station and took the Piccadilly line to Heathrow.

*

Finn and the team left Hereford at eight. Their first meeting at Heathrow was at ten-thirty. By nine they had crossed the Severn Bridge and were on the M4 heading east.

The Heathrow train was crowded, and the escalator from the underground platform to the concourse above took twenty-seven seconds. Funny how you noticed the detail, Kara thought; how at this stage you saw and heard everything. To her right a group of nuns were struggling with their cases. She ignored the escalators to the terminals, and took the one marked WAY OUT. Twenty-five seconds, she counted subconsciously. She left the escalator and stepped into the sunlight. The airport was hectic around her: the radar scanner, Ground Control tower and Terminal One to her left, Terminal Two in front of her, and the road busy with taxis, cars and service vehicles. She waited for a break in the traffic and ran across.

A 747 was dropping out of the sky, and the sign to the spectator viewing area was on the corner of Terminal Two. She followed the arrow to the end of the building, turned right and right again, into the doorway and up the concrete steps, children's voices echoing from above, and the stairs smelling of fresh paint.

Eight sets of steps – she was still counting. Not that the detail mattered. She stepped on to the roof of the terminal. The 747 had landed, an Airbus following it in and the lights of two other planes in the sky behind it. An aircraft landing at Heathrow every thirty-eight seconds, she remembered.

There were two viewing areas, one in front of her and another slightly higher and to her right, the views from both obstructed by new building work. She turned right along the roof, then left and up more steps to the higher of the two areas. There were thirty plane spotters there, some sitting in the smoked-glass shelter and others on the gallery in front. Most were men, a few boys, and all had notebooks, binoculars and airband receivers, the size of mobile telephones, on which they listened to the radio traffic between pilots and air and ground controllers.

'Expensive?' she slipped easily into a conversation. Ten minutes later she left the viewing gallery and went to the cab rank outside Terminal Two. The black cabs were lined up.

'I need a cab for half an hour. Local stuff.'

The driver grimaced. I really want a fare into Central London – she understood what he was thinking. 'How much?' she asked.

'Thirty pounds.'

'Twenty.'

'Twenty-five,' he laughed and opened the door for her.

At the Aviation Hobby shop in West Drayton, in a small line of single-storey shops off the main street, she purchased a Yupiteru airband receiver, a fourth edition of *British Airports*, an Airlife guide to United Kingdom Air Traffic Control, and a copy of *Airwaves 94*. At the British Airways AERAD unit at the side of the 747 hangars on the fringe of the airport she bought the air traffic control/radio navigation charts for Western Europe and Britain, coded EUR/1, and the London area. Plus ground maps, including runways, taxiways, parking stands and remote holding points, for Paris Orly, Amsterdam Schipol, and London Heathrow.

Thirty-five minutes later she was back at Terminal Two. She paid the driver, tipped him an extra five pounds, returned to the viewing area, and went to the café at the rear. The tables and chairs were plastic, a small shop at one end, and a bar with food and soft drinks at the other. Only two of the tables were occupied, both by men listening to airbands. She bought a cappuccino from a vending machine, settled at one of the tables, and checked the page from the ABC flight guide which she had photocopied in Central London the previous afternoon.

*

The hazard warning lights of the vehicles in front of them were flashing, and the traffic on all three lanes of the motorway were at a standstill.

'There has been a major accident on the M4 heading east . . .' The traffic update interrupted the radio station they were listening to. 'All lanes are blocked, and traffic is already tailing back four miles. Motorists are advised to use an alternative route where possible. Police say the motorway will be closed for the next hour.'

'Inform Heathrow we'll be late,' Finn requested Hereford. 'Use the hard shoulder,' he told Steve.

The coffee was weak and the cup was plastic. Kara put it on the next table and checked the page from the ABC flight guide. The flights from Amsterdam were every half-hour at this time of day, therefore she had plenty of time. She unpacked the airband receiver, read the instructions, placed it to her right, and unfolded the Ordnance Survey Pathfinder map. Heathrow Airport was in the centre; the terminals were clearly marked but the runways less clearly so and not numbered. She bought another coffee – espresso this time – and studied the map again, paying special attention to the perimeter fence, the roads which ran along the airfield but were outside the fence and therefore open to the public, and the position of car parks and hotels along that road. Then she placed the British Airports book and the United Kingdom Air Traffic Control guide on top of the map, turned to the pages covering Heathrow, and examined the position of the runways vis-à-vis the terminals and where she was sitting at the moment.

There were two main runways, one to the north of the main airport buildings, and one to the south.

Runways were numbered according to their direction in terms of degrees from the north, she read: the number of degrees were taken to the nearest ten, and the first two figures used as the runway number. Thus direction 274° became 270° = runway 27. The other end of the runway (the other end of the straight line) was 274° minus 180° = 94° = runway 09.

The prevailing wind at Heathrow was from the west, and the majority of landings were made into the wind, therefore from the east. Runways were changed at three in the afternoon so that noise could be distributed evenly over the surrounding houses.

She moved the books aside and studied the ground charts for Heathrow. The runway in front of her was Two Seven Left, and the parallel runway on the other side of the complex Two Seven Right. At the moment, and, more importantly, at the time and date in which she was interested, planes were landing on Two Seven Left.

She checked the time, finished the coffee, and examined the map for air traffic routes over Western Europe, then the map for South England into Heathrow. Aircraft inbound from Amsterdam entered British air space at a reporting point named Refso; at this position British Air Traffic Control would order them to the navigation beacon over Lambourne, in Essex, and from there south-west till they picked up the ILS, the Instrument Landing System, the beam directing them over Central London and into Heathrow.

At each stage, communication between the controller and pilot was on specified frequencies, the controller telling the pilot which frequency to change to at key points. Which meant that plane spotters like those in the café, or the viewing gallery fifty metres away, could follow conversations on their airbands. She moved the coffee to the side, checked the *Airwaves 94* book, switched on the airband, and punched the keys on the right for the frequency on which the next inbound Amsterdam flight would first speak to British Air Traffic Control.

*

Strike convened at ten-thirty.

In a room off the adjoining corridor the Operations Centre was almost ready: the technicians and signallers setting up their systems and checking the equipment with which the teams in the field would communicate with them. Other technicians setting up the secure systems from London to Washington, Paris and Moscow.

In Brussels it was eleven-thirty and the first of the Léopold Group were confirmed as being in the city though not yet making their ways to Rue Léopold. Belgian special forces and their SAS observers were in a holding position, having checked out the target and the firing location.

In Istanbul it was just after midday; Keefer and Bergmann were still in place and the SAS team was on hold.

In Kazakhstan it was three-thirty in the afternoon and the Afghanistan team were already airborne with Alpha and about to go cross-border.

In Washington, Paris, Moscow and London the units which would negotiate the terrorist teams once their locations had been secured from Keefer were about to be placed on standby.

'One question,' Kilpatrick asked as the meeting ended. 'Our source will be inside the room when the attack goes in.'

Therefore do we try to warn him off or get him out? Because his information has been priceless, but if we pull him we risk blowing the entire operation.

'Leave him in.' Langdon glanced at the others to ensure he had their support. 'Shame, but someone has to pay a price.'

The articulated lorry was at an angle across the motorway, cars trapped beneath it and more cars into the back of them. The police BMWs were parked on the hard shoulder, more blue lights in Steve's rear-view mirror. He slowed and stopped, knew what the policeman who told him to wind down his window was going to say.

'Who the hell do you think you are?' Because it's an offence to drive on the hard shoulder. Even more so when you're trying to pull a fast one and we're trying to get people out and hoping to Christ they're still alive.

'No problems, mate.' Steve pulled his ID from his inside pocket.

Finn leaned across from the front passenger seat. 'Need any help?' All of them were trained medics and two of them had spent six months in a hospital accident and emergency department. 'You need any medical stuff?'

The first ambulance pulled in behind them, the paramedics getting out. In the sky above they heard the sound of a helicopter.

'Think we're all right now, mate,' the policeman told them. 'Thanks for the offer.'

'Good luck.' Steve put the Range Rover into four-wheel drive, pulled up the grass verge running on to the hard shoulder, and eased at an angle past the police cars.

'Inform Heathrow we will be arriving in fifteen minutes,' Finn radioed Hereford.

'London. This is BD 104.' Kara picked up the message on the airband. 'Approaching Refso.' The British Midland Boeing approaching British air space.

'BD 104. Confirmed Lambourne Three Alpha arrival for landing runway Two Seven Left.'

She checked the details on the maps.

'BD 104. Descend when ready to flight level one five zero.' Descend to fifteen thousand feet.

'BD 104. Turn left on one five zero for landing on Two Seven Left.' The plane over the Lambourne navigation beacon and turning south towards the Thames, then west up the Thames, over Central London and into Heathrow.

So now I know the standard procedures and the standard instructions from Air Traffic Control for a plane flying into Heathrow from Amsterdam – Kara folded the air control charts and looked out of the window. Because when I'm coming in the bastards will try something. But now I know that if their instructions are any different from those I've just heard, then the bastards in London will be trying to play their games.

She waited another half-hour and confirmed the details with the next flight.

There was one last set of items to research. She switched off the airband, and put the radio, books and maps into her shoulder bag. Terminal Two – she was already thinking ahead: a hire car and a decent cup of coffee. She left the viewing area and headed for the stairs.

Already set up the back door out, Finn. Now I have the front door in.

The Range Rover pulled left off the motorway and slid into the secure compound of the Metropolitan Police station on the perimeter of Heathrow.

'Sorry we're late,' Finn told the Special Branch liaison officer. 'Problems on the motorway.'

'In position at Heathrow and leaving vehicle,' Steve notified Hereford.

'Coffee?' the SB inspector asked.

'We'll take it in one of the terminals,' Finn told him. Because the moment we're in the terminals, even though we're sitting over coffee, we're looking and learning.

They crammed into a police Rover and were driven through the tunnel and into the Heathrow complex. 'Any preferences?' the SB inspector asked.

'Terminal Two.' Because that way they could have coffee and begin checking out the viewing area.

They passed the entrance to the coach and underground

stations, parked alongside a police van at the end of Terminal Two, and began to get out. The bleepers and mobile rang simultaneously.

'Derekson,' Finn answered. Mobiles were notoriously insecure, therefore even call-names were coded. Hereford gave him the scrambler number, Finn clipped on the unit he carried in his pocket, and punched it in.

'London base, priority.' Even on the scrambler the message was carefully worded. Hereford would explain more when he was talking to them on the secure net from the Range Rover. 'Repeat. London base, priority.'

'Back fast,' Finn told the policeman. The SB inspector checked behind, reversed out, and accelerated away.

There were armed police in both the departure and arrival lounges, and police dog patrols by the doors. You haven't killed, Kara watched them. And until you confront that moment, you never actually know whether you can do it. She bought a coffee in one of the cafeterias in the shopping area, then hired a Ford Escort from the Hertz desk, and left the terminal.

It was twelve-thirty. Caz left the classroom, went to the staff room, unpacked her sandwiches, made herself a coffee, switched on the ITN news and waited for the pictures from Bosnia. Same images, she thought; same sniper shooting someone. Nothing about the woman called Helen Rabin in New York, but there wouldn't be, because the East Coast was five hours behind. Perhaps it needed someone like the woman, though; perhaps it had to be someone with the woman's background to stand up and say what a lot of people must be thinking.

The next item was from London, the two women standing outside the House of Commons. They were in their early thirties, and the words on the makeshift placard each carried said simply SAVE BIHAC.

'Saw the lady in New York on the telly last night,' one of them was telling a reporter. 'We thought: if she can do it, so can we.'

'Came down this morning.' Both the women had Manchester accents. 'Left the kids with our mum.'

'What did your husbands say when you told them what you were going to do?' The reporter was also a woman, younger than the two and better dressed, hair stylishly cut.

'They don't know.' The first woman glanced at someone behind her, then back at the reporter. 'On early shift, you see.'

Good for you, Caz thought. She cut herself off from the conversations around her and concentrated on what the women were saying.

'Why did you come down?' the reporter asked.

'You married?' The woman was tall, with longish brown hair. 'You got kids? Because they're killing the kids in Bihac, you know; just like they killed the kids in that place in January.'

In Maglaj, Caz thought; in the hospital in Tesanj. She watched transfixed, totally unaware of the other teachers around her.

'And you think this will do some good?'

'No. It's like Helen Rabin said: we won't change a thing.' The woman hesitated, as if embarrassed. As if, for the first time, she was wondering why she was mounting a protest outside the House of Commons and being interviewed on television about the war in Bosnia. 'But I were sitting at table this morning watching pictures on telly, and I were thinking same as everybody else: poor little beggars in Bihac, poor women and poor little kids. And bloody United Nations was 'iding behind its rules and regulations and doing nothing about it. And nobody was saying anything.

So I thought: *you* do something about it; *you* stand up like Helen Rabin in New York. I know I won't win, but at least I've done something.' There were tears on her face and anger in her eyes.

Incredible, Caz thought.

'And you're going home tonight?'

'Yes.'

But . . .

'Some people said we were doing a good job, and they'd like to join us, but they had to go to work.' It was the other woman. 'They said they'd come back when they finished.'

Except they wouldn't, of course – it was in the reporter's artificial smile. Because it was the sort of thing people said, but didn't actually mean.

The traffic in Central London was almost at a standstill. Steve waited for a break in the line coming the other way, turned right into the barracks, and stopped at the barrier. Finn showed his ID to the sentries, then Steve drove round the edge of the drill ground and parked at the rear of the Centre Block. The offices were at the top, nothing – except for the two security gates – to indicate what took place on the third floor. Finn reported in, collected a mug of tea, then joined the others in the briefing room at the end of the corridor.

The operations major wore civilian trousers and white shirt, tie slightly undone, and the briefing he gave them was little more than Hereford had informed them on the way in.

'Terrorist team in London. No details yet. IDs and location of safe house this evening.'

Strike convened again at three. Everything was in place, Kilpatrick informed them; the assault teams were on standby and the targets were either where they should be, or on their way.

They confirmed the codes to be used that night.

Primary locations to be named after colours: thus Istanbul Blue, Afghanistan Red, and Brussels Green.

Key targets to be referred to by colour-related numbers: thus Keefer Blue One and Bergmann Blue Two, and the Brussels Group to be referred to as Green.

The four cities in which the terrorist teams were located to be referred to as writers; thus London Dickens, Washington Hemingway, Paris Balzac and Moscow Tolstoy.

Something was going down, Marchant knew; something to do with the Léopold Group and Keefer and the Israeli shout. Kilpatrick hadn't been in the department all day though he had phoned regularly, secure line from Downing Street and some of the calls on conference to The Tank, so he could speak to her and Michaels simultaneously.

'The Boss. Now,' Kilpatrick's PA told the team leaders.

They left their desks, hurried to The Tank, and closed the door.

'Any developments?' Kilpatrick asked on a conference call.

'None.'

'Keep checking. Anything comes up, but anything, I need to know. Late night tonight, nobody leaves until I say so.' End of conference, they assumed. 'One other thing. Tell everyone they've done a great job. Tell everyone the High and the Mighty know who cracked it.'

It was late afternoon. In the Operations Centre next to the Cobra room the latest confirmations came in on the secure systems from the field teams.

Blue One and Two in position – Keefer and Bergmann in Istanbul. Red in position – the SAS team in the observation post overlooking the training camp in Afghanistan. Green in position – the Belgian team with SAS observers opposite the apartment in Rue Léopold.

Satellite intelligence indicates higher than usual activity in the training camp, Lessons informed Kilpatrick. Perhaps the terrorist teams weren't in the target cities yet – the trickle of fear crept into both of them; perhaps the teams were still at the camp. In which case the four SAS men on the hillside two hundred metres away were in trouble.

'Inform Red leader,' Kilpatrick told Signals. Just in case. Except the SAS boys would know anyway.

The hotels to the north of the runways were behind her, the perimeter fence in front, and a 747 was descending above her. The light was fading now, the runway lights sparkling in the gloom, and the wing lights of the incoming planes were blinking against the sky.

The authorities could seal off press access within the airport complex, but the television people could still get their camera shots from outside, Kara confirmed. Depending on where she put the plane.

Got it together – it was as if Finn was asking her, briefing her. Checked everything?

Everything covered, Finn. The end might be a problem, of course, but not even you could work round that one. Everything's right up to then, though. Nothing they can get me on, no way the bastards can get anywhere near me.

She drove back to the airport buildings, returned the hire car, and took the underground into Central London.

The afternoon was gone now, the Middle Eastern night a deep purple-black. In London it was two hours earlier. Blue One and Blue Two still in place, Janner informed Strike. Five hours to go now. Give or take. Depending on what was happening elsewhere, which he didn't know.

First operation since he'd been shot up in Bosnia. So what happens tonight, old friend; how do you feel when you go in, how do you perform when you get inside? Be okay, he told himself; the medics had sorted him out and the psychiatrists had told him he was fine. Except nobody would know for certain until the moment he came under fire.

No Kara to pull you out tonight though – the thought hung in the dark. No Kara to come crawling through the mines and the shells. Because Kara was dead. Because Finn hadn't found her when he'd gone back. Because she hadn't shown at the food kitchen in Travnik even though her name was on the list. And if she wasn't getting her food there she wasn't getting it at all. And if she wasn't getting food she was dead.

The Six O'Clock News was just beginning. Caz kissed the boys, thanked the girl who'd collected them from school, and told them she'd make supper in ten minutes. The pictures from Bosnia were always the same now: the guns and the snipers. Nothing from inside Bihac, though, because nobody could get through: TV crews, aid convoys, even the United Nations.

The bulletin returned to the studio.

'This morning two housewives from Manchester came to London to protest about the shelling of Bihac.' The newscaster looked up from a monitor showing him the Bosnia report. 'Tonight they were supposed to be going home.' There was something about the way he said it. As if he actually cared, Caz thought. 'A special report from Westminster.'

The report began, pictures and voice-over. It was drizzling, the buildings dark against the grey of the sky and two women, wet and holding their placards saying

SAVE BIHAC. But not alone. Fifty to sixty others with them, men and women.

'People said we were doing a good job and they'd come back after work,' one of the Manchester women was saying. 'And they 'ave.'

Good on you, Caz thought. I couldn't do that, though, because I'm married to Finn. And Finn is SAS, Finn's signed the Official Secrets Act and goodness knows what else. Finn is a servant of the state. Finn couldn't hold up a placard saying SAVE BIHAC. Therefore neither can I.

Finn and the team helped themselves to tea and sandwiches from the kitchen two doors along, then shut themselves off and began their own session.

'There are three initial problems.' They were seated round the table of the briefing room. A lot more comfortable than many such sessions, Finn thought. 'One: we won't know how many we're dealing with till the very last moment. Two: we won't know the layout, even the location, so we'll be going in cold. Three: it's a quiet job.' The Laundry Boys coming after to clean up and search for clues. 'So we're limited on how we enter and what we do when we get inside.'

'Plus we won't know whether they'll be waiting for us.' Steve was to his right.

'Won't even know whether they'll all be there.' Ken to the left. 'Except it'll be late evening, so the chances are they will be.'

It was the way they always operated. Chinese Parliament style: each man throwing in problems and solutions and thoughts.

'And we won't know whether the door is on a straightforward lock, which we can get past easily, or whether we have to use something else.' Jim, the MOE man – the method of entry specialist on the team. The only one who would be guaranteed employment after the regiment, he often taunted them. 'Except we can't use anything that would wake the targets, let alone the neighbours.'

'Plus we won't know whether they'll have taken precautions. Whether they'll have alarmed or booby-trapped the door.'

The tube train was crowded and the stations were ticking by: Knightsbridge, Hyde Park Corner, Green Park. Time to kill, Kara thought, time to be got through before she sat and stared at the television pictures from Bosnia or lay alone in the room and talked to Adin and Jovan as she talked to them every night. The train pulled into Piccadilly Circus, most of the passengers getting out and the doors beginning to close. No more images of Bosnia, Kara decided; no more talks with Jovan and Adin. The doors were almost shut. She jammed her foot between them, pulled them open, and left the train.

The platform was busy. She took the escalator, left the station, and stepped outside. The early evening was cold, a slight drizzle falling. The statue of Eros was in front of her and the lights and noise and bustle of the West End were all round her. She turned right, waited with everyone else till the traffic lights changed, then crossed Haymarket towards Leicester Square.

The neon lights were flashing on the buildings, and most of the people were well-dressed. She hesitated, heard the blast of a horn, and jumped on to the pavement on the other side as the buses and cabs came at her. The smell of candy floss and toffee and roast chestnuts drifted in the air, the night hummed with the sound of people and traffic and music, and the lights on the buildings and cinemas and theatres were like Christmas decorations. She came to Leicester Square and saw the crowd. Christ – it jolted her. Why police? Why so many? What the hell was going down?

She was thinking calmly, looking for the tails and scanning the area for the way out. 'What's going on?' she asked someone.

'Film première,' the woman told her. 'TV cameras and everything.'

'Who?' Kara asked.

'Arnie.'

She left Leicester Square and turned left into Chinatown.

'Red on standby,' the major in charge of the Operations Centre told Kilpatrick. 'Blue in place. Waiting for Green.'

Afghanistan and Istanbul at the starting gate, just waiting for the Léopold Group in Brussels.

'Blue movement.' The signal was relayed to them.

Blue was Istanbul: Keefer and Bergmann were pulling out.

'Gone back inside,' Janner updated Strike immediately. 'Not One or Two anyway.'

'Green. First contact.'

The first of the Léopold Group. Brussels was moving – Kilpatrick felt the adrenalin. Brussels was going down.

Stand by, Strike told the field teams. Stand by, the operations major told Finn. Standing by, Finn relayed the message to the others. They settled again, ran through the routine again. How they would access the safe house, wherever and whatever it was, plus the routine, as far as they could plan it, once they were inside. Who would go right, who left; who would cover whom. What they would do and how they would get out if it all went wrong.

'Green. Second contact.'

The Léopold Group is assembling, Strike was informed. Looks like it's happening.

'Final confirmation from your governments that we can continue, please, gentlemen,' Langdon requested the ambassadors. 'Everything appears to be in place,' he told the PM on the secure line. 'Do we go or not?'

'Your assessment?' the Prime Minister asked him.

'We go,' Langdon told him.

'Depending on what the others say, we go,' the Prime Minister agreed.

Washington okay, the US ambassador informed Strike.

Moscow okay.

'Green. Contact Three.' Brussels again. Three of the Léopold Group in position.

Chinatown was a mix of shops and restaurants, the wet glistening on the cobbles and the smells of scent and spices filling the air. Time to leave – Kara checked; time to go back.

'Spare any change, please.' The cardboard box was jammed into the rear doorway of one of the theatres, and the girl was sitting in it, a blanket round her shoulders and a small dog tucked against her. 'Spare any change, please,' she asked again.

'What for?' Kara asked

'Something to eat.'

'When did you last eat?'

'This morning.'

At least the girl was honest, Kara thought. 'Why're you here?' she asked.

'My father started fucking me.' The girl spoke without emotion, apparently without feeling. 'My mother didn't stop him.'

'How old are you?'

'Fourteen.'

'Come on then.'

'Come where?' The girl held the dog slightly closer to her.

'Get something to eat.'

'Can't leave.'

'Why not.' Kara crouched down.

'Lose my space.'

'Okay, what do you want?'

The girl's eyes gleamed in astonishment. 'You going to buy me something?'

'Yes.' Because it could be me where you are, could be my Jovan or my Adin. Has been me where you are.

'Burger would be good.'

Kara left the side street, went back to the lights, and found a burger bar. Not that that was difficult, she thought.

'Burger,' she told the assistant. 'Big one. Make it two. Plus two large teas.'

Knew you were coming back, the girl in the box told her. Don't most people? Kara asked, and sat on the ground by her. Only if they want something, the girl said.

Got to go, Kara told her. Good luck.

You too.

Paris okay, the French ambassador informed Strike.

London okay.

'Green. Fourth contact.' Brussels assembled, the Léopold Group in the frame.

'Confirm Blue still in place.' They heard the request to Istanbul, then the confirmation.

'Confirm Red in place.' To the training camp in Afghanistan.

Red's not going to go far, the Brigadier, Special Forces knew the SAS man at the other end of the signal wanted to say. Not much to go far for round here. Unless you were into sheep or mountain goats. And even then I don't fancy yours.

'Green. All in place. Repeat. Green. All in place.' Brussels again. All the Léopold Group present. About to go down, Finn was informed.

'Standing by,' the operations major informed Janner in

Istanbul. 'Your decision,' he told Langdon.

The Foreign Secretary walked the ten metres to the Strike room. 'It's in place.' Which they knew, because the sound was patched through from the Operations Centre. 'May I have a show of hands.'

Each of those present raised his hand.

'Thank you, gentlemen.' He lifted the red telephone and spoke to the operations major. 'Go,' he said simply.

'Blue go,' the operations major ordered Janner. 'Repeat. Blue go.'

'Blue on way,' they heard the signal from Istanbul.

Langdon crossed the room and lifted the white telephone. 'Prime Minister, this is the Foreign Secretary. The operation is under way.'

On the secure lines established for them the ambassadors of the United States of America, Russia and France conveyed similar messages to their respective presidents.

The black of the side street was behind her, and the lights and traffic and people of Shaftesbury Avenue were around her. Kara crossed and went up the street opposite. There was a cinema or a theatre on the corner, she wasn't sure, cafés and clubs on either side, and a sign outside a place on the left, people going in. I know that place – she looked at the sign. Adin used to talk about it. Adin was a jazz fan. One day, Adin had said, he'd take her to Ronnie Scott's. Tonight I'll let you take me, she decided. Tonight you and I will go to Ronnie Scott's. Because tonight is the last time I can do it. Because tomorrow I am on my way. Because the day after tomorrow I pass beyond the point from which I can ever return. She crossed the street and went in.

The Istanbul team had been in eight minutes now, almost nine. What the hell was happening? What was going wrong? The other members of Strike were in the adjoining room; Kilpatrick himself stood at the back of the Operations Centre. No problem, he tried to convince himself. The guys have to get in, sort out the opposition. But sort it out without harming Keefer or Bergmann. Then they have to secure the place and bring in the interrogators. And at no time during this would they have the chance to contact London and tell Strike what was happening.

Ten minutes down – he glanced at the clock again. Almost eleven.

'Green. Confirm everything still okay.' He heard the voice of the operations major and almost jumped, almost thought it was Istanbul coming through to say there were problems. 'Green. Confirmed A-OK.' The Léopold Group in position and unsuspecting.

Twelve minutes had gone, thirteen.

Fourteen minutes, fifteen.

'Red. Confirm standing by.' The team in Afghanistan. 'Red confirmed.'

Sixteen minutes, going on seventeen. It had taken too long. They were in trouble.

'Blue. Blue.' The code from Istanbul. 'Hemingway, Hemingway.' The code for Washington. '6th Street North East. Repeat. 6th Street North East.' The SAS man in Istanbul was good, Kilpatrick realized he was thinking. Address first, so the US team could be on the road. The house number came through, was repeated. 'Blue. Repeat. Hemingway.' The address again. Washington already moving.

Interesting location, Lessons suggested. 6th Street NE was just behind Capitol Hill, therefore the safe house was bang in the middle of where Congressional members and staffers lived. The last place the authorities would have looked.

'Four males.' Blue was giving them details: the aliases

and ages and passport information of the terrorist team in Washington.

'Green go,' the operations major told Brussels. 'Repeat. Green go.'

'Red go,' he told the team in the mountains of Afghanistan. 'Repeat. Red go.'

Should be on in two minutes, Finn was informed.

'We have the first address,' Langdon told Downing Street. 'No, Prime Minister, it's not London. It's Washington.'

In Brussels the first M80 LAW rocket shattered the tranquillity of Rue Léopold. In Afghanistan the first shadows drifted from the hillside and descended upon the sleeping figures of the fresh intake of trainees and trainers.

'Blue. Blue.' Istanbul again. Please make it London. Please may the interrogators have their priorities sorted out.

'Balzac. Repeat. Balzac.'

Paris. Oh fuck, not even Moscow, not even one that really mattered.

'Green down. Repeat. Green down.' The Brussels team. 'Looks good. Pulling out now.'

The apartment on Rue Léopold a blazing screaming blitzed wreck. No survivors, hardly a corpse intact. Three M80 light anti-armour rockets, plus five fragmentation grenades fired in quick succession from a hand-held M79 launcher. One person surviving the first rocket and grenade, though fatally wounded, no one the second, the rest mere insurance.

'Prime Minister, this is the Foreign Secretary. We have the Paris address. Brussels is finished. No, Prime Minister, we do not yet have the details for London.'

Ronnie Scott's was good, Kara decided; Adin would have said Ronnie Scott's was incredible, but she never had been into jazz, never really understood it. She left her drink half-finished, smiled at the cashier on the way out, and began the fifteen-minute trip to the place off the Edgware Road.

'One moment, Prime Minister.' Langdon cupped his hand over the mouthpiece.

'Blue. Blue. Dickens. Repeat. Dickens.'

'London details coming through now, Prime Minister. Yes, I'll keep you informed.'

You're moving, the Ops Room told Finn.

Check communication systems for last time – Finn and the team went through the routine. Check weapons again: Smith and Wessons with suppressors, because for some reason the job was deniable and everyone knew the SAS now preferred Sig Sauers, plus the fact that the action on an automatic made a suppressor itself very noisy. MP5Ks in case it went wrong and reduced Remingtons in case it got really heavy. Lightweight Kevlon body armour vests, ceramic plates inserted front and back.

'Flat 4A. 119 Maida Vale Road.'

'Confirm address,' Finn requested. Because now was the time to sort out any misunderstandings.

'Repeat. Flat Four Alpha. One One Nine Maida Vale Road.'

They left the holding room and went to the Range Rover, the back-up already in position. You got it? Finn asked. Got it, the driver told him. The vehicles turned out of the gates, into the King's Road, then right towards Sloane Square.

'Four targets. Three males, one female.' The Ops Room gave them the details: the aliases and false passports the four were using. The message encrypted.

They were moving north, cutting through the late evening traffic. In front of them a black cab was turning right, the driver pulled into the centre of the road and the cars behind it waiting but the traffic coming the other way not allowing the taxi to cross, therefore slowing them down. The escort car pulled left, on to the pavement. They ignored the horns of the other cars and followed it through, crossed Marble Arch and continued north up the Edgware Road, the traffic slightly thinner now but seeming to move more slowly, Finn and the others ignoring it and concentrating on the job ahead. Pity they didn't know the layout, pity they couldn't put surveillance in first. Pity they couldn't even be sure the four terrorists would be there. They turned left, into Maida Vale Road. Typical flat and bed-sit area, Finn thought, four- or five-storey terraces on either side, cars in residents' parking spaces and the noise of London suddenly just a hum. Comfortable and quiet, just the place to put a safe house, just the street to hide a terrorist team.

'Going in,' he told Control. 'Confirm targets.'

'Three males, one female.'

'Confirm orders.' Because from this point there'll be no time to confirm what we have to do, because there'll be no time for anything. Because from the moment we go in there's only one outcome.

'Confirmed.'

The front door was locked, buzzers to the flats on the right. Names against the numbers but no names against 4A. The lock was straightforward, they cleared it and went into the entrance hall. The smell of polish hung in the air, and the stairs were dimly lit in front of them. Flat 4A theoretically on the fourth floor, except that was hotel logic. Two flats on the ground, so 4A might be on the first. Everything was still quiet, no noise from the flats or from outside, no noise on the stairs as they went up them. Flat 4 was in front of them on the first landing. They turned left. Flat 5.

Turned right. Flat 6. So where the hell was 4A? They

heard the front door grate open, then the sound of footsteps. Woman's, too soft for a man's. Coming up the stairs.

'Blue. Blue. Tolstoy. Repeat. Tolstoy.' Istanbul with the Moscow details. Thank God, or Marx, or Lenin, the Russian thought. Thank Marilyn Monroe or John F. Kennedy or anyone else you want to thank. I don't care as long as we're about to take out the bastards in my city.

'All locations have been acquired,' Langdon told the PM. 'No, Prime Minister, nothing from the London team yet.'

Finn heard the second set of footsteps – man's this time. Heard voices as the man caught the woman up, as they reached the first landing and turned right, around the angle in the stairs. Don't come along here, don't screw it. The voices and footsteps passed them and disappeared in the void above.

Flat 4A. Round the corner at the rear of the building. Lock should be easy, unless it's wired for an alarm or a booby trap. They pulled on the balaclavas. No light under door and no sound from inside. Jim, the MOE specialist picking the lock and slicing through the security chain on the inside. Finn in first, Steve next, then Ken and Jim, streamlights picking out the details and boots making no noise. One door to right, two to left, another in front.

Finn was at the first door on the left, waiting till the others were in position, Steve the second, Ken the door to the right and Jim straight ahead. No way they're not expecting us, no way they don't know we're here. Go – it was somewhere between a nod and an instinct.

Shit, Steve thought, bathroom.

Lounge, Jim thought, sofa bed in corner. One figure on it, beginning to move.

Two beds, Finn thought. Singles, both occupied, both people still awake and turning at him as he came in.

One bed, Ken thought. Fuck, kid in it. Not a kid, a woman.

Steve was already leaving the bathroom and backing up the others.

Male, still turning – Jim double tapped the trigger.

Two males, Finn thought, both getting up. Double tap on one, fast round, double tap on other. Back to first, single shot, then back to second. Check room for anything or anybody else.

Confirm not a kid, Ken thought again. Confirm it was a woman. Which would tie in with the intelligence reports. He crossed the floor, two paces, heard the slight thumps from the other rooms. The woman was moving, turning to him. No kid, he confirmed, double tapped the trigger.

'Two males,' Finn told the others.

'One male,' Jim said.

'One female,' Ken reported.

Bloody bathroom, Steve told them. Empty.

Three males, one female. Numbers tying in with the briefing. Check, Finn told them, make sure there's nobody else. He went back to the bedroom, turned the bodies over and examined the faces, did the same in the lounge. Bastards, he thought, tooled up and ready to go. No one else, Jim told him. Time to bug out, time to clear the killing zone.

Finn went to the last room and saw the woman's back. The blood was seeping across the sheets, and the shadows cast by the streamlight played on the bed and walls. Dark hair, he noticed, tinged slightly auburn. He turned the body and looked down at the face.

'Blue pulling out.' The Istanbul job finished and the team leaving the area. Langdon poured himself a coffee and offered the pot to the other members of Strike.

'Hemingway completed.' The terrorist team in Washington dealt with. Kilpatrick looked at the US ambassador then at Lessons, saw the way the Head of Station's shoulders relaxed slightly and the way the ambassador sagged with relief.

'Red. Task completed. Making for RV.' The team in Afghanistan. Everything going smoothly, so the team heading for the rendezvous point with the Alpha helicopter.

'Dickens completed. Have cleared area.' The London terrorists dealt with and Finn's team already streets away.

It was going to work, Kilpatrick thought for the first time; they were actually going to pull it off. Langdon lifted the telephone and punched the direct line into Downing Street.

'Prime Minister, this is the Foreign Secretary. I have to inform you that the terrorist team in London has been successfully dealt with, and that the threat they presented no longer exists.'

'Thank you,' the Prime Minister told him. 'Please give my personal thanks to those involved.'

'Blue clear of area.' The Istanbul team safely away and the shit hitting the fan in Brussels, the first reports of a major terrorist incident coming in and the area round Rue Léopold sealed off but the Brussels team long gone.

'Tolstoy clear. Repeat. Tolstoy clear.' The job in Moscow done.

'Balzac. Balzac. Confirm address.' Paris, and Paris had been the second location out of Istanbul, the second to go in.

The Operations Centre confirmed the address.

'Negative, Control. Apartment empty. Repeat. Apartment empty.'

Oh God, Langdon saw the expression on the face of the French ambassador. You've done a deal, he suddenly thought; you've agreed to let the bastards go in return for some favour in the future. Except if Paris had done, the ambassador didn't know. And there hadn't been time for that kind of subterfuge anyway.

'Blue,' the operations major spoke to Janner in Istanbul. 'Confirm with Blue One the Balzac details.'

Just time, Kilpatrick thought. No problems yet. At least, no problems which couldn't be overcome. And everything had gone to plan, everything else was correct. So no way Paris could be wrong. A simple explanation and a simple solution. Check the Paris details with Keefer, then Paris could finish the job. Except they couldn't. Because Blue had already said they were on the way out. Therefore Keefer was dead. Therefore they couldn't check the Paris address. Oh Christ, he almost moaned aloud. No problem, he told Strike. Three teams out, the head and the organizing section dealt with. Therefore Keefer's team in France wouldn't know where to go or what to do.

He phoned Riverside on a secure line and stood the department down.

Fiona Marchant woke at six, the sound of Geoff leaving the bathroom, fumbling his way to the kitchen and switching on the television somewhere in the background.

Christ, she heard him call her; look at this.

There was something in his voice. Bastards, he was saying; bloody bastards. She was already out of bed and pulling on her dressing gown, already running down the stairs. Bastards, he was still saying, staring at the television screen. Fucking bastards.

Major terrorist attack in a residential area of Brussels, the reporter was saying: rockets and grenades launched from close range at an apartment block, undisclosed number of people injured, but at least eight dead. Islamic fundamentalists believed responsible. No survivors in the apartment which appeared to be the target of the attack.

She slumped on the sofa and looked at the images.

The briefing was at nine, in The Tank.

'You are aware what happened last night.' Kilpatrick was almost looking relaxed, Marchant thought. 'There are pieces of the jigsaw that you cannot be officially briefed on, but you can work them out anyway. The Prime Minister sends his personal thanks to this department. I understand a message from the White House has also been received Upstairs, and that you will be informed of this shortly.'

He broke the formality. 'Good teamwork, great result.' Because we beat the bastards. Not just the terrorist teams, we also beat everyone else working on it. And if it hadn't been for us there would be four teams out there at the moment, and a whole new terrorist organization to fear. And now that particular threat has evaporated. Okay, so we didn't get the Paris team; okay, so there'll be new organizations and new threats. But yesterday we won. So let's bloody well enjoy it.

I made the connection – Marchant fixed the smile on her face. I spotted the Rue Léopold link, and the Rue Léopold link was a major threat. But three hours ago, when Geoff called me down and I saw the pictures and the devastation and the utter ruthlessness with which the operation was carried out, I actually wondered.

Kilpatrick's PA brought in the champagne. Marchant smiled and took the glass.

The debrief was over bacon and eggs, plates of toast and mugs of tea. The overall operation had been ninety-nine per cent successful, Finn's team was told; an entire terrorist network taken out. Central committee, training camp, recruiter and organizer, plus three out of four teams. Only a team in Paris missed.

'Penny for them?' Steve asked as they left the barracks and began the drive back to Hereford.

'Nothing,' Finn told him. But when I saw the woman's body last night I thought it was Kara.

This Friday little Jovan would be five.

Kara left the hotel, settled her account in cash, took a cab to Waterloo, and caught the 12.27 Eurostar to Brussels, then the 18.20 Lufthansa flight to Berlin. A direct flight from London would have been quicker, but would have left traces of her – albeit tenuous and under a different name – at Heathrow. By nine that evening she was in the safe house in the Charlottenburg area of the city with the rest of the team.

Everything in place and Keefer not knowing. Keefer's money, of course, Keefer's contacts – for the weapons and the passports and the access to the target. But Keefer knowing nothing, Keefer totally unaware. Keefer believing she and her team were still in the safe house in Paris. Keefer not knowing who or where she and the team were now. Not knowing their new identities or their new location or their new target.

Bihac starving, just as Maglaj had starved. Bihac being crucified just as Maglaj and Tesanj and Sarajevo had been nailed to the cross. So time to let the world know, time to make the people sit up and take notice. Time to tell the United Nations that it could no longer let her people down.

Kara's Rules. Kara's Game.

Thanks, Finn.

# Book Three

# 13

Hilary Langdon Carpenter woke at six. Lufthansa flight 3216 Berlin–Moscow had been delayed, the airport informed her at six-thirty. She cursed, told Sammi she could go back to bed, and confirmed the new departure time.

It was three weeks since Rob had been switched to Moscow. Computer head there suddenly on indefinite sick leave, they had been told, Rob to fly in as trouble shooter the next morning. Only for a couple of weeks, which they both understood meant a couple of months. See where something was going wrong – because something was going wrong – sort it out, then hand over to the old head or the new replacement. The sort of role Rob enjoyed, plus a recognition in the company that he was one of the best and the suggestion that a promotion, and a big one at that, was on the way. So he'd not been able to fly back at weekends, therefore Hilary Langdon Carpenter and their daughter Sammi were flying to visit him. A surprise visit, because today was his birthday. So they'd sent him cards, but would only tell him they were visiting when they arrived.

The cab collected them at eleven-thirty. Twenty-five minutes later they arrived at Berlin's Tegel Airport. The traffic was busy, cars pulling in unexpectedly and stopping where they shouldn't. The driver slid between them, parked as close as he could to the departure lounge, and carried their bags in. There was more security than usual, though she assumed there would be after the incident in Brussels.

The queues were already waiting at the two desks open for the Moscow flight. She ignored them and went to the business check-in. The man in front of her was also checking on to the Moscow flight. He was in his early thirties and smartly dressed. French passport but speaking good German, hand luggage only. The clerk checked the computer, gave him his seat number, and handed him his passport, ticket and boarding card.

'Moscow flight,' Hilary Langdon Carpenter told the clerk and lifted her daughter up so the girl could hand her own passport over the counter.

Plain-clothes security hovering near check-in, Kara noted. Probably just out of training school – left hand held slightly too consciously in front of him to stop the left side of his jacket opening to reveal whatever he was carrying underneath. Hard case, though, almost like the El Al guards: smile with the face but not with the eyes, the pupils remaining small and cold.

Franz and Stefani already through – she thought of them by the names on the passports they carried; Alex clearing business check-in and going through now. No problems, but there wouldn't be yet, either from the opposition or from Keefer. Keefer was bound to realize soon, if he hadn't already when she hadn't been in the hotel foyer in Paris for the check call. Plain-clothes security changing, standard procedure: one man or woman in position ten minutes then another moving in and the first moving away. Civilian security people asking the standard questions at the United Airlines check-in area.

She left the news stand and joined the Moscow queue.

Good-looker, the policeman with the bulletproof vest and the sub-machine gun across his chest thought. Early thirties and nice figure; smart though casually dressed, stylish jacket and Levi's. Businesswoman by the looks of the hand luggage she was carrying: airline pilot's navigation bag, fit under a seat or in overhead storage but plenty of room in it. Go to United check-in – the message was in his earpiece. Suspect reported. Female, aged twenty, close hair-cut, ring through nose. White cotton top, baggy purple trousers. Hippy backpack.

Kara came to the front of the queue. 'Good morning.' She handed the passport and ticket across the counter.

'Frau Kussler?'

'Yes.' The passport was in the name of Heidi Kussler, aged thirty-one, and a resident of Cologne.

'Any luggage to check in?'

'None,' Kara told him.

'Hand luggage?'

'One piece.'

'Is it yours . . . Did you pack it yourself . . . Has anyone asked you to carry anything for them . . .' The clerk ran through the routine questions, gave her back her ticket and passport, plus boarding pass, stuck a red security label on her cabin baggage, and told her to have a good flight.

The concourse was busy and the plain-clothes security people had changed again. She passed them and went directly to the first of the departure checks. A woman with a small girl was in front of her, two pieces of hand luggage. Kara joined the queue, showed her boarding pass and passport to the guard on the right, and went through to the baggage screening area. There were five machines, with passengers queuing at each. She joined the shortest, put her case on the belt, watched as it trundled into the X-ray, and stepped through the electronic screening door. In front of her a young man, aged around twenty-five, was asked to open his briefcase. Kara collected her case and walked through to passport control, the official nodding her through as she held up her German passport. Keefer was right; plan it right and you could get away with anything.

It was forty minutes to the switch. She spent fifteen

minutes browsing through the duty free shop, partly to pass the time and partly as cover in case anyone had decided to tail her. Franz was in the cafeteria, sipping coffee, and Alex was in a seat twenty metres away. There was no sign of Stefani, but the woman using that name had gone through fifteen minutes earlier. Kara went to the cafeteria, looked for any tails that might be sitting on the others, and bought a tea.

It was ten minutes to the switch. According to the monitors Flight LH 3216 was now scheduled to leave at 1.30 PM, though there was no indication yet which was the boarding gate. It was five minutes to the switch. The mule wouldn't hang around, she was aware, even though the mule would be a pro. All she'd want to do would be to make the drop and clear the area. It was two minutes to the switch, according to the airport clocks. Their watches wouldn't be synchronized, she and the fixer had agreed, therefore they would go by the clock in the departure area. One minute . . .

She left the cafeteria and went to the women's toilets. Two of the cubicles were occupied; one woman was leaving the washbasins and another touching up her make-up. Kara stood at the third basin from the left, so that the woman was to her left, put the case on the floor to her right, placed the envelope containing the money by the basin to her right, and examined her eyes as if she was wearing contact lenses.

The movement behind her flashed in the mirror.

A woman coming in, dark blue uniform and name badge on her lapel. Navigation bag in her hand the same as the one Kara had placed on the floor, red security ticket on it.

Try to get anything through the normal channels and the opposition would pick you up before you even moved. Some of the electronic detection machines were rumoured not to cover the top of the head, of course, but that wasn't proven, and was too risky anyway. Get somebody airside, though . . .

The woman stood at the basin to her right, neither of them speaking or looking at the other; then she took the envelope and went to one of the cubicles. Thirty seconds later she came out, went to the same washbasin, placed the navigation case she was carrying on the floor, and began to wash her hands. Kara wiped her eye with a tissue, picked up the case containing the guns, left the switch case, and walked out.

Flight LH 3216 Berlin–Moscow boarding at Gate Ten, she saw on the monitor. She went to the pay phones and dialled the number. '3216, 10,' she told the Stasi fixer.

In the departure concourse the destinations above the Lufthansa desks changed and the clerks began to check in the next set of passengers.

'Damn,' it was one of the clerks in the area in which the Moscow flight had checked in.

'What's wrong?' The woman on the next desk glanced across.

'My computer's gone down.'

'So has mine.'

The screens flickered back to life again.

Berlin was behind them, the contours of what had once been East Germany slipping beneath them.

'Coffee?' the chief steward asked the captain.

'Milk, no sugar.' Maeschler was in the left seat, the first officer in the right.

Karl Maeschler was thirty-eight years old and had been a captain with Lufthansa for twelve years. Eight flights after LH 3216 he was due to re-train on 747s for the long-haul runs. Maeschler was married, to a former stewardess, with two children. That morning he had been on standby, expecting not to be called in. In a way he didn't mind: the return trip to Moscow was a relatively short run, and he'd be home in time for the theatre that evening.

The captain has switched off the no smoking signs, the stewardess announced. In business class the purser offered the second round of complimentary drinks.

'Champagne, touch of fresh orange juice,' Hilary Langdon Carpenter looked up and smiled.

'Orange,' her daughter said. 'As long as it's fresh.'

The man who had checked in in front of them was seated on the other side of the aisle, suit jacket still on and hands folded in his lap. Nothing for me, he told the purser.

For one moment Kara was no longer on the plane. For one moment she was back in the corridor of the hospital in Tesanj, Jovan in the bed twenty metres away and Finn at her side.

Your people will always lose, Finn was telling her. Unless you find oil in Sarajevo. Because that was what the Gulf War had been about, that was the reason the Big Powers and the United Nations had moved against Saddam Hussein. Not democracy, or anything like that. To save and protect their oil supplies. So the next time you want Washington and Moscow and London and Paris to do something, remember that you need two things: you need something they want, or want back, and you need them to be afraid of you.

She was back on the plane.

Everything perfect, everything going to schedule. No way any of Keefer's contacts could identify her or the team. And, thirty seconds after Lufthansa 3216 took off, no clue on any computer which of the people on the passenger list might be hijackers, because by now the passenger list no longer existed. And the team Keefer had built around her still thinking she was carrying out Keefer's orders and following Keefer's plan.

She pulled the navigation case from beneath the seat, brushed through the curtain separating economy and business class, and went to the toilet at the front of the plane. The cubicle was just big enough to stand in. She took off her coat, put the case on the seat and keyed the combination of the security lock. The Zastava and Socimi sub-machine guns, and the spare ammunition clips were as she had packed them, machine pistols below and the polythene bags with the other items on top. She took the first sub-machine gun, assembled it and clipped in the magazine, put on the shoulder holster, fastened the M70 in it, and put on the coat again.

'Orange good?' Hilary Langdon Carpenter asked her daughter.

'Not freshly squeezed.' The girl sounded like her mother.

Hilary Langdon Carpenter reached up and summoned the purser. On the other side of the cabin the man who had checked in in front of them stood and made his way to the toilet, another man and woman coming through from economy. Not on, Hilary Langdon Carpenter thought: if you were economy you used the toilets at the rear.

Franz, Alex and Stefani would have been watching her, Kara knew; Franz, Alex and Stefani would be outside, waiting for their own weapons.

Stay with me, Adin, she thought. Look after me, Jovan, she prayed.

Okay, Finn. Let's do it.

* * *

It was thirty-six hours – give or take – since they'd returned from the London job. Last night they'd been in the sergeants' mess till gone four, the other teams returning from wherever they'd been. No one giving details, because no one ever did. The less you knew, the less you could give away under interrogation, even about operations in the past. A good job, though, and everyone home safe. And if someone hadn't made it home, just as Kev and Geordie John hadn't made it from Maglaj, the party would have been a wake and gone on later.

Now Finn sat eating lunch and watching the One O'Clock News on the television.

Sometimes he thought it was the wrong way to wind down. This afternoon, therefore, before he collected the boys from school and cooked tea, he'd go for a run – a long one. Clear his head. And tomorrow he and Janner would make the short trip down to Pontrilas and confirm the anti-terrorist training routines.

Bloody Bosnia – he stopped eating and stared at the images on the screen. Sarajevo cut off again and the Serbs shelling Bihac, which was supposed to be a safe haven. Plus reports that Serb planes had actually bombed Bihac even though it was bang in the middle of a no-fly zone. And the United Nations were sitting back and doing nothing. Not the UNPROFOR guys on the ground, not the men and women sitting isolated and exposed in the hills of Bosnia, the winter about to close in on them. The bloody decision-makers. Or, more correctly, the non-decision-makers. The Contact Group in Europe and the UN in New York. All sitting on their hands and allowing the Bosnian Serbs to pull the strings.

Just like Maglaj ten months ago, the thought crept up on him as he knew it probably would, just like Tesanj.

That was the trouble when you had time after a job. It was when you had time that you began to think about other things; and once you thought about other things your mind slipped from the routines and procedures and drills that you were trained for and that you didn't know when you would need.

The telephone rang. He began to get up, still looking at the screen. The report from Bosnia ended abruptly, halfway through the item, and the programme went back to the studio.

'We are just getting reports of a hijack.' The newscaster glanced at the sheet of paper which had just been handed to him.

One of the Soviet republics, Finn guessed; strange that it should make the main news, though; normally you only read about it in the foreign pages of the broadsheets. He crossed the room and lifted the phone.

'A Lufthansa jet with one hundred and thirty passengers and crew has been hijacked en route from Berlin to Moscow,' the newscaster was continuing.

The Paris team, he thought. 'Yes,' he said noncommittally. Knew what the call was, because once there was a hijack in Europe there was no guarantee where it would end. Therefore, theoretically at least, it might end in Britain. Therefore, again theoretically, they would be involved. Therefore, from that moment, he was on standby.

'Finn?'

'Yes.'

'Fancy a pint?'

'Just heard. On my way.' He switched off the television and dialled Janner's number. 'Jude, it's Finn.'

'You want me to pick up the boys?' Because Janner's just had the call and is on his way in.

'If you wouldn't mind.'

'Anything else?'

'Tell Caz I'll phone this evening if I can. And thanks.'

The photograph of the boys was on the sideboard. He looked at it and wrote the letter. *Had to nip out. Won't be long. Jude's collecting the boys. Will try to phone this evening*. It was the code they had agreed: he was on standby, and it was UK, not overseas. He folded the paper, unfolded it again, wrote *Love Finn* on the bottom, then sealed it in an envelope, put the envelope on the kitchen table, collected his bag and left.

Kilpatrick was a lunch guest at the Cavalry and Guards. He and his host, a businessman with the occasional overseas trip therefore the occasional intelligence connection, were seated at a table in the second floor restaurant overlooking Green Park, Buckingham Palace not quite visible on the far side.

'Possibility of a contract in Beijing coming up,' the host told him. 'Wondered if you and the FCO might need anything.' But before that, of course, you and the Foreign and Commonwealth Office might be able to get me on the short list.

'Telephone for your guest, sir.'

Kilpatrick apologized to his host and followed the waiter across the room.

'Yes.'

'It's the office.'

He recognized his PA. 'Yes.'

'There's a hijacking.'

Keefer's lot, he knew. It was a bit like Northern Ireland, especially the heavy days along the border before he'd moved to Riverside. Think you'd dealt with some of the bastards, then they'd pop up again when and where you weren't expecting them.

'On my way.'

Langdon was in the middle of a BBC Radio interview, down the line from Edinburgh where he had been fulfilling a long-standing party engagement. Bosnia – the interviewer was asking him. Certain Muslim advances, but the Serbs were still shelling Bihac. So what did the UN intend to do about it? What was Britain's position and what effects would a lifting of the arms embargo have?

Bosnia was a long-term problem, Langdon was saying. The UN intended to have troops in-country for the winter, and that was important because it gave some stability, as well as a possibility of working out something via the Contact Group.

'But in the meantime people are dying,' the interviewer came back at him.

'In war situations people are always dying,' Langdon replied slowly and evenly. 'None of us involved in international negotiations ever forget that fact, none of us ever sit round a conference table without having the thought of people dying at the back of our minds. That's why we must continue to seek a settlement, that's what we're striving for at the moment.'

And don't think you can pull that one on me again.

'But what about the Serb shelling of Bihac. Shouldn't the UN be launching an air attack to stop it?'

'The decision whether or not to launch an air attack is not one which rests with the British government.' Langdon began the well-rehearsed answer. 'The decision rests with the . . .'

'I'm sorry to interrupt you, Foreign Secretary.' The interviewer adjusted her earpiece. 'We're just receiving word of a hijacking in Europe.' Ninety seconds to end of programme, the producer told her; hijack story breaking, ask him if there's a Bosnian involvement and try to get him to react. 'Might there be any involvement with Bosnia?'

The missing terrorist team – the shock hit Langdon. 'I'm sorry.' His reply was calm and unruffled. 'You've just heard about it during this interview?'

'Yes,' the interviewer conceded.

'Like you, it's the first I've heard about it. As you'll

appreciate, until we know anything further there wouldn't be much point in my commenting on it.'

The interview wrapped up. Good try, the producer told the interviewer. 'What the hell's going on?' Langdon asked. 'Why wasn't I informed?'

'Returning to London on the two-forty shuttle,' he told Samuelson. 'Briefing on the way in from Heathrow. Provisional meeting of Strike as early as possible in case there's a connection. Find out the Prime Minister's schedule, in case I have to speak to him. Better contact SAS, just in case they come this way.'

'Brigadier, Special Forces has already been in contact,' Samuelson informed him. 'SAS is on standby.'

The Agusta 109 helicopter crossed the Severn and headed east over the English countryside. There was nothing about its appearance to suggest its purpose and nothing about its markings to indicate the identities of the men crammed in the back: the operations officer – this time the squadron major; the team commander, on this occasion a staff sergeant; Finn, the assault group commander, the sniper group commander, a signaller, and the operations clerk. The Range Rovers of the rest of the teams were already on the road, and the plain white van which would carry the back-up gear was already being loaded. It was thirty-five minutes since the news of the hijack of Lufthansa 3216 had been flashed to Hereford.

Heathrow in fifteen minutes – Finn checked his watch.

Establish the holding area where the teams would wait, and set up an Operations Room. It was routine, why he had gone to Heathrow earlier in the week. Borrow a 737, adapt the interior for the passenger and seat configuration of LH 3216 – because Lufthansa only separated business from economy in the minutes prior to take-off. And begin practising. Diversions and approaches, methods of entry and procedures and lines of fire when they were inside. Hope LH 3216 didn't come to London, but be ready for it if it did.

He checked his watch again. Ten minutes to Heathrow.

The strands of cloud drifted around them and the thin ribbon of a river threaded through the green of the forest below them.

'Lufthansa 3216, descend to flight level nine zero.' Descend to nine thousand feet. 'Contact Paris Approach on one two four decimal four five.'

For the first time since the hijack Karl Maeschler's hands had stopped shaking.

'Lufthansa 3216. This is Paris Approach. Descend to flight level eight zero.' Eight thousand feet. Speed two one zero knots, the controller would normally dictate at this point. But speeds at this stage of landing were designed to maintain safe distances between aircraft, and for the past ten minutes all flights into and out of Paris Orly had been suspended. 'Contact Director on one three five decimal zero.'

'Lufthansa 3216, this is Paris Director. Turn left on heading three five five degrees. Descend to flight level six zero. QNH one zero one eight.'

Maeschler swung the 737 in a gentle turn.

One stage over, Kara told herself: the next beginning. Just stick to the plan, stick to the demand and the timetable and the schedule.

'Lufthansa 3216. Turn left on heading two eight zero degrees. Descend to three thousand feet.' After the so-called transition altitude, clearance was given in feet, not flight levels. 'Cleared to lock on ILS for runway Two Five.'

Maeschler banked the aircraft again. 'Landing in two minutes,' he said automatically. 'Your people strapped in?' Funny thing to query, he would reflect later, interesting how even now his training overruled his fear.

'Yes,' she told him.

'Lufthansa 3216. Turn left on heading two four five degrees.'

Maeschler began the final turn. In Paris Orly the security people would already be waiting, Kara thought; the television cameras and radio teams would already be jostling for position.

'Lufthansa 3216, call outer marker.'

So far so good, she thought.

'Lufthansa 3216. Cleared to land. Runway Two Five. Surface wind one eight zero degrees, five knots.'

The lights in front of them were coming up fast. The wheels of the 737 struck the ground, the tyres screeching. Maeschler eased the stick forward, pulling the reverse thrust levers and feeling the power of the deceleration. Oh Christ – he suddenly remembered the hijackers in the cabin. The grenades in their hands and the pins out.

'It's okay,' Kara told him. 'They put the pins back in for landing. They'll take them out again when we stop.'

'Lufthansa 3216, this is Ground. Proceed via taxiway Four Seven to parking stand Mike Ten.'

'Tell them we're going to stand Delta One,' Kara instructed him. Because Mike Ten will be one of the remote stands where the authorities place aircraft they want out of the way. Because the airport's security people will try to keep us away from the television cameras, and the cameras away from us. And the one thing I need above all else is good television coverage of the hijacked plane and live feeds to the world's television sets.

'Ground, this is Lufthansa 3216. I have been instructed to proceed to stand Delta One.'

The aircraft was still moving forwards, the other planes and airport buildings a blur around him.

'Negative, Lufthansa. Delta One is already occupied.'

First mistake, Maeschler would think later: you only gave statements, never reasons.

'In that case Charlie Three,' Kara told him. Or any of the stands fronting the south terminal. And not all of them would be occupied.

'Ground, this is Lufthansa 3216. In that case I have been instructed to proceed to Charlie Three.'

There was a pause.

'Negative, Lufthansa 3216. We have problems with Charlie Three. Proceed to Golf Seven Zero.'

Which was at the far end of the freight terminal, and would therefore keep her even further from the press and the television.

The hijacker had studied the charts, Maeschler realized; she knew exactly where she wanted to go and where not. There was no need for a gun at his head, no need for it to be like the cinema. Her voice was enough; plus the fact that she was standing there in the first place. Please God may I survive this, please God may I live to see my wife and kids again.

'Charlie Three,' Kara told him. 'If it's occupied, tell them to clear it.'

'Hijacked plane is on ground at Paris Orly,' the signaller informed Finn.

They were in the set of rooms, away from the passenger terminals, which had been designated as the holding area. The room which would become the operations centre was on the next floor, and the television monitors with pictures of the CNN, BBC and ITV feeds from Paris Orly were against the wall on the right, the first pictures of the hijacked plane already on the screens.

'Penny for them?' Janner handed Finn a mug of coffee.

'I'm thinking that they seem to be well organized. That they know what they're doing and are doing it well, and that it's one hell of a coincidence if they're not the Paris team.'

But what I'm really thinking is: why now, what's it all about? Generally and specifically. Generally: which groups or organizations might think it's in their interests to hijack a plane? Specifically: what's going on in the world, at this precise moment in time, which someone might try to influence?

They had been on the ground an hour.

'I'm hungry, Mummy.' Sammi was curled into her, right thumb in her mouth. 'Why is that man pointing a gun at us? Why can't we go home?'

'It's all right,' Hilary Langdon Carpenter told the girl. 'Soon everything will be okay. Soon we'll be off the plane and in our nice warm apartment.'

The hijack leader was on the flight deck with the captain, the first officer had been taken off the flight deck and was sitting opposite them, and the other hijackers were spaced along the cabins. Where are we, Hilary Langdon Carpenter wanted to ask. Who are you and what do you want? At least she was British. At least, if the hijackers were Arabs or working for an Arab cause, the first people they would single out among the passengers would be the Jews. Unless they discovered who she was, of course, unless they discovered that among the passengers were the daughter and granddaughter of the British Foreign Secretary. But there was no way they could know that. Except there was, because she'd kept her maiden name, so they could find out from her passport. But to do that they would have to collect the passports and make the connection. And to make the connection they'd need to know the name of the British Foreign Secretary.

'I'm hungry.' Sammi began to cry. 'When are we going to eat?'

Bastards, Hilary Langdon Carpenter thought. Making her child cower in fear like this, making her daughter go without food.

Kara left the flight deck, nodded to Alex to take her place, and walked back down the cabin. Most of the passengers were adult, a few children, their mothers clutching them tight. She heard the whistle from Alex and turned. Radio, he signalled. She went back to the flight deck and nodded to Alex to take up his former position. Ground Control, Maeschler told her.

The radio selector box was on the central console, with buttons for the plane's internal PA system, VHF 1 and 2, HF 1 and 2, the intercom between the captain and first officer, which they never used, and the service intercom to the cabin crew.

There were headsets for the captain and first officer, boom mikes in front and transmit switches on each of the columns. The switches were spring-loaded: on to speak, off to listen. A third headset could be used by someone in the jump seat at the rear of the flight deck, but if that person wished to speak either the captain or first officer had to press their transmit buttons.

Maeschler was already wearing his headset. Kara sat in the jump seat, put the third headset on, and nodded at him.

Maeschler pressed the transmit button. 'Ground, this is Lufthansa 3216.'

'3216. This is Henri Badoual.' The negotiator, Maeschler supposed. 'Is that the captain?' No name, because that would bring the press round Maeschler's house and family like a plague. Although the airline and the German authorities would have that covered by now.

'Yes.'

'Are the hijackers with you?'

'Yes.'

'Let me speak to them.'

Hand away from the transmit switch, Kara motioned.

Maeschler did as she ordered.

'Tell them you've been instructed that the hijackers are not yet prepared to talk to them. Those words, nothing else.'

'I'm sorry . . .' Maeschler began, then corrected himself. 'This is the captain. I have been instructed to say that the hijackers are not yet prepared to talk to you.'

'Karl, let me speak to them.' The use of the first name was deliberate.

I have a woman next to me who's armed and is threatening me even though the gun is at her side, Maeschler wanted to tell the negotiator. I want you to speak to her, but she says no. I want to ask you to tell my wife I'm okay, but I can't.

'I say again. I have been instructed . . .' he paused, then repeated and emphasized the word: '. . . *instructed* to say that the hijackers are not yet prepared to talk to you.'

And for God's sake don't push it any more. Not yet, not so soon. Because there's one in the flight deck with me, and three others in the cabin with guns pointed at my passengers and grenades with the pins pulled out.

'Karl . . .' the negotiator came back at him, an edge of authority in the voice this time.

End of conversation, the woman at Maeschler's side ordered him. Not verbally. With a movement of the hand across the throat. He nodded and took off the headset.

'Well done,' Kara told him.

Remember the course, he tried to tell himself; remind yourself what they said the hijackers would be like and what they would tell you to do. He was trembling again, his fingers and his hands and his body; the sweat pouring off him and the sickness in his stomach, his brain in a whirl. The champagne was on the table and his wife was smiling, almost crying with happiness. I'm pregnant, she was telling him, I'm carrying our child.

'The passengers haven't eaten since take-off.' He tried to force a degree of control into his voice. 'There's an in-flight snack. Should we give it to them now?'

'We could be here for some time. You might think it better to wait.'

'The grenades. Is it all right for your people to put the pins back in?'

'Tell the passengers that's what they're going to do. But tell them not to try anything. Also tell them we're collecting all radios and cellular phones.'

Maeschler pressed the PA button on the selector box. 'This is the captain. We are safely on the ground, so the hijackers in the cabin are going to put the pins back in their grenades. This is for the sake of us all.' He shouldn't have called them hijackers, he thought. But that was what they were, so what else could he call them? 'They're also going to collect radios and mobile phones. Everyone remain seated. Nobody move unless given permission.'

'Mummy,' Sammi Langdon Carpenter whispered. 'I want to go to the toilet.'

'Hold on,' her mother told her. Don't do anything to single us out, she wanted to say. Don't give them any reason to discover who we are and who your grandfather is.

The Rover, plus police escort and outriders, was waiting. Two minutes after the Edinburgh shuttle had docked, Langdon had left Heathrow, Nicholls in the rear seat with him and briefing him as the convoy sliced its way through the exit traffic from Heathrow towards the M4.

'Strike is arranged and the PM's available whenever you want him.' The file was on Nicholls's lap. 'There are two issues, which may or may not be connected.'

The outriders accelerated off the approach road and on to the motorway, lights flashing and cars close behind.

'The first issue is the hijack.' Nicholls gave Langdon the details. 'The plane has now been on the ground at Paris Orly for ninety minutes. Specialist police units are standing by and a negotiator has tried to speak to the hijackers, but the captain has said that they are not yet prepared to talk. The hijackers may or may not be the Paris team.'

'The second issue?'

They were already at the end of the motorway, the outriders ensuring there was no delay.

'The second is Bosnia. The Serbs have been shelling Bihac all day, there are reports of substantial casualties. A number of organizations, plus UN members, are screaming for an air strike. The UN has so far said no.' But the Foreign Secretary would still come under pressure the moment he stepped into his office.

'What's the situation look like?'

'Not pretty.'

'But if the UN launches an air strike, it will upset the Serbs, which might in turn upset the present round of peace talks. Plus it might endanger British troops in Bosnia.'

'Precisely,' Nicholls agreed.

And the press and the public were both fickle, both had short memories. Tomorrow, certainly next week, Bihac would be forgotten.

They were through Hammersmith, the sirens of the outriders and escort car blaring, were heading east along the Thames.

'Any chance of a connection between the hijack and Bosnia?' Langdon asked. Because this is precisely what Riverside warned. Except they got an address wrong and the Paris team disappeared. And except that Berlin wasn't one of the four target cities.

'Kilpatrick is waiting to brief you on that the moment

you arrive.' Perhaps it was a straight answer, perhaps a way out.

Parliament Square appeared jammed with traffic, but a way through had already been carved for them. The Rover accelerated round The Green and into Whitehall.

'I'm briefing the Foreign Sec in thirty seconds,' Kilpatrick informed Fiona Marchant on a secure line. 'Update me.'

'Nothing new,' she told him.

There wouldn't be, Kilpatrick supposed, but there was no harm in hoping. Nicholls collected him and escorted him through. Langdon was sitting at his desk, one of the TV monitors in the corner tuned to BBC and the other to CNN. BBC was on one of the afternoon shows, CNN was just switching from the studio presenter to live pictures from Orly.

'How the hell did they manage that?' Langdon took off his coat. What the hell are the French doing allowing them that access, they knew he meant.

'The hijackers didn't put the plane where the French authorities wanted,' Kilpatrick chose a hardbacked chair at the side of the desk. 'The press had been listening in on airband and were waiting. I imagine they couldn't believe their luck when the plane stopped where they could see it.'

'Was it luck?'

'No.'

'What are the chances of a connection between the Israeli warning and the hijack?' Langdon nodded for coffee. 'Are the hijackers the Paris team?'

Because if so we have a problem; because we got the wrong address out of Keefer, so the French missed the Paris mob; but because the rest of the intelligence was good, we've managed to shift the blame. But we'd better not bugger it up again, otherwise heads will roll.

'At the moment, there's no intelligence whatsoever to say the hijackers are the Paris team.' Kilpatrick was careful.

'On the other hand, it might seem a coincidence if there wasn't a connection.'

'Early days, you mean?' Except that's what you people are paid for.

'Precisely. Nobody's seen the hijackers, they haven't even spoken on the radio.'

'Bosnia's building up again.'

'Yes,' Kilpatrick agreed.

'Any connection there?'

'Possibly, though no one can say for sure at this stage.'

Continue, Langdon's stare told him.

'Bihac is under siege, the focal point of attention. Bihac is a Muslim town. We know that Keefer recruited Bosnian Muslims, though not from Bihac.'

'So it might be that the hijackers are Keefer's Paris team, following Keefer's instructions.'

'Possibly.' There was a slight hesitation.

'But if they're following Keefer's orders, why weren't they at the address where Keefer himself thought they were?'

'Precisely, Foreign Secretary.'

Pemberton poured them coffee.

'What about the passenger list?' Langdon stood up, cup in hand, and began pacing the room. 'Are there any Britons on board?' Which I understand the press have been screaming at us for.

'There's no passenger list,' Kilpatrick told him.

'Why not?'

'The only explanation so far is that there was a pirate program in the Lufthansa computer system.' This is ominous, he had thought when Marchant had informed him. This is not good. This lot know what they're doing. 'The suggestion is that it activated ten minutes after Lufthansa 3216 took off. Probably triggered by another message into the system that 3216 was airborne.'

'So it was installed in the Lufthansa system by the hijackers?' Langdon sat down.

'There's every indication that's the case.' So what about Fiona Marchant, because for the first time Fiona Marchant appeared to have doubts about Riverside. As if the blood in London and Paris and Brussels and wherever else was on her hands. There was a first time for everything, of course, but it was the sort of thing which hung over your head for as long as you allowed it to. And then you made your decision: whether you were in or out. And only you could decide that.

'Yes or no?' Langdon was insistent.

'Yes. It was installed by the hijackers.'

'Why should they do that?'

'To make it difficult, if not impossible, for the authorities to check the passenger details and see which passengers are genuine and which might be using false documents or someone else's identity.'

'Any other way a list could be drawn up? Ticket counterfoils, for example?'

'They've gone missing.'

'The hijackers again?'

'Presumably so.'

'Any questions?' Langdon asked Nicholls. There were none. 'Recommendations?' he asked Kilpatrick.

'None.' Except pray it stays a French problem. 'At least until we know what's happening and have confirmed who the hijackers are.'

The Prime Minister for you, Langdon's personal secretary informed him on one of the internal lines. In his office and needs a briefing from you.

'Five minutes,' Langdon told her. He thanked Kilpatrick, left his office, and took one of the underground passages to Downing Street, thus avoiding the gaze of the sightseers grouped round the security gates at the entrance, and the questions of the press clustered outside Number Ten.

'How do we play it?' The Prime Minister had already been briefed by the chairman of the Joint Intelligence Committee.

'Hard.' Langdon settled comfortably in a wing chair. 'Pressure on Paris. No deals, no concessions.' Give in to one and you give in to everyone in the future. 'Make our position clear.' And hope to hell the French did something behind the scenes, which they had frequently done in the past, and would probably do now.

'No indication yet if there are any Britons on board?' Because the JIC have told me about the computer problem.

'Not so far.'

It was ten minutes to his next meeting. Langdon excused himself, checked on developments with his personal office, and went to the Cobra rooms.

Two hundred metres away the military vehicles moved into position. Kara sat in the first officer's seat, Maeschler to her left, both of them wearing headsets and listening to the BBC World Service on HF.

'Put on the loudspeakers,' she told him.

The speakers were on the flight deck, but by turning them on and opening the door, the passengers in the first rows could hear the news on the radio. And once those passengers had heard, the details would soon be passed to the others.

'The hijacked Lufthansa jet with an estimated hundred and thirty passengers on board is still on the runway at Paris Orly Airport.' The newsreader was male, his voice slightly echoing.

Be all right soon. Hilary Langdon Carpenter held her daughter tight to her and listened mesmerized. It was as if they were talking about someone else; as if she was back home listening to an account of something else happening to somebody else.

'A special report from our reporter at Orly.'

'Lufthansa 3216 is a hundred metres from me.' The reporter spoke live. 'The French have brought in a negotiator, but so far the hijackers have refused to speak to him.' He played the recordings of the messages between Maeschler and the negotiator. 'For reasons which they have not explained, the authorities have not been able to confirm the number of passengers on board, or their nationalities.'

The newsreader moved on to the next item. 'In Bosnia, the Muslim town of Bihac is still under heavy artillery fire from surrounding Serb forces. A report from our correspondent in Sarajevo' . . .

. . . The bridge was the problem. Because that was where the snipers were waiting for you to cross. And you had to cross because you were on one side and the food was on the other . . .

Kara was back in Maglaj the day it all began. The guns pounding and her son crying because he was hungry. Please God, may they not be waiting today. Please God, may they not get me. Because today my husband is on the front line, and I do not know whether he is dead or alive. But because my husband is on the front line, probably only three hundred metres from the bridge I am about to cross, he cannot go for the food while I look after our son . . .

She was dressing Jovan, pulling the clothes tight around him.

. . . Therefore I have to go. But because my husband is on the front line, waiting for the next attack, there is no one to look after my son. Therefore I have to take my precious little Jovan with me. Because unless he eats soon he will die. But in trying to reach the food the two of us might die anyway . . .

She was stepping into the cold.

. . . Therefore, when I reach the bridge and begin to run across it, I will pray that the sniper who killed old man Samir yesterday and little Lejla the day before, is looking the other way, or moving position as the snipers do, or warming his fingers round a mug of hot coffee, or glancing up and taking a sip of slivovic . . .

She was shutting the door and hurrying down the road, her feet slipping and Jovan in her arms.

. . . Therefore when I begin to run across the bridge I will hold my little Jovan in my left arm, so that my body will be between him and the sniper. And when I try to make it back I will hold Jovan in my right arm, so that I am again between him and the sniper . . .

She was seeing the bridge in front of her, the people sheltered in the lee of a building and the man at the front rocking backwards and forwards and counting down from ten.

. . . Please God, protect me. Please God, may the shells not fall again until I and my little son are safely home . . .

. . . She was back on Lufthansa 3216.

Strike convened at five: Langdon in the chair, the Russian, French and American ambassadors occupying the seats at the end of the table closest to him, and the intelligence chiefs – with the exception of Duvalier, who had been recalled to Paris – furthest away from him.

'Updates,' Langdon began. 'Ideas, intelligence?'

He enjoyed this: enjoyed the tension and the drama and the difficulties it threw at him. Enjoyed this moment at this time in this room. Okay, so there were a hundred and thirty people sitting sweating on a plane in Paris, but that wasn't his fault.

Still waiting on the hijackers, he was informed.

They moved on.

Any developments on the passenger list, any suggestion that someone important might be on board ... Any thoughts on the possible link between the Paris team and the hijacking ... The latest situation in Bosnia and the pressure on the United Nations to do something about the shelling of Bihac ... Possible links between Bosnia and the hijacking.

'You are aware of traditional links between my government and the Serbian government in Belgrade, plus the Bosnian-Serb government in Pale,' the Russian ambassador reminded them.

'You understand that my government is under increasing pressure from Congress to take a more active part in assisting the Muslims.' The American.

'You appreciate that if that assistance goes too far then my government will pull its troops out of UNPROFOR.' The French ambassador.

For God's sake – Langdon held out his hands. We're not the Contact Group, we're not at loggerheads in the UN Security Council. We're mature consenting adults, and if we can't find a way out, then God help the rest of the world. Plus it's our necks on the chopping block, which is even more to the point. Because Keefer's Paris team weren't where they were supposed to be, so now we risk being held personally responsible. Therefore the buck stops here, gentlemen. And whilst we all care deeply about Bosnia and world peace and all that, we all care even more about our own personal and political careers.

Caz left school at five-fifteen. The day had been hard, but it had also been rewarding. Remedial teaching was like that. God help the rest of the staff who worked full-time, though. At least Finn was at home; at least he was collecting the boys and making supper.

Jude's car was at the side of the house, not Finn's. Caz

parked, looked at the house in case the boys were waiting at the window, and ran inside. The children – the boys and Jude's two – were round the table in the kitchen, eating toad in the hole and baked potatoes. Jude looking fine, anyone else would have said. Jude looking as she herself suddenly looked, Caz realized. The smile on her face and the stress in her eyes.

'Looks good.' Caz took off her coat, kissed the kids, and made a show of tasting the supper. 'Any left for me?' She hugged them again, followed Jude into the lounge, and shut the door.

'There's a hijack. A Lufthansa jet.' There was no need to say Finn and Janner were on call, because Finn and Janner were on the anti-terrorist team, and if there was a hijack which might in any way affect them, or might require their assistance or intervention, then *ipso facto* they were on call.

'Where?' Caz asked.

'Flying out of Berlin. It's now in Paris.'

At least it wasn't a British plane, at least it wasn't in Britain and didn't involve Britain. At least the Europeans all had their own anti-terrorist teams, so the chances of Finn getting involved were slim.

'Finn called as soon as he heard.' Jude poured them each a gin and tonic. 'Asked me to pick up the boys. He left this for you.' She gave Caz the envelope.

One of the boys came in. 'Where's Dad? I thought he was picking us up.'

'Dad's had to go away for a couple of days.' Caz tried to smile, tried to sound reassuring. Tried to sound as if nothing was wrong. As if Finn didn't do what Finn did. She put her arm round her son's shoulders, and went back to the kitchen. Laughed and joked with the children and listened to what each had done at school that day. Poured them each another orange squash and went back into the lounge. Opened the envelope and read the letter. Switched on the television, sat with Jude on the sofa and waited for the news.

The plan of a Boeing 737 was pinned to the wall of the holding room, and the television monitors carried live feeds from the CNN, BBC and ITN cameras at Orly. So what was going on, Finn wondered. Who were the hijackers and what did they want? It was five minutes to six. Janner came in, and the teams sat at the tables and waited for any updates the news might carry, even though they had already seen the pictures and heard the recordings of the conversations with the pilot.

Interesting times, Langdon thought, interesting place to be. He and the other members of Strike had assembled again in the Cobra room. His dinner engagement that evening had needed to be curtailed. Not cancelled, because of who else was going to be present. But cut short, which always helped create or reinforce an impression anyway.

'Gunmen hijack Lufthansa jet en route to Moscow.' The bulletin began, the summaries first and the newscaster's voice hard and penetrating. 'A hundred and thirty passengers and crew on board. Tonight the hijacked plane is on the ground at Orly Airport, in Paris.'

Caz sat transfixed; watched and listened to the details of the hijack, the conversations between the negotiator and the pilot; the live pictures and interviews from Orly itself, the 737 sitting isolated and exposed. It was bad enough when Finn was away, when she didn't know what exactly he was doing or the dangers he might face. But this, in its way, was worse. Even though logic said he wouldn't be involved.

Today's other news, the newscaster was saying. Unemployment figures and politicians' statements ...

Something about the royal family . . . A film star shocking everyone with a see-through dress.

'In Bosnia, the UN safe haven of Bihac is still under fire.' The newscaster moved on to the next item. 'In New York and London the peace protests grow. A report, first, from our correspondent in Sarajevo.'

Artillery shells are pounding Bihac at the rate of one every two to three minutes, the report was saying. Pressure is mounting on the UN to mount an air strike, but every indication is that this will not take place.

The bulletin switched to the next item.

'In New York it began with a survivor of the concentration camps; in London with two housewives from Manchester. Now the peace protest is growing.' The pictures were from Westminster. At first there had been just the two, then sixty, the following day a hundred – men and women, all ages and classes. Now there were nearer five hundred, standing and sitting on The Green in the centre of Parliament Square. The police presence larger and more obvious now, but the policemen talking with them, and people bringing them food. The protest outside the United Nations in New York was also growing, the reporter was saying; similar protests had begun in Paris, Berlin, and Amsterdam.

Caz stared at the screen. This is what I've been thinking about, this is what I've been asking myself about all day. Because I believe what they believe. And if I believe what they believe, why am I leaving it to them to say it? Why aren't I there with them? Because, in a way, I have a commitment to Bosnia that they don't have. But they're standing outside Westminster, and I'm watching it on television.

But I can't do what they're doing. That's also what I've been telling myself all day. Because I'm married to Finn. And Finn is SAS, Finn's signed the Official Secrets Act. My country right or wrong, and all that. Therefore he can't stand up and be counted. So I can't either.

The light outside the plane had faded. Keefer would know by now, Keefer would be suicidal. It was a long time and a long way from the black market in Travnik, Kara thought, an even longer time and a longer way from Maglaj.

It was fifteen minutes past seven, local time.

'Tell the negotiator that in three hours exactly we're going to open the main passenger door,' she ordered Maeschler. 'Tell him that when we do, any security people shouldn't be closer to the plane than they are now.'

Why are you going to open the door – Maeschler felt the fear. What are you going to do? He pulled on the headset and pressed the transmit button.

'Ground, this is Lufthansa 3216.'

'3216, this is Ground. Badoual speaking.'

The report from the protest at Westminster ended abruptly. Behind her Caz sensed the children were going to ask her something, and began to turn towards them, began to get up.

'The pilot of the hijacked plane is about to talk to the French authorities.' The newscaster's delivery was terse. 'We are going live to Orly.'

'Ground, this is the captain again. I have been instructed to pass on a message.'

Caz waved to the children that she would be with them soon, and stared again at the image of Lufthansa 3216, the cigar-shape of its body glinting in the searchlights which played on it, the half-light eerie around it, and the voices of whoever was talking echoing and far away, yet human and close to her.

'In three hours exactly, the hijackers will open the main passenger door. When they do, they do not wish any security personnel to be closer to the plane than they are now.'

'3216, this is Ground. May I speak to the hijackers?'

Maeschler saw the shake of the head. 'Ground, this is Lufthansa 3216. Negative, repeat negative. They still won't speak to you.'

Kara rose and went to the door. 'Collect the passports,' she told the gunman called Alex. The hijacker flicked on the safety of the sub-machine gun, hung the weapon from his shoulder, took a sheet of adhesive labels and a pen from his coat pocket, and turned back down the aisle.

What's going on, Hilary Langdon Carpenter wanted to know; what game are you playing? Why the hell do you have a sheet of sticky labels in the middle of a hijack? She held Sammi tight against her and wished she was in economy, that she hadn't singled herself out by travelling business.

'Passport.' The gunman called Alex towered over her.

Oh God no, she thought.

Please no, the family five rows back prayed. This is how the Nazis began in Germany sixty years ago. This is how the Palestinians singled out the Jews in previous hijackings.

Thank God she was British. Hilary Langdon Carpenter felt in her handbag and passed the gunman her passport. He opened it and checked the last page. 'The girl's as well,' he told her in English. 'She's not on yours.'

She felt in her handbag again and gave him Sammi's passport. So what do we do now, you bastard? Why the hell have you got a sheet of sticky labels with you. Are you going to give us each one, then play a game? Are we going to draw lots; and if so what's the prize?

The gunman peeled two labels off the sheet, stuck them on the passports, and wrote the seat numbers of the passport holders on the labels.

Maeschler watched from the door of the flight deck. This lot have thought of everything – the fear was fresh now, and different. The passports, okay, because now they would know who was on the plane. But why the door? Why in three hours exactly? Why the precise time?

He turned back to the flight deck and looked at the woman in the right-hand seat. 'The Bihac shelling. That's what this is about, isn't it?' In the front of the cabin area the passengers heard his voice. 'You're a Muslim, aren't you? This hijacking is about Bosnia.' Which is why you're collecting the passports. To see if there are any Serbs on the plane. And if there are then you'll make an example of them. Which is why you're going to open the door.

'I am what you call me.' The passengers towards the front heard Kara's voice and hung on her reply. 'First the world called me a Yugoslav, then a Bosnian. Now it calls me a Muslim. So perhaps I no longer exist in my own right. Perhaps I am only what the world wants me to be.'

The children were talking and laughing in the kitchen, the news bulletin was ending, and the phone was ringing, the boys asking her something from the doorway.

So what are you thinking about, Caz? Who are you thinking about? I'm thinking that when I watch the pictures of Bihac being shelled I'm seeing another place almost a year ago. That when I hear my boys talking, I cannot but remember another little boy. Except he's no longer alive. Because he was killed even though he was in hospital.

She turned and smiled at the boys. 'I'm sorry. What did you say?'

They asked if Jude's children could stay a little longer, if they could play together. Of course, she told them; as long as it's all right with their mum. The phone was still ringing, Jude answering then putting her hand over the mouthpiece and holding it towards her.

Finn . . . Caz mouthed. Jude nodded and gave her the phone, took the children back to the kitchen and closed the door.

'Thanks for calling.' Caz tried to hide the anxiety in her voice.

'You got the note?' Finn was calling from a pay phone in Terminal One departures. People hurrying past him and the occasional airport announcement echoing over the Tannoy.

'Yes. Thanks.' Where are you? What are you doing? If it's about the hijack, tell me the plane isn't coming to England. Even though you've already told me in the two lines of the letter.

'Nothing much doing at this end. I should be home in a couple of days.'

'You need your passport?'

He laughed. 'Shouldn't think so.'

There was little more to say. Because someone from Five might be tapping in, just running the standard security check; or someone might be getting a crossed line.

'I'll phone when I can,' he told her.

'Thanks.'

'Have luck.'

It was a typically Irish thing to say, she thought, a typically Irish way of saying it. 'You too.'

She put the phone down and went into the kitchen. Jude was washing up. 'Finn,' she explained, even though Jude knew it was Finn. 'They're on a standby, presumably the hijack. They're not leaving the country, he thinks they'll be back in a couple of days.'

And the two of us will wait, will pray they don't get involved, and that if they do they come out of it okay.

'Why don't you stay tonight?' Because we're both scared stiff, we both need each other. 'Why don't you nip home and get the kids' things. I'll cook some supper and we'll open a bottle of wine.'

The relief showed in Jude's eyes. 'Why don't I?'

*

Strike reconvened at seven. A short meeting, Langdon suggested, because they all had things to do. Why should the hijackers open the aircraft door – they focused on the one subject. What were the hijackers planning to do? The intelligence side of Strike should examine the options and report to the main committee at nine, the French ambassador suggested. Because it was his country that the hijackers had decided to land in, his government who were screaming blue murder down the secure line for ways out.

'Agreed.' Langdon excused himself and left for his dinner engagement.

There was nothing like leaving such a committee; nothing like arriving slightly late at a function and having to explain you were unable to stay long. Especially when you were Foreign Secretary, there was an international crisis running, and there were TV cameras there to record the relevant parts of the speech your office had already circulated.

A hundred and thirty passengers and crew – it was in the back of his mind. An awful lot of lives, so thank God Lufthansa 3216 was in France. Thank Christ it wasn't a bigger plane, though – the first seed was planted. Thank God it wasn't an Airbus or a 747 . . .

Caz and Jude finished dinner, stacked the plates to one side instead of washing and drying them as they normally would, and opened another bottle of wine. Hell, if the lads were here they'd be on a second bottle now, so why not their wives?

'You think about her very often?' Jude poured them each another glass.

'Since they started shelling Bihac I haven't stopped thinking about her.' It was time to be honest. 'I used to think about her, on and off. Her and the boy. The husband as well, but mainly her and the boy.' And when I look at my boys it crucifies me.

They sat in silence and wondered where the conversation would take them.

'I sometimes feel guilty, you know.' Caz played with the glass. 'I suppose I feel really guilty when I look at Helen Rabin, and Bet and Tracey Bailey.'

A Jewish survivor of the concentration camps outside the UN, and a couple of hairdressers who'd married two brothers from Manchester and who were still outside the Houses of Parliament. Funny how their names slipped off the tongue now.

'Because they're doing something and you're not.' Jude was no longer relaxed. Jude was staring at her as if she was staring at herself in a mirror.

'Something like that.' Caz was still playing with the stem of the glass. 'Finn's the problem, of course. Not directly. But Finn's like Janner. Queen's shilling and Official Secrets Act and all that.'

'Would you go if it wasn't for Finn?'

Which is also to say: would I go if it wasn't for Janner? Because in a way I have an even greater reason to feel guilty than you, because it was my husband she pulled out of the minefield. And now someone like her is being killed again, someone like her son and her husband is dying because they're shelling Bihac and the UN is doing nothing about it. Okay, the UN say they can't, because of the rules under which they're there. But sometimes that's not good enough; sometimes you have to say: enough is enough.

'Yes,' Caz told her. Emphatically, no hesitation. 'If it wasn't for Finn, I'd go.'

'Even though it won't achieve anything.' Jude was still staring at her, still remembering the night Janner was caught in the minefield. 'Even though Helen Rabin and the girls from Manchester admit it won't make the politicians change their minds.'

'Perhaps you might change something. But even if you don't, aren't you under an obligation to try anyway?'

'Even for your own peace of mind?'

'More than that.'

'Kipling, you mean. It counts not if you won or lost, but how you played the game.'

'No,' Caz told her. 'Not Kipling. David Stirling.' Who'd founded SAS when he was still half-paralysed from a parachuting accident in World War Two. 'That's who I really mean.' She'd met him once, when he was old and fragile and had come to Hereford to open the new barracks. Had watched him with awe, the light still blazing in his eyes and the belief still burning through. 'Finn and Janner, that's who I really mean.'

She shrugged. 'I'll check the kids.'

The landing was quiet, the sounds of sleeping from the boys' bedroom. They all wanted to sleep together, they had said, had pulled the mattresses from the other room on to the floor for Jude's children. Caz opened the door, peered in and listened to the breathing. Then she left the room and sat on the top stair. The tears were running down her face, so that she could barely see.

It was Finn who had taken the Queen's shilling, not her, she told herself. Finn who had signed the Official Secrets Act. Not her. Love you, Finn. Know you love me. But I'm not you, Finn. I'm me.

She heard Jude on the stairs, looked up and wiped her face.

'You all right?' Jude sat beside her.

'Yeah. I'm fine. I'm going to London.'

'You mean you're going to join the demonstration.'

'Yes.'

'In that case Mum will look after the kids.'

'Why?'

'Because I'm coming as well.'

Strike convened again at nine. 'Updates,' Langdon began. They ran through the predictable headings, the fact that there was nothing they, the members of Strike, could do at the moment.

'There is one thing we could do,' Langdon suggested, almost casually. He had talked it through with Nicholls, though not Kilpatrick. Had worked out how and when he could introduce the idea. Whether he would gain or lose by introducing it.

'What?' The American ambassador reached in his pocket for his cigar case.

'There's a possible connection between the Paris team and the hijacking.' Langdon slipped into committee mode, as if he was reading the minutes of a previous session at which they had all agreed.

'Yes.' The agreement was unanimous as he understood it would be.

'There may also be a connection between the hijacking and Bosnia.'

'Yes.'

'There's also an immediate problem about Bihac. World opinion appears to be on the side of the Muslims.' The word *appears* was carefully chosen and perfectly pronounced, the meaning clear and understood. A few bloody demonstrators in New York and London and now a couple of other capitals; a few bloody women whose husbands should keep them in order, plus a handful of blokes who were either trouble-makers or queers or both. And the press buying it, because the press always did. 'Public opinion says we should send air strikes in to stop the shelling of Bihac.'

So what's the solution, what can we do now and how will it help us?

Langdon leaned forward slightly, fingers wrapped together then unlocking and pointing to emphasize what he was saying. 'Suppose we threw those things together, came up with something which helped us.'

'How?' The American bit the end off the cigar and lit it.

'Suppose we said that the hijackers are Bosnian Muslims. Not just that. Bosnian Muslim fundamentalists. Militants.' Which is what the bastards are, of course. And everyone is afraid of the fundamentalists, the madmen from the Middle East. 'That way we associate Bosnia and Bihac with the fundamentalists, and with the hijackers. And that might take pressure off us to do something about the shelling.' Because the West is always being accused of not doing enough in Bosnia, and this might give us the justification for that stance. Even though most of the people in Bihac didn't even know what the inside of a mosque looked like.

He sat back and allowed them time to consider.

'We couldn't be seen as the source, of course.' The Russian ambassador, eyes like a fox and summing up what they all thought.

'So we leak it. That way we win if we're right, but we don't lose if we're wrong.'

'There's one problem.' The American drew on the cigar. 'If we leak the fact that the hijackers are Islamic fundamentalists recruited in Bosnia, how might this affect the way they conduct themselves?' He drew on the cigar again. 'Especially towards the passengers.'

'We're off the record?' Langdon asked.

'Yes.' The Frenchman.

The French were past masters of what one might call close intrigue, Langdon thought. Hell, they all were. Them as individuals, or their countries. Or both.

'The fate of the passengers is obviously of prime importance.' Except . . . it was in the intonation.

'Of course.'

'But at least it's not a 747 . . .' With nearly four hundred passengers and crew. If you take my drift. 'Even something like an Airbus . . .' With around two hundred. 'It's still a hundred and thirty lives, of course . . .' But perhaps we're getting off lightly; perhaps the price is hardly a price at all.

Off the record, of course. As we said at the beginning.

The Operations Room had been set up: secure communications, links with the snipers, monitors for the surveillance cameras, plus screens for the live feeds from Orly. Bunks, tables, chairs and cooking facilities in the holding area, one of the rooms with television sets also showing the feeds from Orly. A 737 already sealed off in the hangar fifty metres away. And no one knowing they were there.

It was ten minutes to nine. Finn left the Ops Room and went downstairs to the holding area. So what were the hijackers going to do when they opened the door at fifteen minutes past nine? Fifteen minutes past ten at Orly, because Britain was one hour behind.

Nine-fifteen was bang in the middle of the mid-evening news bulletin, of course, which was why the hijackers had been so specific about the time. So the hijackers were about to wind the game up a notch. Probably open the main door and have one of the hijack team standing in full view of the world's TV cameras, the pictures transmitted live, because everyone would be waiting. The hijacker with a bandana over his face and tooled up like there was no tomorrow. The whole works: sub-machine gun, pistol, probably grenades as well.

It was five minutes to nine. Caz and Jude sat in front of the television and waited. Jude's mother was already driving up from Ross-on-Wye so they could leave early in the morning. A shopping trip, Jude had said. Janner and Finn away, and she and Caz had thought they'd treat themselves to a couple of days.

It was ten o'clock Paris time, the evening dark and the plane silent; Maeschler hunched in the private world into which he sometimes retreated, Kara opposite him examining the passports the hijacker called Alex had collected.

'This is the Nine O'Clock News from the BBC World Service,' they heard the news bulletin. 'Developments on the hijacking of Lufthansa 3216.'

What developments – Maeschler jerked himself awake. Because I'm sitting in the middle, and I haven't seen anything.

'According to well-informed sources, the hijackers are believed to be Bosnian Muslim extremists. In Paris the hijacked plane is still on the ground. In Bosnia, the shelling of the Muslim enclave of Bihac continues. The UN says there will be no air strikes to stop the shelling.'

Because the Muslims in Bihac are Islamic fundamentalists, like the hijackers, Maeschler understood what the bulletin was saying. Therefore madmen and fanatics and killers. And the last thing we want is the spread of Islamic fundamentalism up through Europe from the Balkans.

So what are you going to do now – he glanced at the woman behind him. Because you had something planned, and now they've made you change it.

'In a speech in London this evening, the British Foreign Secretary Richard Langdon said that the United Nations was doing all in its power to alleviate the problems of Bihac.'

'Bosnian Muslim fundamentalists believed responsible for the Lufthansa hijack.' Finn saw the television pictures and heard the headlines of the bulletin. 'Hijacked jet still on the ground in Paris. Bihac still under bombardment, but UN says no air strikes.'

Black propaganda – it stood out a mile, though only if you understood it. A government leak to the press and the press therefore giving the politicos an excuse to play hard with the hijackers. Plus an excuse not to intervene in Bihac. The politicians turning the hijack to their advantage and the media falling for it as they always did.

Perhaps the politicians were right in getting their retaliation in first, though. But the authorities were lumping the hijack and Bosnia and Bihac together. And for Bihac read Maglaj. And in Maglaj the politicians had effectively killed Kev and Geordie John, and almost killed Janner and Max. In Maglaj someone called Kara had saved Janner and Max, and he'd promised her the world. Bloody politicians. Suggesting a connection between Muslim fundamentalists and the poor bastards in Bihac. Because by accepting the connection, the average man or woman in the street would think that the people in Bihac were the same as the madmen from North Africa and the Middle East. And therefore the pressure on the UN to do something about Bihac would be diminished and the lives of the men and the women and the kids in Bihac would be sold.

'So what do we do?' Jude's face was white. Because it was okay to support the protest in London before there were any political strings, but if the Bosnian Muslims have hijacked a plane, then how could she and Caz stand up and support them.

'The woman in Maglaj wasn't an extremist, and it's people like her that they're killing now. Little Jovan wasn't a terrorist, and it's kids like him who are dying now.'

'But what about tomorrow? Because apart from the hijack, it might also influence the demonstration. Might mean people don't support it.'

'All the more reason for us to.'

'Okay. We go.'

They turned back to the television. 'The hijackers have alerted the authorities that at fifteen minutes past nine they will open a door. Our cameras are there, we will go live to see it . . .'

The passports were in a bag on the floor and the passenger list she had compiled from them was on her lap, certain names and seat numbers asterisked. Kara summoned the gunman called Alex, gave him his orders, then left him standing in the door of the flight deck and went down the plane – Zastava in one hand, spare magazines in her pockets – and talked to the other two hijackers.

It was thirteen minutes past the hour.

'Open the door,' Kara told one of the stewardesses. 'Take the child from seat 39B,' she told another.

Thank God not me or my daughter, thought Hilary Langdon Carpenter; thank God we're British.

It was fourteen minutes past nine London time; the door in close-up on the TV monitors.

'The door is opening,' Caz and Jude heard the voice of the television reporter.

'I can see figures inside.' Maeschler listened to the voice of the radio reporter.

'I think it's a stewardess,' the CNN reporter was saying. 'She's holding something. She's holding a child.'

You don't have to kill them, Maeschler pleaded silently. You don't have to kill anyone.

'I can see someone else,' he heard the radio reporter. 'Someone else moving into the doorway. One of the hijackers. He's armed.'

Sub-machine, Finn thought automatically. Looks like a Socimi. Hijacker male, apparently well-dressed, scarf over his face.

'The hijacker is putting the gun over his shoulder.' The BBC TV reporter. 'He's bending down, taking something from his pocket. He's giving the girl a sweet.' The incredulity was in his voice.

There was enough power in the searchlights for the cameras to pick up the details: the stewardess stiff with fear and the girl clinging to her neck but taking the sweet, thanking the man with the gun and putting the sweet in her mouth; the three still framed in the doorway. This is a game, Finn thought, but most things are. This is the hijackers responding to what the authorities said about them.

'Tell them,' Kara told the captain.

'Ground, this is Lufthansa 3216.'

'The captain is speaking to Ground Control.' It was from both the ITN and BBC reporters. 'We can listen in, hear what's being said.'

'Lufthansa 3216, this is Ground.'

'I have a message from the hijackers. They say they are not Islamic fundamentalists, as has been suggested in news reports.' Maeschler glanced at his notepad. 'They say they are ordinary people with a just cause.'

Bastards, thought Langdon.

'The hijackers also say they will announce their demand at ten tomorrow morning, Paris time. That is all.'

Maeschler pulled off the headset, and slumped in the seat. On the TV screens the figures disappeared and the doors closed.

'You asked about food,' Kara said.

'Yes.' Maeschler tried to pull himself upright.

'If you wish, perhaps now is the time to distribute it.' The front passengers could just hear. 'It's all they'll get until the hijack is over.' So whether they eat it now, or save some, or whether the parents give theirs to their children is up to them.

'How long will the hijack last?'

'Two, three days.'

'It's not much for that time.' Why are you looking at me like that? Maeschler wanted to say; why are you making me respond to my own statement. 'But it's more than the people in Bihac will be getting.'

'Your words, not mine,' Kara told him.

'Assessment,' the operations major asked.

They were seated round one of the tables in the holding area.

'No indication yet how many hijackers there are,' Finn summarized what they knew to this point. 'They're professional. They're also ahead of the game, witness the way they came back at what I assume was an official leak. They may or may not be the Paris team. They denied being fundamentalists, but didn't deny being Bosnian or Muslim.'

'Anything else?'

'Not at the moment,' Janner told him.

The plane was quiet; the food had been distributed, most passengers eating a little and saving some. It was mid-evening, the dark settled round the airport and the spotlights still playing on the fuselage. Maeschler sat hunched in his seat, a bottle of mineral water in his hands, staring at the pattern of lights outside.

'What are you thinking?' Kara asked.

He shook his head and she waited.

'You changed your plans, didn't you?' Maeschler spoke at last. 'You weren't going to make a passenger stand at the doorway, even though you'd collected the passports.'

Perhaps – it was in the woman's stare, in her eyes. Who are you, he wondered, what are you? Why are you doing this? Because there's something about you I don't understand.

'What were you really thinking?' she asked.

'I thought you were going to kill someone.'

What do you really mean – her stare said.

'I thought you were going to kill me.'

'And when I didn't?'

'There are two answers. The first, obviously, is that I'm glad you didn't kill anyone.'

'And the other?'

'When I thought you were going to execute someone, but it wasn't me?'

'If that's the other thing. Then yes.'

'I was relieved that it wasn't me.'

'And now you feel ashamed?'

'Yes,' Maeschler admitted.

'Don't be,' Kara told him. 'Every passenger and crew member on this plane feels the same.'

'Lufthansa 3216, this is Ground.'

'Ground, this is Lufthansa 3216.'

'Lufthansa 3216. Do you want anything? Water or drinks or food?'

No – Kara shook her head.

'Ground, this is Lufthansa 3216. She says no.'

The plane had settled; two hijackers on, two resting, in a shift system.

Sammi was asleep against her. Hilary Langdon Carpenter looked up and saw the woman looking at her.

'Interesting middle name,' Kara told her. 'Is it significant?'

'No.' Too fast, they both knew, too clear. If it wasn't significant there should have been a hesitation, even a query.

'The British Foreign Secretary is called Langdon.'

Hilary Langdon Carpenter tried to avoid the eyes.

'I assume the British Foreign Secretary is your father. It wouldn't be your middle name if he was your husband.'

Lie, Hilary Langdon Carpenter thought. Except she

knows. Because your face and your eyes and every part of your body have already betrayed you.

'My father.'

The holding area was quiet, some of the team sleeping, others playing cards, Finn and Janner drinking coffee. The IO – intelligence officer – came in, and poured himself a mug.

'The hijack leader is a woman. It's just come through. The French asked the captain if the hijackers wanted anything: food or drink. Previously the captain had referred to *them* or *they*. This time he referred to *she*.'

'Any doubt about it?'

'No. We were monitoring it ourselves.'

The office was quiet, the light dimmed, the red boxes on the floor and the stack of papers on Langdon's desk. Things to get on with and a country to help run, despite the inconvenience of Lufthansa 3216. European Union session in Brussels in the morning, problems expected, and his aides burning the midnight oil. So the bloody hijackers hadn't bought it when he'd tried to run the Islamic scam past them, but what the hell. It was all a game really. And the bloody plane was on French soil, not British.

'The PM for you,' Nicholls told him.

'Which phone?'

'He's here in person.'

Langdon was halfway across the room when the Prime Minister came in. The PM's looking old, he thought. The PM's aged years since this afternoon. They shook hands, almost formally, and sat down in the armchairs by the fireplace.

'Nightcap?' Langdon suggested.

'Brandy.'

Langdon poured them each a stiff measure. The PM *was*

looking rough. Please not another scandal in the party. Please not something involving the PM himself. But if it *was* something involving the PM, something which might make the PM consider resignation, and the PM was consulting him first . . .

'Your wife has just phoned me.' The Prime Minister balanced the glass on the arm of the chair and looked straight at him.

'Yes?' Slightly puzzled.

'She's just had a telephone call from your son-in-law.'

So . . .

'Lufthansa 3216.'

The slightest panic now, the slightest clenching of the stomach and the tightening of the throat.

'I'm sorry, Richard. Your daughter and granddaughter are on it.'

# 14

The black was around him and the wraiths were closing on him. Langdon was running as fast and as hard as he could, but did not seem to be moving. He and his daughter were walking in the grounds of the house near Salisbury, Sammi running ahead of them. The swan skimming low over the river and Sammi on the bank and reaching for it. Langdon was breaking away from his daughter, running towards Sammi. Sammi was toppling forward, everything in black and white and the river running fast. He was trying to get to her but his legs were moving in slow motion.

In Paris it was an hour to midnight.

Maeschler's children were coming towards him, arms and hands stretched out, and his wife was smiling at him and handing him a beer. Except it was like a film and the projector was running backwards, so that the children's hands were moving away from him, the figures growing distant instead of coming closer, and his wife was walking backwards away from him, the smile and the laugh melting into her face as if it had never existed.

In Paris it was midnight.

The phone in the apartment was ringing and Hilary Langdon Carpenter was picking it up. The voice was telling her the flight had been cancelled and she and Sammi had been transferred to another, and the faces and bodies of the passengers were dancing in front of her like garrotted marionettes. Hilary Langdon Carpenter was at the airport, getting off the plane and telling Sammi they were going to the sun instead, but getting on the Moscow flight anyway.

In Paris it was one in the morning.

The figures on the computer screen in front were exploding, the bodies hurtling red and torn across Rue Léopold towards her. Fiona Marchant was standing in the street, the faces without heads laughing at her and the heads without bodies taunting her, the bodies without limbs teasing her. A hand attached to nothing holding hers and the blood seeping on to her fingers.

In Paris it was two in the morning.

Keefer was laughing at him and the Paris team were looking back at him as they boarded LH 3216. Kilpatrick was trying to get on to the plane, the light coming into the bedroom even though he had pulled the curtains tight. He was on the plane, looking round and relaxing. Telling the captain to have a good flight and seeing the captain's face but the face was Keefer's.

In Paris it was three in the morning.

At last she was doing something about Bosnia – Caz was almost pleased that she was not asleep; at least she had made a decision, gone her own way for the first time. The night was dark around her but the confidence and the excitement and the knowledge that she was right brimmed through her.

In Paris it was four in the morning.

Today she would take it on a stage – Kara sat in the first officer's seat, on the right of the flight deck, and stared at the lights of the airport in the distance. She checked the time. Something else about today – it was in the recesses of her mind. Nothing personal, she told herself, especially that personal, that important. She pushed it away and concentrated on what she would do over the next hours.

In Paris it was five in the morning.

I go in first – Finn lay on the bunk and rehearsed the moves. Steve to my left, Ken and Jim behind. Shouting at the passengers to keep down and hoping they do, hoping the only ones standing are the hijackers. I go right, Steve goes left to check flight deck and toilet. Photos of aircraft crew on wall of briefing room, so you can recognize them, separate them from the hijackers, when you go on.

The dawn was coming up, cold and grey and featureless. The sky was overcast and a light drizzle was falling. It was six in the morning, almost a day into the hijack. This time yesterday she had been consumed by nerves, now she felt cold and detached, as if there was no way off the road in front of her and no place to go to except where the road took her. Kara left the flight deck and checked the cabins.

Everything seemed in order, Maeschler thought, everything seemed under control, but that was how it would be at the moment. The hijackers hadn't issued their demand, therefore hadn't said what they would do if their demands were not met; therefore the authorities had no reason to intervene. He stood and tried to stretch the stiffness from his body, tried not to think of his wife and children.

Hilary Langdon Carpenter watched as the hijack leader passed her. Bastards – the word drummed through her head. Why pick on the weak and the innocent? People like her and Sammi had done nothing wrong, so why had the hijackers descended on them; why the hell had Fate or God or Chance or whatever you called it decreed that she and Sammi be on this bloody plane?

Things like this happened to people who deserved it. It was those who called it upon themselves, either by their colour or their creed or their nationality or their poverty, who were bombed and shelled and flooded by monsoons and baked by droughts. Who had their limbs chopped off and their throats cut by the death squads. Whose parents were butchered in front of them or whose children were taken away from them. But that was their lot in life, not hers. That was what they became accustomed to, therefore they felt less, grieved less. So damn you, God, what an unjust bastard you are, to put Sammi and me on this bloody plane with these bloody killers.

It was seven in the morning.

Langdon had already been at the Foreign and Commonwealth Office forty minutes. He left his office, crossed to Downing Street, and took breakfast with the Prime Minister. Make sure the PM kept him in post, he told himself as they sat down; don't want to lose control of Strike, because if he did he couldn't protect his own. Except he couldn't protect them anyway.

It was seven-thirty.

Finn and Janner and the teams left the holding area, went to the hangar where the 737 was positioned, and ran through the details again. The numbers of passengers and crew. The number of doors – two at the front, two at the rear, plus emergency doors over each wing, all of them able to be opened by handles from the outside. The internal configuration and seat layout – specifically where the panelling separating business from economy was positioned. Weapons the opposition were known to be carrying – from the television pictures. Weapons and ammunition they themselves would use in the confined area of an aircraft interior. Lines of approach, timings, codes and diversions. Not that they would be involved in any solution, not that Lufthansa 3216 would come their way.

The train from Newport to London Paddington was at 7.39. Caz and Jude booked the parking for three days and bought their tickets. Patrol orders next – they laughed at the thought, as if it was a regimental briefing. Caz checked she had time and phoned home, heard Finn's voice on the answerphone saying they couldn't take her call, and asking her to leave a message.

'Hello, love. It's me. I assume you'll work out that I'd leave this message for you.' Because if I'd recorded it at home anyone else phoning in would hear, but by leaving it as a message I know that only you will hear it, because only you and I know the code to activate the answerphone. 'Jude and I are having a break for a couple of days. Doing a bit of shopping. The boys are at Jude's with her mother. Everything's fine. Love you. Back on Sunday.'

Strike was briefed at eight. Lufthansa 3216 was still on the ground in Paris, Bihac was still being shelled and the United Nations was still refusing to launch air strikes to halt the bombardment.

This is not a fair world, Lord, and you are not a fair God . . . Langdon shuffled the papers in front of him and sought to cover his feelings. What right have you to do this to me? What have I done that you have singled me out thus? How have I sinned that you have decreed that the world should be against me?

Langdon was looking rough this morning, the US ambassador thought.

The poor sod must be going through hell, Kilpatrick reflected. Daughter and granddaughter on board the hijacked plane, the Chief had told him: for his ears only, so he knew how to protect the Foreign Secretary and play the best innings for Riverside. Money in the bank so far, so don't draw on it unless you have to.

Langdon tried to ignore the hammer thumping in his head, tried to pull the shreds of his mind together. 'We obviously can't react until we know what their demand is, but do we have any preliminary thoughts on what it might be and how we should prepare for it?' When it was over he'd make sure they paid, make sure they suffered. Make sure they wouldn't come out of it alive. Because they were holding two of his. But he couldn't deal with them, couldn't do what was really necessary, precisely because they *were* holding two of his.

'The demand will probably be specific.' Lessons, the American HoS in London.

'And if so, then that will indicate who they are.' Brizinski, the Russian. 'It might also give us the ammunition we need to back up our overall position on Bosnia.'

'Assuming the demand is connected to Bosnia, which it almost certainly is.' Lessons again. 'It might be even more specific, might even be related to Bihac.'

In which case the hijackers might play into their hands, the French ambassador suggested. Because at the moment world sympathy might lie with the Muslims in Bihac, but if a plane of innocents had been hijacked on their behalf, then that balance might swing the other way. Particularly if 3216 was lost, the Russian reminded them. And which he himself had brought up yesterday – Langdon's face was immobile. But yesterday was a different time and a different place and a different world.

'Specifically?' The American asked.

You've both talked this through, Kilpatrick thought. That's why Leonid Brizinski brought it up and Ed Lessons is giving him the freedom to continue.

'If the hijackers were Bosnian Muslims, and if they were responsible for the deaths of a hundred and thirty people on Lufthansa 3216, then the whole position in the Balkans would change.'

Which, in essence, is what we agreed yesterday – Langdon tried to fight the panic in his body and his brain and his soul.

'Then world support for the Muslims might evaporate; then we could put pressure on the Muslims to agree to a solution acceptable to the Serbs. And the Croats will go along with it because they've already changed sides twice and will go along with anything which delivers them what they want.'

'But what about the people on Lufthansa 3216.' Langdon tried to disguise the U-turn in his position.

The Russian stopped cleaning his glasses. 'As you yourself said, if their suffering was not in vain, if their deaths led to peace, if the loss of their lives meant a stop to the war in the Balkans and the possible spread of that conflict to other parts of the region . . .'

'On the other hand, it could be that the hijackers make their demand more general; that they avoid the problems of being specific.' Kilpatrick tried to cover Langdon.

This isn't you, Lessons thought: you're too sharp to pass on the possibility of anything which might stop something like the Balkans fiasco. So what is it, what are you playing at? Something's up and you haven't told us. Something about your Foreign Secretary, because you're protecting him. 'Only thirty minutes before we know,' he suggested. Therefore no need getting our knickers in a twist over it now, as you British would say.

Thanks Ed, Kilpatrick thought. But now I owe. And we both know it.

It was ten minutes to nine in London, ten minutes to ten in Europe. Television and radio transmitting live pictures and sound from Orly, the media tuned to the VHF frequency Lufthansa 3216 was using and standing by to broadcast the demand.

The BBC and ITV pictures were better this morning, Finn thought; CNN was spending too much time filling in with irrelevant statements from reporters, what the Americans – and increasingly the British – called stand-ups.

When they got to London they'd have to buy fresh batteries for the transistor, Caz decided. The train was twenty-seven minutes from Paddington, a family in the next seat making a noise. She and Jude huddled together and listened to the report from Orly on the BBC.

'In Paris, the hijackers are about to make their demands' – Kara and Maeschler listened on the BBC World Service. The door of the flight deck was open, the passengers behind straining to hear. 'In Bosnia the town of Bihac is still being shelled. The United Nations is seeking a meeting with Bosnian Serb leaders to ask for a cessation to the bombardment, but has refused Muslim requests for an air strike. Radio messages from Bihac suggest that buildings adjacent to the town's hospital have been struck, though these reports have not been confirmed.'

'Tell the negotiator I want to speak to him.' Kara was in the right-hand seat normally occupied by the first officer.

'Ground, this is Lufthansa 3216.'

'Lufthansa 3216, this is Ground.'

'Ground. Is the negotiator there? The leader of the hijackers wishes to speak with him.'

'Lufthansa 3216, this is the negotiator.'

Maeschler nodded. Kara leaned forward and pressed the transmit button on the column.

'This is the leader of the hijack team.' Even though they knew the leader was a woman the voice still shocked. 'My demand is about the war in Bosnia-Herzegovina.'

She was going to screw it, Langdon thought; she was going to give the others their excuse for sacrificing the plane.

'The demand is to the United Nations, and the governments of the East and West, and to the people of the world.'

There was a silence, almost a hesitation. Bastard, thought Hilary Langdon Carpenter; for making my daughter and me suffer. Remember me to our children, Maeschler prayed to his wife; tell them how much I loved them. Don't let us down, Caz asked silently. They heard the voice of the woman again, speaking slowly and clearly and calmly.

'Stop the war in Bosnia-Herzegovina. Save the women and the children.'

What the hell do you mean – Langdon almost lost control. What the hell are you going on about? Specifics, the members of Strike almost screamed. Give us something we can use. Give us ammunition to come back at you, so we can use you against your own.

'You mean help the Muslims,' the negotiator asked. 'You mean stop the shelling of Bihac?'

'I mean what I said. Stop the war. You, the United Nations; you, the governments who have prevaricated for so long. You, the people, who can tell your governments what to do. Save the women and the children. Serb and Croat and Muslim. Because they are all suffering, all dying.'

Goddamn, the American ambassador swore quietly.

Incredible, Caz thought. Okay, so hijackings were wrong. And thank God the hijacking was in Europe. But in a way she and the hijacker were saying the same thing. Except she and Jude and the women in New York and London were merely asking the UN to save Bihac. But the hijacker had taken their argument a stage further and was asking the world to save all the women and all the children.

'Lufthansa 3216, this is Ground. Can you clarify please.'

'Ground, this is Lufthansa 3216.' The captain's voice now, not the hijacker's. 'That is the message, that is the demand.'

'Lufthansa 3216, this is Ground. I understand that, but let me speak to the hijackers.'

No point, Finn knew; she's said all there is to say, and she won't say anything more. He waited another five minutes, re-ran the tapes, then left the room and returned to the hangar and the 737.

*

Strike reconvened at ten London time, after its members had conferred with their respective governments and organizations.

'It's too early in the day for the UN to react.' And thank God for that, Langdon thought. Except it removed one more degree of power from him. But he was powerless anyway. Unless he could strike a private deal with the hijackers, he began to think. So work it out: what he could do and how he could communicate it to them. 'When they open for business I anticipate calls for an extraordinary meeting of the Security Council.'

You're stalling – Lessons studied him. Yesterday it was charge of the Light Brigade, but today you're holding back.

'Intelligence?' The French ambassador turned to the men to his left.

'The demand wasn't specific, which rules out certain reactions.' Lessons took the lead. 'Either the demand is very simplistic, or very sophisticated. We obviously haven't had time to run it yet. Give us this morning.'

'What about deadlines?'

'The hijackers haven't mentioned a deadline yet.' Which might be an oversight or a calculated move to give us time to think it through.

'What about Lufthansa 3216?' The Russian ambassador. By which they all understood he meant the previous suggestion that Strike sacrifice Lufthansa 3216 as part of a wider game plan for Bosnia.

Get out of that one – Lessons looked at Langdon and waited for his response.

'I suggest we wait and see what you boys come up with,' Langdon replied.

Too sharp and too quick, Lessons thought. And Langdon knew it.

*

The tourist buses were circling Parliament Square, and Westminster Bridge seemed full of trippers photographing each other against Big Ben. Caz and Jude left Westminster underground station and turned into the square. The police seemed everywhere, Caz thought; not just in the usual places outside Parliament. She looked towards The Green and saw the women. There were men as well, of course, but the overriding impression was of women. Standing or sitting, peacefully and respectably. Some old – a lot of them older than she had imagined; some young. Between five hundred and six hundred, she thought. She and Jude crossed Whitehall, waited for the traffic lights to change, then crossed to The Green, smiled as someone welcomed them and made a space for them.

Behind them two other women were just arriving. 'Come far?' one of them asked.

'Ross-on-Wye.' It was what they had agreed. 'You?'

'Glasgow.'

There was something special about today. Don't say it, Kara told herself. Don't even think it.

An Air France 747 was coming in to land, its livery glinting against the sky.

'A 737 carries a maximum 16.2 tonnes of fuel and burns fuel at the rate of 2.5 tonnes per hour at cruise,' she checked with Maeschler.

'Yes.' He accepted that she would know and wondered only why she was asking.

'How much did you take off with from Berlin?'

'Thirteen tonnes.' Nine for the flight, plus emergency.

'Which gives a total flying time of just over five hours.'

'Including the emergency fuel.'

Still fuel – her look said. 'And we've used up around two hours so far?'

The thirty minutes into the flight to Moscow, to the

point where the hijack had taken place, plus the thirty back to Berlin, then the hour or so over Europe and into Paris.

'Yes.'

'So we have three hours left.'

'Less. We burn more fuel when we're landing and taking off.'

Kara told the gunman called Alex to cover the flight deck and walked down the aisle, the sub-machine gun in her right hand, safety catch on.

Bastard – Hilary Langdon Carpenter watched, looked at the way the other passengers were looking at the hijacker, saw the way some of them no longer recoiled from her.

Halfway there, Adin; going to make it, Jovan, going to stop you dying. Kara turned back to the flight deck, the gunman in the doorway moving aside for her.

'Tell them we're taking off,' she instructed Maeschler.

He was almost expecting it, Maeschler thought. 'Ground, this is Lufthansa 3216. Permission . . .' He felt the woman's movement, short and hard, hand over the microphone of the headset.

'I didn't say to ask for permission; I said to tell them.'

'Lufthansa 3216 to Ground. We are leaving. Instructions for taxiing, please.' And now they'll delay; now they'll want to know what we're doing, and the negotiator will ask to speak to the hijackers.

'Lufthansa 3216, you are cleared for takeoff. Proceed to runway Two Five by taxiways Four Seven and Four Five.'

'I need the first officer up here,' he told the hijacker.

'Get him,' Kara told Alex.

Ten minutes later the wheels lifted off the runway, the plane climbing hard and the undercarriage thumping as it locked into place.

'They didn't care.' His own words took Maeschler by surprise. 'The only thing they wanted was to get rid of us.'

'Did you expect anything else?' Kara asked him.

*

Lufthansa 3216 leaving Paris, Strike was informed; Lufthansa 3216 airborne. Thank God – it was on the French ambassador's face. Probably not enough fuel to reach Moscow – the Russian ambassador hoped his calculations were correct – and if they'd wanted to go to Moscow they would have done so in the first place. Easily make London though, Langdon thought.

Lufthansa 3216 airborne, Finn and Janner were informed. They left the hangar and went to the Operations Room.

Lufthansa 3216 has left Orly – the news was passed round The Green, those demonstrators with radios telling others; no indication yet which way it was heading.

'Control. This is Lufthansa 3216. Request routeing for Schipol.'

Not within his sphere of influence, Langdon thought. Not within their area of responsibility, Finn and Janner shrugged but stayed in the Ops Room. Lufthansa 3216 has left French air space, the update crept through the demonstrators on The Green; Lufthansa 3216 has requested directions for Amsterdam.

The cloud streamed below them and her ears popped as they descended.

'Lufthansa 3216, cleared flight level nine zero. Contact Amsterdam Approach on one three one decimal one five.'

It was sixty-five minutes since she had told Maeschler to inform Paris they were leaving and fifty-eight since the 737 had lifted off from Orly.

'Check ATIS.' Kara was in the jump seat. ATIS – the Airfield Terminal Information Service, the details of runways and landing conditions recorded on an automatic message and updated every twenty minutes.

Maeschler checked the Schipol landing chart for the ATIS frequency and dialled it up.

'This is Amsterdam Information Bravo.' They heard the recorded message. 'Runway in use: Two Seven. Surface wind two six zero, nine knots. Overcast at four hundred feet. QNH one zero one eight.'

The runway was Two Seven, and the wind on the runway was from a direction of two hundred and sixty degrees and a speed of nine knots. QNH was the local pressure setting in millibars which pilots set on the aircraft's altimeter to tell them their height above the runway. Above a so-called transition altitude a standard altimeter setting of 1013 millibars was used.

'Lufthansa 3216 from Amsterdam Control. Descend to flight level six zero.' Six thousand feet. 'Contact Director on one one eight decimal nine.'

At least they were clear of the French, Langdon thought; because in some situations the French were prone to acting independently. His daughter and granddaughter still on the plane, though – it was lodged immoveably in Langdon's head, controlled every movement he made and every thought he had.

'Lufthansa 3216, this is Amsterdam Director. Turn left on to one eight zero degrees. Descend to five thousand feet.'

Langdon shut part of his brain off from the discussions in the Cobra room and listened to the communications on the VHF feed.

'Landing in five minutes,' Maeschler told Kara. 'Make sure your people are strapped in.'

They were twenty miles out.

'Outer marker in two minutes,' the first officer told Maeschler.

'Landing on automatic,' Maeschler informed them both. Because that way his mind would be free to cope with any problems which might arise. Vector on to the ILS for whichever runway they had allocated him, he knew Amsterdam Director would tell him next. The Instrument Landing System transmitting a radio beam from the end of the runway. Lock on to it, then the aircraft would follow the beam down.

They dropped into the cloud.

First TV pictures from Schipol, Finn noted in the Ops Room. CNN and BBC almost simultaneously, ITV thirty seconds later. Good work by all of them, though once 3216 left Paris the networks probably had all the airports covered. The image was similar in each, though the cameras were in different places: the runway grey and seemingly featureless, and the cloud low. He saw something moving in the ITV picture and focused on it. Something red, something near the runway. A second shape moving.

'Your office for you, urgent.' Kilpatrick handed Langdon the telephone.

'I can see the runway.' Caz turned up the volume on the transistor so the demonstrators around her could hear the reporter. 'The airport is waiting, all other planes have been stopped, and the cloud is hanging over the runway.'

'Problems with Amsterdam . . .' Nicholls began to tell Langdon.

'Lufthansa 3216, this is Amsterdam.' They all heard the voice. A different voice, not Amsterdam Director. 'Lufthansa 3216, Amsterdam is closed. You are denied permission to land.'

'Keep going,' Kara told Maeschler. 'They're bluffing. They don't want us there, but if we don't land here nobody will let us land.'

'Outer marker in one minute,' the first officer's voice was calm.

'Find out what the hell they're playing at,' Langdon told Nicholls. 'Patch me through to their Foreign Ministry now.'

'Amsterdam Director, this is Lufthansa 3216. Am continuing the approach. Request vectors for the ILS.'

'Lufthansa 3216. You are denied, repeat denied, permission to land.'

The cloud was around them. So what do we do – Maeschler glanced at the woman behind him. Go on, she told him. No pulling back.

'Self-position to lock on to ILS,' Maeschler ordered the first officer.

Because at this point they may be trying to stop us, but we don't actually need the vector directions to guide us on to the ILS. Therefore dial up the frequency of the outer marker beacon and let the autopilot swing them towards it, and at the point where the ADI compass needle was at twelve o'clock they'd be heading straight for the runway via the outer marker, and therefore coming down the ILS beam.

'Amsterdam playing silly buggers,' Nicholls informed Langdon. 'No response from the Ministry. Apparently they've placed fire tenders across the runways.'

'Amsterdam Director, this is Lufthansa 3216.' There was no panic in Maeschler's voice. 'I confirm that I am continuing the approach.'

'Locked on to ILS,' the first officer told him. 'Approaching outer marker.'

'Two minutes to landing,' Maeschler told Kara. 'Gear down.'

The first officer pulled the landing-gear lever and the hydraulics lowered the wheels. Kara heard the thud and saw the lights on the control. 'Three greens,' the first officer told Maeschler. The landing gear locked into position. Okay, Maeschler turned to the woman and smiled.

'Lufthansa 3216.' The voice was harsher. 'You have been refused permission to land. Amsterdam is closed.'

'There are fire tenders at the side of the runway,' the

radio reporter was saying. 'I can see them clearly now.'

The tenders weren't at the side of the runway – Finn studied the television pictures. The tenders were actually on the runway. The Dutch really were trying to stop the plane from landing.

The cloud was thick around them. 'Passing outer marker,' the first officer slid into the familiar routine. 'One thousand five hundred feet.' They began the stopwatches.

'Lufthansa 3216. The runways are blocked. Repeat. The runways are blocked. Fire tenders have been placed across all runways.'

'They're bluffing,' Kara told Maeschler. 'Keep going.'

'One minute thirty seconds to landing.'

I don't believe this – part of Langdon's brain was panicking now. I can't believe this. What are the Dutch playing at? Why the hell are they doing this to me?

'Amsterdam Director. This is Lufthansa 3216. Request landing clearance.' The landing chart was in front of Maeschler. 'Repeat. This is Lufthansa 3216. I request clearance to land.'

Because I have four hijackers and a hundred and thirty people on board, and unless you let me land we might all be dead.

'Negative, Lufthansa 3216. Repeat. Negative.'

You're playing it wrong, Finn almost turned away in disgust. This morning all she asked was for the killing in Bosnia to stop and for the women and children to be saved, and now you're trying to kill her. Or at least that's how the world will see it. Because the world is listening to you. And all you're doing is putting the world on her side.

Perhaps the Dutch were going to do what they themselves had discussed, the Russian ambassador suggested to Strike. The aircraft intent on coming in and the Dutch intent on stopping it. And if 3216 crashed, then at least part of their problem would be solved. Okay, so they wouldn't be able to attach the blame a hundred per cent to the hijackers, but they could go a long way.

His kith and kin – Langdon felt the frustration and the desperation again. His flesh and his blood. And the Dutch were going to kill them.

'One minute to touchdown,' the first officer told Maeschler.

The cloud was still thick around them.

'Lufthansa 3216. Clearance denied. The runways are blocked. I repeat. The runways are blocked.'

'They're still bluffing,' Kara told Maeschler. The 737 began to rock slightly. 'What's that?' she asked.

'We're coming down the ILS beam,' Maeschler told her.

'Yes.'

'The beam originates at the far end of the runway.'

'So why are we rocking?'

'Because there's a metal obstruction between us and the beam source.'

Because the bastards really have blocked the bloody runway.

'Thirty seconds from touchdown,' the first officer told him.

One press of the go-around button and the throttles would advance automatically to the go-around power setting, and the autopilot would pitch the aircraft up to a climbing attitude. Decision altitude for non-automatic approaches 200 feet, 50 feet for autolands. After that you were committed. After that you'd hit the runway anyway. And once you were down you were staying down. Okay, you could get off again, and okay, he'd done it. But that was in training, with an empty plane and a runway that stretched for miles. Because once the wheels touched, the weight on them automatically deployed the spoilers. And once you'd closed the throttles on landing, it took nine seconds for them to run up to full power, and nine seconds was a long time at a hundred and sixty miles an hour.

'Three hundred feet,' the first officer told Maeschler. The cloud was thinning; below and in front of them Kara saw the approach lights. They broke through the cloud. Hell, there really was something wrong with the runways. Keep going, she told Maeschler. You can do it.

'Two hundred feet.'

I *can* do it, Maeschler thought. There's just enough space. I think. 'Amsterdam Director. This is Lufthansa 3216. We are visual with the field.'

'The runways are blocked, 3216. I repeat. The runways are blocked.'

'Amsterdam, this is Lufthansa 3216. Continuing. Request clearance.'

'One hundred feet.' The first officer's voice was still calm.

'Lufthansa 3216. Go around.'

The TV monitors were showing the first pictures of the plane now, nothing else in the sky. Every channel going live on it, CNN global. The fire units are still on the runways, the CNN reporter was almost shouting. Lufthansa 3216 is thirty seconds from landing. I can see her coming in. No movement on the runways, the fire units still in position.

'Lufthansa 3216, I say again, go around.'

'Keep going,' Kara told Maeschler. 'Decision altitude,' the first officer reminded him.

'Landing,' Maeschler told him. 'Brakes on max.' The automatic braking system was graded one to three, with maximum above three for emergencies.

Please God save them, Langdon prayed. Please God spare their lives.

'Lufthansa 3216. For God's sake pull out.'

'Fifty feet,' the first officer told Maeschler.

Here goes, Maeschler thought, and disconnected the autopilot. Because autopilots were good and computers ruled the world. But this was *his* life, the moment *he* decided whether he lived or died, and there was no way he would risk a circuit blowing or a glitch in a system sending him to the big airport in the sky, even though they had worked hundreds, probably thousands of times before. The klaxon shrieked and the red light flashed on the control panel. He pressed the button on the stick to cancel it, eased the stick back and flared the 737, changed the rate and angle of descent to land, throttles coming back and the nose lifting up.

'Pull out, Lufthansa 3216. I say again. Pull out.'

You have to let them land, Caz thought. You can't kill them. To her right a nun began to pray, everything and everyone silent, even the noise of the traffic suddenly dead. Just the two voices: the radio reporter at Schipol and the nun praying aloud in Parliament Square. There was a television crew near them. Filming the nun, filming them all as they listened and waited.

They were over the green lights, over the start of the runway.

'The fire tenders are still there,' the reporter was screaming now.

The wheels bounced hard on the tarmac, the runway lights flashing past them. Maeschler hauling back the reverse thrust lever, the plane slowing, and the engines biting and screaming. In front of them the fire tenders were bright red against the grey of the runway.

'Lufthansa 3216 is halfway down the runway,' the reporter was shouting. 'Lufthansa 3216 is almost on top of the fire tenders.'

I'm not going to make it, Maeschler thought. His head and his brain were calm. 'Overriding the brakes,' he told the first officer. He pushed himself back in his seat, using it as leverage, and slammed his feet on the pedals. 'Come on the brakes with me.' Even though he was talking fast, Kara noted, his voice was still controlled.

'On brakes,' the first officer said.

The plane was in close-up on two screens, in wide shot on another. They're not going to make it, Finn thought. They were pushing down as hard as they could, Maeschler's face clenched tight and the first officer shaking with the effort. 'The brakes are screeching and there's smoke flying from the wheels.' The radio reporter tried to calm himself, try to control his voice. Still not going to make it, Maeschler almost swore.

The tenders pulled on to the grass at the side of the tarmac. Two seconds later the 737 passed the point at which they had been positioned.

Not a bad landing, Maeschler told the first officer. Great landing, Kara told them both.

The intelligence section of Strike met at midday, Kilpatrick in the chair this time.

Perhaps he ought to phone Fiona Marchant. It was her problem, her decision, but at least he could say he understood. Except he couldn't, because that would sound so patronizing he'd scare her off for ever. But he'd phone anyway, suggest a drink, ask her if she'd come up with anything. Ease the transition for her if she wanted out and open the door for her if she wanted back in.

'Ed,' he asked. 'You or Leonid want to kick off?' Langdon wasn't going to hold out much longer – the realization took root, and once it had taken root it began to grow. Langdon was so close to the edge he was about to become a liability.

They ran through the familiar positions on the hijack, then opened the discussion up.

How the incident at Schipol would affect the hijackers ... Whether the demand was simple or sophisticated ... Whether the hijack leader meant what she'd said, or whether what she'd said was a code to them for something else . . . How, in phrasing her demand, she had won support . . . What courses of action within the Bosnian conflict were now available, and which closed down.

They poured coffee and expanded the discussion to include the wider Bosnian context.

The nature and effectiveness of embargoes on Serbia, and whether this would persuade Belgrade to continue or to stop supporting the Bosnian-Serb government in Pale . . . Whether a solution could be gained, or speeded up, by assisting the Muslims . . . Whether an alternative might be to let the conflict come to a bloody but quicker conclusion . . . The possibility of one side requesting the UN to withdraw, and the consequences if this happened . . . Whether, in five, perhaps ten years, the region would be redefined along lines the UN hadn't even contemplated . . .

They broke again, called for fresh coffee, and began again.

'Seems to me the Lufthansa affair might give us the window on Bosnia we've been looking for.' Ed Lessons was deliberately relaxed, deliberately emphasizing the *us* to mean the guys in Intelligence rather than the politicians who apparently made the running.

'How so?' Kilpatrick gave his tacit support.

'The diplomats have been pissing in the wind for three years, paying attention to us when it suited them, but ignoring our advice most of the time.'

'So . . .' Kilpatrick asked.

'Radical times.' Lessons sat back and pulled out a cigar, took his time lighting it. 'Radical solutions.'

'How radical?' Brizinski.

Lessons leaned back again and pulled on the Havana. 'Wet jobs,' he said at last. Remove certain individuals and you removed certain problems. Okay, they were all aware of the old adage about better the devil you know. But remove certain problems and you might achieve movement.

Achieve even the first movement and you might be on your way.

'While the politicos have their bollocks in the wringer and need us to get them out,' suggested Kilpatrick.

'Precisely.'

'How wet?'

'Goddamn downpour.'

When Kilpatrick telephoned Marchant fifteen minutes later he was informed that she was not at her desk; when he telephoned a second time she answered on the third ring.

'Anything you come up with, let me have immediately,' he told her.

'Number?' she asked him.

He gave her a direct line into the Cobra room. She waited till he rang off then stared at the screen. So what are you going to do, she asked herself. Because if you're out, there's no coming back. But if she was in, then she knew what to expect.

Today was a special day – the thought crept up on Kara, even though she tried to return it to the dark of her mind. Today . . .

It was time for the next bulletin on the BBC World Service. She sat in the right-hand seat, Maeschler to her left, and listened.

'The hijacked Lufthansa jet with a hundred and thirty passengers and crew on board left Paris this morning and is now on the ground at Amsterdam's Schipol Airport . . . In Bosnia there are unconfirmed reports that buildings near the hospital in Bihac have been hit . . . The UN has again stated that no air strike will be launched . . .'

In the cabin behind, Hilary Langdon Carpenter held her daughter close to her, the girl on her left, closest to the aisle, one arm round her.

'There are additional reports, also unconfirmed, that one shell might have struck the hospital itself.'

For one moment Kara was no longer in the plane. For one moment half her mind was back in Travnik, was back in the room at the side of the house on Tobacco Road. The day Finn had changed everything. The day Finn had told her to start it all . . .

. . . The woman was thin and stooped and badly dressed, and the boy at her side was white with cold and shivering.

'I'm sorry.' The woman's face was tight with hunger and fear. 'My son hasn't eaten for three days . . .'

. . . 'You have children?' she asked Maeschler. In the cabin behind, Hilary Langdon Carpenter allowed sleep to overtake her, allowed her arm to fall from its protective grip round her daughter.

'Two. Boy and girl.'

How can we sit here and have this conversation, he wondered. How can I discuss my family when the Dutch authorities almost killed me? 'Franz and Heidi,' he added without thinking. 'Franz is four, Heidi's two and a half.' . . .

. . . So what do I do, Finn? I'm a slut and a thief and a whore. I'm so far down I can never get back. So far gone over the edge that I can never come back . . .

. . . In the cabin behind, Sammi left the seat and stood in the aisle, walked down the plane a few paces, then stopped, looked round and put her thumb in her mouth. Nobody stopping her or taking her back to her seat.

'You ever married?' Maeschler asked Kara.

'No.'

'Children?' he asked, as if she had answered yes.

'No.' . . .

. . . You have to be ready, Kara. For the next time the

Chetniks start bombing the hospitals and the West stands back and wrings its hands and does fuck all. For the next time the UN lets your people down.

Time to change it all, Kara.

Time to run it by Kara's Rules. Time to play Kara's Game . . .

. . . In the cabin behind, Sammi turned and walked back to her mother's seat. Walked past the seat and stood in the doorway to the flight deck.

'Actually, I had a little boy . . . Actually he would have been five today.'

'What was he called?' Maeschler asked, almost gently.

'Jovan.'

Strike met again at two.

Langdon was looking even rougher, Lessons thought, Langdon was going through hell. So why? Kilpatrick knew, because Kilpatrick had been briefed to cover Langdon's back; but Kilpatrick wasn't going to say a dickie bird, as the English would put it.

'Recommendations,' Langdon brought the meeting to order.

'Preliminary recommendations,' Kilpatrick set out the ground rules.

'Of course.' Langdon nodded his agreement, Of course I can cope; of course I remain in control, both of the situation and of myself. Of course I am not allowing my personal situation to interfere in any manner whatsoever with my diplomatic and political roles and judgements.

'In a way, the response to the hijackers' demand rests with the United Nations, most specifically the Security Council.' Kilpatrick waited for Langdon's response.

'The Security Council has been called for tomorrow.'

'On Day Three of the hijack and forty-eight hours after

the hijackers issued their demand.' Lessons's voice was flat, apparently neutral. The UN operating at top speed. The UN a great place for high-paid jobs and cocktail parties, but the UN in need of a bomb under it.

Langdon shrugged. Not my fault. It was in his stare: our man isn't in the chair at the moment, so our man can't pull the strings. His eyes were sunk and the skin round them was ringed in black.

'The Security Council is going to have to say yes, it will try to stop the war in Bosnia-Herzegovina, because it has to.' It was Kilpatrick again. 'Perhaps the hijackers will buy this, perhaps not.'

Because a group as efficient as this lot are bound to know that whatever the Security Council agrees won't be worth the paper it's written on. Which was what Strike Two had spent the previous hours discussing.

'But consider an alternative scenario. The hijackers assume the Security Council will say it will do all it can, but they know it's a sham. The hijackers also assume that a committee like this will be formed, because it's the obvious thing to happen. And the hijackers know or assume that we'll be wondering what they're really saying. Because in one way their demand is so simplistic it's unreal, but in another way it's so sophisticated that it might actually provide an avenue to some sort of movement.'

'How?' The French ambassador.

'Because it's not just opening the door to radical solutions, it's also giving those with radical solutions leverage within the corridors of power.'

'What radical solutions?' The Russian ambassador.

'The obvious ones,' Kilpatrick told him. 'Identify key people, pressure them through the back door. The sort of deals everybody's been reluctant to think about in the past.'

We're missing something – it was like the first movement of the tide, there then gone, like a string of seaweed or a piece of flotsam on that tide, washed up then washed away.

'Plus?' The American ambassador sat forward.

So what is it that we've missed and why is it important? Why am I suddenly thinking that we've got it all wrong? That whatever Ed and Leonid and I haven't seen would put a whole new interpretation on everything?

'We sort out the leaderships. Remove or have removed those who are the warmongers, and arrange for others to take their place. Internal opposition, like we've all done elsewhere. Wet jobs where necessary. Road accidents, shootings, whatever works. Possibly by our own people, but preferably using locals.'

Which we've all done round the world, in tiny little places that weren't really going to affect anything or anybody. But which we're pussyfooting on in a conflict which might set Europe alight, and which might set Russia and the US on different sides again.

Except there's something which Ed and Leonid and I should have spotted – the tide washed in again, slid out without leaving any indication that it had been there. And Ed and Leonid know this, or at least they are now sensing it.

'Interesting,' Langdon stalled. At least no one had raised the question of sacrificing the passengers on Lufthansa 3216 again.

'And you think this is what the hijackers are assuming we'll think and do?' The American again.

'Who knows?' Kilpatrick was careful. 'Our feeling, however, is that there's a strong possibility.'

The tide washed in again. So what the hell is it and why aren't I seeing it? Your office for you, a clerk informed him on one of the non-priority phones. Not now, he thought; not here and at this moment. Urgent, the clerk told him; priority. Put it through, Kilpatrick decided. He smiled at the meeting and waited.

'Yes.'

'It's Fiona. You said if I spotted something.' Fiona was still in.

'What?'

She told him.

Go to his office, he instructed her. Shut the door and use his phone. He gave her the number of a direct line into the Cobra room. He was in a meeting, he told her, and would be putting her on conference. So the others could hear her and she could hear them. One of his people, he explained to Strike; might have something.

The phone rang. 'You're on conference,' he confirmed to Marchant. So continue. Fiona had made her decision, he thought.

'Start point,' she told them. 'Square One. Are the hijackers the Paris team? We've assumed they are, but there are certain unanswered questions about them. Why weren't they where they were supposed to be; why did Keefer give us the right intelligence for everything else, but the wrong for them?'

We know this – Langdon almost interrupted.

'Apply those questions to the hijackers,' Marchant told them. 'Put them in the context of the hijackers' demand.'

It was beginning to come, Kilpatrick was aware. To his left, Brizinski was beginning to see. Lessons the same to his right. 'Explain,' he said.

'The hijack team . . . We don't know how many there are, but we know the leader is a woman.'

Correct . . .

'We also know from Keefer that the leader of the Paris team was a woman.'

Except that was something we got from Keefer towards the end, Kilpatrick thought, and I suddenly don't remember whether we passed it on or kept it to ourselves. You kept it to yourselves, Lessons and Brizinski looked at him.

Money in the bank for a rainy day. No problem though; we can talk about that later. Because we're suddenly on a roller, so let's not get off.

'Yes.'

'The hijackers are fundamentalists, and one of Keefer's groups.'

Yes . . .

'But suppose they're not.' Marchant's voice echoed slightly on the conference system.

Yes . . . but a slight uncertainty.

'We assumed that we missed the Paris team because Keefer gave us the wrong information.'

Yes . . . strong again.

'But suppose we're wrong. Suppose Keefer himself believed what he was saying was correct. And remember that he was pumped full of sodium pentothal at the time, so it's illogical to think he was telling us anything other than the truth.'

Lessons pushed his chair back and stood up, paced the room his side of the conference table. 'So when we were looking for them, the Paris team wasn't in the wrong place by accident. The Paris team was AWOL.' Absent without leave. 'At that moment in time – from that moment in time – the Paris team was operating independently. Of Keefer, of the fundamentalists. Of everybody who thought they were running them.'

Yes, Kilpatrick thought. But it still didn't feel right. Still didn't feel a hundred and fifty per cent.

'They use what Keefer can offer them.' It was the Russian, Brizinski. 'They use his training, use his facilities. They use him like the fundamentalists thought they were using them.'

'Then they go native. Own target, own rules, own game.' They were throwing it among themselves, ignoring the politicians. 'Which explains the demand, explains why it wasn't what we were expecting.' The electricity buzzed in the air. But how does this help me – the voice was lost and alone in Langdon's head. How does this get my daughter and granddaughter back? The others were still talking, still throwing the ideas between themselves: Lessons, Brizinski and Marchant.

Not Kilpatrick.

'What is it?' Marchant asked him.

'I don't know.' He shrugged, looked at the others on his side of the table. 'We're not there. We're getting there, but one of the basics is still wrong.' And unless the basics were right, they were getting nowhere.

'Go off the wall,' Marchant told him. 'Go lateral on it. Go back to Paris. Go back to before Paris.'

Kilpatrick saw it. 'We're saying that the entire hijack team, four people, were part of this conspiracy. We're saying that the entire team decided on a course of action. Decided to appear to go along with what Keefer told them; used him, then went their own way.' Because that's too much of a coincidence. 'But you don't need the entire team to go renegade. You only need one.'

'You only need the leader.' Marchant.

'And she's the only one of the team in contact with Keefer.' Lessons again, pacing again, pulling out a cigar and chewing on it, offering one to Kilpatrick and Brizinski as if they were the only people round the table.

'So the others think they're following Keefer's orders.' Brizinski, turning and nodding at Lessons.

'What about Keefer's death?' The US ambassador, the first time any of the politicians had contributed.

'Irrelevant,' Marchant told him. 'She probably doesn't even know. But it doesn't matter, because she's a loner. Keefer or no Keefer. Fundamentalists or no fundamentalists. Léopold Group or no Léopold Group. She was always out there by herself.'

'So even now the rest of the team think she and they are still obeying Keefer's orders?'

'Yes.' Kilpatrick.

'So how can we use that against her?' The American ambassador.

'We can't. Unless you want a bunch of fundamentalists in charge of Lufthansa 3216.'

Please no, Langdon prayed.

'Plus you couldn't anyway,' Kilpatrick told them. 'Because to use it against her we'd have to let the members of her team know. And we can't, because she controls the communications, and the first thing she'll have done is collect any personal radios or cell phones the passengers were carrying.'

And all the time the other hijackers thought it was for their security against us, rather than her security against them.

The silence settled. 'How'd she do it?' someone asked. 'Why?' If we're right. But the way it's shaping up we're not too far off the mark.

'God only knows. She does, of course. But I doubt if anyone else ever will.'

The ladders were against the fuselage of the 737 and the door was in front of him, Steve to his left and Jim and Ken tight behind. Stand by, Finn heard the voice of the operations major in his earpiece, stand by. First diversion in – he ran through the routine; second diversion in, then he moves. Door open and on to plane. He goes right, Steve left, Jim and Ken behind them and covering them.

'Green go. Green go.' The first diversion. Not for real, because they couldn't get a chopper in the hangar, but the unit running along the wing anyway. Later today, perhaps tomorrow, they'd go to Brize Norton and run it with the chopper.

'Blue go. Blue go.' The second diversion, Janner's team. Stand by, stand by, Finn was rocking gently. Everything for real suddenly, even in the run-throughs, because if you didn't get it right now, you wouldn't get it right on the night.

'Red go. Red go.' Finn was opening the door, the men behind pushing him up and in.

When they were inside the teams stopped and studied their positions. Then they ended the exercise, left the hangar, returned to the crew room, pulled the gear off, and made themselves coffee. 'The diversions aren't synchronized properly,' Finn told them. 'Run-through again in thirty minutes.' He left the crew room and took his coffee upstairs to the Operations Room.

The pictures from Schipol were the same. 'Anything new?' He sat at one of the desks and looked at the screens.

'Nothing,' the operations major told him.

'Development in Bosnia.' One of the intelligence people came in. 'There are more reports that the hospital in Bihac has been shelled. The suggestion is that a number of people have been killed.'

. . . The hospital was quiet and the corridor was cold and bleak and without hope.

Why the guilt, Finn?

Because I killed Jovan and Adin.

You didn't, Finn. You didn't kill Adin, didn't kill Jovan.

I did. Because the night you saved Janner and Max, the night we cas-evacced them out, I said I couldn't take Jovan on the chopper. But I could have. And if I had then he and Adin would both be alive . . .

The afternoon was warm, the demonstrators sitting on the grass, some of them organizing a list of people offering floor space for those from outside London. Caz and Jude put their names on the list, explained they hadn't eaten that day and would be back in half an hour, then left The Green and walked up Whitehall.

The voice of the news presenter on the radio was fading. Have to get some batteries, Caz told Jude. She held the set close to her ear and heard the words. 'It has now been confirmed that the hospital in Bihac has been shelled and a number of people have been killed.'

They reached Trafalgar Square and turned right along the Strand, bought some new batteries for the transistor from a television and radio shop, and some sandwiches from a take-away. The traffic was heavy and the pavements were packed with shoppers and tourists. They sat on the steps in Trafalgar Square, put in the new batteries, turned on the transistor, and began to eat. Heard the next bulletin. 'It is now feared that most of those killed in the hospital in Bihac earlier today were children.'

'Problems,' the intelligence captain told Finn. The poor people, Caz thought, the poor little mites. What the hell are the hijackers going to do, Langdon wondered.

The light was suddenly losing its sparkle and the voice of the newsreader on the World Service suddenly far away. Kara sat in the first officer's seat, staring at the section of the airport in front of the plane and waiting for the next World Service bulletin.

'It has now been confirmed that at least ten children were killed when shells struck the hospital at Bihac.'

'Contact Ground,' Kara told Maeschler.

'Ground, this is Lufthansa 3216. The hijackers wish to speak to you.'

'Lufthansa 3216, this is Ground.'

'This is the leader of the hijack team. I want a set of steps to the main cabin door in ten minutes. The ground crew to place the steps in position then withdraw. I don't want the ground crew to be your security people. Nobody to go on to the steps.'

Coming to you, the producers told the TV crews at Schipol; something big about to break, they told their programme schedulers. Interrupt normal programmes, the schedulers told the duty presentation officers. News flash and go straight to Schipol. Caz and Jude left Trafalgar Square and ran back to the television shop in the Strand, stood on the pavement and looked at the images from Amsterdam on the sets in the window, listened to the live report on the radio. What's happening, someone was stopping and asking, a crowd already gathering.

She's going to kill me, Hilary Langdon Carpenter thought; she's going to take her revenge on the UN and the Serbs and honest decent politicians like my father by executing me and my daughter.

I was beginning to trust you, Maeschler thought; I was beginning to think that you were different from the other three. I was actually beginning to believe you when you asked the world to save the women and children.

Something going down at Schipol, Finn told the teams in the crew room. Start watching.

What's going to happen – Langdon tried to keep the fear from his face; what are they going to do?

We know what they're going to do – Marchant watched the monitors. We know what logically they should now be doing – she corrected herself. But I didn't think the hijack leader would do it. I actually thought I was somewhere inside her head; not far, but at least somewhere. And now I know I'm wrong.

The steps trundled across the tarmac. Security people operating them, of course – Finn was totally focused on the details, would run and re-run the tapes later, examine the small things nobody else noticed, hope to find a weakness in the hijackers' defence and therefore a way in.

Kara left the flight deck, told the man called Alex to take her place, went back down the cabin, and gave the other woman her orders. Door opening and steps in place – Finn focused on the monitors. Ambulances standing by a hundred metres from the plane, paramedics waiting, and hospitals in the area all put on full alert. No hijackers yet, but there wouldn't be. Don't do it, Caz prayed; please don't do it. The first figure appeared in the doorway. One hijacker, female – Finn noted the details: 7.65mm Scorpio machine pistol in right hand, 5.56mm Zastava submachine gun over shoulder, and scarf over face. No passengers in view.

She's already shot someone, Kilpatrick thought; she's already done the job. But if she has, then why the steps? Christ, she's going to do it in public. So perhaps I'm wrong, perhaps she's an extremist like the rest of them. But even so, why the steps? Why not just do the job in the doorway then drop the body on to the runway? Not my daughter and my granddaughter, Langdon prayed; please God not them.

'Tell the women and children to stand in the aisle,' Kara told Maeschler.

Not me, Hilary Langdon Carpenter prayed. Why me, why Sammi? Can't we do a deal, can't you let me live so I can use my influence with my father?

The first woman rose and stood in the aisle, child clutched to her. A second.

'Get me Ground,' Kara told Maeschler again.

The women and children were huddled together. I saw a photograph like this once, Maeschler thought: it was of the women and the children going into Auschwitz. I also saw another photograph like this once: the handful of survivors after their village had been ethnically cleansed in Bosnia.

'Ground, this is Lufthansa 3216. The hijack leader for you.'

Langdon was going to throw up, Kilpatrick suddenly thought; Langdon was barely able to keep it together.

'This is the leader of the hijack team. This morning I asked the United Nations, and the governments of the East and the West, and the people of the world, to stop the war in Bosnia-Herzegovina, to save the women and children. This afternoon the hospital in Bihac was shelled and ten children died.'

She switched off the mike, left the flight deck and returned to the cabin. The door was open to her right, and the women were huddled in front of her, the children clutched to them, and the other hijackers guarding them.

What's happening, Finn thought; what's she going to do? Don't screw it, even though you are the opposition. Because you've done a good job so far: getting the weapons on board, calling the authorities' bluff in Amsterdam. Even the demand; perhaps especially the demand. So don't blow it now.

The hijacker at the door moved aside and another figure appeared, something held to her. Walked, almost stumbled to the top of the steps. Dazed and bewildered and too stunned to react. Christ, Finn thought; it's a woman and a kid. Don't shoot them, Caz prayed; please don't kill them. The hijacker was still in the doorway, the woman and child beside her, the woman petrified with fear and unable to move, and the child clutched tight to her. What's happening, Marchant wondered; what has the hijack leader told the woman to do? The woman edged forward, out of the door and on to the top of the steps, a gentle breeze blowing and her hair ruffling in the wind.

'They're releasing the women and the children . . .' Caz heard the voice of the radio reporter and watched the image on the screens in the window. 'The hijacker is letting the women and children go.'

The woman came down the steps, walking unsteadily and holding the rail. Reached the bottom and stood still. Glancing forward to the ambulances, then back at the hijacker in the doorway. For one moment she did not move, as if she did not know what to do or could not understand the instructions she had been given. For one moment it seemed as though she was going to go back up the steps. Then the hijacker in the doorway waved the Scorpio and the woman nodded, as if she had at last understood, as if she at last believed. The child was huddled into her. The woman looked at the hijacker again, nodded again, then she turned, left the steps, and began to walk across the runway. A second woman appeared in the doorway of Lufthansa 3216 and stood by the hijacker, a child clutched to her. The hijacker in the doorway nodded and the woman began to walk down the steps.

Kilpatrick's attention flicked from Langdon's face to the TV monitors then back again.

The first woman was fifty metres from the plane and the second was at the bottom of the steps and beginning to walk, another woman at the top. One of the two children she had with her was a babe in her arms, and the other was at her side and clinging to her skirt, the mother's arm tight around the child's shoulders. The voice of the radio reporter was almost breaking. 'The women and children are crossing the runway. The ambulances are waiting for them. The first woman is at an ambulance. They're wrapping a blanket round her, putting a blanket round her child.' The next woman appeared in the doorway, a girl in her arms. Kilpatrick glanced from the monitors towards Langdon and saw the moment his eyes glazed. Saw the moment Langdon recognized the woman and the girl in her arms.

That was why Langdon was off course this morning, Lessons suddenly understood; because he had family on the plane. So how does Langdon behave now? How would the rest of them counter the fact that Langdon would go soft on the hijackers because they'd given him back two people whom Lessons assumed were Langdon's daughter and granddaughter?

The last figures left the steps and began the walk, the woman white-faced and tight with fear, and the girl at her side clutching her hand. Behind them the steps were empty, a solitary hijacker in the doorway. No more women on the plane, they all knew, no more children. Full debriefings tonight, Finn assumed, in-depth questioning of the women and possibly the older children, get the first details of the hijackers from them. How many there were and how they were armed; where they stood and how and when they slept.

The cameras were tight on the last couple. Without warning the girl stopped, turned back to the plane, and waved.

Strike reconvened thirty minutes later. So how will Langdon behave now, Lessons wondered again. How would the rest of them counter the fact that Langdon had gone soft.

Langdon shuffled the papers in front of him and called the meeting to order. 'Radical solutions . . .' he addressed Kilpatrick, Lessons and Brizinski. Including the wet jobs, they knew he meant. 'Sounds good.' He turned his attention to the American and Russian ambassadors. 'The idea of using Lufthansa 3216 . . .' The notion of sacrificing the plane and its passengers, they understood. 'I think we should pursue it.'

Only a hundred and thirty passengers – Lessons studied Langdon's face – so it was cheap at the price. A hundred and thirty minus the twelve women and children, so it was even cheaper.

It was six-thirty, the women leaving The Green and Caz and Jude assigned floor space at an address in Stoke Newington with a woman who had also joined the demonstration that morning. In a way the woman was like them, Caz thought: not the traditional protester, not long hair and burning eyes. The prejudices we don't even realize we have.

They took the tube to Finsbury Park and waited for the 106 bus. There was a telephone kiosk on the other side of the road. They'd just phone home, Caz and Jude told the woman, would speak to the children. They could phone from the house, the woman said. They didn't want to impose, they told her. Because if they phoned from the house it would leave a record of Jude's number, and the number wasn't Ross-on-Wye, it was Hereford.

'Everything okay?' Caz asked the boys. The images were still stark in her mind. The radio reports of the landing at Schipol that morning, and the release of the women and children that afternoon.

'Saw you on the telly,' they told her.

'How?'

'In London, you were next to a nun who was saying a prayer.'

And if they'd seen her and recognized her, then others would. And if Finn phoned, they'd tell him as well. So what's the problem, she asked herself; if you're going to stand up and be counted, then you're going to stand up and be counted.

'How did I look?' she laughed at them.

'You looked good.'

*

It was seven o'clock. Finn left the holding area, walked through the airport to Terminal One, and telephoned home from the pay phones in the arrivals lounge. Sorry we can't take your call – he heard his own voice on the answerphone; if you want to leave a message, do so after the tone. Caz and the boys doing something, he assumed. He left a message that he'd phone back later and went to one of the cafeterias.

So why, Finn? Why tell the hijacker she's doing well, even though she's the opposition? Why tell her that she'd done well getting the weapons on board 3216; that she'd done a good job calling everyone's bluff in Amsterdam? Why tell her not to screw it when the news came through that the kids had been killed in Bihac? Why keep analysing what she's doing and telling her not to blow it?

He finished the coffee and phoned home again, phoned again, again at nine. Caz and the boys wouldn't be out this late, even if it was Friday. Unless there was a children's party, but he would have known. And if something had come up unexpectedly then Caz would have left a message for him. He rang off, dialled the number again, then the code to activate the messages on the answering machine.

'Hello, love. It's me.' He heard Caz's voice. 'I assume you'll work out that I'd leave this message for you. Jude and I are having a break for a couple of days. Doing a bit of shopping. The boys are at Jude's with her mum. Everything's fine. Love you. Back on Sunday.'

He put the phone down and called Janner's number. 'It's Finn. Thanks for looking after the boys.' Hope they're behaving themselves; yes, please, he'd like to speak to them. Having a good time, he asked them; getting the homework done? Yes, he'd be home soon. No, he hadn't seen Mum on the telly.

What was she doing on the telly, he asked. What programme? Yes, he'd look at nine o'clock; see if he could see her. In the background, of course; behind the nun who was saying a prayer that the plane would land safely, but he wouldn't miss her because she was wearing the coat she'd bought at Christmas.

The night above was dark, but the area in front and around the plane was bathed in floodlights. Tomorrow she would do it, tomorrow she would take it to the last stage. What was it that Finn had told her?

It is not the critic who counts, not the one who points out how the strong man stumbled or how the doer of deeds might have done them better. The credit belongs to the man who is actually in the arena; who, if he wins, knows the triumph of high achievement and who, if he fails, at least fails while daring greatly.

Therefore tomorrow she would go into the arena. Tomorrow she would dare greatly.

The Nine O'Clock News was just beginning. 'A child's farewell to the hijacker who gave her her life,' the newscaster was saying, the girl turning back to the plane and waving, and the frame frozen on the screen.

The item ended and the rest of the teams left the crew rooms and went to the makeshift canteen. With you in five minutes, Finn told Janner. Waited. Watched the other item from Bosnia: the shelling of the hospital and the deaths of the children. Saw the demonstration in Parliament Square, the nun praying as Lufthansa 3216 came into Schipol and the faces behind. Then he left the room and went to the canteen.

They were in the kitchen of the house in Stoke Newington: Caz, Jude, Linn and Mike sharing a bottle of wine, the children asleep upstairs. The kitchen was a semi-basement, modern and full of light in the daytime, the doors at the rear leading on to the garden, a sofa bed in the corner.

'Your husbands don't know you were at the demo, do they?' Linn asked. 'And now they've seen you on the TV.'

Typical solicitor – Linn's husband tried to laugh it off.

'No, our husbands didn't know we were coming. And yes, mine has now seen me on the television.' And he wouldn't have missed me, because the boys saw me, and he would have phoned the boys, and they would have told him.

'Problems?' Linn's husband asked.

So how will you react, Finn? What will you *really* think?

'No, no problems.'

Janner was sitting by himself. Finn fetched a tea and joined him. Someone began to sit down with them but Janner nodded him away.

'What's up, Finn?'

'How'd you mean, what's up?'

'I mean, what are you thinking?'

'Nothing.' Finn corrected himself. 'Not a lot.'

'What exactly?'

'Actually,' Finn said at last, 'I was thinking about Maglaj and Tesanj. I was thinking about Kara.'

'Perhaps you're not the only one,' Janner told him. Bihac being shelled, the hospital being hit and the children being killed. So what is it, Janner? You asked Finn what he was thinking, so what about you? You're thinking about Istanbul, that's what you're thinking. You're thinking about something Keefer said towards the end, when he was still pumped full of sodium pentothal but after the interrogators had got the key details from him. Something he said about the woman who was leading the Paris team.

'You really want to know what I'm thinking?' Finn asked.

'Yes, Finn, I really want to know.'

Okay Janner, you and me, and nobody else. Because you and I were there.

'The night we got Jovan to hospital in Tesanj, the others found somewhere to bed down, and Kara and I waited in the corridor outside the ward Jovan was in. We talked about a lot of things.' What sort of things . . . Unspoken, just a turn of the head. 'I told her that her people would never win, that unless they found oil in Sarajevo the West would never really help them.'

'What else did you tell her?'

'Nothing else.'

Which is not true. Because I also said that next time the United Nations let her people down, and if she wanted to do something about it, she should have something the West wanted. But I won't tell you that because it doesn't matter any more, because she's dead. And it isn't relevant anyway.

# 15

Caz and the others left Stoke Newington at eight, Linn's husband running them to Parliament Square. The morning was bright, though a little cold. There wouldn't be too many on The Green yet, partly because it was a Saturday and partly because it was still early. Which was why she and Jude had decided to stay overnight, why they had decided to come this morning. Because when there were few of you everyone mattered.

Trafalgar Square was quiet and Whitehall was empty except for the police vans. They stopped, left the car, and walked into Parliament Square. Yesterday there had been seven hundred of them, today there were nearer a thousand.

The teams had been practising since seven: first diversion, second, first assault team goes in, second, third. At fifteen minutes to nine they broke, at ten to nine Finn collected a coffee and sat next to the intelligence major.

'The passenger debriefs.'

'Yes.'

They were sitting on a desk in a corner, the room silent, almost eerie. Just like one of the RSGs, Finn thought. He'd been down one once, part of an exercise. An attack on a Regional Seat of Government, one of the underground bunkers for use in the event of nuclear war: four levels in a hollowed-out hill in Essex. Everything ready for World War Three – desks and chairs and bunks, even the blankets folded on them and the notepads and pencils perfectly in position. Everything ready, just like the Ops Room now. Then the Cold War had ended, the threat of the ultimate mushroom had lifted, and the RSG had been decommissioned. Just as the Ops Room wouldn't be used, because 3216 wasn't their problem, and wouldn't be.

'One of the debriefs suggested an Englishwoman was among those released,' Finn asked. The details had come in overnight and the teams had been briefed on them immediately.

'Yes.'

'So why isn't there a debrief from her, why aren't we talking to her?'

'There's a problem.'

'What exactly?'

'One of the women passengers released *was* English. She had her daughter with her, the girl was also released. A friend of the woman identified her as she was leaving the plane and phoned the *Telegraph*. The *Telegraph* checked with Downing Street, and the MoD slapped on a D-notice.'

'Why, who was she?'

'The Foreign Secretary's daughter.'

Hell, Finn thought. 'And the hijacker knew who she was?' he asked.

'Apparently so.'

'So Langdon owes?'

'That's why they put the D-notice on. Five have already talked to the friend and suggested she forget it.'

It was one minute to nine, London time. One minute to ten in Amsterdam.

'Tell Ground I wish to speak to them,' Kara told Maeschler.

'Ground, this is Lufthansa 3216. The hijackers wish to speak to you.'

'3216, this is Ground. We are waiting.'

Communication from Lufthansa 3216, the intelligence major and Finn were informed.

'This is the leader of the hijack team . . .' The voice was calm and controlled. 'Yesterday morning I issued my demand. So far I have received no response. Yesterday morning I also said I would issue a deadline.' She paused. 'The deadline expires in twelve hours. I repeat. The deadline expires in precisely twelve hours.'

Could you clarify . . . the negotiator asked. You mean ten o'clock tonight . . . What if we are unable to meet it . . .

There was no response.

There was something he had to do in central London, Finn told the operations commander. Something official, he implied. He and the team would be back within ninety minutes and would remain in radio contact throughout.

Strike convened at nine-thirty, London time.

'The radical solutions you raised yesterday . . .' Langdon addressed the intelligence members of the committee. The wet jobs. 'Have you developed this further?' Because the deadline doesn't affect us.

They went into detail.

'The UN Security Council have agreed to an extraordinary session in New York this afternoon.' Langdon looked round the table. 'I think we can pull it off.'

'Pull what off?' Brizinski asked.

'Get our various governments to agree to what you're proposing, get the Security Council to agree to some form of agreement with the hijackers as cover.'

'You said the Security Council's meeting this afternoon?' Ed Lessons, the Langley man in London.

'Yes.'

'What time?'

'Two o'clock.' Langdon played with the wad of papers in front of him.

'Two o'clock their time, New York time?' Lessons was persistent.

'As I understand.'

'Seven o'clock London time,' Lessons pointed out. Eight o'clock European. Two hours to the deadline. 'That's cutting it close.' Because in two hours the Security Council wouldn't have stopped shaking hands, let alone made a decision.

'That's what the Security Council has decided,' Langdon told them curtly, and moved the meeting on. 'The Russian proposition to use the loss of Lufthansa 3216 as a tactic to reduce public sympathy with the Bosnian Muslims . . .'

Interesting how it had gone from a discussion point, one of several, to a proposal, and a Russian proposal at that, Brizinski thought. 'You can't,' he told Langdon. 'The conditions no longer apply.'

'What conditions?'

'When the possibility was raised, the world thought the hijackers were Bosnian Muslim extremists. Since then the hijackers have not only categorically denied it, they have taken firm steps to prove otherwise.'

'But they'd do that anyway,' Langdon came back at him. 'Come on, Leonid, we all play the game, we all know the score.'

'Since then they've also issued a demand which further removes them from the tag of being extremists. Plus they've reacted to the deaths of the children in Bihac by releasing the mothers and children from the plane.'

'It's still an option.

'Losing your nerve, Leonid?' They all knew he was addressing the ambassadors. Losing your bottle? Afraid to put your money where your mouth is? Afraid to go for the one chance we've all been waiting for to get us out of the

Bosnia mess? Because I'm sure your government won't see things your way if you lose them that chance.

Bastard – Kilpatrick looked at Langdon. Okay, sometimes you made dirty decisions, sacrificed people in a dirty way. But that was what you were paid for, because that was who you were and where you came from. And it was always business, never personal. But that isn't the point, is it? Because what really motivates you now is that for thirty-six hours the woman on the plane made you like everybody else: small and scared and screwed by the world. Totally hopeless and no one lifting a finger to help you. Just like most of the poor little sods out there. That's what really pisses you off, that's really why you're gunning for her. Bastard, he thought again. But a bastard who controlled his future, and that of his organization.

The traffic into London was building up. Finn and the team cleared Chiswick and Hammersmith, then cut right to the Thames. Something he should have picked up on – the thought edged into frame; something they all should have noted. The river glistened to their right, the glass frontage of the place called Riverside on the far bank, the austere masonry of the MI5 building on their left, and the spires and towers of the Houses of Parliament rising into the sky in front of them. The tourist coaches were dropping their passengers and the pavements were already crowded. They entered Parliament Square and saw the demonstration on The Green. A thousand people, more than he had expected, and more arriving. Most of the placards they carried the same. SAVE BIHAC. SAVE BOSNIA.

They waited till the lights turned green then pulled forward, cars and taxis crammed around them. Caz is somewhere in there, he thought; wonder how long it would take him to find her. They circled The Green, Finn in the front passenger seat and looking for Caz, then turned left into

Whitehall. Steve waited till the road was clear, swung the Range Rover in a U-turn, and stopped on the left, facing Parliament Square. The only other vehicles parked were two police cars on the opposite side of the road, and three police vans on their side.

'Ten minutes,' Finn told them. None of the others knew why they were there. 'Bleeper or mobile if you need me.' He got out, shut the door, and walked towards Parliament Square.

Behind him a police squad car pulled alongside the Range Rover and waved for them to move. Steve pulled out the ID and held it open. Police or Customs, Military Police or Bomb Disposal – it could have been anything, whatever cover they were using that day. Perhaps even a correct ID. The patrol car pulled away.

Finn waited for a break in the traffic and ran across to The Green. Couple of Special Branch guys snooping around – see them a mile off when you knew what you were looking for. Probably some spotters from Five as well. Checking on people like his wife. So where was she? Something he should have picked up on – it crept up on him again. Something they all should have seen. He wandered through the crowd, smiled as someone smiled at him, thought he saw Caz and moved in her direction then realized he was wrong. Carried on through the crowd. Some people standing, a lot sitting now, especially those with children. The atmosphere was strange, a mix between a party and a protest, even the police chatting with the demonstrators.

Something wrong, something he'd missed. Where are you, Caz? Something he'd not picked up on, and whatever it was, it was important. Perhaps Caz wasn't here, he began to think; perhaps she'd seen herself on the TV and gone home. Not Caz, once Caz decided something she'd stick with it. Something that was central to what the hijacker was doing that day, something about the deadline.

Oh hell . . . He left The Green, dodged through the traffic without waiting for it to stop, and ran back to the Range Rover. Try this, he suggested to the team. Priority briefing, he requested the operation commander on the encryptor. Move it, he told Steve.

Caz saw the Range Rover leaving Whitehall and pulling into Parliament Square. Four men in it – she watched as it circled The Green; turned to follow it round, people and faces and bodies between her and it, so that sometimes she lost sight of it. Everything suddenly silent, everything seemingly in slow motion, even though the Range Rover was accelerating fast. Saw it for the last time as it left Parliament Square and turned left along Millbank, along the Thames.

'Who was that?' Linn asked.

'My husband.'

The Heathrow briefing was in the Operations Room.

'We know that the hijack of Lufthansa 3216 is entering another phase. It is my assessment that we are about to become involved.'

The session was Chinese Parliament style, everybody contributing as and when they saw fit, Finn leading and the section commanders and intelligence people round the tables.

'At ten this morning, the hijacker announced a deadline. When she did so, she said the deadline was in twelve hours.'

'Yes.'

'Why did she put it that way? Why didn't she say the deadline would expire at ten tonight?'

'Why?'

'Because she's leaving Schipol. And wherever she is in twelve hours it might not be ten o'clock. Therefore she's going to change time zones.'

Where? the operation major asked.

'She's already established the Bosnia connection, so wherever she goes must be a big player in the Bosnia game. France and Germany are out, because she's already been there, already involved them directly. And in any case, they're both in the same time zone as Amsterdam.' Which leaves three.

'Moscow's too far. She has less than ninety minutes' flying time left, unless she refuels. Which she won't, because that would mean asking for something, which she hasn't done yet, because it would have weakened her position, therefore she won't do it now.

'Washington's clearly out of the game.' Which only leaves one.

The overalls Finn and the team wore were standard airport issue, and the Transit van they were driving was a routine maintenance vehicle. They stood facing west, the northern perimeter fence fifty metres to their right. The public road was immediately outside it, the car parks, hotel and occasional office building facing on to it. The main body of the airport – the terminal buildings and the ground control tower – was to their left. Runway Two Seven Left was on the far side of the buildings, and Runway Two Seven Right stretched in front of them.

This is where she'll park up, Finn thought; this is where it will end. Because the one thing she wants is television pictures, and this is the only place she can guarantee that. Because everywhere else either hasn't got good line of vision, or we can seal it off. And here we can't. Not one hundred per cent. Sure we can do certain things, but we can't do everything. And once we try, the press and the television people will find a way around it. And she'll know that.

So this is the place she'll park. Facing down the runway,

in case she decides to take off. Because if she does decide to leave, even though she won't have any fuel, she won't want the hassle of taxiing anyway. And if she decides that, it might also be in a hurry.

Therefore the plane will be parallel to the perimeter fence, facing down runway Two Seven Right. Therefore the side that is visible from the vantage points outside our control is the right side of the plane. Therefore we go in the left side. The obvious line of approach for us is directly from the rear, because then the hijackers can't see us. But everyone else can, even at night. One way in, though; provided the storm drains were in the right place and big enough.

A 747 trundled past and in front of them, and prepared for takeoff, a line of planes queuing behind it on the taxiways. Runway Two Seven Left – five hundred metres away – being used for landings at the moment, and Two Seven Right for takeoffs, the runways switching at three in the afternoon to spread the noise. Therefore after three, aircraft would be landing on Two Seven Right rather than taking off.

They returned to the Transit, sat in the back, and spread the ground plans of the airport on the floor.

Twenty minutes later Finn briefed the team commanders.

At eleven-thirty the unit which, until that point, had constituted the first diversion left Heathrow for RAF Brize Norton in the helicopter they would use that night, a 737 already on standby for the helicopter crew and assault team to practise on.

At eleven-forty the arrangements were made for the diversion which would precede them.

At eleven-fifty the storm drains which ran beneath the runways and the surrounding grass were inspected to confirm they were wide enough for the assault teams to crawl through, and the cover of the drain closest to the eastern end of runway Two Seven Right was tested to ensure it could be removed easily.

At twelve-thirty white tape was laid inside the drain so that Finn and Janner wouldn't take a wrong turning that evening, and the ladders and equipment their teams would use were laid on the grass beside the drain cover from which they would emerge, and camouflaged down. No radio contact in the drain, but they hadn't expected there to be, so they would have to be in position, heads poking out the top of the drain but camouflaged, for the moment the assault was being counted down. Forty metres from the drain to where he assumed the hijacker would park 3216 was still a long way, though. Especially with the world's press sitting and looking. Please God may the new diversion work, therefore. Assuming she came to Heathrow.

* * *

The sun was orange and the sky was tinged with red. A shepherd's sky, they had called it in Maglaj in the old days. Blood sky, they had called it after the shelling and sniping had started and the cemetery was full and you were afraid to cross the bridge from the old to the new town. But that was at dusk, when the light was fading and the night was gathering. And now it was early afternoon.

The sky was deeper, redder. Perhaps those who clung to the old ways and the old traditions would have called it a sign, Kara thought; perhaps the women would have dipped their heads and hurried the children inside. Only now, because of the shelling and the sniping, they were inside anyway. Except when they went to the food kitchen, but that was a risk in itself.

It was five minutes to two, Amsterdam time . . .

. . . She was back in the cold of the marketplace in

Travnik, her pram piled with the overnight load from Popovekuce and someone arguing with the black marketeer next to her over the price of a kilo of flour . . .

'Tell Ground we're leaving,' she instructed Maeschler . . .

. . . Fifteen marks a kilo, the man next to her was saying. I only have ten – the other man was hungry, desperate. Take it or leave it, the black marketeer was telling him. But my children haven't eaten for days, the other man was coming back at him . . .

'Tower, this is Lufthansa 3216. Taxiing instructions, please.'

'Lufthansa 3216. Proceed to runway Two Five by taxiways Romeo and Bravo.' . . .

. . . The man was reaching into his coat and pulling out a gun, shooting the black marketeer next to her in the face. What good is fifteen marks to you now, he was saying. Was turning away, no one stopping him, disappearing into the crowd . . .

'Thank you, Ground.'

Lufthansa 3216 taking off, Strike was informed. Lufthansa 3216 leaving Amsterdam, the news swept through the demonstrators in Parliament Square.

'Tower, this is Lufthansa 3216. Ready for takeoff.'

'3216, cleared for takeoff. Surface wind two two five degrees, eight knots.'

'Thank you, Tower.'

'Lufthansa 3216 . . .'

'Go ahead, Tower.' Everyone was listening, Kilpatrick was aware; everyone was tuned in to airband or the radio or TV stations transmitting the VHF messages. 'Good luck.'

So what will the captain say, Kilpatrick wondered. How will the captain react? The captain was taking too long to answer, he realized; it wasn't going to be the captain who answered.

'Thank you, Amsterdam . . .' they all heard her voice.

Lufthansa 3216 airborne, the operations commander told Finn.

'Which way are they heading?'

'Nobody's sure yet.' . . .

. . . The blood trickled down the black marketeer's cheek, and the snow on which he lay was frozen hard. One day this would be her, she had thought; one day it would be *her* lying there, a bullet in *her* head and *her* blood running down *her* face . . .

'Ask Control for a routeing for London Heathrow,' she told Maeschler.

Now that the 737 was airborne there were no live pictures on the TV monitors. 'Control.' They recognized the pilot's voice. 'This is Lufthansa 3216. Routeing for London Heathrow, please.'

The whisper spread round the women on The Green – she's asked directions for Heathrow, she's bringing Lufthansa 3216 into London. You were right – the operations commander glanced at Finn. Bastard – Langdon turned to the other members of Strike.

'Lufthansa 3216. Route direct to Refso.' The Dutch controller's English was clipped and precise. 'Then Lambourne Three Alpha arrival.' Refso was the reporting point between Dutch and British air space; Lambourne, in Essex, was a navigation beacon on the route into London from Amsterdam; and Lambourne Three Alpha was the standard routeing from the Lambourne beacon into Heathrow. 'Contact London on one three six decimal five five.'

Maeschler leaned to his right and began to adjust the frequency.

'Check ATIS first,' Kara told him. Because that will tell us the conditions at Heathrow, including which runway we're landing on. Which in turn will tell us our route in. And the authorities may not like the way we're coming in and might try to change it. And if they try, I want to know.

'This is Heathrow Information Charlie. Runway in use Two Seven Left. Surface wind two six zero, eighteen knots. Overcast at four thousand feet. QNH is one zero one eight.'

So now you know – Maeschler looked back at the woman in the jump seat. And everyone else will also know. Because anyone with the right set can pick up our messages on VHF, and those who can't can listen to them being played live on radio and television. Which you understood already, of course. Because you planned it as you planned everything.

It was one-thirty London time, Lufthansa 3216 over the North Sea. The nerves had gone from her stomach now, and her mind was calm. The next time the United Nations let your people down . . . she remembered the moment he had told her. The corridor in the hospital, the night dark and freezing, the children crying and the Serb shells thundering outside. The next time the United Nations stands by and does nothing . . .

Keep smiling on me, she prayed to Adin and Jovan. Wish me luck, Finn. 'Contact London,' she instructed Maeschler.

'London. This is Lufthansa 3216. Approaching Refso.'

Lufthansa 3216 approaching British air space, the Strike committee was informed. About to leave Dutch air space. Now in British air space. Lufthansa 3216 now his problem, Finn thought.

Langdon lifted the red phone. 'Convene Cobra,' he ordered an aide. Cobra would be in charge once Lufthansa 3216 landed in Britain, though Strike would continue to operate on the strategic level and Langdon would continue to head both.

'Lufthansa 3216.' They all heard the voice of the British controller. 'Standard Lambourne Three Alpha arrival for landing runway Two Seven Left.'

'What does that mean?' Langdon demanded.

Kilpatrick crossed to the telephones and asked the flight adviser to join them.

Lambourne Three Alpha was the standard arrival route for aircraft coming in from Amsterdam, the adviser informed them. He was settled uncomfortably at the end of the table facing Langdon. Runway Two Seven Left was the standard runway at that time of day for aircraft coming in from Lambourne.

'Which way do they come in from Lambourne?' Langdon leaned forward.

'You mean the route?'

'Yes.' Because Lambourne is to the east, Heathrow is to the west, and London is bang in the middle.

'Up the Thames and over central London.'

'Over the City? Directly over Westminster, Downing Street, and Parliament?'

'Yes.'

Lufthansa 3216 approaching the Essex coast, Strike was informed.

'Lufthansa 3216. Descend when ready to flight level one five zero.' Descend to fifteen thousand feet.

The air traffic control room was rectangular; low lighting and quiet atmosphere, no smoking and not even soft drinks allowed. The watch supervisor's desk was at the head of the room. Along the left wall were four radar suites, each controlling a sector; another suite on the end wall furthest from the watch supervisor, and four more suites along the other long wall. At each suite were two radar controllers, headsets on and radar screens horizontal on the desk in front of them, the crew chief for the sector standing between them.

The watch supervisor checked the time, left his desk and walked the twenty metres to the third suite on the left.

'How's it going?' he asked the controller in the right-hand seat.

'Fine,' Simmons told him.

'How long can we leave it before we stop everything else?'

Because there are thirty-eight landings and thirty takeoffs every hour at Heathrow at this time of day. Of course we'll clear a window for 3216, stop all landings and takeoffs. Do it too early, however, and we create chaos; too late and we risk adding to the problems.

'Twenty minutes window,' the crew chief told him. 'As soon as she leaves Lambourne.'

'Agreed.'

'3216 over Essex coast,' Simmons informed them. 'Two minutes to Lambourne.'

And at Lambourne he would direct 3216 left, so it would pick up the ILS which would guide it on to runway Two Seven Left.

'Lufthansa 3216 approaching the point at which they turn for the run-in to Heathrow,' the intelligence major informed the Operations Room.

So what are you thinking, Finn?

I'm hoping that my assumptions are correct, that's what I'm thinking. I'm hoping I don't get squeezed in the drain system, because I'm terrified of tight black spaces. I'm hoping the first diversion works, otherwise the press might see us and put it out on radio and television. And if they do, the hijackers will hear, and then they'll be waiting for us.

'3216 en route for Lambourne,' the intelligence major updated the Operations Room. 'Heathrow about to be closed down.'

So what else are you thinking, Finn?

A Boeing 737 has six doors – that's what I'm thinking, because that's what I have to think about. Two at the front, two at the rear, and two emergency doors over the wings. All doors can be opened by handles on the outside. Three toilets where the hijackers might hide: one at front on left, assuming entry is through front port door, and two at rear. And I'm thinking this, and nothing else, because from now on I can only think of what is relevant for the moment I go on to Lufthansa 3216 tonight. And I must assume that I'm going on, because otherwise I won't be prepared. And if I'm not prepared, I'm dead.

'Hold,' the watch supervisor told the Clacton crew chief.

'Hold,' the crew chief told Simmons.

The supervisor put the phone down, left his desk, and hurried to them. 'We need to re-route.'

Getting tight to do it, they knew. Plus 3216 was running out of fuel.

'3216 one minute from Lambourne,' Simmons's voice was almost mechanical.

'Why re-route?' the crew chief asked.

'Orders.' The reply was direct rather than blunt. '3216 can't go over central London.'

'Who says?'

'Downing Street.'

Oh shit, the crew chief thought. 'Which rules out a landing from the east. Which means a landing from the west.'

'That's what they've told us to do.'

'We can't.' Simmons's eyes were riveted to the solid line against the black of the radar screen, the last details of Lufthansa 3216's flight pattern trailing in a cone behind it.

'Why not?'

'Tail wind from the west is eighteen knots.' It was the crew chief. 'Maximum tail wind for a 737 is ten.'

'3216 thirty seconds from Lambourne.'

The supervisor turned, ran to his desk, and punched the number. 'This is the watch supervisor at West Drayton.

We cannot divert 3216 from its planned course because that would involve a landing from the west, and the tail wind is too strong.'

'How much too strong?'

'The maximum permitted wind speed is ten knots and the actual wind speed at the moment is eighteen.'

'The west approach,' Langdon told him curtly. 'Do it.' Because there's no way I'll allow Lufthansa 3216 to fly over central London. No way I'll allow the bloody hijacker to fly over Westminster when I'm sitting in the Cobra rooms below Downing Street.

'3216 at Lambourne,' Simmons said calmly.

The layer of cloud was thin below them. It was time to turn left, Kara knew, time to angle towards London, pick up the ILS beam, then swing right and follow it up the Thames and into Heathrow.

'Lufthansa 3216.' The voice of the controller sounded different. 'Turn right on to two eight five for landing on Zero Nine Left.'

Which is not what you told BD 104 and the other flights when I was listening in on airband four days ago, she thought. In front of her the first officer froze and Maeschler hesitated.

'They're re-routeing us.' She was still calm, still controlled. The Zastava sub-machine gun was across her lap, the M70 was in the shoulder holster and the grenades were in her pocket. 'We should be turning left, not right. Any course above two hundred and seventy means we're going north of the runway.'

'Correct,' Maeschler told her.

'Check ATIS again.'

'Runway in use is Two Seven Left.' The details on the automatic message were the same as earlier. 'Surface wind two six zero, eighteen knots.'

'Tell Control that,' she ordered Maeschler. 'Nothing else, just point out that they're telling us to land with an eighteen-knot tail wind and the maximum is ten.'

'Control, this is Lufthansa 3216. Repeat last directions.'

Something was wrong. Finn ignored the other men round him and concentrated on the exchange.

'Lufthansa 3216. Turn right on to two eight five for landing on Zero Nine Left.'

'Control, this is Lufthansa 3216. You originally told me to land from the east on runway Two Seven Left. Now you're telling me to land from the west on runway Zero Nine Left.'

'Affirmative, 3216.'

'But according to ATIS there's an eighteen-knot tail wind from the west, and the maximum tail wind for a 737 is ten knots.'

There was no reply.

Finn swung in his chair so that he could see the TV monitors. There had been no live pictures of Lufthansa 3216 since the Boeing had left Amsterdam, therefore ITV and CNN were replaying the takeoff and the BBC were running a studio discussion: a presenter and what Finn thought of as the inevitable panel of experts.

'What's ATIS?' the presenter asked.

'Airfield Terminal Information Service,' the flight consultant told him. 'It gives the latest airfield report to incoming pilots.'

'What's the difference between a tail wind of ten and eighteen knots?'

They stopped talking as Maeschler spoke again.

'Control, this is Lufthansa 3216. If I follow your instructions and land from the west, the tail wind will mean that I might run out of runway.'

For the second time there was no reply.

'Is that correct?' the presenter asked the panel.

'Yes.'

'So if they land from the west, they might not make it?'

'They should make it . . .'

'But?'

'There's a chance they won't.'

'And the authorities are aware of that but are still telling them to do it?'

Be careful, the expert warned himself. Wrong answer and he wouldn't be invited as an expert again; right answer and he might jeopardize his government contracts. 'So it would seem,' he agreed.

What's happening, one of the sergeants in the police unit supervising the demonstration in Parliament Square asked the woman next to him. Heathrow's changed the route in, Caz told him. Heathrow's told them to land from the west, but the tail wind from the west is above the permitted speed and it means they might run out of runway. Bloody politicians, the policeman said aloud.

They heard Maeschler's voice again. 'Control, this is Lufthansa 3216. Be aware we are fuel priority.' Lufthansa 3216 running out of fuel, they understood. 'I repeat. Be aware we are fuel priority.'

So what do I say? The radar controller stared at the crew chief: what do I do? 'She's turning.' He picked up the first movement. 'Repeat. She's turning.'

'3216 turning,' the crew chief told the shift supervisor.

'Lufthansa 3216 turning,' the supervisor informed Downing Street.

'3216 turning left,' Simmons told the crew chief. 'Confirm, she's turning left.'

'You mean right.' Because that's what we told her to do. That's what we were ordered to tell her.

'No, I mean left.'

*

There was nothing on the VHF and there should be something. 'What's happening?' the BBC presenter asked the panel.

'One of two things.' It was the flight expert again. 'Either Lufthansa 3216 has turned north. Although that's what Air Traffic Control instructed, and therefore seems unlikely.'

'Or?'

'She's disregarded Air Traffic Control and turned left, which would be the normal route in. Then she'd head south at an angle till she picks up the ILS beam, turn right, and follow the beam into Heathrow.'

'Over London?'

'Yes. Over London.'

'And as of this moment, all other air traffic into and out of Heathrow has been stopped.'

'Yes.'

'So the only plane which will fly over London in the next twenty minutes is Lufthansa 3216?'

'Yes.'

Lufthansa 3216 is out of contact with Air Traffic Control, the radio reporter was saying, we are not sure where 3216 is. Caz held the transistor up so those around her could hear. If 3216 is obeying Air Traffic Control, then they are somewhere north of London. If they are disobeying Control, however, they are east of London and preparing to fly over the capital.

The cloud was around them. 'Locking on to ILS,' Maeschler told Kara. 'Beginning final approach.' The Boeing banked gently to the right, the cloud thinned and the ground was suddenly visible beneath them. The green of the fields below them, the silver of the Thames snaking away from them, and the grey of London in front of them.

CNN, BBC and ITV were all already transmitting pictures from Heathrow, BBC cutting with shots from Parliament Square, and ITV mixing with aerial shots of London from an Aero Spatiale Twin Squirrel jet helicopter, registration number GO ITN, and the pictures sent via microwave into Highgate.

So what you thinking, Finn?

Stand by, stand by, I'm thinking. I'm at the top of the ladder and the aircraft door is in front of me. Steve to my left, Jim and Ken tight behind; Janner and his team at the rear door, the helicopter hovering over the flight deck of Lufthansa 3216, the ops major counting down and the diversions about to go in.

Although that's not all I'm thinking.

What do you mean, Finn? What are you *really* thinking?

'Lufthansa 3216 is approaching from the east.' The radio presenter tried to stifle the excitement in his voice. 'We are receiving reports that Lufthansa 3216 has passed over the Thames flood barrier and is about to fly over the City.'

'We have first pictures of Lufthansa 3216,' the voice of the ITV presenter was suddenly urgent, suddenly dramatic. The monitor showing the shot from the Twin Squirrel, the Boeing slightly below it.

Christ she's low, Finn thought. The television images were almost unreal – the empty runways at Heathrow, the people in Parliament Square, their faces turned up and their eyes searching the sky to the east. The aerial shot from the helicopter of Lufthansa 3216 tracking up the river.

Docklands was below her, Tower Bridge in front then suddenly below, and Westminster and Big Ben drawing her in as if she was on a piece of string.

Finn glanced at the BBC pictures from Westminster – the sky empty in the background and the Palace of Westminster in front, Big Ben to the right and the Churchill statue to the left.

'Lufthansa 3216, this is Heathrow Tower.'

'Heathrow, this is Lufthansa 3216.' Maeschler, the captain, husband of a beautiful wife and father of two pretty children – the papers had found out and published a family photograph. Maeschler the hero who'd landed 3216 at Schipol even though the authorities had tried to stop him.

'3216, you are cleared to land.'

There was a slight delay.

'Thank you, Heathrow Tower.' Not Maeschler this time.

It's not the critic who counts . . . Kara remembered the words. Not the one who points out how the strong man stumbled or how the doer of deeds might have done them better . . .

'I can see Lufthansa 3216.' The radio reporter had slipped through the police cordon and was standing on Westminster Bridge. 'Lufthansa 3216 is coming up the Thames towards me.' Caz was straining, standing on tiptoe, looking to her left, looking downriver. The Boeing was suddenly in shot on the pictures from Parliament Square, suddenly approaching Westminster. Passing over Parliament and framed for one incredible moment between Big Ben and the Churchill statue.

The credit belongs to the man who is actually in the arena, who strives valiantly and spends himself in a worthy cause . . . Who, if he wins, knows the triumph of high achievement and who, if he fails, at least fails while daring greatly . . .

What did you say the motto was, Finn?

Who Dares Wins.

Finn left the building and stood on the tarmac looking east. Heathrow was like a ghost around him, the skies and runways empty.

So what are you really thinking, Finn?

You know what I'm thinking.

Tell me anyway.

I'm thinking about a winter night behind the lines in Bosnia. I'm thinking about how the United Nations blew Kev and Geordie John to Kingdom Come that night. How Janner and Max only survived because someone who didn't know them risked everything to save them, even though she didn't have to. I'm thinking about how I told her that I owed, that the regiment owed, and that none of us would ever forget. Because if you can't help those who help you and yours, then who can you help? If you can't be loyal to those who are loyal to you and yours, then who the hell or what the hell can you be loyal to?

In the sky to the east he saw the first flash from the wing lights of the Boeing.

But that's not all you're thinking, is it, Finn?

The lights were suddenly stronger. The Boeing was over the outer marker, over the approach lights. Over the lead-in lights and the runway threshold.

No, that's not all I'm thinking.

So what else are you thinking, Finn?

I'm thinking about what else I said to her. About how I told her that the West would never help her people unless her people had something the West wanted. I'm thinking about what I said her people should do next time the United Nations let them down.

But there's something else, isn't there, Finn?

Okay, there's something else.

So what is it, Finn?

You want to know? You really want to know?

Yeah, Finn. I really want to know.

I'm thinking that it's her on Lufthansa 3216. Except it can't be her because she's dead. But the hijacker on Lufthansa 3216 is doing exactly what I told her to do.

He turned and saw Janner standing beside him.

The tyres thumped on the tarmac, the engines screaming

as Maeschler eased them into reverse thrust. Eight hours to ten o'clock, eight hours to the deadline and five before the UN Security Council met in New York. Plenty of time for the politicians to sort it out. The deadline wasn't at ten, Finn reminded himself, it was at nine.

Negotiator in position at Heathrow, Strike and Cobra were informed. The hijackers have declined the position Ground Control offered them, and the aircraft is now moving across the taxiways towards runway Two Seven Right. No offers to the hijackers, Langdon instructed. No communication with the hijackers unless they initiated it. No concessions if the hijackers asked for any.

Caz was still looking to the west, towards where Lufthansa 3216 had disappeared. The exhilaration filled her and the sheer emotion of seeing the hijacked plane over Westminster had affected her in a way she had not thought possible. Lufthansa 3216 has now landed at Heathrow, the radio reporter was saying. Lufthansa 3216 has ignored Ground Control's directions about where it should park and is now sitting at the end of runway Two Seven Right.

The exhilaration was evaporating, the excitement and the adrenalin dissipating and the black coming in, the terrible long dark clouds of realization. Caz looked away from the sky and saw Jude staring at her, knew Jude was thinking the same thing.

The hijacker at Heathrow. Finn and Janner at Heathrow.

So where are my loyalties, dear God?

With a cause I believe in more fervently and with more conviction and more righteousness than I have believed in my whole life? Even though the cause might never be won, which is even more reason for believing in it.

With someone I do not know, who has broken the law,

but who has taken that cause farther than I or most others would ever contemplate?

Or with my husband, the father of my children? My friend and my companion and my lover. Whom I have always loved, and whom, at this moment, I love more than I have ever loved before.

The plane was settled and the flight deck was quiet around her.

As long as the cause is a worthy cause, he'd told her . . . Hers was a worthy cause, she had always known, which was why he had told her.

As long as her journey was a righteous and just journey, he'd told her . . . Hers was a righteous and just journey, she had always held the conviction, which was why he had set her upon it.

Kara's Rules. Kara's Game.

Thanks, Finn.

* * *

It was three o'clock, six hours to the deadline.

In Bosnia, according to the BBC World Service, Bihac had again been shelled; in Bosnia the UN still had not called in an air strike. A long time since she and Jovan had cowered under the shelling of Maglaj, Kara thought: so many months ago, so many lifetimes ago, that she could barely remember. So many lifetimes since so many things. She left the flight deck and walked back through the cabins, looking at the passengers but seeing and hearing and sensing only the images of last January.

It was four o'clock, five hours to the deadline.

'We need to speak to Langdon's daughter,' Finn told the operation commander. 'The debriefs from Amsterdam aren't detailed enough and the translations are no good.'

'The request has already gone in and been turned down.'

'In that case ask again.'

It was five o'clock, four hours to the deadline.

'You're not afraid?' Maeschler asked.

'No,' Kara told him. 'But you wouldn't understand.'

'Try me.'

'Like I said, you wouldn't understand.'

'Because you believe in what you're doing?' Maeschler suggested.

'Partly.'

'Partly you've nothing to live for?'

Partly because I always knew that one day it would be *me* lying on the ground, the bullet in *my* face and *my* blood trickling down *my* cheek. But also because if you've been to the edge, chosen to go over the edge, then when the man points the gun at you, you can stare him in the eyes and say fuck you, I've been there, seen it, done it.

But you wouldn't understand, because you're not Finn.

It was six o'clock, three hours to the deadline.

The hangar was sealed off, the 737 in the centre of the floor and the teams repeating the drill again and again. Stand by, stand by. Preliminary diversion in: out of drain, grab ladders, and run to plane. Ladders in place and hide behind the wheels. They were totally focused now, totally committed, full assault gear. Heckler and Kochs, Sig Sauers and Remingtons. Black flame-retardant suits and underwear; boots and gloves; belt with mag pouches and body armour with Velcro pockets and plates back and front; gas hoods and masks, pouch on body armour for UHF radio and mouthpiece in gas mask.

Stand by, stand by. Finn listened to the operation major's countdown in the earpiece. First diversion in, second. Open door and enter plane, hope to Christ the diversions and the stun grenades have worked. He himself goes right. First on to the plane, first to face the opposition. They finished the run-through, left the plane, pulled off the gas hoods and body armour, and went to the crew room.

So what is it, Janner – Finn watched. Why have you left the room? Why are you sitting by yourself next door? He followed him through, closed the door, sat beside him and waited.

'What you were saying last night.' Janner stared at the mug of coffee.

'What about?'

'About when you and Kara were in the hospital at Tesanj, about what you told her.'

'I was wrong, Janner. I was out of line.' Because I let her down, and it was getting to me.

Janner was still staring at the mug. 'When you went back to look for her, you couldn't find her in Maglaj or Tesanj.'

'No.' But you know this, Janner, so what's this all about? Because time's running away with us, my friend. Because at this moment the only thing we should be talking about is Lufthansa 3216 and how we're going to get on and, more importantly, how we make sure we all get off.

Janner sniffed and glanced at him. 'The Israeli warning and the intelligence from Box. New terrorist organization with four teams already running. Organizing committee taken out, recruiter and organizer taken out, teams taken out.' Except the Paris team, of course.

'Yes.' Except that you don't know I did the London job and I don't know where you disappeared to, because even though we might be friends we don't talk about operations. Because the less we know about what other people are up to the better. Because you could be in the same country at the same time as your best mate, and neither of you would know till years later. And then it would only come out over a beer, and then only if it didn't matter.

'The intelligence on the teams came from a man called

Keefer,' Janner told him. 'East German, ex-Stasi. Box located him in Istanbul. My team lifted him and Box interrogated him. On the spot. Sodium pentothal, to get the locations and covers of the hit teams before anyone realized we had him.'

Finn remembered the night: the waiting then the drive through London, the three men and the one woman in the flat in Maida Vale.

Janner sipped the coffee for the first time. 'After Box got the key details they asked some follow-up questions. Not many, and not for long.'

'When the Paris job went wrong why didn't they ask him?'

'It was too late.' Because London had decided no loose ends, no prisoners. 'But Box did ask a number of questions. Who Keefer was working for, obviously; who was paying him and how they were paying him.' The command structure, the details which might lead to other groups or other people. 'Plus they asked him about the teams.'

And . . .

The first frost was down Finn's spine and the first nerves jangled in his brain.

'Backtrack.' Janner put the mug down. 'The leader of the hijack team is a woman.'

'Yes.'

'And the hijack team is probably the missing Paris team.'

'Yes.'

'Where did you look for Kara when you went back?'

'Maglaj and Tesanj.'

'And?'

'Travnik.' But you know this, so where are you taking me? Except I know where you're taking me.

'When were you in Travnik?' Janner asked.

'Last January.'

'The woman who's leading the hijack team was recruited in Travnik last January.'

Finn's mind was spinning. 'But didn't the interrogators ask her name?'

'Yes.'

'And?'

'Keefer didn't know. She never told him. Never gave her name or background or anything about herself.'

'Where'd he find her?'

'She was running a scam on the black market.'

'In Travnik in January.'

'Yeah, Finn. In Travnik in January.'

'Impossible. To be in Travnik, Kara would have needed to leave the Maglaj–Tesanj pocket. And to do that she would have had to cross two sets of front lines.'

Who mentioned Kara in this context? Janner might have asked. Who said that it's Kara we're talking about at this point? Except we both know we are. Which is what this conversation is all about. 'But she did make it through two front lines, didn't she? You found her name on the refugee food list there.'

Coincidence, they agreed. Because time was running out, because they had to return to the hangar and the practice sessions on the 737. Because it wasn't Kara on the plane, no way it could be. Not even Kara in Travnik, even though Kara's name was on the food register there. Because Kara hadn't reappeared, hadn't come for food, even though Finn had waited.

UN Security Council meeting has started, the BBC World Service announced; the meeting early, and hopes for a solution to the Lufthansa hijack rising.

'Your people are ready?' Langdon asked the Brigadier, Special Forces.

The other members of Strike, plus the colonel commanding 22 SAS, were also present, though it would be the last time they would convene as a committee. Lufthansa 3216 was now sitting on British soil, therefore a British responsibility, and the operation procedures for such situations assigned control to Cobra.

'Yes.' It was the colonel who replied.

Langdon nodded. 'It is the present thinking of this committee that unless a solution is agreed, your people enter the plane one minute before the deadline expires.'

'Why?'

'To prevent the hijackers doing whatever they intend to do when the deadline expires.'

'But we don't know what they intend to do.'

'Precisely.'

But deadlines are there to be extended, the colonel was inclined to reply; that's why there's a negotiator at Heathrow. Except you've decided against negotiations, you've decreed that the negotiator shouldn't contact the plane. 'What if the Security Council is still sitting?' he asked.

'Then you proceed as ordered.'

'We can't.'

'Why can't we?' I'm running this show, because I'm the Foreign Secretary and you're a colonel who's not going to make brigadier at this rate. Because we're not just talking about a handful of hijackers. We're dealing with major world issues like Bosnia and the future of the East–West relationship.

'Because there's a certain structure to hijacks or other forms of hostage-taking. We don't go in unless the hijackers kill someone. Break that rule and you create problems for the future.'

'Perhaps it's time to change the rules.'

You're not going to win, Kilpatrick wanted to tell the colonel. So give up now. Save the few political points you have left, because you don't have many.

'In that case could I ask your help? The men who'll go on to the plane don't have enough information about what's happening inside. We know the hijackers have certain weapons, but we don't even know whether they have explosives.'

The colonel's setting you up, Kilpatrick glanced at Langdon. He's allowing you to think you've won, and now he's going to put the boot in. You've screwed him, screwed his men, so now he's going to screw you.

'How can I help?' Langdon asked.

'A debrief with your daughter and granddaughter. They *were* on Lufthansa 3216, weren't they? They *were* among the passengers the hijackers released in Amsterdam.'

In half an hour the dusk would begin to settle. The day was colder now, and the women were leaving Parliament Square. Back tomorrow, they were telling each other; but tomorrow would be different, because the key to what they were demanding was the hijack, and by tomorrow the hijack would be over.

'You're staying tonight?' Linn asked. Caz and Jude had changed, she was aware; ever since 3216 had come over London, ever since 3216 had landed at Heathrow. Before they had been relaxed, now they were tight and screwing tighter.

They should head home. But if they did they'd be on a train or in a car when the deadline expired. Finn and Janner will be okay, they had told themselves; and in any case the UN would sort it out, because this time the UN really had no option.

'If that's all right with you.'

'Of course it's all right. You okay?'

There was no answer, just the smiles which said nothing.

Linn's husband was waiting at Finsbury Park underground. Two minutes, Caz and Jude told him, telephoned Hereford and spoke to the children.

Stand by, the words drummed through Finn's head. Ladder against door, Steve to his left, Jim and Ken tight behind them. Janner and his team at the rear door. Other team on the starboard wing as if they'd just exited the helicopter.

Debrief with the English hostage, he was told. Janner to attend as well, because Janner's team would be second on the plane. He climbed down and checked his watch. It was six-thirty, two and a half hours to the deadline. 'She's here?'

'No, she's near Salisbury. Chopper's waiting.'

This is madness, he said, this is suicide; no way he and Janner should be leaving Heathrow at this point. 'Any news from the Security Council?' He pulled off the body armour and assault suit, and slipped on a pair of jeans and a jacket.

'Yes, but you won't want to know.'

'Tell me anyway.'

'There's a procedural problem; they haven't started the debate proper yet.'

It was seven o'clock; two hours to the deadline and the light gone.

The convoy of official cars, police escort and outriders was waiting, engines running, and the television cameras and lights were in place. Langdon left the Foreign and Commonwealth Office. You've got two minutes because he's in a hurry, the press had been told. No lights in his eyes, the cameramen had been warned: the pressure's on, so we'll play ball as long as you do. Langdon walked to the cameras, ignored the first questions, and said what his advisers had written for him.

'I'm on my way to Heathrow. I have just spoken to the Prime Minister, as well as to President Clinton in Washington, President Mitterand in Paris, and President Yeltsin in Moscow. We all agree that the safety of the passengers on Lufthansa 3216 is of the utmost importance.'

The interview was being transmitted live, prefaced by pictures of the plane at Heathrow. What about Bosnia, one of the reporters asked; what about the demands of the hijackers?

'We all feel a great sorrow about what is happening in Bihac. Nobody can stomach the deaths of children, the deaths of any people who are innocent and unable to protect themselves. The response to the hijackers' demand, however, is the responsibility of the Security Council, not of this government. My responsibility, at the moment, is to the passengers and crew of Lufthansa 3216.'

What about the deadline, he was pressed. The hijackers have released all women and children from the plane, and haven't actually threatened to do anything when the deadline expires. Are the SAS at Heathrow? What will they do when the deadline expires? Have you given them orders to storm the plane?

'Thank you,' he told them.

The minders closed round him, he was escorted to the waiting cars, and the convoy pulled away.

'You mind if I write a letter?' Maeschler asked.

'Who to?' Kara looked across at him.

At Orly and Schipol the airports had been quiet round the plane. Here, however, there always seemed to be movement: vehicles moving and helicopters landing and taking off, sometimes circling above the 737, the noise of their engines almost deafening then receding, then coming back again.

'My wife.'

'You're not going to die,' she told him.

Because if you or any other passenger or crew member

died, it would wreck everything; because then the UN and the governments who've pussyfooted on Bosnia would blame us, say we were extremists. Then the pressure on them to do something would evaporate and I would have lost.

'But you might?'

'Who knows?' she said. 'Write what you want,' she told him.

*My dear wife*, he began. *It is now less than two hours to the deadline. I do not know whether I will see you again, but in the event of the Security Council not agreeing to the hijackers' demands, I wish you to understand what I intend to do.*

The debriefers were waiting, Finn was informed as the Agusta landed. The river was to their right, across the lawn, the house to their left. They left the helicopter and ran inside.

The man and woman were sitting in the lounge, both dressed casually, and the tape recorders were tucked discreetly behind the sofa. Thanks for getting here so quickly – he nodded at them. Know you, he thought as he shook hands with the woman; you were an interrogator at one of the Ashford courses. Right bastard. Except that was your job, and you had to prepare me for what I would face if I was ever captured by the opposition.

The other woman, and the girl, were seated by the fireplace. Hilary Langdon Carpenter and daughter Samantha. Finn shook the mother's hand and made a point of shaking the girl's. You're the ones who'll go on to the plane – it was in Hilary Langdon Carpenter's eyes, the way she stared at him; you're the ones who'll kill the bastards.

He smiled and sat at the back of the room, Janner beside him, mother and daughter on the sofa and the interrogators apparently relaxed in the armchairs opposite them. Begin at the beginning, they said. Plenty of time, just got to get it right. No pressure, nice and easy.

How many hijackers ... It was the woman who led. Two men and two women, is that right ... Are they armed ... What are they armed with ... Do they carry the weapons all the time or do they leave them anywhere ...

Where do they stand on the plane, and how do they communicate ... How often do they talk to each other, and do they move around ... The leader, the woman ...

The details were coming out, the little things which had been missing from the other debriefs. The interrogators were pros, Finn thought; going for the jugular right away without the woman even knowing, turning the normal procedure upside down because they knew he didn't have much time. Hilary Langdon Carpenter was also good though; good memory and good on detail.

Explosives ...

'Yes, they have explosives.'

You're lying, Finn thought.

'What sort?' It was the woman interrogator.

'Hell, I don't know.' Hilary Langdon Carpenter shook her head. Christ, I'm a business-woman, not a weapons and explosives expert.

Of course ... It was in the nod and the smile. 'Where do they keep them?'

'In a pilot's briefcase, you know the sort.'

'You've seen them?'

'Yes.'

'What do they look like?' The male interrogator now. Because I don't know about explosives either. It was in the way he sat back slightly. But the lads here do, so describe what you saw and they'll know what you're talking about.

'I'm not sure.'

Why are you suddenly lying – the woman interrogator looked at her, though neither the interrogator's face nor her eyes changed; why are you trying to screw us, screw these guys here? Because sometime this evening they might be going on to Lufthansa 3216, and the only person who can help prepare them is you. And that's what you've been doing so far. But suddenly you've gone off the rails.

I know why, she thought. Because you want the SAS to go on. And when they do you want them to kill the hijackers. God knows why, because they freed you, gave you your life and that of your child. But now you want them dead. So you're saying they have explosives, even though nobody else has said this, because that plants the suggestion that when the deadline expires they'll blow the plane up. Therefore the SAS have to go in early. And they have to go in with the sole intention of taking out the hijackers before the hijackers take out the plane. So what the hell are you playing at, lady?

She smiled. 'Let's go back to the beginning. When did you first see them?'

Good move, Finn acknowledged. But time's slipping and suddenly I don't know where I stand. Because the suggestion that the hijackers have explosives alters everything. Okay, so nobody else has even mentioned explosives, and we all know you're lying. But the mere fact that you've said it changes the picture entirely. Because Ops will be informed, and Ops will have to assume there are explosives on the plane, because at this stage they'll have no option.

'Four hijackers,' the interrogator was asking again. 'Two men and two women . . . What were they wearing and what do they look like . . . ?'

Hilary Langdon Carpenter was answering confidently, her daughter at her side. Time to be going, Finn thought. He and Janner shouldn't be here, he and Janner should never have left Heathrow.

'The leader.' It was the woman interrogator still.

'Yes.'

The daughter was fidgeting, getting bored.

'The leader was a woman?'

'Yes.'

She's the one with the explosives? Finn knew the interrogator was going to ask, going to begin the check. The girl called Sammi slid off the sofa and drifted to the other side of the room.

'What does she look like? Tell me about her. Is she armed?'

Time to go, Janner indicated. We should be in the hangar at Heathrow going through the entry routine, should be leaving the holding positions and getting to our start points.

'Of course she's armed.' There was a slight irritation now. I've told you, for God's sake, so why ask again?

'What else about her?'

Finn and Janner were getting up, nodding to the interrogators. Speak to you when we're back at Heathrow, see if there's anything else. But get this explosives thing sorted, because we all know it's crucial.

Sure, it was in the nod back. Speak to you in fifteen.

Stand by – the drum was beating. Stand by, stand by. Radio silence as the ops major counted them down. Preliminary diversion going in; out drain and move to plane, ladder in position. Stand by, stand by. Radio silence again as the ops major counted down the last stage. Door in front and Steve on his left, Jim and Ken tight behind. Janner and his team at the rear. Stand by, stand by. First diversion in; second. Go, go, go . . .

'Her little boy was called Jovan.'

The voice was from the far side of the room, almost lost in the dark.

'Sorry?' The interrogator turned and smiled, invited a follow-up.

'She had a little boy once. Yesterday was his birthday.

Yesterday he would have been five.' The girl was standing alone, looking at them. 'He's dead. He was called Jovan.'

Something in the room snapped tight – the interrogator was too experienced not to know it, not to sense it. Too experienced to let it show. She was still smiling, as if it was unimportant, looking at the girl then at the mother. Hilary Langdon almost glaring at her daughter. The mother not knowing what her daughter was saying, the interrogator decided. The SAS men looking as if they didn't understand, nothing showing on their faces or in their eyes. The girl still looking at them all.

Something in the room snapping tight though – the interrogator knew for certain. 'How'd you know?' she asked.

'You were asleep.' The girl looked at her mother. 'I didn't go far. I heard them talking.'

They waited.

'He said he had a boy and girl and asked if she had any children.'

They still waited.

'She said no.'

They were still waiting.

'Then she said that she'd had a son, and he asked her what the son was called, and she said Jovan.'

'Who's he?' the interrogator asked carefully.

'The pilot.' The tears welled in her eyes. 'I'm sorry, Mummy. I didn't mean to do wrong. I just went for a little walk.'

'You didn't do wrong,' the interrogator told her. But you've just screwed everything, because I was about to let the SAS boys go, then I was going to hit your mother about the explosives. And now I can't, because your mother's going to say we've upset you. And she has to tend to you, therefore we can't speak to her any more.

*

It was eight o'clock, one hour to the deadline.

What are you going to do, Finn? We owe, you said; I owe. For ever. Anything you want you get, anything you ask for is yours. No oil in Sarajevo, you also said, so you have to have something else the West wants, have to do something that makes the world afraid of you.

Why the hell didn't you do as she asked, Finn? Why the hell didn't you get little Jovan out on the chopper? Because there was room, and if you had then Jovan and Adin wouldn't be dead now and Kara wouldn't be sitting in a hijacked plane on runway Two Seven Right.

The Agusta dropped over the outer perimeter at Heathrow.

What are you going to do, Janner? Because in slightly less than one hour you enter Lufthansa 3216. And once you're inside there's only one thing you're going to do and one way you're going to come out. But if she hadn't saved your life in Maglaj, you wouldn't be alive to kill her now.

The Agusta touched down. They ran into the building containing the holding area and Operations Room, crouched together inside the doorway for thirty seconds because they hadn't been able to discuss anything in the helicopter.

So what the hell *do* we do, Finn?

What the hell *do* we do, Janner?

They left the doorway and went to the holding room. The teams were waiting, each man kitted up, only hoods and gas masks to put on. Steve, Jim and Ken; Janner's team; plus the team which would constitute the first diversion and which would enter Lufthansa 3216 after Finn and Janner's teams.

'Check the chopper,' Finn told the third team.

'A word,' Janner told his team and led them into the adjoining room.

What the hell's running – it was on Steve's face; what

the fuck's this all about? We should be at our start points now, should be ready to go. Should be crawling up the drains and hoping to hell nothing and nobody is coming the other way.

'There's a problem,' Finn said.

'You remember Maglaj . . .

'You remember the night Kev and Geordie John were chopped . . .

'You remember the night Janner and Max almost died . . .

'You remember the night the woman saved them . . .'

You remember Jovan. How we said we'd go back for him and the mother thought we wouldn't. How we took him to the hospital in Tesanj.

Sure we remember, Finn, but what's this to do with Lufthansa 3216?

'I went back. After we'd left Bosnia and were home here. Went back to make sure Kara and Jovan and her husband were okay.'

So, Finn? Move it, Finn. Because the minutes are ticking away and we're nowhere near ready.

'The day after we bugged out the Serbs shelled the hospital at Tesanj and Jovan was killed. The next day his father was shot dead by a sniper.'

So why are you telling us now? What has this to do with Lufthansa 3216?

'You remember Kara?'

Of course we remember Kara. The realization was coming upon them.

'Kara is the leader of the hijack team.'

How, they asked. How'd you know, they pressed him. What had he said to her and was he sure? And even if he wasn't could they take the chance?

He told them.

'Options?' they asked.

'One: we do the job.

'Two: we pull out and let somebody else do it.

'Three: we sort it out ourselves. Us and Janner's team. Nobody else.'

Another time, or more time, and he might have found another way round it. Another time, or more time, and his logic and his loyalties might have been different.

'That night.' It was Jim. 'The night Kara saved Janner and Max. When she went out first she thought it was her husband.'

'Correct.'

'But when she went back, she knew it wasn't.'

'Correct again.'

'The first time she went, she didn't know it was a minefield. But when she went back for Janner she did.'

'Yes.'

'And if we'd choppered Jovan out, like she asked, Jovan and Adin wouldn't be dead, and we wouldn't be here now.'

'No.'

'So we owe.'

'I owe. Not you.'

'Shit, Finn. We all owe.'

Which leaves Janner's team, because they don't.

They went through to the next room.

'Janner's explained things?'

'Yeah.'

And . . .

'Christ, Finn. If you can't help those who've helped your own, who the hell can you help?'

'Okay,' Finn told them. 'This is what we do.'

It was eight-fifteen, forty-five minutes to the deadline.

The vehicle lights were moving a hundred metres away, planes coming in and landing in front of them, and the noise of the helicopter above was deafening. Kara left the flight deck and walked back through the cabin. Nothing yet from the United Nations, but the UN would leave it tight anyway. And then it was up to the British, what the British decided to do and how the British decided to play it. Plus the other hijackers. She still might make it out. As long as the British didn't go against the rules. And as long as the other hijackers didn't realize, even at the last moment, what she had done.

It was eight-twenty.

The two teams returned to the holding room, the others checking their weapons again while Finn and Janner dressed, the small pack which Finn would carry on his back the only difference between him and the others. The third team came in. 'Chopper okay?' he asked.

'Chopper okay,' they confirmed. So what was all that about? What's going down that we don't know about? Nothing that would affect them, they assumed, otherwise Finn would have told them.

Finn left the holding room and went to the Operations Room. The front wall was covered with monitors showing images from the various surveillance cameras, communications equipment linking the room to Hereford and Downing Street, plus special links to the snipers positioned round the plane. On the wall on the right the three monitors showed the pictures being transmitted live from the BBC, ITN and CNN cameras, the 737 clearly visible on the runway even though the cameras were some way from it. Thank Christ they'd set up the preliminary diversion, Finn thought; hope to hell it works.

'What about the explosives?' the operations major asked immediately.

'Langdon's daughter said they have explosives. No other passenger confirms her account.'

'You're saying she's wrong?' Because I have Downing Street sitting on my shoulder. And next door I have the

Foreign Secretary plus two advisers, the Brigadier, Special Forces and the commanding officer of 22, and two members of the Joint Intelligence Committee.

'You want the truth, Ted?'

'Yes.'

'She's lying. Ask Janner, ask the interrogators.' But she's the Foreign Secretary's daughter, and at this stage you can't take any chances anyway.

'So?' Time to go, they both knew, time for the teams to be at the start points.

'Make sure that Langdon signs for everything. Make sure that if anything goes wrong it's his problem and not ours.'

It was eight twenty-five.

In the basement of the house in Stoke Newington Caz and Jude and the others clustered nervously round the kitchen table and watched the images from Heathrow: Lufthansa 3216 sitting on the runway, an occasional plane landing over it, and the area around and behind it grim and bleak.

'Why there?' Linn asked.

'Probably because she knew the TV cameras would be able to see her,' Mike suggested.

'Why are they allowing planes to land on the runway?' It was Linn again.

'Probably because they have to,' Mike told her.

'Why is there always a helicopter over the plane?' Because at Orly and Schipol they left it alone, kept everything and everyone away from it.

'I don't know.'

It was eight-thirty.

The storm drain was only two hundred metres long; they'd made it in five minutes that morning, and it wasn't that tight really. Down this one, drop a couple of metres, right at the bottom and follow the tape. I don't want to do this, Finn thought; I'd rather be going on to the plane than doing this.

They were in the shelter of a maintenance hangar to the east of 3216, the drain cover off and the teams behind him.

Here goes, he thought. He took the pack off his back, held it instead, and eased himself down the hole. Oh hell – he almost froze; never did like confined spaces. He made himself go on and reached the bottom, knelt and slid backwards slightly, so that he could get his head and shoulders in the drain passage going the right way, and began to wriggle forward.

The drain was damp, the light from the lamp on his head picking the way, and the tape gleaming in front of him. When they'd checked they hadn't been wearing body armour, so that now the drain was tighter around him and the weight of the plates was making him gasp for breath. Good thing they'd put the gear in place at the top of the drain, camouflaged it down so the cache couldn't be seen.

He came to the first turning and eased around it. A hundred metres to go, he told himself. The drain was slightly wetter now. For God's sake, nobody get stuck. He came to the second bend, pushed the bag in front of him and squeezed round. Hell, it was taking longer than they'd thought. Almost there, he whispered to the man behind him. A drain shaft rose vertically above him. Not the right one, though. Good thing they'd worked it out, marked everything clearly, otherwise they could be sitting like rabbits in the wrong fucking field. The drain seemed tighter, smaller. In front of him he saw the arrow pointing up, the tape ending and a shaft rising vertically, the drainage pipe continuing on.

'We're here,' he tried to whisper.

He pulled himself up the shaft and eased the grille of

the drain cover aside. So slowly there was almost no movement. Eased himself up a little more so the top of his head was above the ground, and peered round.

It was fifteen minutes to nine.

In place, Finn told the operation commander. Nothing from the UN, the major told the assault teams. Assume go.

'Recommend Purple.' Finn was aware of the men crammed in the drain beneath him. Purple the code for the preliminary diversion. The cache was two metres to his left and the 737 was forty metres in front of him. Between him and the perimeter fence. Between him and the television cameras. An Airbus came in to land above him and he ducked.

'Radio silence. Purple stand by. Thirty seconds.'

Thirty seconds, Finn confirmed with the man below him.

'Purple counting down. Twenty-five seconds.'

A mile to the east the pilot of the RAF cargo plane – military markings replaced by civilian designations – checked with the men in the cabin behind him.

'Purple twenty seconds.'

'What do your husbands do?' Linn's husband asked. 'Do they work together?'

They were still in the kitchen, still staring at the images from Heathrow on the television, the voice of the reporter mixing with the occasional instructions from Control, picked up on the airband and transmitted simultaneously.

'This and that,' Caz told him. 'Odd-job men really. Sometimes they work together, sometimes they don't.' Getting close to the deadline, she thought. Getting close to everything.

'Mayday. Mayday.' They heard the voice on the airband, simultaneous transmission on both radio and television. The voice stark but in control. 'Mayday. Mayday. Engine on fire.'

'There's a plane coming in with its engine on fire,' the TV reporter was saying. 'I can see it. It's over the lead-in lights, over the runway threshold.'

Over Lufthansa 3216.

Why a Mayday – the doubt was almost hidden in Caz's mind. Why was another plane putting out a Mayday call on the frequency only Lufthansa 3216 was using? The cameras swung away from the 737. In the Operations Room the major checked the BBC, ITN and CNN feeds. Each one was on the incoming plane, following it as it touched down and began screaming to a stop. Each away from Lufthansa 3216.

'Red go. Red go.'

Finn was already out of the drain, pulling back the camouflage and picking up the gear and the ladder, Steve behind him grabbing the other end. Jim and Ken also out, and Janner's team following.

The lights of the airport fire engines were flashing on the TV screen, and the smoke and the orange and red were spitting from the cargo plane. Caz and Jude watched, Linn and Mike dumbfounded beside them. The plane was at the other end of the runway, almost lost in the dark now, but the red and yellow and orange still coming from it.

No pictures of Lufthansa 3216 for fifteen seconds now – Caz glanced at Jude. No pictures of Lufthansa 3216 for almost thirty seconds. The cold gripped her; the arctic certainty of what was happening. A Mayday call and a plane coming in and landing with smoke and flames apparently coming from it. Not an emergency, though, no plane in trouble. The first diversion going in – the cold was permafrost now. Finn and Janner and the boys up to their games. Please God may they live. Please God may the hijacker not die.

The image on the screen flicked back to Lufthansa 3216. Nothing had changed, nothing was different. The plane was still alone, still apparently isolated, the silver of the fuselage almost ghostly in the night and the helicopter hovering over and slightly in front of it. So either she had been wrong, or Finn and Janner and the teams were in position.

'What's wrong?' Linn asked.

'Nothing.'

It was eleven minutes to nine.

Stand by – the drum was beating again. I go right, Steve left, Jim and Ken following. Janner's team coming in from the rear after creating the first diversion. The ladders were in place and the teams were huddled in the cover of the wheels.

'Still nothing from the UN.' It was the operations commander. 'White One. White One.' The first helicopter switch.

The noise from above the plane was overpowering, then drifting away. Through the windscreen Kara saw the shadow move away, then heard the thunder as another took its place.

Standing by, the operations commander told the assault teams. Authorization still required, he informed Langdon. No suggestion that the hijackers have killed a hostage, the brigadier reminded the Foreign Secretary; no threat from them that they will do anything to harm the hostages when the deadline expires.

It was ten minutes to the deadline, nine minutes before the teams would enter the plane. The helicopter was moving away, circling in front and over them, then settling again above the flight deck. No word from the United Nations, Kara thought, but perhaps she had never expected any. *Everything is cheerful, my country is really beautiful when there is no war*, she remembered the poem the girl called Karic had written at school. *These evil people are killing us for no reason, only because we have different names and because we don't pray the same way they do.* So what about the UN, Kara thought, what about the secret committees the politicians in Moscow and London and Washington would have set up, what about the even more secret decisions they would have come to?

Nine minutes to the deadline, eight before the teams were due on board. Assuming the UN didn't deliver, Finn reminded himself; but the UN hadn't in Maglaj, so why should they now?

Eight minutes to the deadline, seven before they were due on board. Latest report from New York, the BBC studio link man was saying. Security Council still in session, the UN correspondent told the network, still no news. 'White Two. White Two.' The second helicopter switch, the helicopter above 3216 swinging up and another taking its place. Nobody enters the plane without your written authorization, the operation commander told Langdon. Pilot on flight deck, one of the snipers directly in front of the plane informed Control; one other person, presumed hijacker, returned to jump seat.

Seven minutes to the deadline, six before the teams would enter the plane. The other hijackers were nervous now, snapping the magazines of their weapons and looking at her. *I'm one of those people whom they call refugees.* Kara thought again of the poem the girl called Karic had written. Karic had been nice to Jovan, even though she was older; Karic had been Jovan's friend. *I cannot explain to you how I feel when I think about all those horrors my family and I have been through.* She checked the time again, looked back at the other members of the team, nodded at them to instil confidence in them.

Six minutes to the deadline, five before they were due on board. For Chrissake may the TV cameras not be able to see them, Finn thought; for God's sake may no radio reporter have night sights and be telling his listeners –

telling the hijackers – they were in position. Where the hell were the United bloody Nations?

No SAS teams on the plane unless he authorized it in writing, the operations major told the Foreign Secretary again. Situation still in hands of civil authorities, the brigadier reminded Langdon; the military still have no authorization to intervene.

'Ground, this is Lufthansa 3216.' They heard the voice of Karl Maeschler and froze. What the hell are you doing – Kara almost tore the headset from Maeschler. What the hell are you going to say?

'Lufthansa 3216, this is Ground.'

A communication from the hijackers, the TV and radio stations were saying, every channel going live.

'Ground, this is Captain Maeschler. I have something to say. I hope my wife is listening.'

Lufthansa 3216 talking to Ground, the ops major told the teams below the aircraft. Hold.

'When I was a boy, I was taught about the Holocaust. I was told that Germany had allowed the Holocaust to happen, and that such a thing must never be allowed to happen again.

'When I was a student, I began to realize the full enormity of what had taken place. When I stood in the concentration camps of Dachau and Belsen and Auschwitz, I vowed that I myself would never let it happen again.

'And all the while the world itself said it must never happen again, that the world would not let it happen.

'And now the world has. Not in Germany, but in Bosnia. The United Nations and the world has stood by and allowed genocide and ethnic cleansing on a scale unimaginable since 1945. The world blamed Germany, but now the world is washing its hands of Bosnia. Even tonight the United Nations cannot make up its mind.'

It was five minutes to the deadline, four before they were

due on board. What's happening, Finn whispered in his throat mike, what's going on? Lufthansa captain talking, the ops major told him; not the hijackers. 'White Three. White Three.' The third helicopter switch.

'I do not know what will happen in the next few minutes. All I hope is that someone will explain to my son and my daughter why the world should always have Bosnia on its conscience.'

He took his thumb off the transmit button and sat back.

'You didn't have to do that,' Kara told him.

'I did.'

Bastard, Langdon thought. 'Authorized,' he told the major. 'Sign,' the major came back at him.

It was four minutes to the deadline, three before they were due on board. 'Everest. Everest.' The teams heard the signal on their earpieces. The code that command of operation had been passed to the military, that authorization to board had been signed. 'Nothing from UN.' They waited. 'White Four. White Four.' The last switch. The helicopter above the flight deck began to move away, slower this time; edged to its left, then back into place.

The noise above them was deafening. 'Blue move, Blue move. Red move, Red move.' The two teams slipped from the cover of the wheels, Finn's moving to the front of the plane and Janner's to the rear, sliding along the ground and climbing the ladder. Nothing from the radio reporter – the operations commander listened carefully. Nothing on the TV pictures, he was informed. 'Okay. Okay,' he told them; thank Christ for that, he thought. Stand by – the drum began to beat in his head. Stand by, stand by.

Three minutes to the deadline, two to the moment the teams went in. Still nothing from New York, Kara thought, but you've just told yourself you were expecting nothing, so why are you surprised? One day it would be *her* on the ground, the bullet in *her* face and *her* blood trickling down *her* cheek. So how would the others react at the end, what would they do when she gave them their orders?

The helicopter was still above them, still deafening them. Steve was to his left, Jim and Ken tight behind them. One minute, counting down. Hijacker leaving flight deck, the sniper told Control, captain also leaving. Hijacker and captain both leaving cockpit, the message was relayed to the assault teams.

Still time for the UN to do something – Caz glanced at her watch then back at the TV set; still time for the Security Council to say they agreed. Her hands were gripped tight and her nails dug into the soft of her palms. Oh God, the helicopter's moving, oh God, it's going over the starboard wing. Oh God, the boys are going in. She was shaking, shuddering, Jude the same to her right. You all right, Linn was asking. What's wrong – her husband was turning to them.

The assault helicopter was still moving, closing over the tip of the starboard wing. Kara was standing at the top of the aisle, the other hijackers in position along the cabin and the passengers staring at her in fear. Maeschler eased past her and sat in the seat which Hilary and Sammi Langdon had occupied.

'Thirty seconds,' the operations major told the teams. 'Counting down. Radio silence.' Still time to pull out – he looked at Langdon. Still time not to commit.

'Fifteen seconds.'

Stand by, stand by.

'Ten.'

The helicopter was hovering over the tip of the starboard wing, almost touching it. The passengers and the hijackers were looking at her; one of the hijackers trembling and the passengers white-eyed with fear and sinking in the seats, Maeschler to her left and the gunman called Alex the closest of the hijackers to her. Time to do it – it was in Alex's eyes, in the way he moved. But Alex had always been that way; the most ferocious followers always had been converts rather than those born into a religion or creed or belief. The Socimi was in Alex's hands though Alex still trusted her, still thought she was going to see it through.

Stay by me, Finn. Wish me luck, Adin; pray for me, Jovan. 'Put the weapons down,' Kara told the others.

Why – it was in their faces, in their reactions. The passengers stared at her, some of them rising slightly from their seats but most still cowering. Because we've won, she told them. There's no longer a need to kill anyone; we have what we want; the world is on our side and something will therefore be done.

'Five seconds.'

Bastard – the realization was in their eyes. Keefer wouldn't do this, therefore what are you doing? Keefer wouldn't have issued a demand like the one you issued – the awareness was upon them now. So whose demand was it; whose cause are you fighting? Why move from Paris to Berlin, why were you the only one to have contact with Keefer? This isn't how the Mujihadeen would act, not how the Mujihadeen would end a hijack. You set us up, betrayed us. Used the Cause, betrayed the Cause. And unless there is blood there is no victory. Unless there is death there is no salvation. Their guns were coming up. Swinging from the passengers. Turning on her.

'Green go. Green go.'

The starboard wing exploded, lights flashing and thunder erupting. Men in black coming out of the helicopter and running along the wing.

Linn was white with shock. You knew – she turned to Caz and Jude; that's why you were frightened, that's why you're even more terrified now. So how did you know, why did you know?

Kara was turning, facing the wing. Confused, almost

panicking. The other hijackers turning away from her and looking instinctively to their right.

'Blue go. Blue go.'

The rear door exploded open, the stun grenades going in. Kara turned away from the wing, the other hijackers also turning and facing the rear. The cabin was reverberating with the noise, the shock waves pulsing through and the noise overpowering. Her head was throbbing, spinning, and her brain was fighting to control itself, struggling to tell her nervous system what to do.

'Red go. Red go.'

Finn opened the door, the men behind pushing him up and in.

Explosions from Lufthansa 3216, the CNN reporter at Heathrow was saying. UN Security Council has just voted, the BBC man in New York was trying to interrupt; Secretary-General has fresh ideas for peace plan, major powers are backing it. Security Council has agreed, Langdon was shouting, screaming. UN has acceded to the demands. Stop them, stop the teams. Too late, the major was coming back at him. Your responsibility, Langdon was telling him. You signed, the major was replying; get him out of here, he told a sergeant.

Finn turned right, into the cabin. Steve going left behind him, checking out the flight deck. Ken and Jim already in. 'Down,' they were shouting in English and German and Russian. 'Get down.'

'Down,' Maeschler screamed at Kara. He ignored the gun in her hand and pulled her on to the seat.

Hijacker, female, four metres away, Finn saw. Still facing the rear, still not aware he was there. Double tap, his training told him, double tap again; while she was still confused by the diversions and before she turned and saw he was there.

Might be her, though; might be the one you're looking

for. Double tap, his training screamed at him. You know what I'm doing, Jim. Therefore cover me. Protect me if I'm wrong.

He was moving, the hijacker turning, face towards him and gun coming up. Not her, not the one he was looking for, but Christ he'd left it late. She was full around, seeing him and pressing the trigger of the Socimi. Double tap, the training took over; double tap again. Double tap third and fourth time. Angle of fire, he told himself. Jim and Ken behind so okay, but Janner coming up the cabin from the rear door, so get it wrong and you get Janner.

'Flight deck clear.' He heard Steve's voice. 'Repeat. Flight deck clear.'

'Toilet clear,' he heard Ken.

He was on top of the hijacker, the body still moving. Male hijacker in front, he registered, half-turned. Double tap, double tap again. Thirty rounds in the mag and counting down, so eighteen rounds left.

'Two down. Repeat. Two down.'

Figure in aisle at rear. Male.

Head rising to his left. Christ, hijacker in seat to his left.

He was already dead, the passenger knew; he was already in the next world. The monsters coming at him, all in black. No faces, just masks as if they were from another world.

Finn saw the face. 'Down,' he shouted, gestured, at the passenger in the seat. 'Get down.'

He turned, switched back to the man in the aisle. The firing was still coming from the diversion team on the starboard wing, more firing from behind him as Jim or Steve or Ken finalized the two gunmen on the floor. Christ no – the third hijacker was facing him, gun at him. Eight metres away. Line of fire wrong and passengers in way, therefore can't shoot but hijacker will, and he'll spray the cabin.

The firing was from the rear – the other side of the third hijacker. Double tap. Second double tap. Third. Thanks, Janner. The gunman falling, spinning. Three down, two male one female. So where was she? Got to find her fast before the third team comes on board.

'Finn, behind you. Finn, behind you.' Steve's voice again. Finn's name first to give him extra milliseconds to react.

He spun round. What, Steve? Jim's covering me, Steve, so I know I'm okay. Why aren't you talking to me, Steve? Why aren't you telling me what's going on?

Because I can't. Because that's what we agreed. Because everything is being recorded. Therefore if I say anything they'll know.

Good man, Steve – Finn was back in business class, passengers screaming and some looking up, most still tucking their heads and bodies down.

Not her, Maeschler was trying to tell them; she's not one of the hijackers; she's a passenger. She's a good person, she ordered the others to lay down their guns. The smoke was still clouding his vision and the explosions were still ringing in his head, so that he was unsure who was doing what and what had happened to the other hijackers. He was fighting them, trying to stop them taking her, trying to stop them dragging her away. One monster holding him down and two wrenching her away.

They were going to shoot her, Kara knew. Going to execute her. No – she was screaming, fighting back. *Her* lying on the ground, the bullet in *her* head. *Her* blood trickling down *her* face. Not now though, dear God. Not yet. So many things still to do. *And now I have only one wish* – she heard the words of the girl called Karic. *To go back to my home. And once this war is over I would like you to come to my country and see how beautiful it is.* I want to see Maglaj again, put flowers on the grave on the hillside above Tesanj; I want to work in the hospital there and rebuild my little house. She was in the toilet, one of the monsters holding her and the other shutting the door behind them so nobody could see.

I can't die in a place like this, she was thinking, trying to move but unable to, the strength of the monster holding her, subduing her. Not here, dear God, not like this. In the mountains above Maglaj, yes. In the hills around Travnik, on the night run to the black market, crossing the front line and the minefields near Popovekuce. But not like this. She was screaming, shouting, no sound coming out. Goodbye, my dear Adin. Goodbye, my precious Jovan. See you soon, my husband. Soon be holding you again, my son.

The monster flicked his gun on safety, slipped the gun over his shoulder. What's happening – she was still shouting, still screaming, still no sound coming out. What are you doing? The monster took off the mask and pulled back the hood.

The other teams were on the plane, the doors open and the emergency chutes out. The television pictures showing the police vehicles surrounding the plane and the passengers sliding down the chutes, the police taking charge and rushing them away. Please may Finn be okay, Caz was still shuddering; please may he not have killed her.

The unmarked vans drew up, the hooded men in black left the plane and ran to them, and the vans screamed away. Christ, Linn was saying on the other side of the table.

The Operations Room was quiet, the men who had manned it slumped shattered and drained. The snipers coming in, plus one of the assault team, Heckler in his hand and hood still on.

'Good show,' Langdon told the operations commander. 'Well done.'

You're finished – he saw it in the major's eyes. You screwed us, but in the end you screwed yourself. Because you didn't wait for the Security Council vote; because the hijackers laid down their weapons; because there were no explosives on the plane.

Still won though – Langdon looked at him, looked at the man in the assault gear. Still got her, still got the bastard. Still gave her what she deserved. And you did it for me.

'All hijackers accounted for?' the major asked the man in the assault gear.

The man in the balaclava nodded.

Told you, Langdon turned in triumph. Because in the end that was the only thing that mattered; in the end she was the only one I wanted.

'How many?' the major asked.

'Three hijackers. Two men, one woman.'

'You mean four.' Langdon felt the fear grip him.

'No.' Janner pulled the balaclava from his head and Langdon saw his face, saw his eyes. 'I mean three.'

The late night traffic was busy, cars pouring through central London and armed police on the streets. The Range Rover stopped outside Victoria Station and the men got out. Large men, dressed casually, three glancing round them and one in the middle, the woman beside him.

'You all right?' he asked her. 'You've got your way out.'

'Of course,' she told him.

The concourse was crowded around them.

'Thanks, Steve.

'Thanks, Jim.

'Thanks, Ken.'

She turned to the last one, the others getting back in the car.

'Thanks, Finn. Ciao, Finn.' I don't know what to say, Finn. 'See you, Finn.'

The debt repaid, Kara. Me and Steve and Ken and Jim, Janner and Max. One hell of a repayment, though so don't ask again. 'Ciao, Kara. Go, Kara.' Don't let me down, Kara, don't let yourself down.

She turned and walked into the station. Even before she had disappeared into the crowd the Range Rover had pulled away.

* * *

Sunday morning was cold, almost bleak. When Caz arrived home it was eleven-thirty and Finn was in the kitchen with the boys. Good to see you – she kissed them. You don't know how good it is to see you – she hugged Finn, put her arms round him.

'You all right?' he asked.

'Yes.' Although I'm not. Because I'm thinking about the woman on the plane. I'm thinking about how brave she was, even though you might argue that what she had done was wrong. I'm thinking that all she really did was to take what I did a hundred stages further. And now she's dead. And in all probability you killed her. Of course I'm glad that you are alive, which is such a ridiculous thing to think I can't believe I thought it. But at the same time I think of her and I grieve for her.

She hugged him again, kissed him again. 'For God's sake don't do it live on the TV next time,' she tried to joke when the boys had gone upstairs. He made her tea and toast, and sat with her.

'You want some time by yourself?'

'If you don't mind.'

He went upstairs to the boys. She left the kitchen and went into the lounge, switched on the television and watched the news programme, watched the repeat of the last minutes of the hijacking of Lufthansa 3216.

Slipped in a video cassette and recorded the programme.

That morning the Foreign Secretary had tendered his resignation and the Prime Minister had accepted it, the newscaster announced. In London there still remained the mystery of the so-called fourth hijacker.

'The situation is always confused,' a studio expert explained. 'The passengers released in Amsterdam apparently talked about four hijackers, two men and two women. Yesterday evening, however, the SAS – and the government have not confirmed it was the SAS – killed three when they stormed 3216.'

The clouds were over her, dark and heavy. I don't want to watch this, she thought, watched anyway.

'How could that happen?' the interviewer asked. 'How could there be a discrepancy?'

'It could be the passengers released at Schipol made a mistake. They were, after all, under huge physical and psychological pressure during the hijack. It could be that the SAS missed one hijacker last night. The task of an assault team, after all, is not to kill, it's to secure the release of the passengers. Therefore once they'd achieved that, they left, as we saw in the video pictures. Then it's up to the police.'

The programme played again the last moments of the hijack: the men coming out of the helicopter then the sounds of explosions and shooting; the aircraft doors suddenly opening, the emergency chutes snaking to the ground and the first passengers sliding down them. The police moving in, the vans drawing up, and the men in black jumping into them and being spirited away.

'A textbook operation?' the interviewer asked.

'I think you could call it that,' the studio expert agreed.

I don't need to know this, Caz thought again. So why am I looking at it, why am I listening? She turned off the programme and re-ran the cassette, even though it was illogical, the clouds darker and the depression engulfing her.

Finn and the boys were coming downstairs, telling her they were going swimming. Fine, she was telling them. How can you be so calm, Finn – she looked at him. How can you do what you did last night and be so normal this morning?

Finn and the boys were outside and the tape was running, the passengers coming off the plane and the vans drawing up, the men in black running towards them and getting in. Finn and Janner's teams, she knew, because Finn's and Janner's teams always stuck together. Another van drawing up and the four men of the third team piling into it.

She stopped the tape, re-wound it, and played it again.

The passengers were safe, and once the passengers were safe then the hijack was no longer Finn's and Janner's responsibility. Because they'd done their job and got the passengers off. And at that point their job had ended, even though one hijacker was unaccounted for.

She re-wound the tape again and watched it again. Sat back and tried to think it through.

Say there were four hijackers, and so far the police hadn't found a fourth even though they would have been interviewing the passengers all night. So why hadn't they found her?

Why *her*? Because the passengers released in Amsterdam had talked about the four hijackers being two men and two women, and last night the SAS had killed two men but only one woman. Perhaps she disappeared into the night; perhaps she slipped off the plane with the rest of the passengers then slid away in the controlled confusion which followed. Got on one of the vehicles whisking the freed hostages from the scene and hid under a seat or posed as a policewoman or airport worker. Except the police would have had that covered, because that was what they would have been trained to look out for. So she didn't leave the plane with the passengers, and the only other people to leave the plane were the SAS assault teams.

Caz re-wound the tape again, watched it again. She could have escaped as cabin crew – the thought was almost buried in the confusion which filled her mind. She'd got weapons on to the plane, so she could easily have got a uniform; it was the sort of thing she would have planned for, organized for. But the crew left the plane with the passengers, so were covered by the police.

Caz was still looking at the screen, at the figures in black running from the plane. Not the sort of image Finn would have liked, she thought; the regiment didn't like doing its hunting in public, especially not on live television. She was still looking at the figures, trying to see if anything or anybody was slipping into the darkness behind them. She re-wound the section of tape and looked at it again, re-wound it and replayed it. Studied the detail. Studied the figures in black running to the pick-up vans. Discarded the figures running to the third van and concentrated on those running to the first two. Other figures in black around them, covering them.

I see it . . .

I see what they did . . .

She played the tape again and began to count.

But why? What the hell had been happening last night? Why the hell had Finn and Janner and their teams done what she suddenly knew they'd done? Because without a reason it was illogical.

An informant or an agent, someone from the regiment who'd penetrated the terrorists but had to go along with the hijack to protect his cover. Except the missing hijacker was a woman. Okay, the regiment trained women, and women had served in Northern Ireland and a few other places. But not like this.

So why?

The cold was coming upon her, but not just any cold. The cold of a winter night, but not just any winter night. The merciless cold of a winter night in Bosnia. But not just Bosnia. The awful biting merciless cold of a winter night in Maglaj, the guns pounding the OP on the hillside, Finn and Ken and Steve and Jim cutting throats and calling in the hot extraction, and Janner hauling Max through the minefield.

I don't believe this . . .

I can't believe this . . .

The boys were getting in the car. She went outside to them. Dad will be two minutes, she told them; asked Finn to come inside, asked him to sit with her.

'I know you can deny what I'm about to say. I also know that you can't confirm it.'

Which gives us the way. Because by denying it if it's not correct, and not confirming it if it is, then you can tell me without telling me. But only if we both want it.

Finn sat still, looking at her, not speaking.

'The hijack leader,' Caz began. 'I don't know why she did what she did.'

Because I told her to, Finn thought.

'And I don't know how you worked out who she was.'

We almost didn't.

'And I don't know where she is now.'

Neither do I. Because that was part of the deal, debts repaid and all that. How'd you know – his eyes and his silence asked. How did you work it out?

Caz leaned forward and played the tape. There'd be an explanation, of course. If anyone else spotted it; if anyone else asked. But you had to know what you were looking for to even begin to see it. So nobody else would. Especially given the presence of other figures in black around the plane and covering them as they came off. She stopped the tape, re-wound it slightly.

'Start counting . . .' she told Finn.

'First two vans . . .' she told him.

'Yours and Janner's teams . . .

'Four men per team . . .

'Therefore eight men on to Lufthansa 3216 . . .

'Nine off . . .

'The hijack leader, the woman. It was her, wasn't it? The hijack leader was the woman who saved Janner and Max in Maglaj, the woman you all owed.'

And last night you repaid her. Because if you can't be loyal to those who are loyal to you . . .

Deny it if I'm wrong. Don't confirm it if I'm right.

Finn looked at her. 'The boys are ready.' He leaned across and kissed her. 'I'd better not keep them waiting.'

# EPILOGUE

It was early autumn, the sky blue but the first hint of cold in the afternoon air.

The last time he'd been here the snow had been on the ground and the ground itself had been hard with ice. The last time he'd knelt here there had been two names on the simple wooden pillar at the head of the grave, now there were three. The last time there had been the grave of another woman next to the one at which he now paid his respects, now there was not.

A year ago today he and Janner had stood at Heathrow and watched Lufthansa 3216 come out of the sky. Which was why he had come today. More correctly, why he had chosen today to come.

Bosnia had moved on, of course; perhaps predictably, perhaps through the machinations of unknown hands; perhaps in its own way, or perhaps what had taken place at Heathrow had changed or influenced things. Perhaps the new ceasefire would hold, perhaps the peace negotiations really would get somewhere this time, perhaps not.

It is not the critic who counts, he reminded himself, not the one who points out how the strong man stumbled or the doer of deeds might have done them better. The credit belongs to the man who is actually in the arena, who spends himself in a worthy cause. Who, if he wins, knows the triumph of high achievement and who, if he fails, at least fails while daring greatly.

But only if the cause is a just cause and the road is a righteous road.

The sound was from behind him, no more than a rustle in the grass. He heard it yet remained still, bending forward and tending the grave.

'The day NATO and the United Nations changed their minds . . .' she said. 'The day NATO and the UN decided to remove the Serb gun emplacements that were shelling Sarajevo, the day everything changed. You and the boys were in the hills laser-targeting in the air strikes, weren't you? You and Ken and Steve and Jim. Janner and his team. You were the ones who made it possible.'

He shrugged. Because that was operational, and you never discuss anything operational.

'Thanks, Finn,' she said.

She was close to him, standing just behind him.

'So where is Kara now?' he asked.

'Kara died. You can see she's dead. Her name is on the grave.' The third name on the pillar at the head of the grave on which he had laid the flowers.

'When I was last here there was another grave, that of a woman called Asra.' Even now he remembered the grave and the name on it.

'Asra is alive.'

Because unlike Kara, Asra can be alive. Because no one is looking for her, no one is hunting her. Even though nobody except you and Janner and the boys know who Kara was. Even though nobody except you knows who Kara now is. If Kara still exists. But sometimes someone in one of the security agencies stumbles on something they aren't expecting . . . Sometimes an analyst runs a search through the databases and comes up with something he or she didn't know was there . . .

'So where is Asra now?' Finn asked. 'What is Asra doing?'

'Asra's fine, Asra's happy. Asra works with children now. She's training to be a doctor.'

Printed in Great Britain
by Amazon